PRAISE

BRU

CH00822542

Winner of the 2020 Gene
Year, Australian Boo~ ~~~~~~~ ~~~~~~~

'More like a hand grenade than a book, with its excoriating satire and explosive view on our political and economic trajectory . . . audacious writing with something here for everyone . . . moments on every page that keep narrative tension bubbling away.' **Rohan Wilson,** *Weekend Australian*

'An entertaining and thought-provoking romp with authentic dialogue with characters that are all complex and multi-dimensional . . . Rose writes with emotional intuition [and] has that eminently readable interiority that only a novel can bring.' **Louise Swinn,** *Saturday Paper*

'*Bruny* throbs with the clash of rapacious development versus a simpler life . . . Crisp and evocative writing makes this a hugely enjoyable page-turner.' *Marie Claire*

'Heather Rose takes no prisoners in this hugely entertaining satirical novel.' *Readings*

'Among her intense political intrigues and deep concerns about the directions Australian society is taking Rose inserts moments of deep tranquillity . . . often passionately didactic and cautionarily disquieting, *Bruny* is thoroughly entertaining and endearingly Tasmanian.' **Katharine England,** *The Advertiser*

'An expert storyteller, Rose has mastered the contemporary realist novel . . . Is there nothing she cannot do with her words and skilled imagination? No vignette or internal dialogue is here that doesn't enhance the complex tale she is making . . . Believable, relatable people, families, romance, grief and the terser political narrative all come together with magnificent brio.' *The Age* and *Sydney Morning Herald*

'*Bruny* sits where the political and the personal intersect, and meditates mostly on the wheeling and dealing of politics, the complexity of modern life. Rose leaves no stone unturned, she covers it all: agriculture, economics, stability, jobs and growth, environmentalism, family, loyalty, betrayal, corruption, power . . . you'd be forgiven for thinking [Rose] is psychic.' **Keeping Up with the Penguins**

'Seamless and enormously entertaining story-telling for readers of all stripes . . . Packed with swipes that Tasmanians especially will have no trouble recognising.' *Illawarra Mercury*

'A tense work of fiction that will slap its readers in the face as to how close and possible it feels, in our current cultural and political landscape.' **AustCrime**

'An intelligent and timely literary, political thriller—another highly thought-provoking read from the very talented Heather Rose.' **Booklover Book Reviews**

and lives. Pondering the parameters of this storyteller turns out to be almost as tantalising in this book as mulling its deeper questions: What are we? What is art? How should we live?' **Dominic Smith, author of** *The Last Painting of Sara de Vos*

'Framing a love story around a long-durational performance work, where the passage of time is essential, is a profoundly original idea. I loved this book.' **Marina Abramović**

'This captivating work explores the meaning of art in our lives and the ways in which it deepens our understanding of ourselves . . . Rose also combines intriguing characters with a laser-sharp focus on art to produce a gem of a novel.' *Library Journal,* **starred review**

'Clever, genre-bending . . . A portrait of human desire and human failing, but perhaps most profoundly, human striving for something greater than self. Rose's melancholy book resonates with emotion, touching on life's great dilemmas—death, vocation, love, art.' *Publishers Weekly,* **starred review**

'Deeply involving . . . profound . . . emotionally rich and thought-provoking.' *Booklist,* **starred review**

'From its conception to its last page, this book challenges our perceptions of where life ends and art begins . . .' *The Australian*

'The narrator's voice gives the novel a quiet power, as if the universe was filled with a non-meddling benevolence. There's a cinematic quality too, with even minor figures sketched in with sure and affecting touches. *The Museum of Modern Love* is alive with the surprise and challenge of presence in many of its forms—it is a very generous book indeed. Images and storytelling have been intertwined since the first human beings gathered by a painted wall to tell tales in the firelight. Heather Rose's *The Museum of Modern Love* works with these ancient ghosts with exquisite care and intelligence. Positing grief and art as deep echoes that corroborate the transitory nature of our lives, Rose brings the reader to a place of acceptance despite the inevitable darkness. With rare subtlety and humanity, this novel relocates the difficult path to wonder in us all.' *The Christina Stead Prize 2017*

'A meditation on love and creativity . . . Special kudos to the author for a pedantry-free examination of art's ability to change lives—and for this novel's tacit implications of the vanishing space between fact and fiction.' *New York Journal of Books*

'A moving book that invites the reader to revel and re-evaluate.' *Booktopia*

'Rose brings a skilled and at times almost mischievous artistry, not least in effecting narrative surprises that both disorient and persuade.' *Sydney Review of Books*

'A glorious novel, meditative and special in a way that defies easy articulation.' **Hannah Kent, author of** *Burial Rites*

'*The Museum of Modern Love* is that rare and lovely thing: a novel of ideas that blooms into a persuasive illusion of real life . . . The lapidary brilliance of Rose's sentences is never overblown and her style is one of prescient, unflustered beauty.' *West Weekend Magazine*

'. . . few Australians have chosen to write fables that take shape-changing as their central theme. *The River Wife* tells her story in intimate, seductive prose. A love story must engage readers and persuade them to believe as well. And this one does. The emotions are unfalteringly subtle and persuasive.' *Sydney Morning Herald*

'A cool and luscious fable of love . . . (with) all the hallmarks of the great love stories—passionate and tantalising, elegiac and profound . . . there are echoes of Oscar Wilde's fairy tales, Anna Livia Plurabelle from James Joyce's *Finnegan's Wake*, and even Murray Bail's *Eucalyptus*. Replete with sensuous, evocative language.' *Canberra Times*

'From the first pages of *The River Wife*, the reader is struck by the beauty of the prose. There is a fluid brook-like quality to the writing. [A celebration of] the beauty of nature and the enduring power of story.' *The Age*

'A strange, beautiful, lyrical book, set in modern-day Tasmania, about a woman who every night changes into the form of a fish . . . This book walks the shadowy borderland between fiction and fable, prose and poetry, myth and magic realism. It is a love story, an exploration of the importance of story to the making of self, a paean to the beauty and power of nature, and a warning of the dangers of not listening. Utterly haunting, exquisite, and unique.' **Kate Forsyth**

Heather Rose is the Australian author of eight novels. Heather's most recent novel, *Bruny*, won the ABIA 2020 General Fiction Book of the Year. Her seventh novel, *The Museum of Modern Love*, won the 2017 Stella Prize. It also won the 2017 Christina Stead Prize and the 2017 Margaret Scott Prize. It has been published internationally and translated into numerous languages. Both *The Museum of Modern Love* and *The Butterfly Man* were longlisted for the International Dublin Literary Award. *The Butterfly Man* won the Davitt Award in 2006, and in 2007 *The River Wife* won the international Varuna Eleanor Dark Fellowship. *Bruny* and *The Museum of Modern Love* are both in development for the screen and the play of *The Museum of Modern Love* premiered at Sydney Festival in 2022. Heather writes with Danielle Wood under the pen-name Angelica Banks and their *Tuesday McGillycuddy* children's series has twice been shortlisted for the Aurealis Awards for best children's fantasy. Angelica Banks is also published internationally. Heather lives by the sea in Tasmania.

HEATHER ROSE

BRUNY

ALLEN&UNWIN
SYDNEY · MELBOURNE · AUCKLAND · LONDON

This edition published in 2022
First published in 2019

  This project has been assisted by the Australian Government through the Australia Council, its arts funding and advisory board.

The excerpt on p. 18 is from 'If' by Rudyard Kipling.

Allen & Unwin
Cammeraygal Country
83 Alexander Street
Crows Nest NSW 2065
Australia
Phone: (61 2) 8425 0100
Email: info@allenandunwin.com
Web: www.allenandunwin.com

Allen & Unwin acknowledges the Traditional Owners of the Country on which we live and work. We pay our respects to all Aboriginal and Torres Strait Islander Elders, past and present.

 A catalogue record for this book is available from the National Library of Australia

ISBN 978 1 76106 877 5

Maps by Guy Holt
Set in Granjon LT Std by Bookhouse, Sydney
Printed in Australia by McPherson's Printing Group

10 9 8 7 6 5 4 3 2 1

 The paper in this book is FSC® certified. FSC® promotes environmentally responsible, socially beneficial and economically viable management of the world's forests.

For everyone who is still awake

'A flow of words is a sure sign of duplicity.'

HONORÉ DE BALZAC

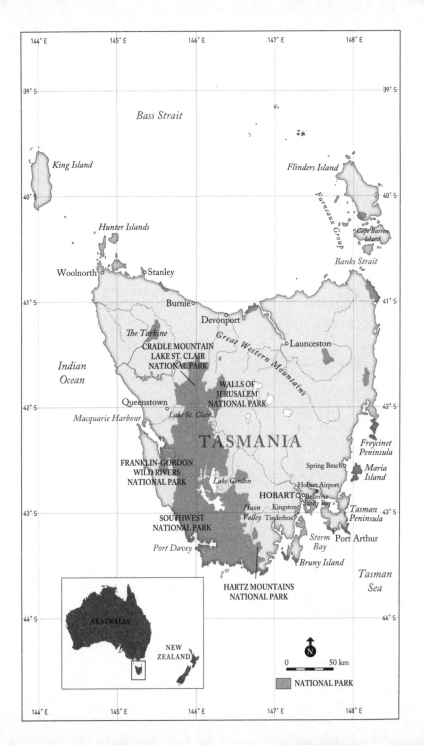

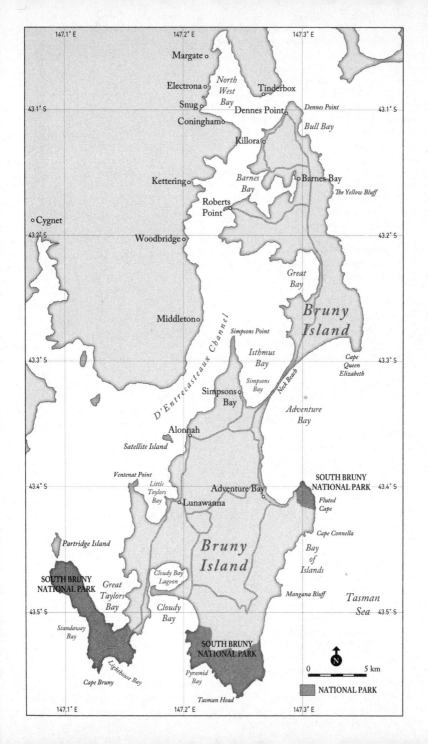

PROLOGUE

A Pacific Gull is winging its way down the wide course of the Derwent River. It dips its dark-tipped wings past a curve of headland and slides west into the D'Entrecasteaux Channel. There, behold, at the mouth of the channel is an enormous suspension bridge, as high as the Brooklyn Bridge and two hundred and twenty-seven metres longer.

For the last one hundred years and more, the only access to Bruny Island has been by boat or the two vehicle ferries running morning to night across the channel. Now, after four years under construction, the bridge is three months short of completion. Cables tension the entire structure, curtaining the sky. Two roadways, reaching from shore to shore, come to an abrupt gap over a calm indigo sea.

At the near shore, where the bridge begins, is a hamlet called Tinderbox. It is here, on the beach, that the Pacific Gull lands. The night and the tide are at ebb. Dawn is a promise on the horizon. There are no lights on in the homes and no traffic on the road.

The far shore, Bruny, is one of the largest and most popular islands off the Tasmanian coastline. It is almost one hundred kilometres in length, half as big again as Martha's Vineyard but without the mansions, wealth or famous seasonal occupants. Bruny is a long stretch of farmlands, eucalyptus forests, green and gold hills, and long white beaches. For those who come to holiday, it's a place for fishing, swimming, and simply sitting on your deck with a beer or a glass of wine and thinking about how good life is. Tasmanians do quite a bit of that, given the chance.

Permanent residents on Bruny number just a few hundred. Several thousand shack owners swell the island population through summer and school holidays. And more than two hundred and fifty thousand tourists visit year round, staying in the hotels, cottages, caravan parks and national parks, filling the restaurants, buying local chocolate, local cheese, local whisky, gin and vodka, local salmon, oysters and local wine. If Tasmania is the new France for global gourmets, Bruny is the new Cote d'Azur. Tourists fill cruise boats and bus tours, car parks and craft stores. It is for the tourists, the Tasmanian government says, that the great bridge is being built.

As dawn arrives, a large speedboat becomes visible, tucked under the cliffs at Tinderbox. It is steel grey, more an absence of light than a presence. Four divers surface beside the boat and clamber aboard. A fifth person emerges from the boat's cabin and swings a winch into action. The gull lifts from the shore and flies towards the boat, alighting on the roof beside the radio antennae. The divers lose their masks and fins, then shrug off their tanks and lower their weight belts to the deck. Four large catch bags are winched out of the sea. The contents are heavy and unmoving. No wriggling fish, crayfish or abalone. Everything is done with as little noise as possible. None of them remove the balaclavas they are all wearing.

'That bloody drill . . .' says one of the divers.

'Let's move,' says a second, surveying the shore and the sky.

They look towards the bridge and fall silent.

The boat engine comes to life and the gull lifts away. Within moments the boat is heading south out of the bay and leaving a widening wake down the channel. A security guard for the bridge comes out of his office on the hill at Tinderbox and notes the disappearing boat. He scratches his chin and frowns. He calls his colleague over on Bruny Island. It goes to voicemail. He calls again. Still no answer. The boat is mid-channel now and moving fast. He calls another number and looks to where he knows the foreman lives on North Bruny.

'Yep,' says the foreman. Dan Macmillan doesn't sound like he was asleep, though he was when the phone rang. He's quickly alert.

'Can't raise Clarke,' says the security guard. 'Just had a strange-looking boat close by. Don't know when it came in. Didn't hear it.'

'Is it still there?' Dan asks.

'Headed down the channel now. Reckon you can see it from your place.'

Dan gets out of bed and walks into his lounge room. The distant hills are just catching the early light, their forested peaks aglow. Dan picks up his binoculars on the bookshelf and surveys the water. He finds the wake and travels his gaze along it to the speedboat moving south fast. Too far away now to see much, but it's no recreational fishing boat. He's sure about that. It looks like a military vessel, almost invisible against the sea.

'What's that doing here?' Dan says more to himself than the guard. 'No-one called you?' he asks.

'No. Just saw it come out under the cliffs.'

'Clarke see anything?'

The security guard sighs. 'Can't raise him. It's quick though. Quiet too. Navy?'

'Maybe,' says Dan. 'Pretty sure we don't have boats like that.'

From either side of the channel, the two men observe the great bridge and the colour coming back to the world. The wake settles and the channel resumes its vivid calm. The vessel is out of sight.

'I'll go down and take a look,' says the security guard.

'Check carefully. And ring Hobart,' says Dan. 'Find out what you can. Maybe someone forgot to tell us something.'

'Will do. Let's hope it's nothing.'

'I'll go wake Clarke,' says Dan.

❧

An hour after the boat disappeared down the channel, Dan Macmillan is on the shore at Dennes Point. The sky has faded to a blue so pure it looks freshly invented. He sees no sign of anything to concern him on this side of the bridge. The security guard has done the same on the Tinderbox side. Nothing. Dan has also woken Clarke and roasted him. Now he's walking back towards the jetty. The only breeze is a zephyr rounding the point, gently ruffling the bay's calm, casting mirrored shards of light across the channel.

Dan is thinking of coffee and scrambled eggs when a deep rumbling shatters the morning's calm. He spins around to see the bridge tower on the Tinderbox side quiver then shake. As he watches, the one-hundred-and-sixty-eight-metre tower drops into the sea. It takes with it cables and a large section of bridge roadway, all disappearing into the D'Entrecasteaux Channel.

Later, Dan remembers everything happening in slow motion. The bridge squealing like a meat grinder on metal. The cables straining, several vertical cables snapping, the noise of giant whip cracks. The sea churning and roiling. Shock waves rushing erratically towards the shore. The second tower shivering too, but holding. The bridge screaming and groaning until it settles in a twisted slump, cables swinging loose in the morning air.

Residents come out to gape. After some time, police sirens are heard coming from Hobart. The media is in quick pursuit. By mid-morning, a flotilla of voyeurs aboard yachts, speed-boats, dinghies, paddleboards, windsurfers and kayaks is being held back by two police launches. On radio and television, the expression 'terrorist attack' is used.

The premier, John Coleman, a large man with a salesman's smile not in evidence on this occasion, says that an outrageous act of barbarism and sabotage has been enacted upon the Tasmanian people. The leader of the Opposition, Maxine Coleman, who happens to be the premier's older sister, says it's hard to fathom that such a thing could happen in Tasmania and that all Tasmanians will be in shock.

By evening, every media channel in Australia is running a version of TASSIE TERRORIST STRIKE as its lead story. The federal police are raking through files that might indicate a suspect or suspects. There are helicopters and naval boats out searching for that disappearing speedboat, but they find nothing. It's as if it has evaporated.

Leaders of several bridge protest groups are taken in for questioning. Marinas from Hobart to Kettering are searched for evidence of explosives. There's some roughing up and the usual standover tactics, but no-one bends. There are no obvious leads but a world of suspicion. The bridge has had four years of serious opposition.

The Pacific Gull is now long gone. It has flown on to more isolated stretches of coastline, searching for yet another place to feed and rest. The bridge drama, however, goes on. There is an election coming, and the premier is keen to show that he's not bowed by any of this.

'I want to reassure Tasmanians,' John Coleman declares that first night on television, the broken bridge behind him, 'that we will not be diminished by today's violent assault on our peaceful community. Nor will this shocking act dissuade us from fulfilling my government's brilliant vision for Tasmania. We will find these terrorists and bring them to justice. The Bruny Bridge continues to be a project of national significance. Come March next year, the bridge will be open on schedule, and the next chapter in the success story of Tasmania will begin.'

CHAPTER ONE

As the hours went by, the truck began to smell more and more of men. If we were passing through towns blasted to rubble, I couldn't tell. All I knew was that we were squeezed into the back of a truck, part of a midnight convoy entering a stronghold of land I had observed only on satellite images.

When we finally drew to a stop, it was after dawn. I slipped the niqab over my clothing. The truck doors opened on a bleached dusty street with the usual piles of rubbish. Decomposing plastic bags were caught on thorn bushes and underfoot my boot broke an abandoned plastic fork. It was twenty-eight degrees and 6.30 am.

The compound had traditional dun-coloured walls. Half of our security detail went ahead, assessing the place for threats and traps. When they returned with the all-clear, we entered the home along a short corridor that opened into a wide, central courtyard. It was a beautiful home—or at least it had been. The ornate circular fountain at its heart was dry now. The citrus trees had been stripped of fruit. The mosaic floor and intricate stonework spoke of history. The black flags and the militants armed with M16s at intervals along the walls spoke of now. And there was a cage with a charred body within. A small American flag had been stuck into the corpse.

Instantly I was recalling the film posted two days ago of an American soldier burned to death. He had been the same age as my own son—twenty-seven. They had doused him with petrol and set him alight. He had flung his body against the bars while the watching men cheered. There are many things in my life I'd prefer never to have seen. It comes with the job. We had not expected to find him here. We hadn't known this was the place.

I glanced at my travelling companion and saw that he was flushed with rage. I breathed and calmed myself. This meeting had been months in the planning. The deal we were here to make was mine, but my mouthpiece was an American ex-president.

The emir was waiting at the far end of the courtyard under an arched ceiling. Ignored, I went to stand in the shade of the rear wall without comment. I was the invisible, irrelevant woman veiled in black cloth. This anonymity is twofold; it provides a strange protection from scrutiny, and it makes it easier to observe people.

The emir and the ex-president sat and were served tea by a boy. The ex-president laid out the terms. We were offering to exchange fifty men for one hundred and thirty-six women abducted into sex slavery.

'These women are not your concern,' the emir said to the ex-president. 'They are not my concern. They belong to the men who own them. They have been bought and paid for. What are you really seeking? You have come a long way.' He had a lean, bearded face with a beaked nose and dark, inscrutable eyes.

If the world knew we were looking to return Daesh militants held captive, there would be uproar. I had been working on the release of the women for years. This was the last of those still alive, we believed.

A Daesh recruit receives an additional monthly stipend for keeping a sex slave. And the slaves they had taken en masse were Yazidi women. We knew they were broken, diseased and severely damaged. Under the laws of *sabaya* a man is entitled to rape, beat and punish his slave. Some had been as young as seven when they were captured. They had been slaves now for over seven years.

The caliphate had open passage to the sea through Turkey thanks to President Erdogan, and it was expanding across the Syrian border. So much for Daesh being crippled. This was what the US withdrawal had done. That was the message of the US flag in the body.

I have learned through my years in this role that violent extremists can appear perfectly reasonable even when their extremism has obliterated charity, mercy and clarity. The emir had a political science degree from the London School of Economics but had returned home after the death of his father in Abu Ghraib prison at the hands of US interrogators in 2004. His brothers had disappeared in Fallujah. Our intelligence said he had a wife and two daughters living in Saudi. I knew he had agreed to this meeting because, with access to the sea, everything had changed.

In these situations, I quiet my fear as if it were an animal. Fear is how you get yourself killed. Or you kill someone else. I would have liked to pull out a hidden weapon and open fire on all of them. But I didn't have a hidden weapon. We had been carefully searched. Not quite well enough to find the tracking device under my skin, but enough to make me feel quietly violated.

More than twelve million people now lived under this regime. I had seen the tens of thousands of refugees made homeless. I knew how many Yazidi daughters had died. In all this, I did not forget what the emir had lost nor the horror he had witnessed. Or how he had chosen to disconnect himself from the world he once inhabited. I would kill to protect my children, I have no doubt of that. But when I saw a man like the emir, I wondered about the power of an ideal. The certainty of a belief. Would I ever kill for an ideal?

The ex-president said, 'A caliphate without mercy and compassion will never be viewed as anything but a threat to its citizens and its neighbours.'

'Christians have killed millions of my people without cause,' replied the emir. 'What was the war in Iraq if not an assault by a Christian coalition on my people? Where was this Christian compassion when my father was murdered? When my brothers were thrown into a mass grave outside Fallujah?'

This is negotiation. It's emotional, sometimes predictable and rarely simple.

'But we share—' began the ex-president.

'You think I can help you,' the emir interrupted. 'Perhaps I could. But what is fifty brothers when five hundred are joining us every week?'

This was an exaggeration, but in truth we had no idea. If it wasn't five hundred each week now, it might well be by next year.

'Our brothers in captivity will find a way of making their deaths glorious. If that is in your prison, or in your streets, then beware. We will restore justice. Because everything we do is for the glory of Allah.'

There was a pause and the emir turned to stare at me. 'What is this woman doing here? She is saying nothing but you are listening for her.'

'You know, Emir,' said the ex-president, 'that Ms Sheppard is from the UN. She is here to ensure these women are returned home.'

The emir inspected his hands. 'Perhaps we burn a slave every day until our brothers are returned to us. Perhaps we send out a call to our brothers across the world to also burn a woman every day. We start here with Ms Sheppard.'

Our security tensed. The courtyard stilled. Even the breeze ceased.

My name is not Ms Sheppard but he would never know that. I was simply a long, black-robed vision of woman. All the emir could see of me was my eyes and that was going to have to be enough.

'My death would be a very small death, Emir,' I said. 'The killing of women will not give you the homeland you seek. The women we want returned are half-dead anyway. Before they die as slaves, they can secure the lives of fifty of your brothers. Consider it a good return on investment.'

'I repeat that these women are of no value to me,' said the emir, turning back to the ex-president. 'What else did you come all this way to offer me?'

'A seat at the new UN Council for the Middle East,' I said.

The ex-president was caught off-guard. Everyone knew his position on this. If he had known I would make such an offer, he would never have agreed to this meeting. This resurgent expanding caliphate, emboldened by the shift in US policy, fed by the trade of oil and weapons, was a virus. Some argued that only by giving it recognition, and making it answerable to the global community, would it find its way to human rights. Others, like the ex-president, had invested everything in its demise. But he was no longer in power.

The emir observed the ex-president and smiled. 'Go on,' he said.

'Your role,' I said, 'would create recognition of the caliphate as, if not a country, a state. You are going to need to broaden trade. With your growing population, you need food security and humanitarian aid. Your background in economics makes you the right choice.'

'Is that so,' he said.

'We are offering you the chance to give this land of Allah a voice on the international stage,' I said.

The emir had taken this palatial home. Perhaps he imagined his grandchildren playing in the courtyard one day. This was revenge for Abu Ghraib and Fallujah. But it was also a celebration of the brothers and sisters who had killed and injured people in London, Berlin, Paris, New York, Sydney, Los Angeles—and all the cities yet to come. The offer was risky but it played to his world view. He believed the EU would falter and the West would fall. If he had to put a timeframe on it, he would have said within ten years.

'What assurance can you give me?' he asked. It was evident he cared little for the men, nothing for the women and, unsurprisingly, a great deal about power.

There was a long pause. Would it work? I wondered and I waited, my eyes down.

'I am guessing that would be mine,' said the ex-president at last, although I could see that it killed him to say it.

The emir smiled. 'One hundred brothers. Fifty women.'

The bargaining began.

Back in the truck, the ex-president said to me quietly, 'Tell me what we just did?'

I met the trucks transporting all the women home. There were powerful scenes of reunion, but within a few hours each of the women fell into an almost catatonic state. I had warned their families that this would happen. When the enormous effort to survive was no longer required, they would go into shock. Only with time and gentle coaxing, with tenderness and love and family members to lure them back, would some of them emerge, so deep was their trauma. We know this from thousands of women rescued and returned the world over. None of them truly recover. They simply learn to go on, each in her own way. Some kill themselves. Two of these women were only fourteen now, and one of them had been bought and sold fifteen times.

I was at one of the girls' homes when I heard a strike had destroyed the home of a Daesh leader and a nearby training camp in northern Iraq. White phosphorous was used—an American weapon of choice. The American State Department was vehemently denying any knowledge. The Iranians were being blamed. There was only a handful of survivors and the emir was not among them.

The ex-president rang me. I took his call under a sky of membranous clouds.

'You could have trusted me, Astrid,' he said.

'I did, sir,' I said.

'And the caliphate being on the Council for the Middle East?'

'I have no idea what you're talking about, sir,' I said.

'I was right to trust you too, Astrid,' he said.

Later that same day I got a call from my brother, JC, John Coleman, the premier of Tasmania. He said someone had blown up the new Bruny Bridge. He had a war on his hands, a war about progress. There was an election coming and he needed a conflict resolution specialist.

He said, 'It's your home, Ace. It's your island. We need you. I need you.'

He was very persuasive but I resisted.

Then a text message came. It said: *Call your brother. Say yes. Tell him you changed your mind.*

And suddenly I was heading back to Tasmania.

CHAPTER TWO

Hobart airport. Scene of my great escapes from Tasmania. There, waiting for me, was my sister Max. Not Maxine Coleman, leader of the opposition I can see everyone noticing, but my very petite older sister, hugging me. JC, our brother the premier, had offered to send a driver but Max had scoffed.

'I'm picking you up, Ace,' she'd said. 'Of course I'm picking you up.' Ace. That's me. Astrid Coleman.

Elsewhere a political family like ours would be impossible, even ludicrous. But you get used to it in Tasmania. We're a very small population on a very southern island and we've been marrying each other for two hundred years. There are relatives around every corner, and if you meet someone new, it will usually take less than five minutes to work out who you have in common. My brother and sister are the second generation of politicians in our family but Max is the first woman. We are sixth-generation Tasmanians. Everyone knows about the Colemans. Everyone has an opinion about us.

Hobart airport had been made over. No more tractor ferrying bags across the tarmac to an outdoor collection point. Now there were high ceilings, glamorous wall claddings, polished floors, cafes, and two baggage carousels complete with a biosecurity dog sniffing the luggage. Two huge video screens advertised the new art gallery and the convict ruins, and reminded visitors to drive on the left side of the road. Maybe Hobart had become part of the modern world. Maybe. I guess if there were bombs going off, it really had.

Outside the airport, as we walked to Max's car, the air was still the same over-oxygenated blast, the sky aqua with high cumulus clouds and a chilly breeze blowing in from the west. It was November, late spring, with a Tasmanian summer on the horizon. I hadn't spent a summer in Hobart in ten years. I'd been home less than a handful of times since I left for university in 1981.

Surprisingly, Max didn't mention politics on the drive into Hobart from the airport. Not right away. She behaved as if I was simply home for a visit and such visits happened almost regularly. We began with my children (Tavvy and Paul) and Maxine's cats (Paul and Tavvy). And, of course, our parents.

'Of course, she will have to move one day,' Max said, referring to our mother, 'but for the meantime Phillip is an angel, as you know. Although I think he misses Dad and even blames himself for not being there when the last stroke happened. Mother had insisted he sit with her while she had her nails done.'

'Should I feel guilty?' I asked.

'Because you weren't here? Or because you've left all this to me?'

'Both,' I said.

She shrugged. 'It's the way it is,' she said. 'And you're here now.'

A whole shopping precinct that hadn't been there on my last visit had sprung up on the highway from the airport. Outdoor stores, carpet stores, hardware and brands I didn't even know.

'It's been dry,' I added, observing pale paddocks sprouting new subdivisions on the left with houses and units in muted greys, browns and creams. All my life, farmlands had accompanied the highway into the city. Now a low-level sprawl of stucco, corrugated iron and paling fences slid by beside us.

'It's dry everywhere,' said Max. 'Up north too. The Midlands is already struggling. We're right down on the water reserves. It's going to be a tough summer for farmers. And it's going to bugger up the hydro.'

'Wasn't Tasmania running on diesel?' I asked. Clean, green Tasmania was technically one hundred per cent hydro-powered. Until the rain stopped falling.

'Yes,' said Max. 'All through last summer. And back in 2016. Plain stupid. Cost taxpayers a bloody fortune. And it'll happen again. Using the last fifty years to predict rainfall is as about effective as using eye colour to predict baldness these days. It's only a matter of time before the rest of Australia gets their renewables sorted and there won't be the premium for what we send out of the state. Meanwhile, Tasmanians are paying so Melbourne, Sydney and Brisbane can keep their air conditioners on. They're not big thinkers, his lot, as you know.'

This is one of those landmines in my family. They're not big thinkers means JC is not a big thinker. And he's my twin. I have learned to stay mute at times like this, step around the IED and move on.

We topped the rise and the mountain came into view. I took a breath and my heart did something warm and wobbly. Mount Wellington ascends behind Hobart, a slumbering bear of purple slopes, glades, streams, towering gum trees and delicate ferns. It's the great wild magnet for everyone who lives on the city's slopes. Every Hobart resident knows to look west, back over the mountain, to assess what to wear for the day.

Our father had taken us walking on the mountain through every season as children. We'd stand on Sphinx Rock and stare down at the city and the river, and he'd quote poetry to us. Kipling.

> If you can keep your head when all about you
>> Are losing theirs and blaming it on you,
> If you can trust when all men doubt you,
>> But make allowance for their doubting too . . .

What he was giving us was a recipe for public life, but we hadn't known it back then. I hadn't seen him in a year, not since his last trip to New York.

'Have you got time to go see Dad together?'

'I can't today. I'm sorry, Ace, I'm due back. But it's only a walk from JC's. I know he'd love to see you.'

'Will he know who I am?'

'Of course,' she said. 'And it's not easy.'

'Any change?'

'No,' she said. 'I told him you were coming. He seemed pleased. It's bizarre how well he communicates, considering.'

❧

As we crossed the Tasman Bridge over the Derwent River, I glimpsed the arc of something huge beyond the distant palomino hills to the south. It had to be the Bruny Bridge.

'So there it is.'

'Yep, can't miss it,' said Max.

'It's huge,' I said.

'That's one of the problems.' Max gave me a wry smile.

'So who's the likely bomber?' I asked. I'd had the whole thirty hours of travel time from New York to Hobart to think on this, but heading home so suddenly had made me feel tired in a way I hadn't acknowledged for a very long time. I'd planned on catching up on a few movies but, in the end, I'd finished some paperwork for the person taking over my role at the UN and slept.

'Maybe someone in the BFG. The Bruny Friends Group.'

'Cute name,' I said. 'They're shack owners, yes?'

'Lots of them. But they're residents too. The BFG tends to attract the new arrivals, not the people who've had a place on the island for a hundred years—although a few of them have joined the cause. But the really vocal members are the sea changers and tree changers. "Climate change refugees", they like to call themselves. Burned-out corporates. Lawyers, media people, a few actors. I'm sure you know the trend. Buy an old Federation home with a bit of land. Seems incredibly cheap after London or Sydney. Get a few bees. Plant an orchard or a vineyard.'

'Get a Fowlers bottling kit. Go to a cheese-making course . . .'

'Yes,' said Max. 'They're everywhere.'

'They're in Maine too,' I said. 'And upstate New York.'

'Well, they're a big part of the Bruny and channel population. And they're highly organised. Led by Gilbert Farris, as I'm sure you know by now.'

'Did you read *Homogenocene*?'

'No,' she said. 'I hear it's heavy going.'

'The loss of diversity is killing us . . . In a nutshell, fifty per cent of what was once here in terms of individual species is gone. It heralds the end of human life as we know it.'

'Cheery,' she said. 'Just like him.'

I looked at her.

'He takes himself very seriously,' she said.

'What's he doing in Tasmania?'

'What everyone else is doing. Escaping. Funny how they don't though. When something like this comes up, it's as if they can't wait to reclaim some missing part of themselves.'

'Their stress,' I said.

And we chuckled.

'You said yes to him,' Max said, and I knew she meant our brother, John.

'I also said yes to coming home for Dad,' I said. 'And you.'

'And Mother,' added Max.

'Yes,' I said, and we exchanged one of our looks.

Here was the rub. It was always the rub. Max was our older sister but JC was my twin, our little brother. Technically Max is our half-sister, because she was born the year before our parents met. Max's father had been much older and he'd died in awkward circumstances when our mother was just twenty-two. Our father, Angus Coleman, Labor MP in the Tasmanian parliament, fell in love with the beautiful young widow and the rest is us. The media liked to drag it out from time to time, referring to Max's 'half-sister' status to the premier, but for me it has never been an issue. Not for our father either. I'm never sure if JC feels the same. Let's face it, politically Max is a major thorn in JC's side. At moments like this, it can get a little murky for any number of reasons, families being what they are.

Max navigated the traffic as we entered the city and passed the docks where the fishing boats moored and the fishmongers plied their daily wares. The whole place was looking a little more modern. New hotels, more people. But the same deep blue river and architectural mistakes.

Both of us were looking older. Max's lines had settled around her mouth and neck. Her short pale hair, pink suit and lemon blouse were camera ready. Max has the vigour of a Stepford wife, yet I could feel her weariness too. Maybe it's just that we're women of a certain age, had our fill of looking after people and doing their bidding. I've seen Max's breed of weariness in so many political figures. Good people run by their desire for public service but worn down by it all. The being on call, the critics, the staff, the volunteers, the voters, the media, the election cycle. The stories that are only half true, the back-stabbing, the compromise. The brain that never stops churning. People trading their values for a little bit of legislation in the hope it will change the world. And, if they're women, everything it takes on top of that.

'Have you heard the latest plan?' Max asked.

'For Mother?'

Max shook her head and smiled. 'No, for the bridge.'

'Tell me,' I said.

'They passed new foreign labour laws in federal parliament this week. It's finally happening. We're going to have three hundred Chinese construction workers on the bridge.'

'I heard,' I said.

'So he can cut the ribbon on March fourth and it's on the front page of every paper election morning,' said Max. 'Bar another bomb, I don't think anyone can stop the bridge. It's too big an investment.'

'So I'm not really needed?' I asked.

Max made a face. 'Probably not. It was a good thought. Bring in an outsider who's not really an outsider. He'll cop more flack than you over the nepotism thing. Of course, I've put out a statement saying I think we must be proactive and that I support your appointment wholeheartedly. The community needs solidarity right now. People are really shaken up. The bomb was a dark turn no-one anticipated.'

'What are the polls saying?' I asked.

'There's a new one in the paper today. He's on thirty-eight per cent as preferred leader.'

'And the Greens?'

'Their leader is Amy O'Dwyer,' she said, one hand momentarily lifting off the steering wheel and rubbing her forehead. 'I'm sure that's in your briefing notes. She's a Cygnet girl. Incredibly beautiful. Looks like a young Penelope Cruz. Smart, too. The Greens were running at twenty-one per cent, but since the bomb they've dropped a couple of points. Still, young Amy is running at thirty-five per cent as preferred leader. The public like her.'

'Ouch. JC will be hating that.'

'I'm hating that,' said Max.

I quickly did the calculation. If JC was on thirty-eight per cent and the Greens leader was at thirty-five, that meant Max was on twenty-six per cent or less as preferred premier. In our family, statistics have always been personal. In New York, I rarely told people that my brother and sister went up against one another in elections. Even for New Yorkers, who are almost impossible to surprise, this raised eyebrows.

'So what did we pull you out of?' asked Max.

I thought back to the Yazidi women, the body in the cage, the air strike.

'The Middle East,' I said to Max.

'You okay?' she asked.

'Sure,' I said.

There are many things I do not tell my family. Things I can't explain.

෯

Beyond the city we took the road past the university and deep into the affluent riverside suburb of Sandy Bay. The tinted windows of the car did nothing to block out the visual nightmare that was the steep urban sprawl of Churchill Avenue. You could be forgiven for thinking some great monster simply spewed the rendered houses with their double garages, mirrored-glass windows and tiled balconies out onto the hillside at quarter-acre intervals. There were slums in Rio that, but for a coat of Dulux and a few pool fences, would entirely resemble Hobart's second-highest income-per-household suburb.

Max pulled into a driveway barred with high white gates. She leaned out and pushed the buzzer. A brief exchange took place between her and a distant female voice. The gates opened onto a paved driveway lined with agapanthus and white standard roses leading up the hillside.

'So this is how he lives now?' I asked.

'A man of the people,' Max said, then her voice became subdued. 'Ace . . .'

'Yes?' I said.

'I know it's not what you're here for, but there's something really fishy about the bridge. Too many unanswered questions. In a way, it's not surprising someone tried to blow it up.'

I waited.

'Nothing about it adds up for anyone other than certain people with their heads in the sand.' She gazed at JC's ahead.

'Okay,' I said. 'And you're right: I'm not here for that. I'm here to get everyone settled down. No more terrorists.'

'I understand that,' said Max. 'You're here to smooth things over for him. Buy him time so that on the fifth of March he wins office again—I get it. But you and I need to talk, sooner rather than later.'

We were at the top of the driveway. Max killed the engine.

'How about an early-morning walk?' I suggested.

'Sounds good,' said Max. 'Let's give you a few days to settle in first, though. Let you hear his side of things.'

I nodded. 'Maybe Monday morning?'

'The old Regatta Pavilion, six am?'

'Okay. It's still there?'

'It is,' she said, smiling, and I smiled too. It was an old haunt. Scene of many an act of misspent youth. Or, possibly, well-spent youth considering how serious our lives had become since those days.

We got out of the car and proceeded to unload my bags from the trunk.

'If you're on his side, Ace,' said Max, 'I know you can't be on mine. At least, not so he can tell. Nothing new in that! By the way, they're having a lunch for you on Sunday. To welcome you home.'

'And you're not coming?'

'Course I am—wouldn't miss it,' Max said, jumping back into the car and starting the engine. She wound down the window and called, 'Stephanie will pick up Mother and I'll bring Dad.'

'Astrid!' came a voice, and there at the front door was Stephanie, JC's wife, in jeans and a striped blue shirt, looking every bit the ageless blonde Sandy Bay wife. Stephanie, who had arrived in our lives like Araldite about fifteen years ago and insisted everyone stick together. She and Max waved to one another as Max departed. Behind her, two girls emerged from the house.

'Girls, it's Aunty Astrid!' said Stephanie. 'She's finally home.'

Then we were all embracing.

CHAPTER THREE

Even unfinished, bombed and listing to one side, the Bruny Bridge was still an extraordinary piece of design. It towered over the channel, dwarfing the hills and dominating the sky. It was a curved six-lane single span, far bigger than the Derwent Bridge that crossed the river to Hobart. Hobart was a city of one hundred and twenty thousand people. Yet this huge bridge— longer, higher, wider—was taking people to a remote island with a population of only six hundred.

Living in Manhattan, I've learned a distinct appreciation for bridges. The UN is on the East River. For years I crossed the Manhattan or the Brooklyn Bridge, cabbing back and forth, or taking the subway through the tunnel to Prospect Heights, until we moved to the East Village, after Ben and I separated. Such an inadequate word—separation—for that chaos, but if you've been through it, you'll understand. I've seen impressive bridges in my travels. Seen quite a few blown up too. The former Yugoslavia in the 1990s. Enough said. But this bridge was truly audacious. Perhaps Washington Roebling felt the same when he envisioned the Brooklyn Bridge back in 1869. Though let me say, every time I look at the Brooklyn Bridge, I see the largely unrecognised Emily Roebling, his wife, who got the thing finished after Washington got the bends and was bedridden. She was the first female field engineer and she learned it all from scratch. Same thing with Canberra, Australia's capital city. The architect mentioned is always Walter Burley Griffin. He had the lake at the heart of the city named after him. But it was his wife, Marion, who drew up the plans. Don't get me started.

The Bruny Bridge had been designed by the winners of an international design competition—Santiago Calatrava and Satoshi Kashima—legends of bridge design. The result was spectacular, even in its injured state. Considering it was costing two billion dollars, I supposed it ought to be.

Standing beside me, observing the damaged bridge, was Frank Pringle. Frank was JC's chief of staff and number-one adviser. He and I had just come from a meeting on the rebuild program with my brother and a room full of people in the premier's boardroom back in Hobart, a twenty-minute drive upriver. I had just witnessed my brother in action as premier of Tasmania for the first time. He'd been premier for almost eight years but, watching him, it was still a little unbelievable.

He'd introduced me very formally as Dr Astrid Coleman from the UN, proud to have this connection even though I wasn't here under that brand. I was here as an independent consultant, though 'independent' had taken a battering in the media, given my family connections. JC hadn't called me Astrid in decades. I was always Ace, since we were teenagers. Because they were my initials, and because I was good at poker and

Cheat. Any game where I have to hide the truth, that's always been my specialty.

Across from the executive building, where we were meeting, was Parliament House. I felt as if I had grown up in those green-carpeted corridors, visiting my father's office, sitting in the gallery while he debated gambling licences, forestry licences, hydro dams and new schools. He was a politician for forty years, our father. Minister of this and minister of that, but never premier or even deputy premier. Now his son was premier, but for the other side of politics. None of us had quite forgiven JC for that betrayal of Dad's legacy.

The meeting in JC's boardroom had not been easy. The forensics on the bridge were still incomplete. Divers would be down there for days yet, but it was evident what was required. Repair the bombed tower. Repair and re-tension the damaged vertical cables. Rebuild the road sections. Sounded easy in principle, but on a massive structure nothing was simple. Still JC had been adamant.

'Whatever it takes, this bridge has to be open, and the traffic flowing, on March the fourth. That's why you'll have an extra three hundred skilled workers and the budget to get it done,' he'd said. JC's an inch taller than me. I wouldn't be surprised if he's two-hundred and fifty pounds now, and it's not muscle. I've lost track of metric living in the US for so long. He's a big man.

The chief engineer was also tall, but lean with long grey hair that made him look unsettlingly like Gandalf. He was loath to commit to a new schedule when the damage was still being assessed. Mick Feltham, the bridge director, had been equally adamant. Escalating the schedule spelled trouble. More than trouble, it spelled death. He reminded us that twenty-six thousand people had died to build the Panama Canal. Under a fanatical director, they were crushed in tunnels, drowned in concrete and died in the thousands from yellow fever, just to get the canal finished so the bridge director could collect an enormous personal bonus. Mick Feltham was not that man. He wasn't prepared to have a death on his hands because of an unrealistic schedule. But the word 'bonus' had hung in the air.

I could see JC weighing up what kind of a bonus it would take for Mick Feltham to get the job done. Then he placated the man. This was how he got his nickname—not because J and C were his initials, but because he can be convincing in an almost biblical way, even when you know you're being worked over. JC has that most dangerous attribute: charisma. People warm to him. People trust him.

'Nobody wants a death, Mick,' JC said. 'I don't want a death on my hands. None of us do. We're not expecting you to risk lives. But I trust you to solve this.' He'd paused and smiled at Mick Feltham. 'You've done this kind of thing before, Mick. That's why I knew you were the man for the job. It's been a long few years. Your family's probably worn out by it too. But it's so close to completion. Look at it this way—if we don't have the bridge finished by March fourth, we let the terrorists win. We let terrorists win the world over. You don't want that. I don't want that. Our families don't want that. None of us want to live in fear. This bridge is a symbol, Mick. You know that. It's a symbol of hope. It's a big, beautiful, literal and metaphorical bridge between old Tasmania and new Tasmania. A new vision for Tasmania. Real prosperity. And you're the man we've trusted to deliver that for us.'

The federal minister, flown in that morning, looked like he might shed a crocodile tear. His name was Aiden Abbott, but on social media he was known as Aid-n-Abet and he was the Minister for National Protection. His portfolio stretched from border protection to internal affairs and he was enormously powerful. With his dark suit and balding head, he might have come straight from the set of *The Sopranos*.

'Anything you want to add, Minister?' JC asked.

'The prime minister sends a personal directive: *Make it happen*,' said Aid-n-Abet. 'So, Mick, I'm here to make sure you have everything you need in order to make it happen. We're giving you the workers. We're getting you the steel. We've called in a world-class conflict resolution specialist to settle the protestors.' Here he nodded to me. 'We're doing all we can to assist you.'

I could see that whatever bonus Mick Feltham was going to ask for, the feds would pay. I wondered when that would occur to Feltham.

JC turned back to Gandalf and asked him again if it could be done. The chief engineer looked sadly at Feltham, then at JC, and said that, as he'd said before, more investigation was needed. They'd only had a week and they were still assessing the damage. The suspension cable had been damaged back at the anchor point, torched, and that was going to present some problems. But it was the footings deep in the seabed that were the real issue. Until he knew repair was possible, he couldn't be sure.

'If it can be repaired, are we good to go?' JC asked.

The chief engineer took a breath and said, 'Yes, Premier,' guessing correctly at last that this was all he was really there to say.

The federal minister nodded. He applauded everyone's commitment, slapped Mick Feltham on the shoulder and told him he was a good man, shook hands with the chief engineer and said he had every faith in him, and then Aid-n-Abet was gone back to Canberra via a fifteen-hundred-dollar-a-head fundraising lunch with JC and party donors at the famous art gallery just outside Hobart, while Frank and I came down to the site.

❦

It was a breathtaking view. We had stopped at this vantage point on the headland above Tinderbox so Frank could show me the bridge. In Hobart, upriver, the Derwent was probably about the same width as the Hudson between Manhattan and New Jersey, but here at the mouth of the river it was four times as wide. Blue-forested hills stretched away on the far shore towards the Tasman Peninsula, one-time convict headquarters of the British government. The bleakest, coldest, most savage of all the British penal settlements. When we were growing up, the idea of a convict in a family's past was scandalous, but now it had become fashionable to claim a thief, a forger, a con man.

Between Bruny and the Tasman Peninsula was Storm Bay, a wild, exposed bit of sea that can be as benign as a lizard in the sun and then as fierce as a she-wolf protecting her cubs. Beyond the broken bridge was the northern tip of Bruny, and the village of Dennes Point. North Bruny has always been a far more remote destination than South Bruny, although it didn't start out that way. The first ferry service across the channel ran between Tinderbox and Dennes Point back in the 1800s. Later the service moved down the channel to Kettering, with its mirror-calm harbour nestled under deep green hills.

Dennes Point lacked sufficient rainfall, a pub and a service station—the staples of any town—to draw the hundreds of shack owners who had built their weatherboard and fibro cottages on South Bruny, where there was regular rainfall, shops, cafes and an essential pub. There had been a shop at Dennes Point when we were kids, but it had closed long ago.

Nevertheless, despite its isolation, North Bruny had maintained a determined population of home and shack owners and I was one of them. Not that I'd spent much time there in the past thirty years. But from time to time I'd fantasised about coming home, sitting out on the deck watching my grandkids playing on the lawn. Leaving the world behind for a little bit of paradise. Though how I'd ever get Paul and Tavvy out of New York now . . . Still, it had been a dream. It was probably still a dream, if I thought about it. But dreams had run aground in my life a few years back when my marriage ended, and I hadn't created any new ones. Mostly I'd just trashed the old ones.

The Bruny Bridge was clearly a massive dream. A global statement. Yet it was here at the far end of nowhere. It begged a question. Why? Why was it so very big? Was that just the way of the world now? Taller buildings, bigger bridges, wider roadways, deeper tunnels, bigger wars, greater wealth, greater poverty, shadier politicians?

Young Frank had been silent all the way, giving me time to take in the changes I was observing out the window of the chauffeured car. In Hobart, there were more people in the streets, and more cars on the road than when I was last here, but it was nothing compared to the rest of the world. There was a new highway that peeled off at Kingston and cut across the hills to Tinderbox. There were new houses glimpsed high on the hills. What wasn't new was the vivid blue sky, the wide sparkling river and the feeling of being a very long way from anywhere. Especially anywhere that was crowded, dirty or dangerous.

When we'd gotten out of the car at Tinderbox, I was glad I'd brought a good jacket. The breeze coming in from the west was cold. Tasmania has the most changeable weather I've ever encountered.

In a movie, chief of staff Frank Pringle would be played by a twenty-something Paul Bettany. Frank had the vivid ginger looks and sharp features but none of the mischief of Bettany. Beaten out of him, no doubt, by the boys' school education and the standard economics/law degree from Melbourne Uni, the same degree and university as JC—just thirty years later. This was the boy JC had charged with Tasmania's strategic direction.

'Well, you can't miss it . . .' I said.

'If they'd blown all the suspension wires, we would have been stuffed. I think it was amateurs. Only one tower. Almost certainly those mongrels over there,' he said, eyeing Dennes Point.

'The Bruny Friends Group?' I asked. 'I doubt it.'

'You can make a bomb in your kitchen,' said Frank. 'The joy of the internet.'

'But they must have dived in the dark,' I said. 'That's no simple thing, setting explosives underwater at night. In a current. And they're heavy, bombs like that. They'd have needed special machinery. A commercial-grade oxyacetylene torch for one, to take out that anchor point. They knew what they were doing, whoever it was. And a boat like that. It was a stealth vessel, wasn't it? Not the sort of thing you can rent.'

Frank frowned at me. 'You've been talking to the feds.' He was referring to the federal police, who were now in charge of the whole investigation.

I shrugged. 'You pick things up in my line of work,' I said. Maybe they'd used PETN in waterproof containers, but they'd have needed some way to transfer all that along the seabed. Couldn't have done it with regular air either. The cost would have been huge, putting all that together. Definitely not the work of amateurs.

'The UN,' Frank scoffed. 'What was the mandate? International peace and security?'

I observed him.

'Can't say the world looks like the UN has made much difference, right now,' he said.

I waited. I was a long way from anywhere, here on this headland. That's what I wanted to think.

Frank went on. 'Must be pretty good getting a gig to come home and settle the restless natives of Tasmania.'

I wanted to say, 'Must be good being chief of staff at thirty,' but I didn't. Instead I said, 'You're right, Frank. The UN is not perfect, but its mission is still sound. It's idealistic, but what good mission isn't? Of course, things go wrong at times. After all, it's made up of humans.'

'But with the US pulling out, and everything else going on,' said Frank, 'we all know it's only a matter of time before Europe erupts. These days we need the Chinese on our side far more than the US.'

'I saw the tourism figures,' I said.

'It's not Chinese tourists that are going to make the difference—it's investment.'

'Okay,' I said.

'That's what the people of Tasmania need to understand.'

'You know, Frank, I always think that international cooperation begins with two people.'

'Is that how it works?' he asked.

I was twenty-six years older than him. I'm paid to be nice.

'It is, Frank, it is. And I'm a pragmatist. We've got a long summer ahead. Anything else you want to get off your chest?'

'I told JC it was a mistake getting you involved,' he said.

'You and everyone else, I expect. But sometimes JC is his own man. I know that's never easy for advisers to accept, but here I am.'

'It's so wrong,' said Frank. 'You're his sister. No matter how the premier and your sister want to play it, it looks bad and it's going to backfire. Probably on all of you.'

'And, Frank, I'm a Tasmanian. I happen to own a house right across there. You a Tasmanian, Frank?'

Frank shook his head.

'Where did you grow up?' I asked. I knew the answer, but it usually doesn't pay to let people know you've backgrounded them.

'Northern Victoria, up on the Murray,' he said.

'Your family still there?'

He nodded curtly. They were. His mother had a clothing store. His father owned the local service station. Frank was a country boy made good.

'Well, then, I expect you understand what it means to come from a place that's in your bones.'

Frank shrugged.

Life is wiser than you. That had been my profound thought upon waking at 2 am. I have them from time to time, these little text messages that arrive in my brain. I think sometimes I should write them down. *Thoughts for Life.* But I don't. If that little thought was true, then I had to trust that somehow Frank was the wise choice here for JC and for Tasmania. I had to trust that I was in the right place at the right time.

'You think they'll find them?' I asked. 'The bombers?'

'Absolutely,' said Frank. 'Nowhere to hide.'

I looked down the channel at the hills disappearing back into the World Heritage-listed area that stretched all the way to the west coast, hundreds of impenetrable miles away. Sure, nowhere to hide. Unless you wanted to.

Looking across to Dennes Point, I thought I could see the roof of my house, though I might have been wrong. It had been so long. The houses continued right along the waterfront now, and there were more up in the hills.

'It's got busier over there,' I noted.

'Not really,' said Frank. 'All the action is at Adventure Bay. North Bruny will always be a backwater. The bridge isn't going to change that. People will just drive right through. A bit of noise and they've made all this fuss for four years. Tasmanians will make a fuss about anything. Over there, and down at the other BFG camp you'll see in a minute, they really think they can beat this bridge, but they can't and they haven't. Even with all their celebrity supporters.'

He paused and then he said, 'Soon enough, someone is going to talk. And then people are going to go to jail for a very long time. No-one can keep a secret here. I'm sure you remember that. Now, if you've done enough sightseeing, let's go.'

CHAPTER FOUR

The construction site was a village of demountables comprising the 'offices' of the bridge. It sprawled across a hill previously used for sheep, swelling the population of Tinderbox from forty-seven to four hundred and twenty on a daily basis.

'We also acquired a private swimming pool,' Frank said, pointing down the hill as the chauffeured car took the last curves to the site. 'It never went through the proper channels with local government, so it became a bit of a compulsory acquisition. We filled it in.'

Frank was a future despot.

We passed under the flyover that connected the new stretch of highway with the bridge, and entered the site. We both stepped out of the car and showed our ID. Security had been drastically increased. We were scanned with a metal detector. I was surprised we weren't x-rayed. How could anyone be trustworthy? What if Frank had another agenda? Maybe he was quietly an anarchist. Maybe I was. In my line of work, you learn to trust nobody, even when you've known them a very long time.

Nobody had imagined a bomb. Maybe a little graffiti. Or a high-wire, attention-seeking activist wanting to be the latest viral sensation. But a bomb? This was Tasmania. Possibly the quietest place in the world.

On the side of the small valley was BFG site number one— the Bruny Friends Group. There was a white farmhouse at the top of the hill and below it were tents of every shape and colour. Vans, caravans and cars were squeezed into every inch of a steep terraced paddock. In the middle of the paddock, either side of a big weathered marquee, were two twenty-four-sheet posters. One poster read: HALF DOWN, HALF TO GO with a cartoon of the bridge being blown up.

The other read: NO FOREIGN LABOUR. PROTECT TASMANIAN JOBS—black type on a white background.

After four years of protest, the encampment looked like a tired festival. Music was pumping through the air. People were wandering about or were seated on the grass watching the site below, or possibly taking in the view.

'Quite a crowd,' I said, as we got out of the car.

'There's been a fresh influx since the bombing. They think they've got wind of a victory.'

'R.E.M.,' I said, '"Drive".'

'They fire up early and don't stop till the shifts are done,' said Frank. 'Apparently it's become the Protest Playlist on Spotify. You get used to it,' he added.

'I guess you come and go,' I said.

He stiffened a little in his two-button suit. He had the current look, Frank. A nautilus shell of hair above a crew cut, the serious weightlifter body, the narrow size eleven shoes, the pale blue patterned socks. A man going to that trouble gets up around five every morning. I guessed the red hair had caused him problems at school. Maybe he'd had a bully for a father. The guys who look like they've worked out since their teens, there's always a story. The pursuit of power was so often revenge for men.

'It's not the music that upsets people,' Frank said. 'It's the chanting. The ferals tend to do that towards the end of the day, when everyone's heading home. Surprised they're here today. Maybe for your benefit.'

I turned and looked up at them. I waved. A couple of people waved back. Step one in getting to know each other.

'You'd think they'd be lauding the workers, not trying to destroy their morale,' Frank said. 'It's just another front for the Greens.'

The Greens. The political movement that had started right here in Tasmania back in the early seventies and birthed a global movement.

'They really don't know their history,' said Frank.

I waited.

'Greatest lie ever told is that communism would be a brilliant idea if it worked. It's actually one of the most evil ideas humanity has ever aspired to. Those people up there, they want people like you and me to pay them to sit about, live in their hay bale houses and wear their vegan shoes. They get raided pretty regularly for drugs. But they rebuild. Even the police have grown weary.'

Or sympathetic, I thought. It's always a mistake to think of protesters as 'the other'. Usually they were your neighbours, sometimes your children and even your friends. The BFG, from what I'd read, were not a front for the Greens. Their membership was far more diverse than that. I'm not paid to have a political perspective. If Frank was trying to determine whether I was aligned with my brother, my sister, or even the Greens, he wasn't going to get any joy from me. In my work, it's not about alignments. It's about perspectives.

Frank then pointed out the various staff facilities—kitchen and cafeteria and the various offices for the director, HR, engineering and media. Signage, pathways, efficiency.

'Normally there's about four hundred men on site,' he said. 'Two shifts, seven days a week.'

Down by the waterfront, there was still a children's playground, a red slide, rubber-tyre swings and an old roundabout that I thought I remembered.

'Anyone make use of it?' I asked, eyeing the swing.

Frank merely shook his head. 'It was the local park before we took over,' he said. He was a serious young man.

※

When we entered the executive building, the admin staff stared. A late-thirty-something woman got up from her desk. She introduced herself as Karen, assistant to Mick Feltham, the bridge director, and showed us into a large meeting room with a table big enough to seat twenty, although there were only half that many present. Mick Feltham was there, plus the chief engineer, the head of procurement, the head of manufacture, OH&S, PR, union and HR.

On the walls were framed artist's impressions of the project complete with traffic, sailing boats and road systems. The windows looked out on the bridge and all the way to the narrow beach and rocky flats where we had played—me, Max and JC—as children on family picnics.

Karen offered me tea or coffee. I asked for a long black, one sugar. The men had already helped themselves to a pile of sandwiches on a central platter. I eyed the sandwiches but, despite being hungry, avoided the food. A man could pull that off, eating while talking, eating while commanding a meeting, but not a woman.

I've spent more than three decades learning to read people. It's like sniffing the air for rain. This room had complexity. There was wariness and resentment. There was also relief and straight antagonism amidst the usual blend of curiosity and hostility that came with my job, and with my being a woman in a room full of men.

I circled the table and shook everyone's hand and then I said to those still standing, 'Please take a seat.'

I remained on my feet. Frank tried to catch my eye as if he expected to make the opening remarks. I continued.

'So, hello,' I said. 'As you all know, I'm Astrid Coleman, and I'm a conflict resolution specialist. I usually work in war zones for the UN, but I've taken leave to come help out here. I understand Mick has already briefed you on this morning's meeting with the premier?'

Mick nodded. So did a couple of the other men.

'I know it's been a very difficult week,' I continued. 'I'm here to ensure that things settle down.'

'Yeah, but with foreign labour.' A man in a high-vis vest with a Balkan accent had spoken. Alec Brankovic, rep for the CFMEU, the Construction, Forestry, Mining and Energy Union—one of the most powerful unions in the country. I had a file with all their photographs. I had their names and faces memorised.

'Yes, Alec, it is going to take foreign labour. That's a federal decision.'

'It's a fucking outrage.'

'Alec, right now, I'm just giving you a heads-up.'

He stared, and then looked away.

I scanned their faces. I scanned myself too, noticing I was nervous. I paused to breathe, lower my energy. I suddenly felt out of my comfort zone. But this work *was* my comfort zone. Were my nerves showing? Maybe not to the people around the table, but it was unsettling me. Tasmania. It was Tasmania. The people around that table looked like people I'd once known. My teachers, the fathers of my friends. They had the outdoor faces of Tasmanians—a bit similar to Americans who worked the land. Like they knew distances, sunshine, weather and hard work. And right now these people were rattled.

Tasmanians have a history of being extremely good at protests. When they band together, they have created protests on an international scale. They have stopped their rivers being dammed for hydro schemes, and pulp mills being built. They've stopped forests being destroyed, hotels and landing strips being built in national parks, and salmon farms taking over waterways. I knew that in the time I had, I could only make a show of fixing this resistance to the bridge. On top of that there was the additional irritant of foreign workers.

I'm a fraud, I thought. That's why I'm nervous. They can tell I'm a fraud.

I am not a fraud, I told that voice. I'm good at this. Shut the fuck up.

I breathed again and wriggled my toes in the steel-capped Blundstones I had dragged out of the back of my wardrobe when I was packing for this trip. Nothing like steel caps when you're the only woman in the room, and often the only one unarmed. And nothing like a Blundstone boot for making Tasmanians think you're okay too. Once Tasmania had been home to Blundstone like Oregon was home to Nike. But the boots haven't been made in Tasmania for years. Now they're made in China and they don't last. Mine are more than twenty years old, from the good ol' days.

'So the aim is to get this bridge opened on March fourth next year,' I continued. 'That's going to come round fast. I think you'll all agree it's going to take something big. I want to know from each of you what that something is. Don't tell me now. I want you to think about it over the weekend. What will March the fourth next year look like? How will the community be feeling when there are cars going over this bridge, boats going under it? How will you be feeling about the job you've done?'

I paused again. The bomb had clearly spooked them. If one could go off at dawn, why not any time of the day? Why not on their shift?

'You all know the new security measures. No-one gets on or off this site without clearance. This bridge now has additional surveillance day and night. The federal police are determined to solve this.'

I wasn't telling them anything they didn't know, but it seemed to soothe them a little.

'I have one-on-one interviews with each of you on Monday and Tuesday. I look forward to those conversations. I'll also be conducting interviews with community leaders, supporters, protestors and people further afield who have expressed an interest in this project. And beyond that, there'll be meetings to keep all of you—the people employed and the community, everyone—informed of progress over the remaining months.'

There was almost an audible groan.

'I guess you've heard all this before,' I said, offering a wry smile. A few people nodded, a few glared. A few simply stared out the window, as if they had far better things to do.

'Let me assure you that any information you wish to share with me will be treated as confidential.'

Was that a snicker moving around the table? Had I amused them or insulted them? Okay, here was the bit that was always going to get tricky.

'So, let's acknowledge the elephant in the room,' I said. 'My brother is the premier and my sister is Maxine Coleman, leader of the Opposition. The fact I have equally amiable relations with them both perhaps gives you an insight into my ability to be discreet. And possibly why I left here at eighteen and went to live on the other side of the world, where I have stayed ever since.'

That caused a chuckle. They looked at me with new interest. I had them now. I should have started the meeting with that, remembered that Tasmanians need the personal touch. They need to know you're connected to them somehow.

'So what I am going to need from all of you is an under-standing of the issues you see at work, out in the community, around your dinner table, or even in your own head. I need to know what you're experiencing here, and out there, when you leave this site.'

I watched them reflect on the things that were said to them at the dinner table, at the pub, what their kids brought home from school and the playground. The way the music from the protesters, and the chanting, got in their heads.

'I'm not going to take up any more of your time now, other than to say that seeing the bridge for the first time in person, it is truly remarkable. I know it's probably been a very long four years for some of you. To see what's happened to it must be hard. But I do reassure you that the premier is totally committed to seeing the project through and keeping you all safe in the process.'

'And his Chinese workers,' said Brankovic.

'Yes, you will have the assistance of skilled Chinese labour,' I said. 'The project stands to benefit from that.' I wasn't here to sell them anything, but it needed to be said.

'Your union can make all the fuss in the world, but it won't change anything, Alec,' Frank interjected. 'If you take action, we can sack you all and bring in more of them. That's the law.'

'You and your laws,' said Brankovic, and the room got quiet. 'The more laws you make, the less rights people have. Have you noticed that? This government, it has crippled the unions. And when you do that, you cripple families. Everyday working people who have no comeback with their pay and conditions are losing out big time. I come from a country where I've seen this before. A government running over its people's basic rights to privacy and protest. You should be very careful working for a government like that. It's a greasy slope. Not just slippery, greasy. Because someone is always making you pay.'

After the last election, JC's majority government had passed protest laws that meant anyone in Tasmania communicating an opinion harmful to the government or government activities received a five-thousand-dollar fine. Those billboards on the hill were very risky. Any activist getting in the way of the normal activities of a business, or was found protesting on a business premises, copped the same fine and, if they reoffended, got a jail sentence of up to five years. The bill had been opposed by environmentalists but they'd lost in court.

'You ought to read your history, Frank,' Brankovic said. 'But you are far too young to think you might learn something from that.'

I could feel the support he got for that in the room.

'Soon enough, Tasmanian workers, Australian workers, will be forced to accept Chinese rates of pay,' he added.

'Alec, that will never happen,' said Frank. There was a flush at his neck. 'The Chinese workers will be paid three times their usual pay. This is a win-win.'

'What's that, twenty cents an hour?' said Brankovic.

'The foreign workers' pay is commercial-in-confidence, and you know that,' said Frank. 'These men will go home a lot richer than they arrived. I would have thought you'd be supporting that, Alec.'

'I hope,' another man said, also in fluoro, bald, fleshy. He was the head of manufacturing at the plant across the bay at Electrona, 'there's a lot of translators coming with them.'

'They're bringing translators,' said Frank.

'It's going to be a huge problem,' said Brankovic.

Nods went around the table. There was an air of *I can't believe I've lived to see this day.*

I observed Mick Feltham. He had the look of someone who was going to retire after the bridge was done. He'd take his wife on a cruise and then maybe move to the shack. He'd kick the football with his grandchildren, and when they asked him did he really build the bridge to Bruny, he'd say, 'I sure did.'

The world is a machine that feeds on people. There's always a cost. There are always broken marriages and messed-up children. Happiness—simple happiness—maybe it doesn't really exist anymore. Not in the world I saw, anyway. When it did happen, it was fleeting at best. Somewhere in the great rushing wind of conflict, refugees, climate change and capitalism, it had dissipated. It would be easy to blame capitalism but it wasn't just capitalism. It was this idea that everyone had a God-given right to live as they pleased. Now, in the US, there was a righteous, well-armed underbelly wearing their brown shirts and creeping deeper into America's psyche while the Democrats might as well have been talking underwater.

When the GFC happened back in 2008, the money to bail people out in America went to Wall Street and Silicon Valley. East Coast and West Coast. But it was the places in between— the 'flyover zone'—where the real pain was felt; where the homes were lost and the suicides happened and the kids went without decent food and schools. Lots of those people had bought the messages of the far right. Men and women, young and old, with their Christian creed and their right to bear arms, had elected themselves a leader who was going to save them. But he hadn't and America was paying the price. Australia had been teetering on the brink of right-wing extremism for years. Across the world there was a deepening sense of powerlessness. In Europe, a lot of people were overwhelmed by the tide of refugees and the influx of Islam. Now there was also the fear of speaking out. Of being seen as racist and xenophobic, anti-multiculturalism, anti-progress. The chaos of Brexit was really the desperate bid of the English to salvage whatever values they'd surrendered back in the 1950s. The growing movement to dismantle the EU was the same. What were our shared values? Nobody seemed to know, other than to look to the past. But you can't wind back time. There was trouble coming. We could all feel it.

Back in the meeting room at Tinderbox, I said, 'We're all delighted that it looks like the bridge can be repaired, Mick. That the damage wasn't worse. I can only imagine how personal it feels to all of you to look out there and see it.'

They turned their heads in unison and took in the mutilation.

I flicked open my notes for the first time and scanned my itinerary. 'So, in your emails, you'll discover a schedule of one-on-ones. Frank, would you hand out the hard copies?'

Frank stood and said, 'We need everyone to make themselves available. No excuses.' He handed a bunch of papers to the man next to him who took the top sheet and handed the rest on.

Frank looked as if he was about to say more, but I spoke again.

'Let me add that I know I sound American these days—it's a hard thing to avoid after thirty-plus years away—but I am a Tasmanian. I grew up here, and I have a shack over there on North Bruny. On the hill. What happens here, with the bridge, this is personal to me too.'

There was a silence. This was personal for all of us. I could work with that.

'Now, any questions before we finish up?' I asked.

There was silence, and then the head of manufacturing said, 'What if it can't be done? By March? It makes no sense to rush it now. Except if you wanted to be re-elected.'

The ripple of smirks went around the table.

'Look, from my perspective, getting the community aligned, it takes the time it takes. You can't hurry these things. That aside, there is a schedule, but that's Mick's area of expertise, not mine. I recall, Mick, you've worked miracles on deadlines before. The new Launceston power scheme for one?'

Mick looked as if someone had stroked his feathers. As I said, I do my homework.

'If that's it, then let's bring this to a close,' I said. 'Thank you all for your time. I look forward to speaking with each of you next week. Enjoy your weekend.'

With that, I walked out of the room and back out into the reception area. Karen stood up again and, with a smile, handed me a paper bag.

'You must be hungry,' she said. 'I put this aside for you.'

I thanked her. I am a fan of the thoughtfulness of women. Then I crossed the foyer and headed towards the waiting government car.

Inside the muted interior, behind the tinted glass, I wondered why that had been tougher than I'd imagined. Not tough the way militias were tough, or religious fanatics, or women returned from captivity. But the feeling of injury. They were bruised. As if the bomb had damaged them. Or maybe it went deeper than that. The daily dissent wherever they went. Working on this bridge was costing them.

The government chauffeur said nothing and I blessed him for it. Frank was moving towards the car. The person walking with him was Mick Feltham.

'It's what it is,' I heard Frank saying. 'Premier's relying on you.'

'At least she doesn't waste time,' Mick said. 'See ya, Frank.' And he turned back towards the buildings and Frank got into the car.

'All right,' he said. 'Well, I think that went well. They do good pies near the ferry terminal, if you're hungry.'

I held up my lunch bag. Frank frowned. 'Okay,' he said.

The car exited the worksite, and took the road that would connect us with the highway to Kettering.

Frank said, 'JC told me about your house there at Dennes Point.'

Frank making small talk. Good, I thought. A small power shift.

'Haven't seen it in a long time,' I said.

I wondered what would have changed over there in ten years. Apart from the bridge, maybe very little. This was what I relied on: that while the world went to hell in a handbasket, Tasmania stayed pretty much the same, decade after decade.

CHAPTER FIVE

W e could have taken a boat across from the construction
site, but I'd requested otherwise. I'd also offered to go
on from Tinderbox alone, but JC had insisted Frank accompany
me today. I think he wanted to show Frank that his objection
to me being here was unwarranted.

It had been a long time since I'd been on the Bruny ferry.
And despite what everyone said, I was sure it wouldn't be operational in a year or two. The bridge would do it in. There
weren't enough ferry devotees to make it worthwhile. It was the
market reality. And I wanted to understand the communities
that would lose all the passing trade.

We drove through the tiny suburbs of Howden, Margate,
Snug, past Coningham and Oyster Cove, along the winding
rural road until we descended into Kettering. From there the
road continued on to Woodbridge and eventually wound back
to Cygnet, if you didn't veer down Ferry Road. All these places
named in honour of our British overlords. The new King of
England is still Australia's figurehead. If the crowd at the
airport, and the people I'd observed in the streets and shops were

anything to go by, Tasmania was still almost entirely an Anglo-Saxon population of people schooled in British manners, habits, food and government. It was possible Tasmania had changed, beneath the surface, but I doubted it. Other than people who looked like tourists, I had hardly seen a non-Caucasian person.

The channel used to be a place of orchards—cherries, apricots, apples. The apples had mostly gone in the seventies when Britain joined the European market. Tasmania had grown an abundance of potato varieties back then too, but they had gone when one of the multinationals insisted on farmers growing a single potato variety suitable for making fries. A few years later, with all that diversity lost, the multinational moved on to another country with cheaper labour, better subsidies. Looking at the countryside with its weatherboard farmhouses, paddocks, fences and tidy gardens, I wondered if the latest venture was alpacas or health spas. Sheep's cheese or sloe gin.

The Bruny ferry crossing is twelve minutes or so. The wait was much longer. There were vehicles lined up across the bitumen car park in neat lines. I went into the cafe with Frank and got coffee. I took it back to the car and ate my sandwich. It was a Reuben and I wondered if someone thought of that especially for me, coming from New York. If so, I appreciated it. The silverside was good. The sauerkraut was excellent and the cheese just right. Not toasted but delicious. I was suddenly homesick for New York. The trees had been bare when I'd raced home to pack for this trip. The wind rushing through Union Square had grown icy in the weeks I'd been gone to the Middle East. Suddenly everyone was in black puffer coats and beanies.

When you live in the East Village, you can walk two blocks and wonder what part of the world you're in and if you're safe. Near the East River, in Alphabet City where the avenues go by letters, even today the code is still A for adventure, B for beware, C for caution and D for dead. I live in a fifth floor walk-up on East 4th Street between Caution and Dead. It's fine to go to the grocery one block over, but not to the one across the road. Sometimes it's good to be a white person and feel unsafe. It reminds me what my children have to go through every day. What the people I work with go through every day. Of course, for most women, fear is a state of daily awareness. But at six feet tall and trained to defend myself, I've probably had less of that than many women. I love the East Village. I love its edginess that's so unlike the West Village. I love the little library on Tompkins Square Park and the coffee at Third Rail and Momofuku's shrimp buns and chicken noodle soup. It was hard to believe I was there just the other night with Tavvy and Paul having a last dinner before I left again. Though they're both grown up, and I leave Manhattan often, something about being here, waiting for the Bruny ferry, made me feel very far away from them. I hadn't given them this. In a way, I thought I'd been saving them from it. From the smallness of a life here in Tasmania. I'd escaped. I'd wanted them to have a different life. A bigger, more colourful, more international life. Well, they sure got that, but maybe I'd been wrong. That's the downside with parenting. There's no going back.

The chauffeur started up the car and drove us onto the ferry. It was the same old beast as the last time I was here. Salt-sodden, rust-eaten, painted up and practical. A double-decker ferry carrying buses, a couple of trucks bearing the branding of building contractors, residents, and all those tourists in their rental cars, all keen to see Adventure Bay, Cloudy Bay, the lighthouse, the Neck. It was easy to spot them. They were the Asians and Indians with their cameras and slightly jaunty holiday wear at odds with the practical clothing worn by the locals. Clearly Manhattan wasn't the only place where the black puffer jacket was the outdoor uniform. My briefing notes told me that South Bruny had an abundance of visitor accommodation, cruises, fishing trips, shops, cafes, wineries, history and diving. On the long pristine beaches, fairy penguins came ashore after dark, shearwaters nested in the sand dunes and there were dawn vistas from isolated lookouts. Two hundred and fifty thousand tourists a year were proof that whatever Bruny offered, people liked it. It made sense to build a bridge. So why was everyone so het up about it? Why had someone wanted to blow the thing up? Was it just that Tasmanians will protest anything that comes in the guise of progress?

'Why do you think Tasmanians are so upset about the bridge, Frank?' I asked, sipping coffee.

'Because everyone here is inoculated against change. And the worst of them are the sea changers and tree changers who have done more to change the place than anyone.'

'But it makes sense, yes, to let tourists have better access to Bruny? I mean, they're coming anyway,' I said.

'There's plenty of room,' said Frank. 'The place is booming. People ought to be grateful.'

'Yet people smell a rat. Is it the size of the bridge? The two billion dollars? I mean, the scale of the thing, it doesn't quite add up, does it?'

'What's to add up? Tasmanians complain all the time about being the poor cousin and then, when the federal government finally gives them a golden goose, they turn up their noses at it.'

'So there is no other agenda? Something everyone's missing?'

'You've been here twenty-four hours and you're already talking conspiracy theories?'

We were parked on the lower level of the ferry, so I got out of the car and took the stairs to the upper deck. There, leaning against the railing, I surveyed the channel. It was dark denim blue. A five- to ten-knot south-westerly was ruffling the water. I breathed in the salt air. Most places I've travelled, I've found beauty, but in Tasmania, each time I come back, I get hit with it all over again. The beauty here is of a different order. Something to do with the light and the air that is so crisp and unpolluted it almost hurts to take a deep breath at first.

Further along the deck, a young woman emerged from a minibus in a floral dress with a garland around her head. Other women emerged from the bus, also in floral dresses and high heels. One had a camera, and she began to photograph the garlanded woman, who posed as models do, assured of her beauty, at ease with her body and her smile, slightly embarrassed at all the attention. The breeze was stiffening as we moved into the channel, and the wind blew her dress up, revealing black lace underwear. All the women laughed.

'Come together, ladies,' said the photographer, and snapped them as they cuddled and laughed. Being November, it occurred to me that this was probably a Melbourne Cup party. Australia's favourite horse race inspired social events across the country. Even in Hobart.

I noticed that men were emerging from the cars around the women. As if they could smell the scent of fresh oestrogen, these older men in blue singlets or polo shirts, with their beer guts and jowls, sauntered about taking off their caps and rubbing their balding heads, puffing out their chests, nodding to one another and covertly staring at the women, like roosters assessing the hens. Are you serious? I wanted to say to them. Don't you know how old you are? They are never going to look at you!

Along the railing, three Chinese women had dressed for this ferry crossing in blue striped t-shirts, white pants and sneakers. They photographed one another, but when they saw the male attention the floral women were getting, they moved further down the railing. They looked a little lost.

A passing yacht heeled to starboard, heading up the channel. The Chinese women returned to their car. The floral women resumed their seats on the minibus. I looked north and took in the dramatic expanse of bridge, huge even from this distance.

Driving off the ferry, we followed the traffic up over the hill. At the North Bruny turn-off, only one other car took the road to Dennes Point. The rest of the traffic headed south.

The road had been upgraded, widened and sealed in anticipation of the bridge. Gone were the tight gravel corners and corrugated surface. Now it was a four-lane tarmac carved through farmlands. Only as we reached Dennes Point did the roadworks end, and we diverted to the old road. We could see the last section that, when complete, would sweep over the hill, down past the 1800s red-brick farmhouse, to the bridge.

We passed my house on the left. I didn't mention this to Frank. Perhaps he already knew. I was relieved it was on this old section of road away from the bridge traffic. So was the new cafe and local art gallery that had opened a few years back. And there was the bridge up close, winged, injured, a giant beast fallen on one knee.

We pulled in by the jetty. It had been upgraded too—lengthened and widened for equipment and supplies. We got out and walked a short distance along the shore to the head-quarters of the BFG.

'Very well funded, as you will see. They pretend they're not a political group, so donations are tax deductible,' Frank sneered.

'Like churches,' I said.

Frank did not reply.

BFG number two camp was very different to the one across at Tinderbox. Over there it was hippie music festival. Here it was neat rows of temporary cabins, portable toilets and shower facilities clearly marked. Rental recreational vehicles were parked in neat lines. People were seated at outdoor tables, engaged in conversations. There was an attention to order. And no music. People paused and observed us as we walked in. Frank's suit and tie was decidedly out of place and I was glad for the outdoor pants and polar fleece jacket I was wearing. I blended in. The blackboard outside the kitchen tent announced today's lunch as vegetarian lasagne with garlic bread and salad at fifteen dollars a serve. There were water tanks and duckboard to protect the shoreline and almost a military air. Somewhere in this camp, I thought, were people who knew how to lay explosives. But why now? Why after almost four years? Why not wait until the day it opened, with all the politicians present to watch it blow? When the international media were going to be here in force for the whole event. Why *now*?

Maybe they got desperate. It was a long time to maintain a protest. Every day and every night. No, I decided. These people had sticking power. Four years, through one election cycle and into the next. Why, I wondered, not for the first time, were Tasmanians so good at protesting?

I recognised Gilbert Farris immediately. If you were casting Farris in a movie, you'd want a character actor. Michael Shannon would do just fine. The same sociopathic tendencies, easy smile and hard eyes.

Farris bought the property at the end of the beach a year before the bridge project was announced. He'd thought he was retiring from the world to work on his next great tome on the human species. But then people began crawling over his little bit of paradise. Bridge designers were imagining caissons and cables, engineers were considering wind and tide, torsion and tension. Soon enough, boatloads of workers were being ferried back and forth from the pier by his house and Farris's haven was suddenly the scene of one of Australia's most significant infrastructure projects in years.

I've known a lot of men like Farris. Because of the privileges afforded them, they are eminently employable. I'm menopausal. I know I can sound tough about men, but I've had fifty-six years for things to simmer beneath the surface and now they're bubbling up. My daughter Tavvy—Octavia—calls them cis-gendered white males, but to me the ones like Farris are just husbands. They tend to have wives who for years worked full-time while their men built careers. Women who raised children, did the ferrying of provisions and sports bags, ran the social calendar, oversaw the homework and house-work, the soccer fixtures and the swimming lessons, loved these men and ensured with all their care and nurture and support that these men of words, ideas and inventions fulfilled their greatness. And this greatness was made evident by the world bestowing that word—genius—upon them. And having had it bestowed, they carried this word as they might carry a great shield bearing their names and icons.

Maxine and I had both gone to a Catholic girls' school. Our mother had not exactly behaved to type, but we had been trained to be good. Compliant. Well-behaved. Charming. Never laugh too loud. Never interrupt. Never tease a boy. Be of service. Do the housework. Make the beds. Cook the meals. Honour thy father and thy mother and thy brother. Pretend sex never happens.

Everywhere I've travelled, regardless of skin colour, religion, economic or political circumstances, it's men who've created the violence and viciousness of the world. It's the way it is. There've been a few exceptions, of course. Maggie Thatcher. Ruined the lives of millions in her own country and a few in the Falklands too. And Aung Sun Suu Kyi. I don't excuse the savagery that's happened under her leadership, but she never had the real power or authority. It was all show. The Myanmar military were always in control after she was elected. She spent twenty years under house arrest, under that same military regime. Lost her sons, her husband, and God knows what else.

One woman I knew, also in Asia, was under house arrest for three years. Every night, the militia sent in a different soldier to rape her. Every night. After three years, there was an election. Government was restored. She was freed. That's what democracy can do.

But people get immune to violence when it's all they know, and all I know is that men enact it everywhere. And usually they enact it in the name of some kind of God, even the God of Economics. I try not to go down this road, getting cynical, but it comes with the territory. Like the bad dreams, and the sweats that follow loud bangs or when I hear a child scream. I don't sleep well. I get jumpy in four-wheel drives. It would be easy to think of it as PTSD, but who isn't a little bit fucked up by the modern world?

CHAPTER SIX

Gilbert Farris was the bestselling author of seven tomes, including the controversial bestseller *Homogenocene*. He had been insisting loudly on every news outlet that the BFG had had no part in the bombing. They'd never advocated violence. But the BFG, he had clarified, applauded any effort to delay the completion of the bridge. I'd sat through hours of footage JC's people had prepared for me, giving me the media history over the past four years and more.

'This bridge has no good part to play for Tasmanians,' Farris had said on an ABC special on the bridge back when the federal government, heading to the polls six years ago, made it a key election promise for Tasmania.

'Imagine what two billion dollars transforming the Midlands into arable land for growing crops would do,' he had said.

He came up well on camera, if a little oafish. His nose was getting fleshy, his jawline too. But he had the same pale blue eyes that had made him look penetrating in his YouTube lectures and on the jackets of his books.

'What would two billion dollars on wind farms do? Imagine even ten per cent of that spent on Tasmanian schools!'

Farris reprised this once we were seated outside a large portable office. The Bruny Bridge swept forty or fifty metres above us. The government had compulsorily acquired a narrow stretch of Farris's land for the flyover, and it was said that he had used the money to fund the BFG.

There were two women flanking him.

'Maggie Lennox,' said the first, a striking older woman in a bright orange jacket and a strand of pearls that whispered Paspaley. 'That money poured into Tasmanian schools would change an entire generation.'

Maggie Lennox had a South African accent. 'And this is Jenny Singh,' she said.

'Public relations,' said Jenny Singh. She was my age, all generous curves, red lips, liquid black eyes, a floral headscarf and sunglasses dangling from around her neck. She'd previously been head of PR for a multinational in Zurich before sea-changing to Bruny. Farris might be their star mouthpiece, but it was Jenny Singh who had landed so much of the press that had advanced the BFG's agenda.

We all sat in deckchairs with the bridge ahead and above us. Frank took out a handkerchief and dusted off his highly polished shoes. Farris was observing me. I turned to Singh. 'Do you live here at Dennes Point?' As I said, I never let people know I've backgrounded them.

'We're at Adventure Bay,' she said. Adventure Bay was on South Bruny, about an hour's drive. 'Where all the tourists end up. We've had years of resisting hotels and high-rises down there. And we're losing. We're all losing. We didn't move here to find Bruny becoming Miami or the Gold Coast. Bruny Island is a small community. A really active community. We moved here because we don't like crowds. We don't want our roads congested, our wildlife killed. There's no planning on water reserves or even toilet blocks. No planning on sewerage. This government has no idea . . .'

'You have an accommodation business, yes?' I asked Lennox.

'Maggie owns *Solitude*,' said Singh. *Solitude*. The high end of the high end of Tasmanian tourism. Word was that Oprah and Reese Witherspoon had stayed there recently with Witherspoon's kids. It was price on application, tailored services. Starting price apparently some twenty thousand US dollars per week.

'And the cafe and gallery here at Dennes Point too,' Singh added. 'It provides all the food for the camp.'

'This isn't just about economics,' said Farris. 'It's about a loss of place.' He had an abrasive quality. 'Tasmanians are like small, furry animals with no predators. Well, they have a predator now, and it's a monster.'

'People are distraught,' agreed Singh.

I had taken in the CCTV surveillance at the camp on approach. The BFG had eyes on every part of the project, and they had eyes on themselves. Smart. And they had a high-powered telescope trained on the worksite back over at Tinderbox. Farris was happy to point that out.

'We don't miss anything,' he said.

'So you got film of the bridge being blown up?'

'We handed it all over,' he said. 'As soon as we began this protest, we knew they'd want to disable us. And they've tried.'

'I suggested the cameras be installed right from the start,' Jenny Singh added. 'I was sure things would get nasty. Two billion dollars, after all. The government was always going to try to wipe us out.'

'That's the way you people work, we know that,' said Farris.

You people . . . I didn't bite. 'What does your footage show of that morning?'

'That it was dark,' said Farris. 'Security saw nothing until the boat was halfway down the channel. Godawful explosion. Woke everyone in Dennes Point and at Tinderbox. I was in the kitchen making coffee and felt the tremor. Thought it was a bloody earthquake. Then that far pylon just collapsed. The whole thing shook like a guitar string, then it started twisting. I thought the whole bridge was going to go.'

The Bruny Friends Group had formed within twenty-four hours of the bridge being announced, and they'd been going ever since, gaining momentum with members and funding. They were highly engaged, well informed, well resourced, articulate and well connected. Because Farris was involved, many high-profile visitors had been drawn to Tasmania to see the bridge and support their cause. In short, they were the worst sort of protesters for a government or a corporation.

'You've been at this a long time, and you've built incredible awareness,' I said. 'You've got about forty per cent of Tasmanians supporting you. Why haven't you succeeded in stopping it?'

Lennox sighed. 'It's beautiful,' she said. 'You know. You see it, even looking like it does now. People come here and they see the architecture, this feat of engineering, and they love it.'

'They don't see the island trampled with tourists,' said Singh. 'They don't see the damage to birdlife or wildlife, the threat to the fairy penguins and shearwater rookeries. It's more than a loss of place, though Gilbert is right, it is that too. It's the death of a way of life. You put a bridge in and it stops being an island.'

At this they all nodded. *Island.* Tasmanians are island people. Bruny Islanders even more so. It's a very different identity to that of someone from the American Midwest, the mountains of Europe, the veldts of Africa. There is always the awareness that we are somehow water-bound and water-dependant. The water is friend and foe. Every child is taught to swim and every year there are drownings—fishermen, surfers, jet ski riders, swimmers. We are water people. If this bridge was being built to join Tasmania to mainland Australia, Tasmania would, I imagined, be absorbed into mainland Australian culture within a decade or two. I was sure Tasmanians would resist that with everything they had, despite the economic advantages. Because to live on an island isn't just a location. It's a sense of belonging. It's history and sacrifice. It's a choice to be remote. It's a kind of metaphor.

Manhattan is an island. It's easy for people to forget that, but I never do. I am sure that's why I felt so at home there when I first arrived for university. I was between water. Surrounded by water. There was the smell of salt in the afternoon breeze that blew through Midtown. I could watch the sun set over New Jersey across the Hudson. There was the possibility that, if we had to, we could close the bridges and the tunnels. Of course, no-one had seen an attack coming by air. But the premise remained. An island was both a stronghold and a bolthole. It was also a choice to live on land that might be prey to the

sea level rising, to tsunamis, hurricanes and king tides. These
new arrivals to Bruny—the Farrises and the Singhs and the
Lennoxes—these sea changers with their ideas of an old age
far from the madding crowd, and the residents who felt that
sense of island deep in their bones, it was probably the same for
all of them. The longer they'd been here, the deeper it went.
And right here on Dennes Point was the micro reality of being
an islander in the face of a very macro bridge.

❧

'Why was it blown up now?' I asked them.

I thought Maggie Lennox was going to answer, but Farris
interjected.

'It's always about who has the most to gain,' he said.

'This is fabulous publicity,' said Singh. 'It makes all the
protesters look like terrorists. Public sympathy is now on your
brother's side, just as he's going into an election.'

'Gilbert is right,' said Lennox. 'Someone is benefiting
from this.'

'Yes,' said Singh. 'The Chinese.'

'The Chinese?' I asked.

'The Chinese!' said Frank who had, until now, maintained
a polite silence. 'The Chinese are Tasmania's biggest investor.'

'They don't let us go there and buy land and businesses
willy nilly,' said Singh, 'in case you haven't noticed. The same
in Switzerland. Smart places don't. They protect their assets.
And land is our asset.'

'So is beauty,' said Maggie Lennox.

Frank scoffed.

I gave him a look. He leaned back in his chair and stared up at the sky. 'A one-hundred-million-dollar golf course and health resort on the east coast. A three-hundred-million-dollar investment in the dairy industry. Do you people have any idea of the employment that creates?'

'Precious little, actually, Frank,' said Gilbert Farris, 'if you bothered to do your own analysis and didn't simply believe the press releases of the Chinese government.'

'Frank,' I said. 'Can we have a moment?'

I got up and indicated for him to walk with me. Quietly, once we were out of earshot, I said to him, 'I really appreciate the time you've given this today. And I'm sure you've heard all this before.' He was shorter than me, which is often helpful. 'How about I meet you up at the cafe when we're finished here? Or if you want to head back to Hobart—I know you've got better things to do.'

He looked at me and acquiesced. 'Don't hatch any new theories without letting me know,' he said, without smiling. 'You're sorted for tomorrow, yeah? I heard the foreman's taking you back over. He'll pick you up at the jetty.'

I nodded. He turned and gave Farris, Singh and Lennox a short wave and walked away.

'Too young for the job,' said Singh when I returned. And no-one disagreed.

'So the Chinese . . .' I said.

'It's chequebook colonialism,' said Farris. 'They're buying our island one property at a time, and everyone refuses to see it as a problem. They have their so-called Buddhists here filming everyone. They're building their global database of faces, even here in Tasmania. They're going to make a killing selling that to ASIO one day. Or the CIA.'

'How dare they film us!' said Singh. 'At every festival or public event, they're there. They don't have my permission.'

'They don't have to,' said Farris. 'And they've been pushing the foreign labour laws for years. Now, they've got them. The perfect scenario. It was always only a matter of time. And Tasmanians—your brother and his cronies especially—are too stupid to see it.'

Australia had never allowed foreign labour en masse before. But now it was brand-new law. Ironically, it had been the far-right White Nation Party that had supported the legislation to pass it through parliament. They'd been promised more funding of apprenticeships, a promise that may or may not be kept depending on the outcome of the next election. A new era was dawning for Australia. Globalisation of labour had arrived. Not via the internet with Paypal, Indian web developers and online shopping, but with a foreign workforce building infra-structure right here in sleepy Tasmania.

It was not going to be easy, managing the media around that. Racism was sure to rear its ugly head. But, then, humans doing anything together is not easy. Why is that?

'So the Chinese orchestrated this?' I asked.

Singh nodded. Lennox was looking uncomfortable.

'The Chinese Communist Party to be precise. They're playing a long game and we're sitting ducks,' said Farris. 'We're playing chequers and they're playing Go.'

'You know all this happened in the wake of the visit from the Chinese president?' said Singh.

'The bombing?'

'No,' said Farris, 'the announcement of the bridge. The Chinese president came, and within twelve months we have a massive increase in Chinese investment in hotels and real estate. They even paid to extend the runway at the airport so planes can fly direct between Hobart and China. Then the federal government suddenly comes up with two billion dollars for a bridge to nowhere made from Chinese steel. And Tasmania signs up to China's Belt and Road Initiative. That's how your brother is getting the backing to keep his spending spree going.'

'Ask your little brother about the Chinese,' Farris continued. 'It's a bit like the Bin Laden family being flown out of New York after September 11. No-one dared ask the Saudis what they were doing sheltering the fountainhead of al-Qaeda. Still don't. And no-one asks about the Chinese here. Here it's all good for business. They own the fish farms, the dairy farms, the wind farms. Woolnorth on the west coast, our biggest wind farm, was paid for by taxpayers but was sold to the Chinese. Now it's owned by the Chinese government. Not just a Chinese company—the Chinese government. Because we need the cash. We've got a debt-laden Ponzi scheme that's meant to fund public service retirees and we need the cash. You can't sell the dams; that's legislated, at least for now. But you can sell the wind farms. What were the terms? Don't know. Commercial-in-confidence, of course. It's a joint venture between two governments, and governments have to protect their commercial position. *Not.*'

Maggie Lennox said, 'I do not, personally, feel that we have anything to fear from the Chinese. I believe that China is simply doing what any powerful nation does. What the US has done, and the British before that. They are investing in their allies. I know that's new and hard to accept for some people, that we have become an ally of China, but we live in a global world. I'm much more concerned about what's behind this investment from the federal government's perspective. That's where I think we should be focusing our attention. And the state government is simply doing their bidding. Possibly without understanding the larger picture.'

We are pawns, I thought. We're all pawns.

CHAPTER SEVEN

The house at Bruny was a tiny jewel box of light in the afternoon sun. It still had its 1940s weatherboard exterior but now it was painted a Greek sea blue. Inside, this ode to Mediterranean summers continued with polished floors and blue and white rugs. On the walls were framed posters of balconies overlooking the Aegean Sea and flowers in terracotta pots. The kitchen still had the original fireplace and a door to the balcony. Stephanie had suggested the deck be widened during the renovations and returned around the house by the dining room. The effect was a length of view up and down the channel and across into North-West Bay. The afternoon sea breeze was in and the water was whipped with white tips.

In the fridge there was beer, three sorts of cheese, fig paste, white wine and a jar of caramelised onions. In the cupboard was pasta, pasta sauce, tea bags, long-life milk, red wine, dry biscuits and sardines. In the freezer I found bread and my favourite Homer Hudson ice cream. In the bathroom were blue-and-white-striped towels and good shampoo, conditioner and body wash. Stephanie had said I'd need almost nothing, and she was right. On the back of the bedroom door there were two dressing-gowns.

Wishful thinking, I thought.

∽

When Granny, our father's mother, died, she left me and Max and JC her house: a little white cottage just off the road into Dennes Point. This was the house our father had grown up in, before he went to school in town to complete his education, boarding with an aunt. Our father's father died in a work accident when our dad was twelve. Fell from a roof. He'd been a carpenter and an early representative for the unions. When JC and I were born, Granny had come to live with us.

'Well, I did it to help your mother, of course,' Granny told me later, when I was a teenager. 'I mean, you were twins!' Looking back, I think she did it so that we actually got the kind of mothering she believed in. I imagine Granny could see from the moment she set eyes on the very young widowed Hyacinth and her little baby Maxine that Hyacinth Coleman was not the maternal type.

Granny had a separate flat in the garden of our house. It was Granny I remember holding the bowl to catch the vomit when I was sick, teaching me to knit and sew, playing cards with us by the fire, listening to my woes about schoolyard bullies and incomprehensible maths.

Once a year, each winter, she went on a holiday. She'd take bus trips across the Nullarbor or up to the Great Barrier Reef, bringing us back bright bits of coral and seashells. I remember the house feeling very empty without her.

During the summer holidays, Granny took us home to Bruny with her. 'Give your parents a break,' she'd say. Dad often came with us. Mother rarely. It was here we got to run wild. Barefoot for weeks on end, so that lacing our feet into new shoes at the beginning of the school year was awful for the first few days.

Granny died when JC and I were seventeen. The first person I had loved and lost. Our father insisted we wait until we had all turned thirty before any decisions were made about the house. He said it was smart to keep it as an investment. So it was rented. By the time I was thirty, I was long gone from Tasmania, resident of New York, with an undergrad in politics from NYU and a PhD in international relations from Columbia, an intern at the UN thinking I was going to contribute to world peace.

JC was in the UK working as a lawyer at a regional firm, and then he moved to a London practice. Max had gone into nursing, specialising in paediatrics, and was working in Melbourne at the Children's Hospital. She became involved with the Australian Nursing Federation.

This was what happened to Tasmanian children. A lot of us left the island in search of bigger dreams. And then, sometimes, we came back. This contingent living interstate and overseas was known by economists and sociologists as *the Tasmanian diaspora*. We were the intellectual wealth that lived away from the island and, if the island was lucky, one day returned.

JC came home at thirty-six because he'd met a Tasmanian girl called Stephanie, only twenty-four, in London. They decided that if they were going to have children, Tasmania was the place they wanted to raise them. They were married, and a few years after that, he and Stephanie produced Ella and Grace, now thirteen and ten.

I remembered the short letter I'd received from our father in his measured cursive hand.

Your brother has decided to run for parliament. For the Liberal Party. I have wished him well. I have explained that due to our political history, my family's values before me, and my values, I am sorry I cannot campaign for him. I have, however, I remind myself, given him the benefit of the Coleman name. Certainly from the media attention his campaign is getting, he seems to have no shortage of support.

'Times have changed,' JC said, when asked by the media how he could reject his father's politics and switch sides. 'Economics isn't what it was back then. Nowadays we need Tasmanian families to flourish, not just survive. I have enormous respect for my father and all he achieved during his time in parliament. But the Labor Party hasn't improved the lives of ordinary Tasmanians. Tasmania needs to play a bigger game if we are going to meet the future well prepared.'

The electorate bought it. He was made shadow Minister for Growth and Development. Three years in, he was party leader. At the next election, almost eight years ago, his party won government after Labor's long run of sixteen years in power. The Tasmanian people had, it seemed, finally forgiven the Liberals for all the corruption around gambling and forestry. Or simply forgotten. Not that the Labor Party had been much better. There had been corruption on both sides.

'Why is politics these days so often the choice between the lesser of two inadequates?' Max had asked when JC became leader of the Liberals. 'I'm so proud of him, but you know JC—he's going to be impossible if someone good doesn't emerge on the other side.'

By then she was the head of the Australian Nursing Federation and a fixture in the media. So Max came home too, bringing all her nursing activism with her. Our father doorknocked every day for a year for her. Max was elected in his old seat for the Labor Party the same election JC became Premier.

A very public fall from grace six years ago by the then Labor leader (he was discovered to have taken bribes to buy his support for tourism development in national and state parks) saw Max made leader of the Opposition. Nothing like putting in a woman to clean up the mess, she had said at the time. They became serious rivals, JC and Max, and yet somehow they kept turning up for Sunday lunch, for Christmas Eve, for Good Friday fish and January barbecues. How it worked, exactly, nobody really knew, but Dad, in his calls to me in New York every Sunday without fail, told me Max still looked at JC the way older sisters who love their younger brothers look at them. And he said he'd seen JC put his arm around Max while turning the sausages at the barbecue, and they'd laughed together like two comrades who knew the war would be over one day. This had heartened our father no end, thinking we could all still get along.

'You're family a long time,' he used to say. Before he started quoting Shakespeare.

Once they were both back in Tasmania, Max fell for a cottage at the Bay of Fires on the far north-east tip of Tasmania, a series of beaches with pink granite rocks and aquamarine sea. JC said he and Stephanie had their hearts set on building a holiday house at Spring Beach, midway up the east coast. Which, after the divvying up, left the little weatherboard cottage on Bruny to me.

It wasn't worth much at the time. It would have been a better investment to sell it and buy up the east coast, too. Land prices up there had skyrocketed two hundred per cent over the next five years. But I'd always loved the Bruny house. I loved the view. I loved the memories of Granny and summers and being free.

About five years ago, Stephanie suggested we set up the Bruny house as a short-stay business. The long-term tenants had given notice and she thought it would be a good earner with the ever-increasing tourist trade. She sent me quotes for restumping, rewiring, a bathroom upgrade and a new deck. The photos she sent showed the house I knew so well. It still had the patterned wallpaper, a wood stove in the kitchen and an outdoor toilet. Stephanie organised builders, painters, plumbers. Sorted new carpet and furniture. It created a friendship between us, all that to and fro of ideas and decisions on colours and costs. And Stephanie wouldn't accept a cent for her troubles, for all the hours she put into the cottage.

'That's what family is, Astrid,' she'd said. 'We look out for one another. Heaven knows, we need to do that more than most families. Besides, it's fun. JC won't let me do anything else on the place at Spring Beach, so I might as well use my new-found knowledge on your place.'

Just after the renovations were completed, the bridge project was announced. There had been a steady flow of journalists, engineers, architects and bridge enthusiasts looking for an Airbnb in a convenient location to the bridge ever since.

'Did you know?' I'd asked Stephanie. 'When you suggested the renovation, did you know about the bridge?'

'Of course not,' Stephanie said. It wasn't a video call, so it was impossible to tell if her face said something different from her voice. We are a political family through and through. She knew how to play the game, I was sure.

When she got the news I was coming home, she'd cancelled the forward bookings.

'Of course you must stay with us, in the downstairs apartment. It's right by the pool and quiet. Much nicer than a rental. And the girls will love the chance to get to know you better. But I'm sure you'll also need to be over on Bruny quite a bit of the time, too. With the queue these days, you can wait for hours for the ferry. This way you have the option of staying on the island. And there's nothing like being part of the community.'

As I said, she's a good woman, our Stephanie.

'I'm thinking I'll spend the night on Bruny,' I'd said to her last night when we'd discussed today's itinerary. 'I'm keen to see all you've done to the house.'

'I'm keen for you to see it too,' she said. 'You haven't had a moment to catch your breath. It's all ready for you. Just take PJs and a change of clothes.'

'How will I get back?' I asked.

'Are you sure you want to come back tomorrow, not Sunday?'

'I need to get back,' I said. JC had given me an office on his floor in the executive building. There was a lot to get underway.

'JC's PA can organise someone to collect you from Dennes Point pier and run you across in a boat and a car could wait for you at Tinderbox and drive you to town. If you left Bruny at eleven am you'd be back in town by midday. Would that work?'

'Easy,' I said. 'I could get a rental,' I added.

'I think you've got enough on your plate without remembering to drive on the left side of the road,' she laughed. 'Wait till you've settled in. And keep your phone on in case there's problems with the weather.'

'Last time I was here, there was no mobile coverage up that end of the island,' I said.

'All that's changed with the bridge. Telstra put up a new tower.'

I sighed. 'I used to think it was the only place in the world I could be unavailable.'

Stephanie nodded. 'Those were the days,' she said.

CHAPTER EIGHT

I lay on the bed and took in the curtains, the lamps, the wooden dresser, the view beyond the window into the garden with gum trees dropping leaves in the lazy afternoon breeze. It was almost 4 pm. I had started at 6 am.

I took out my phone and sent Stephanie a text. *Thank you. It's fabulous. Granny would be amazed! I love it!*

I sent JC a text too. *Met with Farris, Singh and Lennox. And mgt group earlier. All good. Talk tomorrow.*

Then I turned off my phone and closed my eyes. I thought about the meeting with the Bruny Friends Group. I could hear Jenny Singh saying, 'It's the death of a way of life.' I'd heard that one a few times. *The death of a way of life.* Fishermen, subsistence farmers, forest dwellers. A lot of violence these days had its genesis in some kind of environmental disaster if you looked. My career had been spent trying to help people come to terms with the new. Give them some sense of empowerment that wasn't attached to the need for guns and missiles. But weapons were the biggest international trade—all across the Baltic, the Middle East, throughout Asia and Africa. More than one hundred billion dollars was spent on weapons every year. If people could get their hands on weapons, they generally didn't see the need for conversation. It was my job to remind them.

Who exactly had stood to gain from the bombing of the bridge? Officially I wasn't here to solve the crime but, as I said, there are things my family do not know about me. Other roles I'm employed to play. It was highly likely that someone on my meeting list over the coming week had been involved.

Had the BFG been infiltrated by the kind of radicals that would do that? Did Farris really know his fellow activists? And if it had come from within the BFG, what else might they do? Assassinate someone? JC would have to be at the top of the list.

The nationwide media attention JC was getting four months out from an election was priceless. Yes, he'd gained a lot from this bombing. But what about the damage? Was it pure coincidence that the bridge could be repaired by March, but only with the help of skilled foreign labour?

The police divers had also found a bomb on the base of the other tower. It hadn't detonated; infiltrated by sea water. Had that been a coincidence too?

The investigators were saying the charges were detonated remotely, probably from a computer or a mobile phone. Apparently the music festival bombing outside Paris last summer had been activated in Libya. The call to detonate the bridge could have come from anywhere. Whoever they'd been, they'd done enough.

The bombing suited the federal government even more than JC. Mining companies had been lobbying for foreign labour laws to bring in cheap mine workers in the Pilbara for years. The federal government had needed a project of national significance to find a way around the CFMEU, the union Alec Brankovic represented here in Tasmania. Now, suddenly, they had their chance. They'd swooped and gotten themselves a little test case running in Tasmania.

I thought back to the afternoon JC had rung, asking me to come home.

'The Bruny Bridge. Someone's just blown it up.'

'What?'

'They blew up the bridge, Ace. It's a fucking nightmare. I just got off the phone from telling Max,' he said. 'In her official capacity, of course,' he added wryly. My siblings . . .

'There's police everywhere,' he continued. 'The feds are coming in thick and fast.'

'Was anyone killed?'

'No, thank God. Happened at dawn. No-one about, thank Christ.'

'Was it that unpopular?'

'That bridge is bringing prosperity to this island. It's going to take more than a few fucking terrorists to knock it down.'

'Okay,' I said. 'I was just asking—'

'The federal government has called for a special session in parliament tonight to enact the foreign labour laws.'

'Meaning?' I asked.

'We're going to bring in Chinese workers. Skilled bridge workers to add to the existing crew. Without them, we have no chance of finishing the thing on time. It's a project of national significance and there just aren't the workers here.'

'And the deadline is . . .'

'Election day, of course. Watch how the Greens like that.'

'JC, the Tasmanian people aren't going to like that. Chinese workers?'

'They'll like it when the bridge is finished.'

'But you have an election to win, yes? Public opinion?'

'That's why I need a conflict resolution specialist. A good one. A very good one.'

'JC . . . no. You know this isn't my thing.'

'Yeah, it is. It's a fucking war between the people who would have this place stay a little backwater and those of us who want to get with the program and join the world.'

'And the Bruny Bridge is going to do that?'

'Ace, trust me. Yes.'

'It can't be me. Everyone will cry nepotism.'

'Ace, this is what you do. It doesn't have to be under the UN banner. Could you take leave? I'm sure you've got buckets of it. It's your home, Ace. It's your island. We need you. I need you. Tasmanians trust other Tasmanians.'

There was a long pause. Then he said, 'Who did you help today, hey? Today you could help me, Ace. Me.'

There it was. The family rule. Every night at dinner, from as young as I could remember, our father Angus Coleman would ask us at the dinner table: 'Who did you help today?'

Our mother suffered the question in silence for a long time. By the time we were teenagers, she'd started scoffing. She'd begun an affair with the principal of JC's boys' school. Her boss at the time. She'd decided to get a job once we were all in high school. 'Just for pocket money,' she'd said. The marriage had nearly fallen apart, but somehow she and Dad had survived it.

Like they survived everything. Mostly because our father was the kindest person I'd ever known.

Once Max had asked our mother the question. 'So who did you help today, Mum?'

Our mother had replied, 'As if your father's silly ideas apply to me. Goodness!'

Two of us became state politicians and one of us ended up at the UN.

'Let me call my chief of staff in and we'll brief you,' JC had said, thinking he'd won.

But I held out. Said I'd try to come home for Christmas. I wanted to see Dad and everyone else. I'd see if I could help him then. And then I'd received that text. *Call your brother. Say yes. Tell him you changed your mind.*

And so I was here.

ॐ

I breathed. I knew there were things I had to do, but I was getting cold. This felt like the first moment of complete silence I'd had in a long time. The sun was moving stage west, towards the Hartz Mountains. Gulls were flying down the channel. Seals were prodding fish farm nets. Flies buzzed against the screen door. I slid in under the doona. The white linen felt crisp under my fingertips. I dreamed then of New York, of trying to catch a cab to JFK. JC was beside me and Max was in the car ahead, but no matter how much I wanted to get to the plane, it never happened. In the end, I was standing on the tarmac in the dark feeling desperately alone.

I woke suddenly, disoriented, surprised to find I'd slept for almost three hours. My body clock trying to adjust. I wandered through the house and out onto the deck. The breeze had dropped and the channel was a millpond. A bright streak of pink was running like a wound across the western sky. From here the bridge was a monolith. Listing to one side, too large to pick up and dust off, too unwieldy to untangle and start again. It looked like an idea that had been derailed. Perhaps even misunderstood. If I did the job JC wanted, the bridge would be opened without protest on March 4th. JC would be the premier for another four years. Max would be relegated to Opposition again, and there would be tourists by the thousands flowing over the bridge day and night, supposedly bringing wealth and prosperity to the people of Tasmania.

I had to agree with the BFG. And with Max. Something about this bridge didn't add up. No government puts in two billion dollars without a serious payoff. It had to be worth a lot more than two billion dollars to someone. Why had the Chinese brought it in under their Belt and Road Initiative? Tasmania was never going to be able to deliver a payoff like that to the Chinese no matter how many tourists came. The Belt and Road Initiative was in South America, the Pacific, southern Europe and Asia now. Big investments in infrastructure—dams, ports, power stations and roads—and massive loans to foreign governments.

In my experience, the people to worry about most were not the entitled white men. They were easy to peg. It was the people of any gender, colour, race or religion who had implacable ideals.

The bridge smacked of something to do with a vision. I just didn't know what that was yet. But I was going to work it out.

I put on my jacket. Sunset this far south was a long farewell. By mid-summer it would be twilight until after 9 pm. I followed my nose and found the narrow path at the bottom of the street, and in a moment I was down the flight of steps and crossing the road to the beach.

CHAPTER NINE

In regular circumstances, I thought, as I strolled the shoreline, Tasmanians would have found Gilbert Farris a bit of a tosser. But they tolerated him now, I suspected, because he was pushing their barrow. It wasn't that they couldn't have pushed it themselves, but he had more than 13.4 million Twitter followers, and more on YouTube for his lectures. He had famous friends and famous enemies. His ideas for improving the human race included the sterilisation of criminals and incurable addicts, a two-child policy worldwide for those deemed fit to parent, compulsory free education until age twenty-one or military service. He was pro-abortion, anti-guns, pro-meditation and an atheist. He was born and educated in Canada. Apparently his favourite book was Herman Hesse's *The Glass Bead Game*.

Mostly Tasmanians had no interest in being famous. Why else did they live at the end of the world? They didn't like grandstanding. They didn't want a bridge that was going to make them famous. They had a very famous art gallery for that, the envy of galleries worldwide, built ten years ago by a maverick art-loving gambler who needed a tax deduction. Despite a couple of high-profile members like Farris and Lennox, most of the Bruny Friends Group were mums and dads whose property, or simply their quiet summer holiday, was threatened by the bridge. So the briefing notes had said. Yet they'd kept fighting for four years. And now the bridge was in pieces. Farris was more than an activist. He'd become something of a saint. It's dangerous to be a saint. They tend to end up as martyrs.

The horizon was blood red now. The sea breeze had dropped out and the sea was liquid red, edged with pewter. The colours were so remarkable I stopped and simply stared. To add to the wonder, a dolphin leaped twenty metres offshore. Then another. A pod of five or six of them moved away along the shoreline, languidly lifting their glistening bodies in effortless arcs as they went. I took photos, trying to capture all this to send to my children. They were unlikely to care. To them, Tasmania was a bit like Narnia. Somewhere they went on rare occasions and afterwards, looking back, it all seemed a little unreal. I knew the feeling.

Checking the time, I realised it was after 3 am in New York. Paul's girlfriend might respond in the morning, so I included her. *Love you Mum!* would be the note back from Tavvy, my twenty-four-year-old. Accompanied by smiley face emojis. That was fine. Any contact from your twenty-somethings was fine.

I remembered cartwheeling on this beach and making sand-castles, wandering about with a net scooping up tiny sea creatures to examine, doing handstands in the water. I remembered JC getting startled by a huge stingray that used to lie in the shallows on warm days and crying until our mother promised him his own packet of Tim Tams. It was one of the only memories I had of her being here. I remembered discovering when we were teenagers that if I sang 'Don't Cry for Me Argentina' it would drive JC absolutely mad. Suddenly I wanted to run along the beach and attempt a cartwheel. I resisted. Most likely I'd put my back out.

❧

The jetty at North Bruny had once been the main landing platform for people and produce arriving on the island. That jetty had disappeared in my childhood, becoming a narrow, planked thing, big enough to cast a line from, small enough to run from one end to the other in five seconds before throwing ourselves in at high tide. But now that, too, had gone and it was a great working platform for the bridge.

I saw a dusty white pick-up parked beside the road. Ute, I reminded myself—*ute* not *pick-up*. Got to remember my Australian vernacular. The driver was standing to one side, talking on the phone. He had a fishing rod leaning against the rear of the vehicle. He was tall, in dark glasses and a hat that had once, maybe a century ago, been a beige Fedora. He looked up as I approached and gazed at me as he finished the call, pocketing his phone.

'Quite a view from here,' he said.

He thinks I'm a tourist, I thought. Here to check out the bridge.

'It's certainly big,' I answered, my accent no doubt confirming his assumption.

'More than eight hundred thousand tonnes of steel and concrete,' he said, 'by the time it's finished.'

'So you're for it?' I asked. I wondered if Gilbert Farris had his binoculars on us.

'Me?' he said. 'It's an eyesore. But it will put Bruny on the map. Has already, as you can see. Especially thanks to that mob there.' He gestured to the BFG camp.

I nodded.

'The cafe is doing legendary trade with all the visiting journos. Pat at the gallery tells me she could dry a few bits of seaweed and someone would pay a hundred bucks for it.'

'There were dolphins,' I said, 'back there, on my walk.'

'Yeah, they're always good for the visitors too.'

I wanted to tell him that I wasn't a visitor. Tell him that actually I was a Tasmanian and my family had been Tasmanian for generations.

'They break into the fish farms down at Barnes Bay and free all the salmon for people like me,' he said. 'Fish farmers hate them. I've heard their guys shoot them with harpoons if they see them near the nets.'

I frowned. Nasty for Tasmania's image if that went viral— shooting dolphins.

'How are you finding being back?' he asked.

So he didn't think I was a visitor. He knew who I was. I sighed inwardly. There had been a large profile piece in *The Mercury* yesterday created by JC's PR team. Pictures of me and JC and Max as children. A picture of me overseas on UN work. It was meant to reassure people but it had the side effect of making them feel as if they knew me. This was it. No privacy.

'In some ways it's a surprise to find it so unchanged—other than . . .' I indicated the bridge. Then I looked at him more carefully. God, beneath the hat and Ray-Bans, he seemed familiar. I had a dreadful moment wondering if he was someone I'd known years ago. That had already happened to me at the bottle shop last night. A woman who claimed to have gone to school with me had corralled me by the Tassie sparklings and invited me to come out for drinks one night. I'd only the vaguest sense of who she was. She had the benefit of my face on the front of the paper.

'Do you know who blew up the bridge?' she'd asked. 'Are there any leads? God, it's like a spy thriller right here!' Then she'd asked, 'So how do JC and Max really get on?'

I'd escaped, feigning a call I had to take.

He cocked his head to one side and grinned at me. 'Dan Macmillan,' he said. 'I'm the bridge foreman.' He took off his hat and ran his fingers through cropped brown hair. He nodded towards Tinderbox across the channel. 'Apparently I'm running you back across tomorrow morning.'

'Oh, great,' I said. Of course. The Dan Macmillan who lived on this side. Who had actually spotted the bombers' boat as they'd taken off down the channel and seen the bridge blow. I'd forgotten how this happened in Tassie, especially when you least expected it. Someone had once declared that there were six degrees of separation between any two humans on earth, but in Tassie there was maybe half a degree. Talk with anyone here for long enough and you always found someone in common.

I reached out to shake hands. We shared a brief, steady exchange, not the crushing grip I often braced myself for.

'You missed the meeting this morning?' I asked.

'They don't include me in meetings like that.' He grinned. 'I'm a lowlife. Just here to keep the lads on track.'

'You saw it happen,' I said.

'Not something to forget, that,' he said, turning to stare at the bridge. 'So you're here to make us all one big happy family.'

'I guess that's your line of work as well,' I said.

'Yep, too right,' he agreed.

He had a Chris Pine been-down-Texas-robbing-a-bank look. At least six three. Stubble with a touch of grey in it. He looked strong. More Chris Hemsworth than Chris Pine in that way. But rugged. Maybe ten years younger than me. He didn't remove the Ray-Bans so I couldn't see his eyes and it made me search his face harder. He had a pale half-moon scar to the left of his lip, as if he'd been caught on a fishing line as a kid.

'How are the workers going?' I asked.

'The ones I have now, they get a mixed reception if they mention what they do in the pub. And they're pretty sick of crossing the channel at the end of the day in a breeze. But they're on a good wicket. The ones coming, the Chinese? Not sure what they'll get. Ton of trouble, I'm guessing. S'pose you'll be sorting that out for us, eh? Nothing to worry about.'

'If only it were that simple.'

'Well, us little folk are relying on you big folk to make it work.'

Was he being antagonistic? Condescending? Or was this his manner? It was hard to tell.

He moved to the back of the ute and pulled a bucket out from underneath the cover of the tray.

'You live this side?' I said.

'Yep. My place is just down the road from yours.'

It was all so close. He knew my house, knew my family. I had left for this exact reason.

'Do you want the bridge, Dan?' I asked.

'Not up to people like me,' he said. 'We're just cogs in the wheel.'

'So you're impartial?'

'I wouldn't say that. I just know what I think doesn't make a bone of difference. I make sure the thing gets built to specification and on time.'

'So you took over when . . .' It had been in one of the briefing notes. The last bridge foreman had died a year back.

'Yep,' said Dan. 'Damned if I'm going to let it kill me though.'

He had that tradie swagger. The one that seemed to convey that because they could fix most anything, they were God's gift to the world. And they got paid cash, if they could get away with it. That, no doubt, gave a person swagger. But underneath, in my experience of living through several renovations over the years, they were often quite shy. Dan Macmillan didn't seem the shy type. The flannel shirt was untucked, the jeans were worn. He looked pretty comfortable with himself. I wondered what would kill Dan Macmillan. Alcohol maybe. Or a long life.

Dan said, 'They found his car there.' He pointed across to Tinderbox. 'They found his clothes out there, where the road ended at the time.' He indicated the bridge. 'Folded. Neat and tidy.' He paused and then he said, 'Maybe it was a very beautiful sunset. Decided he'd had enough. Nice place to die.'

I hadn't realised it had been a suicide. That hadn't been in the notes. 'Did they find him?' I asked.

'Nah,' said Dan. 'There're great whites in the channel. Smaller sharks too. They come for the fish farms. Nine degrees in the water that day. The cold probably got him first.'

'He was a friend,' I said. I could hear it in his voice.

'He was my business partner,' said Dan.

I have learned not to react when people tell me terrible things, but this blindsided me for a moment. I wanted to kill the person who'd prepared those briefing notes.

'I'm so sorry,' I said. 'I didn't know.'

We stood there in silence until Dan added, 'And my brother-in-law. Met my sister when they were sixteen. Two kids. Yeah. Didn't leave a letter or anything.'

I watched the waves break on the shore beside the jetty. There was human tragedy in the world. It was a fact even here, in faraway Tasmania. A kind of numbness seemed to crawl up from deep inside me, as if it had been waiting there while I took a day or two to acclimatise.

It was Dan who spoke next. 'Your place has scrubbed up well. Bit surprised your brother's been so keen on the bridge. Must want you to have some lights to look out on at night.'

'Maybe,' I said, but what I thought was how JC would like his initials lit up on the highest point of the bridge. That would make him happy.

'What was his name, your business partner?'

'Jimmy,' he said. 'Jimmy Talbot.'

I nodded. The conversation was becoming awkward. I wanted to ask him all about Jimmy Talbot, and I also wanted to evaporate.

'Well, it was good to . . .' I began. But what was good? Again that numbness. What was wrong with me?

'I'll leave you to your fishing,' I said, trying to find any sort of smile. The conversation didn't warrant a smile. It seemed to warrant going to a pub and having a beer together but there wasn't a pub for fifty miles. We'd have to drive to the south end of the island. There was beer in my fridge, but that felt way too intimate.

Dan Macmillan was vital to the project. I'd been here two days. I needed time to consider everyone and everything. Soon three hundred Chinese workers would be all over this bridge and they'd be in his care. I thought about Jimmy Talbot and how the bridge being blown up and the Chinese arriving would sweep away his story. He hadn't even become official. There were no deaths noted on the construction record.

'So I'll meet you here at eleven tomorrow morning?' he said.

'Sure. Thank you. I hope that's not inconvenient.'

'It's fine. It's been a quiet week with the works shut down.'

We both looked again at the cables hanging loose, the missing tower, the twisted roadway.

'Enjoy settling back in,' he said. 'Can't be easy.'

Shaking hands again seemed too much physical contact in such a short space of time, so I nodded.

'I meant with your family,' he said, and grinned. It was a very white grin against his complexion. *Your family.* Was it a sneer? *Your political family.* Or a nod of compassion? *Your very complicated family.* I wished I knew the colour of his eyes.

'Thank you,' I said. And as I walked away I thought that *thank you* had not been the right thing to say. I thought about turning back and saying, 'I'm not staying. I'll be out of here as fast as I can, as soon as you've got the bridge built. I'm not like them, you know. My family. I'm not like them at all.'

But of course it wasn't true. Back at the house, I took out my laptop and wrote a report on the day. I encrypted it and emailed it, along with a request for some supplies to be delivered here to the house. Then I went into the spare bedroom and took the framed print off the wall to give myself a large working space. Tomorrow I'd get photographs printed. Meanwhile I wrote the names of everyone I'd met in thick black pen on white paper. Using Blu Tack from the kitchen, I began a spider's web of connections with JC at the top.

CHAPTER TEN

When I walked in for coffee the following morning, the new Dennes Point cafe was doing a bustling Saturday trade. There were young people and families, a seventy/thirty resident-to-tourist ratio, by the look of it. The tourists were easy to spot taking selfies on the balcony or photographing their food.

Maggie Lennox—cafe owner, *Solitude* owner, prominent activist—was at a table by the window. The cafe had a perfect view of the bridge and Tinderbox hill in the distance. Maggie waved, almost as if she'd been looking out for me, and indicated I should join her. She had beautiful skin, the bonus that older strawberry blondes get for keeping out of the sun. Think Helen Mirren with a careful chignon, nonchalant chinos and cotton sweater, elegant spectacles with peacock blue frames. It was a facade, of course. They all had a story, these white South Africans who made their homes elsewhere after apartheid ended. There was usually a dead relative, a torched farm, or worse secrets.

'Morning,' she said, smiling. 'I was going to call you but, then, here you are. Could we have a moment?'

'Sure,' I said.

'How are you finding being home?'

'It's a little strange, to be honest,' I said.

'I gather you're not a great fan of the place?'

'Tasmania?'

She inclined her head.

'Oh, I am,' I said. 'Of course. I'm a Tasmanian. I have a place here.' I indicated my house up the road.

'Yes, I know,' she said. 'But you've done a good job of staying away.'

There are no days off in a job like this. Not unless I fly away again. While I was here, I was on. Everyone got my phone number. Soon enough, here at Dennes Point, they'd all be keeping tabs on me. Possibly the quietest place was in the apartment downstairs at JC's. But this wasn't a job where hiding out had any value. It was getting amongst it, having these impromptu conversations, when the real work started to happen. When they stopped me for a chat, when I listened, that's how I built trust.

'Coffee?' she asked.

'Double-shot long black,' I said.

'There are some lemon friands just out of the oven. Gluten-free. Dairy-free. My treat. If that's allowed.' And she chuckled. 'Bribery by seduction.'

'Oldest trick in the book,' I said.

Maggie Lennox had an earthiness to her that was compelling. Practical, competent, very good at what she did by all accounts. *Solitude* was her fourth tourism venture in Tasmania.

We shared a little chitchat about New York. She had been many times. These days she stayed in Airbnbs, mostly in the

West Village, but she used to frequent the private Metropolitan Club. 'My first husband had reciprocal rights and we used to love to stay there,' she said. 'The view from the terrace out over the park was divine. But now I hardly ever go uptown unless I'm going to the Met or MoMA. Or the theatre. I've been watching the High Line grow ever since they planted it.'

The coffee and friands arrived. Both were good.

And so we came around to Bruny and her venture.

'Yesterday, you came on the ferry, didn't you?' said Maggie. 'I still find I let go as the ferry departs. I mean, to some extent, by the time everyone's got to the ferry, they're well on the way to letting go. In the case of my visitors, they've usually flown a long way to get to Tasmania. Either we've picked them up, or they've hired a car and navigated their way to Kettering. Did you stop for coffee?'

I nodded.

'I'm sure you weren't served by someone with a tattoo sleeve and a nose ring. It's Elsie or Jean or Matilda, who grew up in the country and who smile as if it's nice to see you. Then there's the ferry and the crossing. The weather is whatever the weather is. The wind hits. Sometimes there's spray and waves breaking over the bow. People are out of their element. It's wild. Maybe a little dangerous. Their phone loses bars. It's unsettling but something else is seeping in even then. That's where the magic begins, crossing the water.'

She paused and I nodded again.

'Then they arrive on the island and they're ushered off the ferry by a bloke in a fluoro vest who doesn't look like he cares a fig for where they're from, their money and their fame or how important they are back home. He's cold. He wants the car moved. Now.'

She was right. This was exactly how it had gone yesterday. How it had always gone, in my memory.

'Of course, they've sealed the road now, so you miss that part of the adventure. Some people had never driven on an unsealed road. The world slowed down when it was gravel. Became a bit precarious. Those corrugations and soft edges. But it's like any other road now.'

Who would have thought we'd get whimsical about narrow, windy, gravel roads, but she was right; I'd missed it too.

'Then they top the rise and see *Solitude* as they come through the gate,' she continued. 'Instantly, their phones drop out. I installed a dampening field that cuts them off at the top of the driveway. No wi-fi, no calls, no emails, no news until they leave. Some of them tell me it's as if five years drop away right then. They stare at the sea. They stand and take it all in. Inside, if it's even a little bit chilly, they find a fire burning. Fresh bread or scones from the oven. There's a view from every window to take their breath away. The air's so clean, they want to drink it.'

'You've gone to a fair bit of trouble,' I said.

'It's been a dream for seven years. And it's been awesome seeing how people respond. That first day they wander about looking a bit stunned. The next day they walk a little further. They eat well. Most everything we serve is grown and raised here on the island, or somewhere in Tassie. They say they've never known anywhere so peaceful. They feel as if they've left the world behind. They get present to themselves, to their lives.

That's why we have a minimum ten-night stay. So they can get past the shock.'

I understood all this. I hadn't been to *Solitude* but I'd been to other retreats.

'And they sleep,' I said.

'They sleep better than they have in years,' she agreed. 'They tell me their dreams get really interesting. No-one disturbs them. Our staff are entirely discreet. It doesn't matter if it's a movie star or a president, a prime minister or a rock star. They can drop all that and be.'

She laughed. 'I know I'm passionate,' she said, 'but I need you to understand, Astrid. I need you to be quite clear on how I feel about a highway and a bridge that gets them here in forty-five minutes from airport to door, with a great big slip lane and traffic noise day and night. This bridge is my nightmare. I won't stop fighting. Everyone laughs and says don't we know we're beaten. But I'm not beaten. None of us are. It doesn't matter that we've been at it for more than four years. We're trying to protect the only thing Tasmania really has going for it in the twenty-first century. Its isolation. Its quiet. Its lack of population. Its remoteness. We need fewer people with more money coming here. I'm not the only tourism operator to have invested millions here on Bruny. Not everyone agrees with me, but most of us can see that this bridge is a dumb strategy. Bruny needs careful planning, not this deluge of visitors we are unprepared for. It will destroy our boutique appeal. So nothing you are ever going to say, on behalf of your brother, is going to change our minds or make us compliant.'

'I understand,' I said.

'Will you let me show you *Solitude*?' she asked.

'I'd love to see it,' I said. 'You've got my number.'

'Here's mine,' she responded, pulling out her phone, finding my number and texting me.

I've met a lot of people. I'd heard their litany in every form. Religious. Political. Ideological. The end almost always justified the means. But then there were these people; people like Maggie Lennox and Jenny Singh and no doubt most of the BFG cohort. The ones who surprised themselves by becoming activists. You can find them the world over. What they had, what they valued, was being threatened or destroyed. Forests, water, fish, land. Here in Tasmania, right now, it was the quiet life.

I knew they'd hold their ground, these protesters. They would fight to their last breath. They would inspire their children to take on the battle, and their grandchildren too. Here were the opponents to the slave trade, the suffragettes, the unionists, the environmentalists, the feminists. Century after century, economic imperatives rode roughshod over people and they tried to stand in the wake of it, a picket fence against a tsunami.

I looked at this dignified graceful woman. In almost any other circumstances, we might have been friends.

'Thank you, Maggie, for the coffee and the food,' I said. 'I'm due at the jetty at eleven. I have to get back to town this morning. As you know, I'm at the information-gathering phase. But I'll be in touch soon.'

'By the way,' she said, 'if you're here for a few months, you're going to need a hairdresser.'

'I am,' I said, smiling. I had been admiring her colour. Let's face it, at our age colour is everything.

She texted me again. 'That's Fabian. He's a whizz with all sorts of blonde.'

'Thank you,' I said.

'Just ask if you need any others. Doctor. Nails. Girl things. There's lots of good people.'

'Not the outpost it once was?' I said.

'It's beautiful. Still an outpost but people have relocated. Or come home. Or decided to stay and create. Twenty thousand tourists a week means we've got some great restaurants. People invest now because they know if they get it right, they're going to get numbers. It's quite the weekend destination, as you can see.' She waved her hand at the cafe cohort. 'Not just here on Bruny, but all over the state.'

'But you'd like less of them on Bruny.'

'I'd like them to catch a ferry. A bigger ferry. More frequent ferries. Just come by water. Preserve the magic. When they start up again,' she said, staring at the tangled bridge, 'you'll hear it loud and clear from your place. It will give you a bit of a sense of what the future might be like. And soon it will be twenty-four seven.'

I nodded.

As I was going out the door, another woman stopped me. She was short, plump.

'Oh, you're that woman, the premier's sister, aren't you?'

'I am,' I said, holding out my hand. 'Astrid Coleman.'

She looked a little surprised but shook mine. 'Jean Henty,' she said. 'Don't worry, I'm nobody, so don't bother remembering my name. I just want you to know we're not all like them,' she said, frowning in the direction of the BFG camp. She spied Maggie Lennox and dropped her head.

'Some of us think this bridge is the best thing that's ever happened to Bruny,' she said quietly.

'And are you part of a group, Jean?' I asked.

'Oh, I'm from Bruny in Action. I think we're expecting you for afternoon tea next Wednesday. Progress. Progress is what this place needs.'

I nodded. 'Wonderful, Jean,' I said. 'I'll see you on Wednesday. Thank you for saying hi.'

She smiled. And then I was out the door, and down the road to the jetty.

CHAPTER ELEVEN

I t was Sunday and our mother Hyacinth (Cynthy to her friends) was seated in the middle of the table between Maxine and my niece, Grace. Mother was wearing a blue dress and pink satin pumps. Her wig today was Marilyn blonde. I hadn't seen her in ten years. There had been photos posted by JC and Stephanie and Max on the private page Stephanie had set up for the family, but Mother didn't like technology, so in terms of conversations, it was landline only.

When I'd embraced her, it had felt like hugging a cardboard box. There didn't seem to be any substance left to her and I felt a wave of guilt and compassion until she looked into my face and said, 'Ah, Astrid, sweetheart, how you've aged! We all do, but some of us do it faster than others.'

'*One may smile and smile and be a villain,*' said my dad as he ambled past.

'What did you say, Angus?' Mother asked, her gaze swivelling with laser precision.

'Don't trouble yourself, Mum,' said Max, handing her a champagne and indicating to me to move our father along.

'*Hamlet!*' called Ella, my older niece, checking her iPhone. 'It's from *Hamlet*.' She pressed a few buttons then looked up at me. 'I'm keeping track, Aunty Ace. He's never wrong.'

With the quote, or the inference? I wanted to ask, but a warning glance from Max dissuaded me.

There'd always been an expectation that dresses were worn by the girls of the family, and suits by boys, for all formal occasions. Sunday lunch, following church, was a formal occasion. I had bowed out of church, but JC, Max, Stephanie and the girls all went. I wondered how my Tavvy and Paul would adapt these days. For Tavvy, being told to wear a dress would probably mean she came in something short, tight and black with her piercings and ink on show. But Paul would have been happy to comply. He was fond of ironing his shirts. Here was order and ritual, compared to the rather bohemian affair that had been the family home in Brooklyn.

Stephanie, observing the scene before her at the table, said, 'Well, don't we all look nice.'

'In my day,' Mother said, 'we socialised on a Saturday night over fish paste sandwiches. We had crepe paper decorations and a five-piece swing band. At the Mossman Hall. They played Buddy Holly and Elvis songs. We dressed properly. Stockings and shoes.'

Our mother had grown up in Far North Queensland before running away to Sydney. It was there she'd met our father after her first husband, also a politician—a senator no less, and thirty years her senior—had died of a heart attack in a Kings Cross brothel. Max had been less than a year old. For years, our mother pretended she had no family. The senator's family had disowned her, showing no interest in Max and paying our mother off. Her family up in Queensland were all dead, so she'd said. Until a sister showed up. I'd been rather impressed by her. I think she was called Frankie. I'd been about fourteen at the time. She'd drunk two longnecks for breakfast. But that was the first and last time we ever saw her.

'Grandma, how old are you?' Ella asked.

'Goodness, Ella, don't you know it's rude to ask people their age?' said Mother.

'People ask me all the time,' said Grace, seated beside Stephanie.

'Well, it's different when you're a child,' said Mother, stretching her neck so she looked even more like an ostrich. Cancer had accentuated her already chiselled bones, and given her a little panic in the eyes. The wig was a plea for another turn, I thought. A turn at being sexy, young and glamorous all over again. After the senator's death, Mother and Max, widow and baby, had been on the front of the *Women's Weekly* in matching white dresses.

If I'd met our mother in a counselling session, I would have thought *shock*. This woman has had a shock. And I would have trodden carefully.

'Manners are everything, Ella,' Mother said. 'You'll learn that in life. It's what separates us from the great unwashed.'

'*Sometimes I am a king, then treasons make me wish myself a beggar, and so I am; then crushing penury persuades me I was better when a king,*' said our father, lifting his face from the onion tart entree.

Max traded a look with me. Ella grabbed up her iPhone and tapped in the words.

'*Richard the Second*,' she said.

'You're quick,' I said.

'Do we have to have phones at the table?' asked Mother.

'Mum, it's her project, you know that,' said Stephanie.

'Even the idea of a child having a phone . . .' said Mother. 'Awful.'

'Or the idea of Dad now only quoting Shakespeare,' I said.

'Oh, well, we could all have seen that coming,' said Mother. And laughed.

There was a pause then Stephanie said, 'We have a lot to be grateful for, and it's so nice to put our differences aside and just be a family.'

She lifted her glass. We followed suit. 'To family,' said Stephanie. 'To Astrid, for coming all this way. For coming home.'

'To Ace,' everyone said. 'To Aunty Ace! To Astrid.'

And our father said, '*They do not love who do not show their love.*' And stood and clinked his wineglass carefully against each of ours.

Stephanie had seated them apart, Angus and Hyacinth, because since the dementia had set in, our father had taken a deep dislike to our mother. They had been married for nearly sixty years. Now he lived in an aged-care facility and our mother remained in the family home with the aide who'd lived in for five years now.

My boy. That was how Mother referred to the endlessly patient Phillip—nurse, cook and cleaner—who was in his thirties and from New Zealand.

The main course was served and Mother embarked on a joke involving Irish people, black people and refugees. Stephanie had diced Mother's lamb roast, but our mother simply pushed the food about the plate and drank white wine as if it were water. At the end of the joke, she erupted into laughter while the children looked surprised, and the adults looked mortified to various degrees, except for JC, who giggled and said, 'Mum, you can't tell jokes like that anymore.'

'Oh, why not?' she said. 'It's only a bit of fun.'

And Angus said, *'There's no more faith in thee than in a stewed prune.'*

Which got everyone giggling. Except Mother.

'It's all very well to laugh at him, but it only encourages him,' she said.

'How are you finding being back?' Max asked me quietly.

'I'm seated between dementia and cancer,' I said.

She touched her shoulder to mine. 'And you thought the UN was a challenge.'

'The UN always looked good compared to this,' I said.

∾

'Shakespeare.' Max had called me when it had first happened.

'Shakespeare?'

'Yes. Some kind of neural loop since this last stroke. It's not that uncommon. Well, the Shakespeare is—I don't think they've seen that before—but the neural loop isn't. Apparently there was one woman who could only talk in Twinings tea varieties, and someone else had to commentate the 1966 Grand Final over and over again.'

'Who won?' I asked.

'Oh, don't, Ace. I didn't ask.' Max had laughed softly. 'I'm afraid his days of travelling to see you are over.'

A silence had fallen.

'I'll come home,' I said. 'As soon as I can sort things here.'

'He would love that. I would love that too.'

I'd intended to follow through. I wanted to see my dad. I wanted to see Max and JC. I'd escaped a long time ago yet a part of me was still here. I put it down to biology because, despite the fact that we replace all our cells every seven years, we seem to go on being what we are. Believing I could escape was futile. But I went on trying, and not coming home made it easier.

Dad had appeared to be delighted when I'd walked into his room my first day back. He was sitting in a chair by the window, dressed in a thick cable cardigan, smart pants and shirt, his silver hair combed. He had a view looking out towards the river with the mountain behind. There were fresh flowers and a speaker on the table playing Maria Callas. At least I guessed it was Maria Callas. Something beautiful. But did he know me?

'How are you, Dad?' I had asked.

'Here we will sit and let the sounds of music creep into our ears,' he'd replied.

I took his hand, his dear, papery hand. The skin thin now, showing every vein and bone. The skin on his face marbled too. His eyes sunken but still bright, as if they were shining with a distant light. He had aged ten years in one.

'I'm sorry you've been unwell, Dad. I'm sorry I didn't come sooner.'

He put his hand atop mine and squeezed it. He said, *'Trust not your daughters' minds by what you see them act.'*

'I'm here for a few months. I'm helping JC with his bridge.'

'Tell me, Juliet, how stands your dispositions to be married?' he asked.

'Ah, well, I broke up with Ben. Almost three years ago now. Do you remember? But I'm better without him. I'm not looking for love anymore, Dad.'

With that he lifted my hand to his mouth and kissed the back of it. I was sure he knew everything, remembered everything. It was only the speech centre that was betraying him. We sat together, the music creeping into our ears, and he nodded off. After perhaps half an hour, he woke and saw me there.

'To die, to sleep. To sleep, perchance to dream. Ay, there's the rub. For in that sleep of death what dreams may come . . .' he said.

'I think death has only good things waiting, Dad,' I replied.

How often I had soothed myself with that thought, walking into a town that had been bombed, a home that had been the scene of unspeakable atrocities, the bodies gone but the blood, the marks on the walls, the stained beds all still there. Or when you have brought together religious leaders, soldiers and rebels knowing that, despite everyone being searched with care, someone may still have a way of blowing everything up.

I wanted to believe that death was a warm place my father would escape to, but really I wanted him to be himself again.

Looking at him as he sat there at the Sunday table, carefully finishing everything on his plate, for the first time it really struck me that I was going to lose him. We were all going to lose him. His body might still be here, but our father was already leaving, trailing his beloved Shakespeare behind him like a long, velvet cloak.

CHAPTER TWELVE

Profound thought: *Time is not an illusion.*

I don't sleep well. I'm a fifty-something woman and if you know one who sleeps well without medication, then congratulate her. It was a novelty for me getting more than three or four hours at a time. Mostly I tried not to fight it. I read a lot through those wee hours, trying to slow the brain. I listened to podcasts. Tried meditation apps. That Sunday night, I'd gone to bed early, trying to settle in to the new time zone but found myself wide awake at 1 am. I considered visiting my dad. I wondered if they'd let me in. Even if he was asleep, it would be good to sit by him, so I walked the few streets to the centre.

'My dad is Angus Coleman,' I said to the night nurse who appeared when I buzzed. 'I know it's late, but I'm here from New York, I'm really jet-lagged and I thought . . .'

'You're Astrid,' she said. 'Of course, it's not really permitted but he's often awake now. A bit prone to wandering about at this hour of the night, if we're not careful. He doesn't mean any harm. I think he likes the company. Such a lovely man. Says the sweetest things to us. *Beauty lives with kindness.* Isn't that lovely? I think he's told me that most every time I've looked after him. Let's go find him.'

We set off through glass doors down a pale peach corridor with peach patterned carpet.

'By the way, Astrid, I'm Robyn Lucas. You were in the year ahead of me at school.'

'Oh, hi, Robyn,' I said. 'I thought you looked a bit familiar . . .'

'I didn't expect you to remember me.'

This was Tasmania. Everyone knows everyone.

Making small talk, I said, 'So did you stay in Tassie after school, or have you come back?'

'Oh, I went travelling for a few months, like we all did back then, and then I came back, and I've hardly left since,' said Robyn. 'I married my first boyfriend, actually, and our children are grown up now.' She smiled. 'I'm a grandmother six times over. My eldest grandchild is twelve. Your sister has been marvellous for us nurses, you know. You've all done so well for yourselves.'

She had a kind, lined face.

'Thank you,' I said. 'And congratulations to you too. Family is quite an achievement, isn't it. So are they here in Tassie, your kids and grandkids?'

'Yes, everyone stayed close by. My eldest works for one of the fish farms. My youngest is with the Symphony Orchestra—marketing not musical. And my middle one is a nurse too. There have been divorces, you know, but they're all good. Does it feel like it's changed much? Coming back? Must be very quiet after what you're used to.'

'It's definitely got busier,' I said.

Robyn frowned. 'Yes, peak hour used to be between five ten and five twenty—when all the public servants knocked off. But now it's any time. We live at Kingston and it's a nightmare trying to get in and out of town. Where did all these cars come from? I can't imagine the bridge is going to help any of that. There'll just be more visitors than ever.'

'You had an older sister, too, didn't you?' I asked.

'Yes, Laura. You've got a good memory. She died five years ago. Cancer.'

'Oh, I'm so sorry.'

'Your mum has cancer too, doesn't she?' she said.

I nodded. 'It's metastasised now.'

Robyn shook her head in sympathy. 'I often wonder whether they might have been able to do more for Laura if we'd lived in Melbourne or Sydney. It was really awful at the end. And we don't have the best technology here. No money for new equipment. Or the new drugs. One of my boys broke his leg a few years back, and it was so crowded in the fracture clinic he had to stand up and wait. When he finally got in to see the doctor, the scales were held together with duct tape. I looked at them and I thought, that's what it's come to. Our public schools, our public hospitals, barely held together with love and duct tape. My husband has been waiting three years for a hip replacement. So much for two billion dollars on a bridge. It's health and education we need here. Feels like everything is for the tourists.'

I nodded again. We had come to a halt outside room 29.

'Still, you're not here for that,' she said. 'This is your dad's room. Let's see if he's awake. You do know what to expect, don't you?'

'I do,' I said.

Dad was sitting in his chair, wrapped in a blanket. He saw me and said, *'Good morning to you, fair and gracious daughter.'*

Robyn smiled. 'I'll leave you both to it. Just let me know when you're going.' She closed the door behind her.

'How are you, Dad?' I asked, pulling the visitor's chair up beside him and opening the curtains so we could look out at the lights of Sandy Bay.

'The web of our life is of a mingled yarn, good and ill together,' he said.

'Yes,' I said. 'That's just what I was thinking too.'

I miss you, Dad, I wanted to tell him. I mean, I missed being here all these years. Close by. My dad had come every year to New York, faithfully making the day-and-a-half trip from Tasmania. He had loved New York. Loved the Metropolitan, took the children there so often Tavvy had said, at the tender age of six, 'Please, Grandad, could we go to the Guggenheim instead?'

I thought how the perfect place for my father to die would be there in the Met, in one of the re-created rooms from the mid-nineteenth century, or marvelling at a painting of the French Revolution.

We had not seen this coming. That our father would go this way. Three strokes in quick succession over the last two months, the first two seemingly benign, other than him being found after the second one on the floor of the State Library. The last he had simply put his head on the table at a cafe. When the staff woke him, he hadn't a clue in the world who he was or how he'd got there. All he would say was, '*To be or not to be, that is the question.*'

CHAPTER THIRTEEN

I was walking from the car park to Sandy Bay Beach to meet my sister Max. It was five to six, and already the sun was up, the light golden, the sea breathless. Years ago, when I first began travelling for my work, I kept a diary. I came upon it when I was packing up the Brooklyn house and moving to Manhattan after Ben and I split. Reading back over it, I was exhausted by myself. The travel schedule. The meetings. The sheer number of people I had contact with on any given day. Sharing this with my daughter, Tavvy, she said, 'Mum, don't you know that keeping a diary is meant to be about writing the high point and the low point of every day, and what made the low point bearable? You can't write it all!'

I wondered what the high point of today would be. At 11 am I had a meeting with the Bruny Progress Society. Bruny Island, I'd discovered, had more interest groups than street names. The Bruny Progress Society did not see eye to eye with Bruny in Action. The two groups fundamentally disagreed on the meaning of the word *progress*. The Bruny Progress Society was against the bridge, and they were against the fish farms, which they said had ruined the Huon River and were utterly destroying the channel. They were also against any further tourism development at Adventure Bay until there was a proper planning scheme that was based on projected visitor numbers, not on the handful of residents who lived there permanently.

Bruny in Action had been started by a local and very successful cheese maker who believed that the bridge was the epitome of progress. His followers believed the bridge was the bright future for Bruny, its businesses and its landowners. The cheese maker and Farris were bitter enemies and there had been several very public showdowns at community events. Bruny in Action was funded, in part, by the biggest aquaculture company. Also, interestingly, they were funded by Friends of China, a tourism body that had sprung up to help Chinese tourists on their Tasmanian visits. Friends of China was funded by the Tasmanian government and, I discovered, by the Shenzhen Association, which was a front group for the Chinese Communist Party. This, in itself, was not unusual, I quickly discovered. Most organisations in Australia with links back to China also had links back to the Chinese Communist Party. It wasn't advertised, but there was plenty of research.

The Adventure Bay Residents Group was against the Adventure Bay Friends Group and the Birdwatchers of South Bruny did not see eye to eye with Birdlife Bruny. The latter had sprung up only with the arrival of the bridge project, whereas Birdwatchers of South Bruny dated back to the 1950s, so I was told. Then there was the BFG, which had attracted a lot of people who didn't agree on anything else but did agree a bridge was not what Bruny needed.

A few marriages were split down the middle, wife in one camp, husband in the other. Children and grandchildren, too. A grandmother or grandfather was in the Bruny Progress Society while a child or grandchild was in the Bruny Friends Group. The Adventure Bay Progress Society, an offshoot of the Bruny Progress Society, had got a spike in membership a few years back when the government had tried to log the hills behind the bay.

'Pretty much like sucking the lilies out of the Monet, to wipe out those forests,' one of the Progress Society people said. 'Same with this bloody bridge. You finally find a bit of peace and, suddenly, the whole bloody world wants in. Want to be able to drive right to it.'

'It's like expecting daily flights to Antarctica but no harm done to the place,' said another. 'Well, it's the same here. You can't have wilderness and crowds.'

'It's like porridge and pesto,' said the Monet wit. 'Some things just don't go together.'

✍

If you google, you can find a counter showing the world's population. It ticks fast because around three hundred and sixty thousand people are born every day and around one hundred and fifty thousand die. Net result: the population of greater Hobart is being added to the world every twenty-four hours. Glaciers are melting, soil is drying out, sea levels are rising. We're a tumour, the human race. And like a good tumour, we'll keep on growing as long as we can. This is possibly today's low point. I think Tavvy would want me to work harder for my low point, because this is not a new thought. Luckily, at that moment, I spotted Max.

She was coming down the path wearing a pink beanie and dark glasses. I grinned. Here was my sister. Not thousands of miles, four airports and the whole wide Pacific away, but here. Here, on her home turf. Maybe this was the high point of today. We had always looked alike, even though we only shared fifty per cent of the family genes. I was the tall version, she the short one. But still, we're a pair. Light brown hair dyed variations of ash blonde, unusual amber eyes, our mother's cheekbones and small ears. Our hands honed by piano lessons, our calf muscles by ballet. Max had been better at both than me. I grew too tall to ever look right in a pas de deux. I'd had an urge to learn jazz piano, but I wasn't allowed.

'Jazz is for drug addicts,' our mother had said, and that was that.

By twelve, and five foot nine, I gave up ballet. By age fifteen, and six feet, I gave up piano. Just flat refused to go to lessons.

'You have to stop growing, Astrid,' Mother said. 'No man will ever marry you.'

People suggested basketball, and I did play for a couple of seasons, but the truth is when I was younger I was pretty uncoordinated. I used to like jogging until I got shin splints. Swimming suits me. I like walking too. I've done some yoga over the years.

Though she won a few events through school at the Hobart Eisteddfod, it wasn't music that called Max; it was activism. Max out in the south-west protesting the damming of the Franklin River. Max in Western Australia protesting something—maybe forests, maybe gas exploration, I can't remember. Max with the Aborigines and their tent embassy in Canberra.

It was that trip that really got her thinking about politics. She came home and said, 'Did you know the Aborigines weren't allowed to vote until 1962? And that the first woman elected to the federal parliament was a Tasmanian?'

'There's always room for more,' our father had said.

'One politician in the family is quite enough,' our mother had added. A quote that's remembered with some amusement.

So far Max hadn't opted for federal politics.

'I can't leave Tasmania with these short-sighted blokes in charge,' she'd said, when we discussed it. 'I can do more here.'

But had she?

When I hugged her on the sand dune, I was reluctant to let go.

'You okay?' Max asked.

'Sure,' I said. 'It's nice to see you.'

'You too,' she said.

There were lots of dog walkers on the beach. A few of them glanced at Max, recognised her, gave a little nod, offered a 'Morning'. Max nodded to each of them in return, said, 'Good morning,' and smiled. She is a very good public person.

We'd had years of being the children of our father at all the election events, the debates, the afternoon teas and barbecues. We were highly trained social creatures. But mostly, as we strolled along the shore, I could see that Max was trying to be anonymous. It was, after all, just after 6 am. Hence the beanie and the dark glasses, the grey marle hoodie and navy track pants that somehow consumed her form so that her five-two frame seemed even smaller.

'Making progress?' Max asked.

I gave her a bit of a rundown on the groups and clubs and associations of Bruny. The Day Walks Club as opposed to the Bushwalking Club, the Quilting Network and the Knitting Network.

'I know,' she said. 'It's straight out of *The Life of Brian*. You know, the Judean People's Front and the People's Front of Judea.'

'Splitters!' we said in unison. You have to be a certain age to really appreciate Monty Python.

'And that's before any of the government departments or the political parties and their side groups—unions, business clubs and environmental groups,' I said.

'We are passionate people,' Max said.

'Present company included,' I added.

'Oh, they've tamed me, really.'

'The Labor Party?' I asked.

She sighed. 'I'm a pale shadow of my former self. I think compromise is going to kill me.'

We arrived at the boatsheds at the far end of the beach and lost the view of the mountain. The Tasman Bridge was ahead, the godawful casino too—a seventies thermos of concrete and glass that had been emboldened by an eighties conference centre. It still had a revolving restaurant at the top that did a circuit every hour, but the bottom floors were given over to pokies.

Tasmania was the Nevada of Australia: the gambling state. JC's last election campaign had been funded by millions from the family who owned all the casino infrastructure, the machines and most of the state's pubs and clubs. There were no disclosure laws in Tasmania. It took years for the election funding figures to come out under freedom of information, and by then the electorate had surrendered to the inevitability of it all.

It nearly crippled Max, that election. And then, somehow, she rallied. 'I will never watch democracy bought again; I'll never play the game the same way,' she'd said on one of our calls.

And now it was all beginning again. I was going to see firsthand the way Max was going to play the game.

We stopped for a moment and took in a narrow beam of light spearing the river. Granny used to tell us there were so many whales back in the first days of Hobart that you could have walked to the far side of the Derwent across their backs. Acres of whales breeding and birthing and then harpooned to light the streets of London. So many barrels of whale oil harvested in Hobart that it caused a glut in the market and nearly crippled the trade. By 1900, the whales in the Derwent were all gone. There hasn't been a whale sighted in the river for well over a hundred years now.

Max was talking about the bridge. 'I mean, I asked again and again for the raw data. The studies don't add up. The metrics are all wrong. The projections are skewed. We had some huge fights, me and JC, on the floor of the house. But it was always a done deal. People love this idea of majority government, but what they forget is that majority governments run roughshod over due process when they don't like what the people are saying.'

I frowned. 'That sounds like heresy from a party leader.'

'It's always a fight. Why does it have to be a fight, Ace?'

'Isn't that just politics?'

'But why? I mean, there are some basic things we could all agree on.'

'Like a business plan for the state?'

'Ha!' she snorted. 'I think JC believes the bridge is that. It's too big a project for us to fight, so I've had to go along with it—publicly, at least. But in the party room, I'm the cat among the . . . well . . .'

'Guinea pigs?' I suggested. And we both chuckled.

'And the people of Hobart . . .' Max paused.

'Are completely divided on this bridge,' I said.

'That they are,' she sighed.

'They're divided on the salmon industry, too,' I added.

There ought to be a name for the kind of overwhelm that happens when you realise there are too many things to fight. If it's not environment, then it's human rights. If it's not human rights, it's women's rights. Law and order. Gun control. Invasive species. Water pollution. Tax reform. Refugee policy. Education. Health care. The list is endless. And the Australian healthcare system looks like a Mercedes-Benz compared to the burned-out jalopy the Americans have. That makes me more angry than anything, living in America. How the poverty is so vicious when so many people have so much. The divide is ugly and nobody wants to talk about it, not really. The poor people keep voting for the people who have everything—as if they honestly believe those people will change their lives for them. Meanwhile, the schools get more broken, people get dumber and sicker, and the rich just keep on getting richer and richer. It's *The Hunger*

Games, but nobody's noticed. Australia is probably twenty years behind, but it will get there soon enough.

'I keep asking myself who wins,' said Max. 'Who wins if the bridge is blown up? And it would be easy to think Farris and his supporters. All those shack owners at Adventure Bay who are fighting the hotels and the high-rises. Or the business owners who rely on the ferry traffic down Kettering way.'

'But whoever did it, didn't do it properly.'

'No. They injured it . . . and an injured bridge creates a reason to enact the foreign labour laws,' said Max.

We turned and headed back along the beach. I have a feeling there's another version of me in the future. A relaxed, funnier me. Maybe I do a bit of painting. I have a fabulous lover. I drink peaty whisky, read all the classic novels by the fire and never open a newspaper. I'd like to know that woman. She might sit on the balcony of the Bruny house, looking out over the channel, watching dolphins. Did I want that great bridge to look out on every day? There were worse things to look at. It was a very beautiful design. It was the traffic and what the traffic meant I wasn't sure about. But I'm not paid to want the bridge or not.

'So you think JC got some mates?' I asked very quietly, once the next passing dog walker was out of earshot.

'No,' said Max, shaking her head. 'He's many things, our brother, but I don't think he's that. But I do think, just between you and me, that someone in Canberra might have got busy. I mean it's crazy, right, but it's fishy. It's only damaged enough to need a whole new round of skilled workers to finish it by election day. And they're clever. It's not replacing Tasmanian jobs, it's in addition to—so who can really complain?'

'Not a year's worth of damage,' I said. 'Not six month's worth of damage. Just the right amount of damage.'

'You know, the second bomb that didn't blow . . . that would have sunk any hope of having it repaired by the election.'

'Same if they'd totally severed the suspension cable,' I said.

'The thick plottens,' said Max. An old joke from childhood.

'Yes, but you know what they say: if you have to choose between conspiracy and stupidity . . .' I said.

'Put your money on stupidity,' said Max. 'I know.'

'There're no leads at all?' I asked.

'You'd probably hear before me,' she said.

There were boundaries and they were never clear cut. I reported to JC. I wasn't free to discuss my findings with Max. How much Max knew, how much I knew, what JC told either of us, what I gleaned working alongside his people and in doing my job, it was a delicate process. To say nothing of the other job I was here to do that nobody knew about.

'You love a good mystery, Ace. Doesn't it feel like a mystery? We're just missing the lead character. We need a heroine. You have the VIP pass. You can pretty much ask any question you like under the guise of "conflict resolution". You're perfect for the part.'

I gave her a glance. 'You don't think JC would notice if I started asking around?'

'I think people would feel a whole lot better about the bridge if they felt in their guts that it was all as simple as the government wants them to believe.'

'You're working on me,' I said.

'Sorry,' she said. 'You're right. It's just, having you home, I actually feel for the first time . . .'

'What?'

'I don't know. Like I've got my friend back.'

I nodded. 'Me too,' I said.

In paint, that colour on the horizon is called Prussian blue. Prussian blue is also an antidote to heavy metal poisoning, which is ironic because the Derwent River has received the daily outpourings of a zinc smelter just ten minutes north of the city these past hundred years or so, and it's still going strong. Social licence is a powerful thing. Communities forget sometimes that they hold all the cards. They are the voters. The taxpayers. Society relies on a willingness for us to act as a group. Without the group, there's anarchy. But within the group, there's immense power. That's why JC's new protest laws were so effective. They deterred not just individuals but whole communities from speaking out.

I thought of Dan Macmillan saying, 'Us little folk are relying on you big folk to make it work.'

I had wanted to talk more to Dan when he ran me over to Tinderbox in the Zodiac on Saturday morning. But after our initial greeting, neither of us spoke. The noise of the boat, the breeze and something about him had made me silent. He was hard to read, I thought. What had made him that way? His business partner had suicided a year before. That could do it. Deaths like that linger a long time. But it seemed to go deeper with him. I wondered what his story was.

I'd done a little research over the weekend. His company website had a brief bio noting he'd served in the Australian

Army and had been deployed in East Timor, Afghanistan and Iraq. Rank—Corporal, 3rd Battalion, Royal Australian Regiment (1999–2003), Special Air Service Regiment (2003–2011). A paratrooper. There was no photo. No Facebook page or anything else either. No newspaper articles or court records. I did find two photos of him from a few years back with a young woman who claimed him as her brother and the uncle to the two children he was also photographed with. This must be the widow of the partner who suicided. Nothing else. Being ex-military Dan would have knowledge and contacts. But motive? And, more importantly, means? Who had bank-rolled the bombing? Who had the means to employ a highly trained team to cripple a bridge in the dead of night and then disappear in a stealth vessel? I wondered if Dan Macmillan was the kind of bloke who might bomb a bridge?

CHAPTER FOURTEEN

Day after day, my job for JC was to go from meeting to meeting, face to face, person to person across Hobart, up and down the channel, and up and down Bruny. I was sewing together a tapestry of community concerns that might somehow help everyone to coalesce. But these people had already participated in community meetings. Many of them had signed petitions, written letters to the paper, sent emails, organised crowdfunding, sat in the public gallery of parliament, sat on the lawns of Parliament House. All the things anyone against the bridge could do without getting arrested.

In some ways, any attempt on my behalf to meet with them as a group was just inflaming the situation. And the year was drawing to a close. People had Christmas and school holidays on their minds. I went gently. I had lots of one-on-one meetings. I identified key voices within the protest groups. I listened to their stories and assessed opportunities for collaboration and alignment. I ate scones and asked questions. I drank cups of tea and I listened some more. I reflected. I applied my training. And I observed my own inner dialogue. That is often the real barometer of the underlying machinery in conflict. We are all a cocktail of emotions. Even Supreme Court judges voting against a woman's right to an abortion or for a refugee's right to a visa are driven by emotion. Understanding exactly what that is, that's the way to bring about change. But it can be delicate and unpredictable.

The more I listened, the stranger it all got. Here was a huge bit of infrastructure that would join two islands together. But, somehow, despite the enormous investment by the federal and state governments, the jobs it had created and the vision it aspired to—to make Bruny a global destination—Tasmanians weren't buying it. Forty-three per cent of people in southern Tasmania didn't support it. The people who disagreed came from across the political spectrum. And for them, because Max and JC were aligned in supporting the bridge, the one person they felt they could rely on, even though it went against the grain, was the bridge's one political opponent: Amy O'Dwyer, the leader of the Greens.

Amy O'Dwyer was a wide-eyed, dark-haired, articulate beauty. She was warm and vivacious and the latest polls had thirty-five per cent of voters wanting her as the next premier. JC's support had dropped to thirty-six. Unlike us Colemans, Amy did not come from political stock. Her parents were Americans who had sea-changed to Tasmania in search of a quieter, safer world. Both were employed at the university. Her father was a plankton scientist, her mother taught history. Amy had been Steiner-schooled. She told me all this over dandelion coffee at the only good cafe in the southern town of Cygnet.

Cygnet is the Byron Bay of Tasmania, before Byron Bay got money. There's no surf, but there's the hippie culture, an annual folk festival and a Sunday farmers' market with excellent organics. In the sixties, Cygnet was a farming community of small-to-medium landholdings raising cattle and sheep. Neat white weatherboard homes with large barns and plants in white-painted rubber tyres. When farming became more precarious, a new kind of land lover moved in. White weatherboard had become sunset orange and daffodil yellow, with Tibetan prayer flags fluttering in the breeze across the front verandahs, gardens run to seed and motor vehicles with bumper stickers saying JC: DON'T BELIEVE IN HIM and NO BRIDGE TO BRUNY. The JC one amused me.

Amy had run for the lower house of the Tasmanian parliament at age eighteen and was the youngest person ever to have been elected in Australia. The national media loved her and had elevated her to pop star status. Everyone said she was bound for the Australian Senate but, so far, she had made no moves in that direction, saying she was a first-generation Tasmanian and this was where she was focused.

'It's inconceivable that we're not all more concerned,' Amy was saying, severing a vegan caramel slice. 'I battle with solistalgia all the time. You?'

'I'm not sure,' I said. 'It sounds uncomfortable.'

'It is,' she said. 'It's a deep melancholia for the assault the world is experiencing. Our home is fast becoming a place we're not safe in. And it's much worse if you're on some low-lying island in the Pacific. Or a refugee in some camp for the last ten years.'

'Ah,' I said.

'Scientists like my father are the most depressed people on the planet right now. Do you have children?'

'I do.'

'What do they do?' she asked.

'They're both in New York. My daughter's in international law and my son's in virtual reality.'

'Virtual reality,' said Amy. 'Our grandchildren, maybe even my children, will walk in virtual rainforests and swim over virtual coral reefs. And you know what? There're a lot of people who don't think that's a problem.'

'So how do you feel about the bridge, Amy?' I asked.

'We Greens have been the best strategists for Tasmania in the past forty years,' she said. 'We are the reason Tasmania is experiencing this tourism boom. Because we imagined a clean, green island and it turns out we were right. Clean, green and remote was what people wanted. So it's a double-edged sword for us. I mean, we've been so successful at selling Tasmania as a destination that now we're being overrun. Our special places are being overrun. Neither of the major parties are doing anything about it. It's crazy. I'd hoped all these tourists might shame the government into doing more to protect our wild places. But it hasn't. And the communities down the channel—the bridge is going to mean lots of them close down without the through traffic. No matter what anyone says, people aren't going to take the ferry when they could drive straight across. It's like Mount Wellington and the cable car. They promised that the road would stay open, but within eighteen months the developers had convinced the government to close the road. Now we have to pay to get up our own mountain, as if we were the tourists.'

I hadn't taken the cable car up the mountain yet, but it was visible from just about everywhere in Hobart. And the shuttle buses taking tourists to its base added to the traffic congestion.

'There are more than two hundred family businesses in the Huon beyond sheep and cattle. Cheese makers, fruit growers, wineries and cafes, the Heritage Centre, art galleries, the Apple Museum, distilleries and breweries. All of them will suffer when the bridge opens. Those people have laboured for years to grow the reputation of their region, to build their brands, and now all that passing trade is going to dry up.'

Amy had the manner of someone who got a lot of airtime. Single child. Media darling.

She continued. 'There's a hundred-page feasibility study on the bridge. Have you read it?'

'I have,' I said.

'Then you'll know it doesn't assess in any depth the impact on the wider community. How was that allowed to happen?' she asked.

'So why is the bridge going ahead?' I asked. 'You must have a theory.'

'Some people think they're going to give Bruny duty-free status. Make it like the Jersey islands—a tax haven. But I have a feeling they're going to sell the whole thing to the Chinese. Still, good luck getting anything out of your brother on that, even if you are the one asking.'

'Sell Bruny?' I frowned. I had not seen that coming.

'Well, the three major grazing properties there are now owned by the Chinese. And there's a Chinese Buddhist centre that's got planning approval on the hill above the Neck on South Bruny. There are planning applications for five hotels owned by Chinese consortiums at Adventure Bay, Cloudy Bay and at the lighthouse. One of the beaches north of Adventure Bay has been leased to the same company that's building the huge golf resort up the east coast.'

The one Farris had mentioned. 'Will those applications be approved?' I asked.

She nodded. 'Almost certainly. You have to understand, there are two types of Chinese. The ones who came here to escape the Chinese Communist Party, and the ones working for the Chinese Communist Party—working to roll out the Chinese Communist Party vision around the world. The China Dream. And it feels like the first type is being outnumbered by the second in Australia right now.'

'Tell me more,' I said. I could feel a conspiracy theory brewing in the fresh dandelion coffee that had just been delivered to the table.

'The Chinese are smart,' said Amy. 'Do you know they have this long-term vision of China as China One, Africa as China Two and Australia as China Three? They have a population problem and that means they have a food shortage coming at them, unless they start farming elsewhere. Australia has welcomed them. Well, their money at least. We've sold them huge tracts of farming land. And Tasmania has especially welcomed them. More of our farming land has been sold to Chinese interests than any other state of Australia.'

'And the bridge is somehow part of that plan?'

Amy laughed. 'Your brother signed up to the Belt and Road Initiative. We've become part of their plan. The bridge is being built with Chinese steel bought from a Chinese company, and it's going to be completed by Chinese labour. The loan structure? Nobody's telling us anything. Commercial-in-confidence. Look at the Chinese Buddhists. They've been here for years. They're part of our culture now. But they film everything.'

I thought back to Jenny Singh and her concerns. 'Why do you think they do that?' I asked.

'They're tracking us,' she said. 'What happens to all that footage? I know we think Chinese and camera are like bread and jam, but they pan across every dignitary, every face in the crowd. You watch. I can guarantee that when the Chinese workers come, the Buddhists will put on a huge celebration. It will be like Chinese New Year. There will be dumplings and fireworks and a Chinese dragon dance. And there will be camera operators documenting every person in the crowd.

'And you know what makes me mad?' she added. '"Jobs and growth." The answer to every problem is jobs and growth. Even if the jobs are all cleaning rooms and serving beers. I mean, is that the best we can offer our children? The Silicon Valley types and the financial whizzes, you can bet they want something more for their kids. But the rest of us? Casual labour at a measly hourly rate. No benefits. No security. That's why the Greens are so committed to a universal basic income trial here in Tasmania. We are the poorest state. It could make such a difference here.'

Amy O'Dwyer reminded me of my daughter: passionate, smart and a product of the twenty-first century. All knowledge was available if you were willing to seek it out. If I had to guess Amy's primary value set, it would be community, knowledge, family . . . after that I didn't know.

She leaned closer. 'You know, I once put up a dinner with myself at a fundraiser. Master Chin, the head of the Chinese Buddhists, bid for it and he won. So I go and have a very nice dinner with Master Chin and some of his community. When I got home, I found an envelope in my coat pocket that had twenty thousand dollars in it. I rang your brother and told him. Ask him. He'll tell you. I rang him at eleven pm. And of course I gave it back. But you can imagine how seductive it was. There I am, a few glasses of wine down, in the privacy of my own home, and I discover I'm twenty thousand dollars richer.'

I gazed at her.

'Amy,' I said, 'if there is some kind of organised plan to have a greater Chinese presence in Tasmania, how would the government do that? How would that get past Scrutiny and Estimates?'

'It already has,' she said. 'The Chinese Buddhist retreat on South Bruny, for one. I always say, if you want to spy on people, you do it in full view. If you want to hide, you do it in a city. And if you want to have access, you do it under the guise of religion. The retreat—it's got an electronic cage around it. Your phone drops out if you stand by the fence. Apparently they've put in six satellite dishes. It's wired to the world.'

I frowned.

'Let me tell you another story,' she said. 'There're only about a dozen Tibetans in Hobart, but when we knew the Chinese president was coming to Hobart a few years back, we got together. We knew the president had an early meeting at Government House, so we set up on the corner. When he emerged, the first thing he'd see would be the Tibetan flag and photos of the Dalai Lama. We didn't know how long he was going to be—but ten am comes and goes. Then, at ten thirty, four buses arrived full of young Chinese people. Turns out, two aeroplanes had been chartered from Melbourne for all these young, male Chinese university students, organised by the Chinese embassy. They started unfurling these huge Chinese flags—four or five metres long and two or three metres deep—on these massive wooden poles. Basically surrounded us. We were starting to feel a bit threatened. So I went over and introduced myself to the police, who were keeping an eye on all this. This is before the protest laws, of course, when we were free to do this sort of thing. I told the most senior officer, an inspector, that we were getting jostled. He said, "Well, give me a wave if it gets worse." Within the next ten minutes, the students were trying to lever us back and we wouldn't move. The Tibetans were getting pretty angry. I mean, you can imagine why. So I waved to the inspector, and he came over. I told him they were physically trying to move us and telling us we had no right to be here. So he goes up to the ringleader of the Chinese students and says, "Back off." And the young man says, "No, we're entitled to be here." The inspector says, "These people were here first." And the Chinese leader says, "But they're being disrespectful. They're waving the Tibetan flag." The inspector hitched up his trousers, puffed out his chest and said, "Mate, in Australia you can wave any damn flag you like, wherever you like—now back off.'"

Amy grinned at me.

'And there's a photo,' she said. 'You can see us totally surrounded by a sea of Chinese. The president went past in his motorcade, and he looked me right in the eye. Me, standing there with my huge portrait of the Dalai Lama. And he knew who I was.'

She paused. 'That inspector, by the way, is now the chief of police.'

'But it's too late,' she continued. 'Short of a coup, we're about to get Chinese workers on the bridge day and night. We've already sold or leased our dairy farms and wind farms and beaches. Stanley, and now that huge development at Freycinet. Cruise ships in Wineglass Bay. Our historic landmarks, too. Heritage homes. If they're not already gone, anything worth having is in the process of going. They've done it in plain sight, with government support and, in many cases, with the assistance of the very healthy bank account of the Chinese Communist Party. It's a juggernaut. Gilbert Farris calls it chequebook colonialism and I think—'

At that moment, a very good-looking Asian man in a dark suit and striped shirt approached the table. Amy looked up and beamed. He leaned down and kissed her on the cheek. She blushed. Then she turned to me. 'Charles Lee, meet Astrid Coleman.'

'How do you do, Astrid,' said Charles Lee. 'I've heard a lot about you.' He had an American accent. West coast.

'It's good to meet you, Charles,' I said, standing to shake his hand and collecting my bag to leave.

'Oh, I thought you might have questions for Charles. He's the communications director for Tourism Tasmania. Started four months ago. And don't worry, he's not working for the CCP. I had him vetted.' She laughed, and he smiled.

'She really did,' he said.

'You're Chinese, Charles?' I asked.

'Born in San Francisco. Taiwanese parents.'

'He's a McKinsey boy,' said Amy.

'Ex-McKinsey,' said Charles, grinning. 'Always a sign of sanity.'

'Between you and me,' said Amy quietly, 'Charles is not very happy about the Chinese Communist Party getting so much traction in Tasmania.'

'I'm just here to sell Tasmania to the world,' said Charles, holding his palms up.

'And sometimes being bilingual helps?' I asked.

He gave me a grin. 'It does.'

The thick plottened indeed.

'How do you feel about the current tourism numbers, Charles?' I asked.

'My role, as I see it, is to ensure Tasmania remains unique but the industry is also able to thrive. It's a delicate balance. Acquisition and dispersal.'

'You need them to come, and you need them to travel around the state?'

'Exactly,' he said. 'So, although Amy doesn't want to acknowledge it, the bridge is a key part of that strategy. The ferry is romantic. Nostalgic even. But it's not fulfilling the needs of the passengers. The queues are too long. We need more efficient dispersal. And reasons for people to travel.'

'We need higher-value tourism and lower numbers, in my world,' said Amy. 'Which makes people in government, and the industry, a little nervous.'

Charles smiled at her the way people who are newly in love do. Or maybe most people looked at Amy that way. She was ridiculously beautiful.

'So how did you two meet?' I asked.

'We sat next to each other from LA to Sydney. It was serendipity! Charles was on his way to start this job,' said Amy. 'I'd been to see my grandparents. We are a Qantas romance.'

I wondered how JC felt about this relationship.

Amy appeared to hear my thoughts. 'I think it's making your brother's government a little nervous. Afraid I'll turn him into a greenie.'

'And is she?' I asked.

Charles laughed a little uncomfortably. 'Of course not. But I love it here already.'

'Me too,' I said. 'It's home.'

It startled me, that. Was Tasmania still my home? It felt like the place had swallowed me whole. I was in a movie I'd never imagined. Roger Deakins was in charge of lighting—the epic skies, the marbled seas. Scorsese was in charge of direction—the family intrigue, the cast of character actors. But who had the plot? And, if it was a movie, someone was sure to die before that bridge was finished.

❧

It was Friday again. I sent a text to Stephanie saying I'd be on Bruny. I caught the last ferry. Max was right. I love a mystery. Amy was right. If you want to spy on people, sometimes it's simplest to do it in full view.

CHAPTER FIFTEEN

December 1st and a large white Christmas tree had been erected in the lobby. Tinsel and baubles were strung along the reception desk. The whole crazy thing seemed to start earlier every year, and come round faster. I greeted Michelle, the early-morning regular on the front desk, and swiped myself through. Then I rode the elevator to the tenth floor, where JC and his team had their offices. Here too a Christmas tree had been situated in the waiting area, this one smaller, dark green and heavily adorned in gold. The meeting with the Chinese delegation was scheduled for 9 am. It was just after 7 am. I took care of some paperwork and emails in my office, then emerged at 8.45 am.

Frank Pringle was adjusting his tie in a mirror in reception.

'You arrived early,' he said.

'I did, Frank. No rest for the wicked.'

He looked a little wired, Frank. Maybe it was a post-gym flush, or maybe it was a little white powder to start the day.

Moments later, two swarthy men with receding hairlines and pinstriped suits came through the doors from the lift lobby. One was the federal Minister for National Protection, Aiden Abbott, who had been in that first meeting I'd attended the day after I'd arrived. Aid-n-Abet—the most powerful man in Australia bar the prime minister. Some said even more powerful. Basically, anything that happened on Australian soil, or in surrounding waters, or wherever he chose to focus his gaze, was part of his portfolio. Abbott's aide looked so like Abbott that I could only assume he'd been hired specifically for that reason. The man on his heels was Barney Viper, deeply conservative federal Tasmanian senator and puppet master of the Tasmanian Liberals; JC's Maker, so I was told.

Viper had a trowel-shaped face with large teeth, a pallid complexion and an unsavoury reputation as a bully. He had also been blessed with a voice that belonged to a cartoon hyena. He was accompanied by Gavin Plumb, Tasmanian Minister for Infrastructure, who was almost as fat as JC but only half his height. Max called him Tweedle-Plumb. Forgive me if I don't seem to like politicians, family aside.

The last to arrive were the Chinese. An older man in a dark suit and red tie was introduced as Gao Enzhu. He was accompanied by a younger woman, May Chen, and a young man whose name was simply given as Edwin. It seemed the older man was the representative of the Chinese government, and Chen and Edwin were aides but I immediately pegged May Chen as secret service. Edwin too. May Chen was the sort of lean, serene Asian beauty designed to reinforce all those stereotypes men had of Asian women. But I glimpsed a tattoo on the underside of her wrist, and when she held out her hand to me, her eyes were warm.

JC emerged from behind the closed door of his office at 8.55 am accompanied by two members of staff. He was wearing a navy double-breasted suit that only enhanced his impressive corpulence. I noted a silver dragon tiepin on his blue tie. The dragon appeared to have glowing ruby eyes. I wasn't sure this was such a good choice in the present company, but maybe it had been a gift from a previous Chinese delegation.

A small forest had been felled to achieve the polished panels, table, sideboards, chairs and parquetry floor of the premier's boardroom. Myrtle, sassafras, blackwood, Huon pine. Even the large video screen, upon which an artist's impression of the completed bridge was hovering, had a timber surround. On the boardroom table was a silver platter of large Tasmanian-shaped biscuits, iced and topped with hundreds and thousands.

JC took his place at the head of the table with the view out over the river behind him. A mistake, I thought. First, he was partly in silhouette. And second, it was so enticing to look at the sparkling river and not at my brother.

It was the sort of day Tasmania does well. A little breeze was catching on the river's surface, sending the morning light into paroxysms of pleasure. A few white clouds decorated the vivid blue Southern Ocean sky. It was a day that looked as if all would be well. Julian of Norwich, a nun who had taken a man's name, as was customary at the time, had immortalised these words: *All shall be well and all shall be well and all manner of thing shall be well.*

If only it were true. Still, the words had been like a mantra through the devastation in South Sudan, the horrors of Myanmar, the ravages of Mosul, the savagery in Nigeria, the brutality in

Turkey and . . . *all shall be well and all shall be well and all manner of thing shall be well.*

I drew my thoughts back into the room. JC was waxing on the significance of this meeting. He had our father's wavy fair hair that had greyed to silver and the same grey eyes. He hadn't always been a big man, JC. As a teenager, he'd been a rower, tall and well-built. Even into his thirties, he'd been fit. This morning he was articulate, charming, and a little dull. The benevolent leader with the best interests of his people at heart.

There it was again. Altruism. It was only ever a short step between believing you are the *right* leader to believing you are the *only* leader for your people. Mussolini in Italy, Hitler in Germany, Putin in Russia, Trump in America, Erdogan in Turkey, and now the Eternal Fragrant President of China. Left or right, it didn't matter. We can rattle off a few bad women leaders over the years, but the list of deplorable men has been endless.

Frank Pringle took over from JC to walk everyone through the current status of the investigation into the bombing. There were a couple of leads but nothing concrete and no arrests. Apparently ASIO was now involved. Interpol, too. I would have thought there had been ASIO agents here since day one, assessing the scene, but I said nothing.

'The federal police think it unlikely it was done from a Tasmanian base,' Frank said.

Next, Tweedle-Plumb went through the logistics of the foreign workers. Their accommodation would be at a recently decommissioned refugee camp. The camp was out of town and surrounded by a six-metre cyclone-wire fence topped with razor wire. There was twenty-four-hour surveillance. The federal police were contributing extra security to bolster the Tasmanian resources, but it was hoped it wouldn't be needed.

There was a short interchange between the older Chinese man, Gao Enzhu, and May Chen.

'How much resistance are you expecting?' May Chen asked in her Oxford English.

Viper spoke. 'None. That's why Doctor Coleman is here. We have employed her to ensure any dissent is nipped in the bud. Historically, Tasmanians are a peaceable people. That's why Cadbury built its empire here in the early 1900s. Yes, we've had our share of protests, but they were drummed up by radical leftists. Ridiculous short-sighted protests by economic vandals. But the Tasmanian people want this bridge completed. The latest poll shows that overwhelmingly. Up another eight per cent since the bridge was bombed. Protesters are almost entirely made up of Bruny shack owners and channel residents. And the Greens. They're no match for this government.'

May Chen translated this and the older man spoke. She listened and then said, 'We think it would be unwise to underestimate the potential loss of public sympathy for the bridge—following the bombing—when Tasmanians are faced with a foreign workforce being bussed through Hobart to the bridge every day. Also, we must consider those working onsite. Such a sight, with foreign workers, has never before been seen in Australia.'

'The hydro schemes back in the fifties,' Tweedle-Plumb said. 'They were built by foreign labour. Slavs and Poles and Krauts.'

'But not Asians, Senator,' said May gently. 'And they were a long way from Hobart. Not visible to everyday Tasmanians.'

'We had the Hmong people at Salamanca market for years before they moved to northern New South Wales,' said JC. 'Tasmanians liked them.'

'But they grew vegetables,' said May Chen. She and I exchanged a glance. This conversation wasn't surprising either of us.

There was another exchange between May Chen and Gao Enzhu.

'The Chinese government,' said May Chen, 'and our Eternal Fragrant President, would like this to be an opportunity for exchange with the Tasmanian people. Our government is proud to be participating in this project. Tell me, what efforts will be made to ensure that the integration of local and foreign workers is positive?'

The Chinese president had recently consolidated his power under the new title of Eternal Fragrant President and had appointed himself to the role for life. I couldn't help but suppress a smile, imagining a spate of Chinese restaurants emerging: Eternal Fragrant Lotus Flower, Eternal Fragrant Floating Dragon, Eternal Fragrant Harmony . . .

But May Chen's question about the integration of the workers was not about logistics. It was a cultural question. When the Chinese wanted to woo the world, they did it with culture. Plays, architecture, ballet, design, opera, art, film, poetry. Shame they'd killed a whole generation of creatives under Chairman Mao.

'We have briefed our advertising agency,' said JC's PR person. He was a bearded young man in a pink shirt and deeper pink floral tie. 'But these things take time. Obviously we will create good news stories.'

'Shame it's not footy season,' said JC. 'We could have a special match. Or table tennis? Could we have a tournament?'

May Chen smiled beatifically, to her credit. There was chuckling around the table from Tweedle-Plumb, Abbott and a couple of JC's minions. Viper was humourless.

Aid-n-Abet said, 'Yes, but it's not simply a matter of advertising or PR. Am I right? I think we need to devise an appropriate community engagement strategy.'

Everyone but the Chinese nodded.

'We could have an update on TasInvest,' suggested JC. 'Get the president back. Ace, what do you think? You're on the ground.'

'The question is time. The workers are about to arrive. The community is tense,' I said. 'Public sympathy for the bridge may be up, but overwhelmingly people believe investment would be better placed in other projects for Tasmania. Even among those *for* the bridge, there's a distinct sense that they want this bridge to be a wholly Tasmanian project. They're not happy about foreign labour. They'd rather the bridge took longer to build. If those people for the bridge but against foreign labour start seeing eye to eye with those against the bridge, that could become a very large group to neutralise.'

'Why the fuck do Tasmanians have to be so bloody combative?' said Abbott.

'A lot of good people have tried to answer that, Aiden,' said Viper. *Aiden.* Not *Minister.* Viper was a minion in comparison to Abbott, never given any significant role in the federal government even though the Tasmanian people kept re-electing and re-electing him. But here, in this room, Viper wanted everyone to see that he and Abbott were equals.

'Mr Gao?' said Abbott to the older Chinese man. 'What would your government wish to see put in place?'

May translated, and there was a brief exchange.

'We have taken the liberty of preparing some materials,' she said. 'Premier, if you will permit . . .'

'Of course,' said JC.

The young man, Edwin, walked over to the video equipment and began navigating the various remotes and devices. The electronic blinds were lowered, the room was dimmed and, within moments, a short film began playing on the large screen. This was such an impressive display of expertise with unfamiliar technology—I hoped everyone in the room realised they'd just been one-upped.

The words *A Bridge between China and Tasmania* appeared on the screen. The Eternal Fragrant President appeared and spoke of the importance of this project for China and Tasmania. The film was both dubbed and subtitled.

'Hello, people of Tasmania. I loved my visit to your beautiful island during the wonderful TasInvest Conference. My eyes were opened to the beauty and bounty of your magnificent home. I wish my country to continue this important engagement with Tasmania. I wish to extend the support of the Chinese government to ensuring the prosperity of Tasmania. This sharing of workers, for the first time, is the beginning of a program of mutual economic exchange and cultural enrichment. A small delegation of Chinese workers will help to fulfil a Tasmanian dream to join Bruny Island to mainland Tasmania. But it will also join Chinese workers and their families with Tasmanian workers and their families.'

At this point there were cutaways of Chinese families playing with their children in a park, walking along a boulevard and sharing a family meal, and then there was an extended table with both Chinese and, presumably, Tasmanian people, sharing a meal together, playing cricket in a park and looking as if they were all having a fine time.

'If such an exchange proves helpful to both Tasmania and Australia,' the president continued, *'then this will pave the way for a future where many things are possible.'*

The film went on to outline the Tasmanian buses that had been acquired by the Chinese government for the duration of the workers' stay. There was footage of the buses under-going their makeovers, and an artist's impression of the finished product: buses emblazoned with images of the completed Bruny Bridge. There were also illustrations of banners erected all the way from the Chinese accommodation into the city, and then down the highway to the bridge site—each banner emblazoned with the Chinese flag and the Australian flag side by side.

'And to demonstrate our commitment to the people of Tasmania,' the president's dubbed voiceover continued, *'the Chinese government will stage three nights of Chinese music and theatre, providing an opportunity for Tasmanians to share in some of the most loved stories from Chinese culture. To welcome the Chinese workers, the Chinese Buddhist community will perform a dragon dance ceremony through the streets of Hobart, culminating in a fireworks display and a feast at the Peace and Reconciliation Park at Macquarie Point.'*

There was footage of a dragon dance complete with a glit-tering dragon weaving its way through the streets and awestruck children waving both Chinese and Australian flags. Then there was a magnificent eruption of fireworks.

The film concluded with an animated logo entwining Tasmania's tiger logo with the Chinese dragon and the words: *Together with Tasmania.*

JC flicked his dragon tiepin and nodded. Frank nodded too. The PR person from the government looked a little confused. Aid-n-Abet and his aide both nodded. Viper smiled. May Chen and I gazed at one another as chess opponents might.

The platter of Tasmanian biscuits was passed around. JC took one and bit into it. Abbott asked if he could take some home to his children. Everyone laughed and Viper dispatched a staff member to make that happen. Tea and coffee was served. The bearded PR boy said something to JC, who waved his hand to brush him off.

'How are the workers being flown in?' I asked.

'There are direct flights from Hobart each week to China carrying fresh milk. The workers are coming in on the return flights,' said Frank.

Aid-n-Abet said, 'And your government has signed a deal to acquire the additional steel to repair the bridge from Shoughan International under the Belt and Road Initiative?'

'Onto ships next week and delivered by the end of the month,' said Viper, 'as I understand.'

'Excellent. Really excellent,' JC said, dusting hundreds and thousands from his fingers onto his plate, and wiping his hands on a folded linen napkin.

Tweedle-Plumb added, 'There's sufficient steel currently in the state, or in transit, to continue the build until it arrives.'

Everyone nodded.

'So, if there's nothing else,' said JC, 'let's get the journos in here, Frank. Mr Gao, Miss Chen, would you join us to outline the next steps?'

'Sir,' said bearded PR, 'it would be good to review the materials and ensure they align with . . .'

I loved his attempt but he was a wet moth going downstream.

'Time is of the essence, wouldn't you say?' said Viper. 'No harm in getting this next step into the public arena. We can deal with tomorrow tomorrow. What do you think, John?'

JC put up his hands as if in surrender and said, 'Agreed. Let's not overcomplicate things, or slow them down. We're all on the same page here.'

'That we are,' said May Chen. 'We have also prepared extra dossiers for the media.'

The meeting dissembled. JC walked over. 'Told you we had it sorted,' he said.

'They make doing business look easy,' I said.

'Makes your job much easier too, all this stuff.' He prodded the red dossiers on the table with their embossed and entwined Chinese dragon and Tasmanian tiger logos. 'Shall we talk later today?'

'Yes,' I said.

'Come up and we'll catch the news at home.'

'Done.'

The last person I passed on the way out of the room was May Chen.

'It's very nice to meet you, Miss Chen,' I said, holding out my hand.

'And you, Doctor Coleman.'

'Astrid,' I said.

'May,' she said. 'You are a conflict resolution specialist.'

'I can see you are too,' I said.

'Let me give you my number,' she offered. 'I hope I can be of assistance throughout this time.'

She handed me her card. I promised to text her so she had my details too.

We both smiled and I left the building.

CHAPTER SIXTEEN

Later that day, JC and I watched the various news bulletins reporting 'a round table between the premier, the federal minister and representatives of the Chinese government'. There were extracts of the film with the Eternal Fragrant President declaring a new global approach to labour. JC was seen saying, *'The relationship between Tasmanian and China goes back over one hundred and fifty years. Now China is once again making a proud contribution to the economic, social and cultural wellbeing of Tasmania.'*

'It went well, yeah?' said JC through a mouthful of corn chips and salsa. 'Bloody terrorists have actually done some good. I don't think there is any way it would have got finished without the bombing.'

I raised my eyebrows. 'Really?'

He crunched and nodded.

'JC, who gave you speech notes about the relationship between Tasmania and China going back over one hundred and fifty years?'

'It was in the media folder. I . . . why are you looking at me like that, Ace?'

'Because it's not quite true.'

'Close enough. They were here for the gold rush back in the 1880s.'

'But not exactly government to government. Not contributing to Tasmania's . . .' I sighed. It made it sound like China had staked a claim years ago and was now coming back for more. That we owed them. This was a regular gambit. But there were bigger fish to fry. 'Tell me why the bridge wouldn't have been finished on time without the bomb.'

'I was getting all sorts of reports.'

'So what would you have done?'

JC shrugged. 'The bomb took care of it. Whoever they were, they did me a favour.'

I scrutinised my brother. Had JC organised a bomb to get his bridge built? Would he be that ruthless? He had traded our father's values to get elected. He had seen the writing on the wall. Labor was on the decline, so he'd done the one thing he knew would break our father's heart. Because it suited him. Maybe he did find a way to have the bridge blown up. Means and motive, when it all came down to it. But, if he did, JC wasn't pulling the strings. He would have been Viper's puppet. ASIO must have been suspicious. Unless ASIO was involved. Unless it was an ASIO operation. After all, this suited the federal government far too well. That would make sense of the vessel. I knew JC was under surveillance. His calls were being listened to. That's how I'd received such an instant instruction to come home. The Chinese would be listening too. Monitoring his emails. Did JC have any idea what he was involved in? Would ASIO and China's MSS or 3PLA collaborate? How deep was this new alliance between China and Australia going to go?

JC went to his whisky collection and selected a tall slender bottle. 'You've got to try this one,' he said. 'We make the best whisky in the world these days.'

He poured generous serves of amber liquid into two crystal tumblers. I recognised the tumblers as the ones I'd sent him for Christmas last year. The wonders of online shopping at Barneys. New York to Tasmania, gift-wrapped, in forty-eight hours flat.

'You do know who supplies Shoughan International?' JC asked.

'Gina Rinehart?' I replied. I should have feigned ignorance.

'Too right. So it's Australian iron ore in that bridge. This is the new world, Ace. You must see it everywhere, yeah? This is globalisation benefiting Tasmania.'

'What I see is the Chinese going to inordinate lengths to make this project a success,' I said, warming the glass and its contents in my hand. 'You signed up to the Belt and Road. I have to ask: why, JC? Was it all part of the federal deal?'

He shrugged. 'You don't get this kind of investment for nothing, Ace.'

'I think there's a higher price somewhere, JC. Sure, the steel contract, plus what's required for the repairs. The cost of labour. But what's with these images of workers' families? Since when did the Chinese care about individual workers? There are no families coming with the workers.'

'I think it's there to remind us that these workers have families like all of us, Ace. China's realising it can't keep a lid on capitalism forever. Selling their labour overseas makes sense.

I mean, that's harnessing their biggest resource. People. We're the first step. They're very family-minded. They plan for the long term. We could learn a lot from that.'

'I think they're way ahead of us,' I said. I wanted to say 'way ahead of you' but it would only irritate him.

'Look, at the end of the day, Tasmania benefits, Ace,' said JC. 'You saw the news coverage. It's fantastic. It's a win-win.'

I reflected on a conversation I'd had with Gilbert Farris the day before, this time at his home on Bruny with his wife, Barbara. 'You've been back a minute,' Farris had said. 'We've been here for ten years now. I've watched the government do deal after deal that's bad for Tasmanians. Most everything done here in the past hundred years has made future generations poorer. Tasmanians have voted for it, believed in the rhetoric, and called it progress. What does Tasmania have to show for all those lost forests? All the polluted waterways? The overrun national parks and lost wilderness? There are tourists swarming over every last inch of the place. And now we're going to lose Bruny too. One of the last truly remote, beautiful, liveable places in the world.'

'There's something about seeing that . . .' I said to JC as we both watched the animated Tasmanian tiger merge into the animated Chinese dragon, 'which makes me uncomfortable. And it's going to make other people uncomfortable too.'

'Fuck, you're starting to sound like Max,' said JC. 'China is our major trading partner. They're also our ally. They've invested heavily here. What they're doing with the bridge is protecting their investments. When there's a real problem, Ace, make sure I'm the first to hear about it. Meanwhile, they're getting our bridge built.'

'All so you can get re-elected?'

'Not just that, Ace. We're part of the future. We promised we'd be that, and here we are changing the world, twin. And we're doing it together. It's allowed to feel good, hey?'

And he chinked his tumbler against mine.

As I let the whisky warm in my mouth and slide across the place my tonsils had once been, I asked him, 'What do you think would bring Tasmanians together over the bridge?'

'There is no together,' he said. 'You know that, Ace. This is Tasmania. People love to disagree. Keeps their lives interesting.'

CHAPTER SEVENTEEN

I was drinking coffee and reading the Saturday paper at the Dennes Point cafe when a voice said, 'I could sit there and drink my coffee and read my paper, or I could sit here.'

I looked up. It was Dan Macmillan. He indicated the empty table next to mine, or the chair opposite me.

'Good morning,' I said. 'Please, sit down.'

He sat and gave me a grin. He looked freshly showered and unshaved.

'I'm not trying to disturb you,' he said. 'Just thought it would be weird if you looked up and saw me trying not to be noticed.'

'Well, enjoy being there and not noticed.'

'Perfect,' he said.

The waitress brought his coffee and he opened his paper.

I had *The Australian* and he had *The Mercury*. I was reading a December feature on *The Year That Was*. This was a look back at Cyclone Pauline, which had chewed up the coastline from Byron Bay to Sydney at the end of last summer. A cyclone so far south had been unprecedented. The warming currents were blamed. The federal government's failure to attend to climate change was blamed. The scientists who predicted it were blamed. The coal industry was blamed. The Greens were blamed. But none of the blame saved the thousands of homes, schools, resorts, businesses, yachts and three runways at Sydney airport.

For the next ten minutes, neither of us said a word. We sipped our coffees, turned pages and navigated the space at the table between us.

At last, I said, 'Okay, I need more coffee. You?'

'Absolutely,' he said.

I got up and ordered. As I was returning to the table, despite the warmth of the morning, rain started splattering on the floor-to-ceiling windows. The cafe was built high above the beach with a view up the Derwent and across the channel. White walls, raw wood, polished timber floors, a wide covered deck filled with patrons, and a kitchen garden below with stairs leading down to the beach. Maggie Lennox was nowhere in sight this morning.

Dan looked out as the weather closed in. 'The boys will be loving this,' he said. Meaning the crew on the bridge.

'Do you think anyone will catch the ferry once the bridge is open?' I asked.

'Shouldn't think so,' he said. 'Maybe there are ferry nuts like there are train nuts. Might get a few of those. But no. It's a shame, but I guess that's progress.'

'Why does the ferry matter to you?' I asked him.

'It was always something to look forward to,' he said. 'I mean, I still look forward to it, and I must have done it thousands of times by now. It's a new experience for a lot of people too—it's an adventure. With a bridge, there's no real feeling of arrival.

I mean, what's happening here now, with the bridge and the sealed roads, fifty years ago a bloke would have given anything to have a highway past his front door. Suddenly he's sitting on a goldmine. These days, someone's gone to the arse end of the world to set up a place for people to stay, and some government sees fit to build a bridge and it devalues her place. I know there'll be people who will be going, "We're sealing the road right by her house. We're giving her a slip road and a sign. What's her fucking problem?"'

'She's very popular, Maggie Lennox.'

'She's a great woman. It's shitty what they've done to her. She's given a lot to the state. And now they're throwing her under a bus. Have you seen her place?'

'I have. It's incredible.' Maggie had given me the promised tour. It was exquisite. 'And you built it,' I said. 'I didn't know you did projects like that.'

'It's Tassie. We pitch for lots of things, big and small. Got a lot of blokes on the books. Have to keep them busy. In the past, I did the smaller stuff and Jimmy did the big commercial.'

I nodded. 'Maggie said. It must be rewarding, seeing something you've made in the landscape.'

He stretched out his legs to the side of the table and partly turned towards the window. In quixotic Tasmanian style, the shower had passed and sunshine was breaking through the cloud cover. The sea looked like crushed linen. 'It's dominated my thought process, building,' said Dan. 'And it's dominated my philosophy. Design is one thing but execution is everything. The central driver is how a structure will perform over a long period of time. How is it going to weather? You want it to stand the test of time. You want it doing exactly what it's doing today in fifty years, in one hundred years. It can look good, but the test is three hundred years' time. Maggie understands that. She's tight—but she's got her eye on the right result.'

'Did you build this too?' I asked, meaning the cafe.

'No, not this. This was the first thing she built on Bruny. Didn't know her then.'

Our coffees arrived.

'Not long ago,' Dan said, 'I was on my way home on the ferry and this bloke appeared out of nowhere on the lower deck. He had this white jacket on, like a lab coat. Tall and skinny, wild white hair—looks like the doc from *Back to the Future*. And I asked one of the crew that I was talking to, "Who's that old bloke? How long's he been here?" And the bloke says, "He's been here twenty-six years. He's our mechanic." Apparently he stays downstairs. Gets on at seven, gets off at four. I've been on that ferry all my life, and I'd never once seen him. Sits down there in his lab coat all day, every day, when he's on, monitoring the pressure gauges and increasing the water flow, turn that up here and that down there. And he watches DVDs all day. Got a whole set-up down there. TV, headphones. That's his life. What are they going to do with him when the ferry stops?'

'What do you reckon he does at the end of the day now?'

'Chops people up, I reckon. Got people dissected in his freezer.'

I laughed.

'And what about the women who sell curry in Kettering?' he asked. 'They'll be out of a job for sure.'

'Do tell,' I said.

'There's two of them in a caravan just near the terminal. They're like Marg Simpson's sisters. They've got these lines on their faces like a couple of Shar Peis, as though they've smoked a billion cigarettes. Their curries are fantastic. They make it all onsite, sitting on crates peeling onions. It's another bit of the channel that we'll lose when the bridge opens.'

'Dan,' I said, 'why do you think Tasmanians protest so well? Why are they so averse to change?'

'Well, we already gave up a lot just to be here.'

'How do you mean?'

'Most of us could have done something else. Gone interstate or overseas. Could have lived bigger lives. Had fancy homes and a fat bank account. And the sea changers, well, they did live bigger lives. But they came here for something else. Quiet. Simplicity. When you settle for Tassie, you've settled for less in some ways; less of what matters out there, more of what matters here. If someone wants to change that, take what you love about it away, you get pretty shirty. Because it's what we have. It's all we have. You'd have seen a bit of that elsewhere in your line of work, I'm guessing.'

'I have,' I said.

'Pretty messy job at times, yeah?'

I nodded. I didn't want to think about all that. 'So, Dan,' I asked, 'what matters most to you on this project?'

'That I don't lose any of my guys,' he said. 'It's a bloody big structure.'

'How do you think the foreign workforce is going to go?'

'Hard to tell. Guess we'll make it work.'

'You seem pretty relaxed,' I said.

'That's why they pay me the big bucks.' As in *not*. He grinned that infectious grin that had such mischief about it. He had the most intensely blue eyes. Paul Newman blue. They were distracting.

'So, you were a paratrooper,' I said.

'Been checking up on me?' He grinned again.

'It's my job to know who I'm dealing with.'

He gave me a long level gaze. 'You think I'm the bomber?'

'Probably not,' I said.

Yet he must have known a fair bit about explosives. He'd have had friends, too, who might have been able to put a team together. But the cost? Someone must have funded the bombing to the tune of several hundred thousand dollars. If Dan had done it, he would have been employed by someone. But would he build the thing and also blow it up? It seemed unlikely. Unless they offered him big money. I thought of his car, the house. He didn't seem like a man who would be motivated by money, but it was hard to tell. More likely it been an order from higher up. Maybe a commanding officer from the old days. That might make sense. He was the only person I'd found who had the right background. And he was trained to obey.

'Way beyond me, a job like that,' he said, as if he knew he hadn't convinced me. 'But the Feds did ask me a fair few questions. I didn't blow up the bridge, Astrid. Jesus. But look at the place. It's paradise. I don't want it to change.'

'Someone really knew how to do enough,' I said. 'Not too little, not too much.'

'Yep,' he agreed. 'Skill.'

'Was it hard adjusting to civilian life after all that?'

'It's why I like working with a crew, I guess.'

'Why did you leave?'

'Our unit was reassigned to mechanised infantry in 2011,' he said. 'The ultimate insult. Hyper fit, top of the food-chain, airborne soldiers got to be carried around in armoured personnel carriers like backpackers.' He stretched out his arms and yawned. 'Still, small-minded decisions are not special to the army. Lots of us moved on. Jimmy offered me a job, made me a partner. Taught me everything I know, really, about business and such. It's been okay, coming back.

'I gotta get down to the site,' he said, looking at his watch as he finished his latte.

'Nice to see you, Dan,' I said. 'Thanks for the chat.'

'You need a lift over tomorrow, Sherlock Holmes?'

I laughed. 'Sunday lunch cannot be missed. Is that okay with you?'

'See you at the pier. Eleven,' he said.

He looked good as he walked away. Tall, strong, a bit solitary. I'd never seen anyone else come or go from his house, but I supposed he had a partner. Despite my job involving endless conversations, I'm an introvert. I like solitary. I need it. I understood exactly what Maggie Lennox's clients were looking for. The difference was, they paid twenty thousand a week for the privilege while I could just close the door. Dan too.

I went to pay but Trixie behind the counter told me it was all good; Dan had taken care of it.

When I got back to the house, I looked down on the rooftop of Dan's house. From the street, it was private and surrounded on three sides by an old macrocarpa pine hedge. A kind of fairy-tale seclusion with an amazing view.

I had once had a beer with an American submariner after an operation. He'd been underwater for fifty-six days on a sensitive mission. I asked him what he'd missed while he was down there.

'Stars,' he'd said. 'I missed the stars.'

I've had prisoners tell me the same thing.

I learned a lot of tough things early. It's taken me all my life to get to the simple ones.

CHAPTER EIGHTEEN

That next week, the Chinese workers came. Two hundred and eighty-nine of them. The number had been carefully considered like a discount price at a bargain store. The first of them were met at Hobart airport by both JC and Maxine and various government ministers. I attended too.

The workers were bussed to their refurbished quarters at Brighton's old refugee camp to settle in. That evening they were bussed to the festivities. The Chinese dragon dance was colourful, the free community yum cha was attended by thousands. Dumplings were drained from steaming saucepans and scooped from hot woks by an influx of Chinese student volunteers from across Australia, all impeccable in kitchen whites and chef's hats. At the Derwent Entertainment Centre, a concert was staged for all the bridge workers and their families, Tasmanians, mainlanders and Chinese. The Tasmanian Symphony Orchestra played with a famous Chinese conductor and soloists from both China and Tasmania sang. Afterwards there were fireworks from barges on the Derwent. And the Chinese Buddhists filmed everything.

Our whole family attended, save for Dad. Mother came in a red wig and cheongsam, flanked by the devoted Phillip.

'A cheongsam?' I whispered to Phillip. 'Really?'

'I couldn't talk her out of it,' he sighed. 'You know how she is.'

'I do,' I said.

⁊

That night I dreamed that I was trying to pitch a tent. My daughter Tavvy was with me. All the tents were somehow incorrect. I had only a fly, but I pitched it against a wall and was happy with it, even though it was ridiculous, as things are in dreams. But when the rain started, Tavvy disappeared and I was alone. I watched the rain begin to flood the paddock, making wide shallow puddles and pooling between hillocks of grass. Now it was impossible for camping. I saw a wooden structure. It was overgrown with bushes but it had once been a children's playhouse. Above the foliage was a tower stained by the rain. A tower would be fine to sleep in, I thought. But the only way up was via a narrow beam. On the other side of the narrow beam, Dan Macmillan appeared. He didn't offer me a hand. He simply persuaded me I could do it myself. He pointed out places where I could put my foot to negotiate the vines. He reassured me that I wouldn't fall. I walked. He smiled. Then I woke up.

I didn't like dreaming about Dan Macmillan. It felt unprofessional. As I showered, the dream kept coming back to me. The silly fly I had pitched. The puddles in the ground and the whole field awash with water. The dark tower overgrown by bushes. Dan assuring me I could balance and walk.

I thought of the dream again as I sat across from Dan in the morning briefing at Tinderbox. He was wearing a crisp, white shirt and I thought of him ironing, and that led to me thinking of him showering, and that led to me wondering if he still made the bed military style. His house was literally down the paddock from mine at Bruny. When I took walks I sometimes heard music playing, and I'd thought about whether I should invite him up for a beer one evening. But I didn't. He was younger than me. I had no idea what he'd make of such an offer.

This morning's briefing wasn't like other morning briefings. Normally Dan briefed his team leaders on exactly what needed be achieved. They got an hour-by-hour weather forecast and the schedules for barges and deliveries. I made sure Dan also got press updates so his team were forewarned of the coming evening's likely media. This meant that when they got home to eat dinner or muck about with the kids and the telly blurted out something about the bridge, they were already informed.

But tonight was the first night of the Chinese workers. Frank Pringle had come south with me for the morning meeting, behaving as if he was the acting Premier.

'So, the moment has come,' Frank said. 'In the next twenty-four hours, labour in Australia will change forever. We'll no longer have to wait for years to build things or to acquire technical knowhow. We'll have the use of workers from across the world. Experts in their field will be able to work anywhere they can be valuable. This means a significant shift for the world's workforce. Geography has been conquered. We've seen this happen in the UK with Eastern European labour and in the

US, where for years they've enjoyed the benefits of a cheaper workforce thanks to the Mexican border.'

Ah, Frank, I thought. You're a little behind the times with this speech given Brexit and the wall between the US and Mexico.

'Here are just some of the projects these workers have been employed on to date,' he said. He flicked images onto the large screen behind him of bridges across canyons, across water, flyovers across cities, rail bridges and car bridges. It had been my idea to give everyone some sense of the skill of these workers. I'd got the images from May Chen. Whether any of it was true, and these workers really had been behind these projects, we were about to find out.

The Tiananmen Square moment happened in 1989. I was finishing my postgrad studies in New York. It shook us all. Since then, the human rights abuses had continued. People go missing every day in China. Particularly human rights lawyers and activists. Anyone who is deemed to have insufficient social credit can disappear. Artists, actors, academics and poets. The control of the Chinese media has been effective. It's very rare for dissent to escape the national borders.

In my game, human rights are not theoretical. It's not white-boards, round tables and talking points. Prison in China is interrogation cells and cages, crowded quarters and a crushing, calculated system of torture designed to make any prisoner, no matter how innocent, confess to whatever the Chinese government wants them to. No lawyers, no phone calls, no contact with the outside world until it suits the government. If you won't comply, there are always family members to incarcerate and torture as well. I was sure these workers newly arrived in Tasmania would all put the Chinese Communist Party above their own interests. There would be no deviation.

∾

At the bridge, the afternoon workers were still onsite. Enormous cranes were working on either side of the bridge. They were rebuilding the tower from the seabed up, repairing and re-tensioning cables, doing the prep work for the road segments. Barges carrying huge floodlights were in place, powered by generators, making the place as bright as midday. I spotted Dan Macmillan ahead. He nodded when he saw me.

'You have something to do with that?' he asked, indicating the Tinderbox camp behind them and the BFG camp ahead on Dennes Point. Both were eerily quiet. Up on Tinderbox hill, there was a modest bonfire. It was a warm, still evening and the sound of an acoustic guitar and singing drifted in from time to time over the construction noise.

'Are they really singing "Kum Bah Ya"?' Dan asked.

'I think so. International song of peace.'

Dan shook his head.

'It's only temporary,' I said. 'But let's enjoy it for now.'

I had worked overtime getting the two BFG camps to agree to let the new workers begin in peace. Australians were good at racism. I was still asked regularly, when people gauged my nationality, how Australia could treat refugees the way it did. But these bridge protesters were not racists. They were activists protecting their patch, their way of life, their economic wellbeing. They were trying to preserve, not destroy. If they protested the first few nights, while the workers were getting underway, and there was an incident or, worse, a death, they would be blamed. The government would forcibly remove them. Show over. The Tasmanian protest laws made that very clear. It was only while they maintained their distance and didn't interrupt the work that they were tolerated.

A siren went off. Buses were arriving. Buses with Tasmanian tigers and Chinese dragons entwined and grand vistas of the finished bridge painted along their sides. Here was the night shift. A sea of Chinese men in orange high-vis vests and white helmets disembarked. Within the group was a small cohort of men and women in suits, also in high-vis vests and hard hats.

Interpreters, I thought.

Behind us the workers from the afternoon shift were gathering. Dan stepped forward. He picked up a microphone. It was wireless, connected to a PA to one side. Now he had workers all around him. He offered the other microphone to a Chinese woman who had stepped forward.

'I'm Dan Macmillan,' he said. 'Bridge foreman.'

The interpreter began translating. Everyone remained standing.

Dan continued. 'Welcome. *Huan ying.*' Some of them nodded. 'So here it is! And you can see we've got some work to do.'

The men at his back were watching. The air was tense. The Australian workers were observing the new arrivals like a patient observing a brain scan, wondering what the doctor will tell them.

'Nothing on this bridge is more important than your safety and the safety of the men on your shift,' Dan continued. 'Here we are on a near perfect night. The weather is calm. The sea is calm. We are calm.'

Already he had them, interpreter and all. He stood with ease, as if he was speaking to each of them individually. He continued laying out his expectations for protocol and systems while they were onsite. This was what he did. This was what he was good at, melding men into a workforce.

It was such a risk. How could all these men, given the cultural divide, determine together exactly how tight the bolts should be screwed and the wires tensioned, en masse, as one mind? And it wasn't just here. Over at the manufacturing site, all the components were being constructed. Steel sections were coming in on barges and being craned into place. Everything relied on expertise and skill and cooperation. It was easy to forget that. Human endeavour relied on cooperation. The construction of buildings, ships, aircraft, dams and bridges, all the great monuments to civilisation.

War was the defeat of that cooperation. In the process, it destroyed the labour of countless human beings. Perhaps that was its greatest flaw. It eviscerated the output of lifetimes. It laid waste the lives of women and men and made of them gravel and dust. The arrogance of that was staggering. But here was a man trying to coalesce a group to do quite the opposite. To give of their minds and bodies to create an engineering feat that would carry people across water for generations.

When Dan wound up his talk, a mixed crew of Australian and Chinese workers and interpreters was transferred onto barges that took them to the Bruny side of the bridge. The remainder flowed onto this worksite and shadowed their counterparts in this hour of crossover.

❦

'They cannot see themselves as adversaries,' Dan had said to Mick Feltham. 'You are asking for sabotage if you let that happen. I know the costs will increase. But we cannot trade budget for safety.'

Mick had given him until New Year. Three weeks of this hour of shared shift—the changeover—with Australian workers and Chinese workers. But after that, it was back to the standard quarter-hour changeover. Feltham had been immovable.

'It's not even his money,' Dan had said to me, as we'd left that heated meeting.

'Small-minded decisions are not special to the army . . .' I said, quoting him.

He nodded. 'Too right.'

It's not just small-mindedness that's driving Mick Feltham, I'd wanted to tell him. This will be his parting achievement. So, no, it's not about money. It's much more than that. It's his legacy.

CHAPTER NINETEEN

Feltham and I had been on our way to the site at Tinderbox in a government car a few days before. I'd asked him about his family. Discovered he kayaked each Sunday with a group of men who were mostly doctors. And then we'd got on to the Launceston dam and that was it. We'd left the government offices, been picked up by the chauffeur and driven down here to the bridge, and he hadn't paused or asked me a single question.

Mick Feltham had a Gene Hackman face, smooth, doughy. He favoured check-patterned ties. He looked reasonable, affable, but he was becoming neither since the Chinese labour had been approved.

I'd wondered how Feltham's wife put up with him. What did they talk about at dinner? Did he really know her? Had he taken an interest in her lately? What did people really do with their lives? As a single woman, it had grown harder to understand the idea of marriage. Why were men the way they were? How had we let them get so self-centred? I'd been married for twenty-five years and what did I have to show for it? Two beautiful kids. I was grateful for them. They were worth every hard day. I'd given it everything I had, but I was still a bit confused. How had it felt so unequal—support for Ben's career and his needs versus the irritation he extended towards mine?

I'd decided while I was doing my PhD that academics were pretty dysfunctional people. My ideas on that hadn't changed, only consolidated over the years. Most of them have never worked a day in the real world. I'd watched the way they behaved, saw the back-stabbing, cliques and paranoia Ben got caught up in. It was as if they were still in high school. Ben's favourite hate over time: gender politics. He'd watched a lot of women rise on the academic ladder while his own career stalled, and he was bitter.

'You women rule the world now, don't you?' he said. 'You're out there outdoing us. But it's not merit. You do know that, don't you? You've rigged the field. And look at you. Flying off here and there, trying to settle us all down. You've emasculated us.'

After we separated, a friend of ours came over with lemon meringue pie and a bottle of Grey Goose. He was a colleague of Ben's but he had also become a friend of mine. He'd had a bad break-up himself a few years before. He told me two things that afternoon that helped at the time. He said, 'Astrid, what I know about relationships is that people stay in them far too long.' Later he said, 'The thing about Ben is if it's not shining on him, he makes it rain on everyone else.'

∽

Mick Feltham was still talking. 'The project was completed two weeks ahead of schedule, under budget, and is a scheme everyone on the team got immense professional satisfaction from.'

177

'Great,' I said, although he would have kept talking without my input, I was sure.

'My grandchildren are going to drive past that dam and tell their children that I built it.'

'On time and under budget,' I murmured.

'Your brother is going to get his ribbon-cutting on March the fourth. He has my word,' Feltham continued.

'So your concerns have been allayed?' I asked.

'Supply chain issues have been resolved,' he said. 'And we have all the men we need now. No reason to doubt that we can deliver.'

I knew Mick Feltham had been offered a huge bonus for meeting the bridge deadline by JC, following that meeting with Aid-n-Abet. There were also penalties for any day it went over. I wondered if Dan Macmillan had been offered an incentive too; Dan's firm was subcontracted to Feltham's. Somehow I doubted it. That would have been smart, on Feltham's part, even fair. But still, I doubted it. I could see he thought Dan was a young buck, even if Dan wasn't young. He was forty-three. I could see Dan rankled Feltham somehow. But Feltham needed him. Maybe Dan's business partner—what was his name again? Talbot, Jimmy Talbot. Maybe Jimmy Talbot had been a more amenable type. But without Jimmy, it was Dan who knew the project inside out. Would have made no sense to bring in another firm at that stage.

'And safety issues?' I'd asked.

'That's Macmillan's problem,' Feltham replied. 'He knows what's at stake. This is a project of international significance.'

I thought about Dan and how what mattered to him was not losing a man. He and Feltham were going to come unstuck somewhere over the next few months.

∽

I'd wondered if Ben's new partner would finally get the man I'd always imagined he could be. I hoped she did. I hoped she didn't get the other man, the one who could take all the light out of a room. I hoped her kids didn't get him either. He was so good at hiding it. And then, when we least expected it, he'd be there. That other Ben. The Ben that rained on everyone. The Ben that could be savage. I hadn't realised, until it was over, that I'd been like a windvane, swinging towards the breeze, trying to sense the incoming storm. I wasn't quick enough. I was rarely quick enough. It could go from calm to chaos in moments, without warning. And then I'd be in peacemaking mode for days. Maybe that's why I chose him. Building a version of my mother and father so it felt like home. Honing my skills at conflict resolution in the bedroom, kitchen and lounge room.

Last year I stood in the window of Dubai's newest and tallest tower and it was then that I really understood what a tiny speck of sand I am. Over my lifetime I'll take some photos, drink some wine, eat food of various types. Eventually, I'll leave an apartment of clothes, furniture and books that will mostly end up in a charity store, and I'll be out of here. Solistalgia? Melancholia? No, just reality.

Suddenly, I knew where this conversation with Mick Feltham was going. Why hadn't I realised it before?

'So, Mick,' I said, 'given the contribution you've made to this state, and this project, if the premier wanted to honour you . . . if he wanted to do that . . .'

He wriggled a bit in his seat. 'You know, there's not a single statue of an engineer here in Tasmania,' he said. 'Politicians. Antarctic explorers. Sporting legends. Soldiers. Farmers. Even a female convict, I believe. But the people who built Tasmania? The engineers? Not a one.'

'So the Tinderbox headland or North Bruny, which location are you imagining?' I asked, as we topped the rise and the car began the descent to the security gates at Tinderbox. I was the premier's sister. He wasn't telling me any of this for nothing.

'Well, I think this side,' he said. 'As the road meets the bridge. A testament to all engineers, you understand. If the premier thinks that's fitting.'

'But a statue of you, yes?'

'I think people will know I earned it,' he said. He settled back into the seat and stretched out his legs. When we stopped to show our IDs, the wind whipped in the open window and blew his tie about.

I had dearly wanted to tell Dan about this conversation, but I didn't. I'm a mistress of discretion. Secrets go in deep with me. And they stay there a long time.

CHAPTER TWENTY

The first fatality on the bridge was on a Tuesday. I heard about it at 4.22 am.

'There's a car on its way to you. A Chinese worker's been lost.' Frank Pringle's voice on the phone. 'Don't know any details.'

I jumped out of bed, shed my pyjamas, grabbed a bra and knickers, track pants and a hoodie. I splashed my face with water, quickly cleaned my teeth, pulled on socks and runners. Four minutes after the call, I dashed upstairs. The lights were on in the lounge room and I could see JC in pyjamas and dressing-gown talking on the phone. I knocked on the glass. He came over and opened the balcony door, waving me in.

'I understand,' he said. 'Yep. Talk later.' Then he ended the call.

'What happened?' I asked.

'I don't know. That was Frank. The foreman is still out searching.'

'A worker disappeared?'

'No, Ace! He fell. These people aren't asylum risks. They've all been vetted for that. Apparently he was eighty feet up. I want you down there to make sure it doesn't get out.'

'Doesn't get out?' I repeated blankly.

'Closed loop, Ace. No-one else is to know.'

'Did he fall in the water?'

'From eighty feet, Ace. No chance of survival, that's what I'm told.'

I thought how what mattered to Dan was not losing a man. I thought about Jimmy Talbot and the suicide. He would make this personal.

JC said, 'We have to hush it up.'

'It'll be on the police radios, JC,' I said. 'And the media will be down there faster than the police launch, you know that.'

'No police. Bad publicity so early in the works. The Chinese are right. We don't let it out.'

'You're taking orders from *them*? JC, this isn't the People's Republic. We can't control what gets out.'

'Yes, we can, Ace. Their workers are not going to be a problem. They won't talk. Macmillan—you're going to have to manage him. How well do you two get along?'

'JC, every one of those workers has a phone. Someone will leak. We're talking about a man's life. This is never going to work.'

'Yeah, it is, Ace. It's already had the lid put on it.'

'You're really telling me the police haven't been called?'

'Fuck, Ace, I know. I haven't been here before. But it has to be this way. I've got . . .'

I heard the buzzer go for the gate. I went and pressed it to let the government car up.

'JC, you have to get police crawling over the place. If it gets out that someone tried to cover this up, that *you* tried to cover this up, you're sunk.'

'I can't go against their wishes, Ace. The Chinese are our partner in this.'

'You can't go against *their* wishes?' Things were getting a little heated now.

'Ace, it's a project of national significance. There are different rules . . . I can't . . .'

'What the fuck are you talking about? The Chinese have to understand that in *this* country, people like transparency. Don't we? *Don't we?* Or has that gone with the bridge? Make the call, JC—or I will.'

'Ace, right now, you don't get to call the shots. And you don't get to go against me. It's one worker. One accident. This gets out, it jeopardises the whole thing. Shut it down, Ace. Those are my instructions directly to you. Shut it down.'

'You're not thinking, JC. How will you explain it when some kid with the family dog comes across the body washed up on the shore?'

'I'm told there're sharks. Nobody washes up.'

I shook my head.

'You're here to do one job, Ace,' he said. 'Put out fires. Get down to the site and ensure the fire is out or it's going burn this bridge down. And if the bridge goes . . .'

If the bridge goes, you go, I thought. But I didn't say it. I walked out of the room and out to the waiting car. So the government was taking instructions from Beijing. Who hadn't seen that coming.

৯

At the site, there were men in fluoro high on the bridge looking like Christmas decorations. Vertical cables were being tensioned with the help of cranes. It was as if nothing had happened here at all.

Frank arrived and came to stand beside me.

'Morning,' he said.

'This is wrong, Frank,' I said. 'This is not a thing you hush up. What happens if someone does find the body? A Chinese body in a fluoro vest?'

'We'll cross that bridge when we come to it.'

'Nothing about this is funny, Frank.'

He had the decency to look embarrassed.

'Who knows it's happened?' I asked.

'You, the premier. Macmillan. The Chinese obviously. They won't talk. They'll bus the workers back at the end of the shift and there'll be a lockdown at their camp. No calls. No internet for a week. Let anyone thinking of breaking ranks cool off. Some re-education. But I'm assured every one of them is party faithful. They understand what's at stake.'

Nature was putting on a breathtaking sunrise. For a moment I felt like I was in a Kurosawa movie. All sweeping vistas and human tragedy. I scanned the water and saw the Zodiac coming into the beach.

'I'll go talk to him,' I said.

Frank nodded.

Dan jumped out and pulled the boat up on the sand.

'Hey,' I said.

'Hey,' he said. He did not meet my gaze.

'I hear there was an incident.'

'Of course you did,' he said.

'And knowing is a problem,' I said.

Dan stared at me. 'Yeah, seems so. Seems that some lives are worth more than others. I wonder where that puts us all, in the long run?'

'You want to tell me what happened?' I asked.

'You want to know? Or you want to hear it so that, when I'm finished, you can thank me, then tell me I need to take a good, long vacation until this thing is done?'

I sat down on a rock. I left a flatter, easier rock to my left. It was first light and there were still long shadows on the beach.

'Please, Dan,' I said, 'I want to know because I want to know. Tell me what happened.'

Dan did not take the flatter, easier rock beside me. He stayed standing. 'It's fucking nuts. I mean, these guys do not do occupational health and safety. I've been hounding them every night. I've got this interpreter, yeah, who's with me through the shift, never leaves my side, but you would swear no-one understands me anyway.'

'They don't wear their harnesses?'

'Not if they can get away with it. They'll unlock them if they think they can do the job easier or faster without it.'

'And then one of them falls.'

'I heard him. I heard him scream as he fell. Then nothing. I yell to one of the team leaders to sound the alarm. It's protocol, right, but suddenly the interpreter's in front of me. "Yes, Mr Macmillan. We will sound the alarm." I'm focused on getting to the bloke before he drowns, if he's even still alive. I mean, if you hit the water from that height . . . But if he's dead, then his family—they'll want a body. I tell the interpreter to call the police. He's running beside me. "Yes, yes, Mr Macmillan, we will take care of everything." He gets out his phone and says to me, "Mine is nearly out of charge. Can I use yours?" And I hand it to him. I should have known then. I'm getting the Zodiac into the water. I see him making a call. I say, "How long? Tell them we have a man in the water." He says, "Yes, yes, everything is under control, Mr Macmillan." Then I'm out there, searching. It's dark. There's a big current. But there're no police. Twenty minutes, thirty minutes. They should have been here. But no-one comes to help. I see that the workers are going on as if nothing's happened. They're all just carrying on. Then I see that the security guards are still back up at the gate. That's when I realise something's not right because they don't know. They'd have been running about like headless chooks. So I come back to shore. There are three Chinese standing on the beach. And this woman, one of the interpreters, says to me, "We appreciate all you have done, Mr Macmillan, but we understand that the chance of survival is extremely unlikely. Less than five per cent." "Where're the police?" I ask. Then she says, "Mr MacMillan, we do not want any problems here in Tasmania. We do not want any problems for the government. We do not want any problems for you. We are not involving the police. Do we understand one another? I have the premier on the phone," she says. She hands me a phone and the premier, your brother, says, "Hello, Dan. Thank you for doing all you can. This is a very delicate situation. We will handle it diplomatically. But now, what's happened there this morning, it requires your absolute discretion. I know you signed the Official Secrets

Act many years ago, when you were in the army. I need you to do your duty again. Do I have your commitment?"'

Dan sighed and rubbed his face. He looked haggard.

'I'm a soldier,' he said. 'You know that. Once a soldier, always a soldier. I didn't think that was true until now. But I could feel myself pulling back my shoulders and standing to attention. I handed the phone back to her. The woman says to me, "There is no missing worker, Mr Macmillan. Everything is as it should be." Someone else gives me my phone. I mean, I couldn't believe it. I got back in the boat. I've been driving around out there ever since. It's all I knew to do. God knows what security are making of it. Me fanging around out there.'

'There are sharks, yeah?' I said.

'The fall would have knocked him out. Let's hope he didn't feel anything. Might have drowned, of course.'

'Oh, God,' I said. 'I'm so sorry.'

'You're very big on manners, aren't you,' Dan said. 'Thank you, please, sorry. I don't like whatever it is you're doing here. I don't like whatever it is your brother and his government are doing here. This is fucked. A bloke is dead. Less than five per cent! If we'd had the police launch out, if we'd done a search, we might have found him. But his life wasn't worth shit, was it? Because of a bridge. A bridge at the end of the world. He came all this way to fix a mess so your brother can get re-elected. You do know that, don't you? The whole thing's so . . .'

'Dan,' I said.

'You feeling good about yourself right now?' he asked. 'Playing politics with people's lives?'

'I tried,' I said.

'Tried what?'

'I wanted the police called,' I said. 'When I heard in Hobart. I wanted the police called.'

I was saying too much. But nothing about this was normal.

'I'm sorry,' I said again. 'It's crazy. I didn't sign up for this either . . .'

I looked at the sun cresting the horizon. The sky was amber and mauve, the sea was luminous. A sea eagle was circling above us. It was a beautiful, terrible morning.

'A couple of months ago, I had to leave the body of a young American soldier behind in northern Iraq. He'd been burned to death. I couldn't get him home to his family. I had to choose between the living and the dead. I dream sometimes that I'm laying his body on the steps of a church in Damascus. It's a very old church. I don't even know if he was Catholic.'

He sat down then, on the rock beside me. We sat there and watched the eagle sweep away across the channel to Bruny, heading south down the coastline. He's going to quit, I thought. He's going to get up right now and walk away. And he'd be right to do that. Maybe I'm going to quit too. Maybe none of this is worth the toll. What was I doing here? Everywhere I went, it was chaos. I was so sick of it.

'I've got to get back up there,' he said, standing up. 'It'll be handover soon. Business as usual, eh?'

'Can you do that?' I asked.

'Can you?' he asked.

'I'm not sure,' I said. I felt sick. Sick and numb.

'Me either,' he said. 'You and your family. You sure you want to belong to them?'

CHAPTER TWENTY-ONE

I figure God has had plenty of opportunities to show his love. Take William Tyndale, who transcribed the Bible into English so that people everywhere could understand it. Surely that deserved a little act of love before they strangled him to death then burned him at the stake in 1536 for heresy.

And what about that little girl Max told me about? Twelve years old, and pimped by her mother and stepfather. Why is it always the stepfathers? Where were the Brothers Grimm on warning us about stepfathers? That was something every woman really needed to fear. Bringing a new man into a woman's life was just about the most dangerous thing she could do for herself or her children. Especially for that twelve-year-old. More than one hundred men of Hobart had used her as a prostitute. At least one politician. There was a notebook, apparently, with phone numbers and names and amounts paid, kept by the girl's mother for accounting purposes. Only the politician was exposed. He blamed his Parkinson's drugs. No-one was ever brought to court or prosecuted. God did not intervene.

Or that little boy who had washed up on the shore in Turkey a few years back. Just three years old and, when the boat from Syria sprang a leak, all the passengers found themselves in the Mediterranean, despite the money paid for safe passage. Only the boy's father survived. Where had God been that night?

I was in a deckchair on my balcony at the end of this long day. I'd texted JC this morning, after I'd seen the Chinese workers get back on their buses at the end of the shift and Dan Macmillan get in the Zodiac and go back across the channel to Bruny. My message to JC was: *Nothing you did this morning was right. Nothing. Going to Bruny. Turning off my phone.*

I went into Hobart and bought a wetsuit. Then I hired a car and I took the ferry and drove all the way down to Cloudy Bay at the far end of Bruny. I was the only person there. I walked a long way along the beach, then I stripped off, put the wetsuit on, and threw myself in the surf. This was my medicine. I bodysurfed wave after wave, and if I sat on the beach afterwards, entirely spent, and let the tears come, then nobody saw. Maybe a seagull, that's all.

Then I came home to the house at Dennes Point and took a nap. I woke up feeling shattered. Now I was a bottle of red wine and a joint down. Somewhere in the channel, the remains of a worker was being nibbled into oblivion by small or large creatures. I wanted an argument with God.

The China I knew had enormous cities with air so polluted people wore oxygen masks with supply tanks just to get through the day. There were cities so polluted, no child born in the last twenty-five years had ever seen a star.

The North Koreans were underfed and traumatised, the Taiwanese were always under threat, as were the South Koreans, but the Chinese were plain overcrowded. There was no personal space other than their one tiny room, their one tiny apartment.

A Bruny resident had told me that she'd stopped her car because some Chinese tourists on the side of the road looked like they were in trouble. She said they were almost catatonic. When she roused them, they kept saying, 'So empty. So empty.' Which she took for an existential crisis, not just the view as they looked at the ocean beach with not a single footprint in the sand.

There were more tourists arriving every minute, getting off planes and descending from cruise ships. Is this how the Aborigines had felt? I wondered. All these foreigners arriving. Arriving and not leaving again. Taking up residence. Making homes in all the best places. Establishing their own rules. Making you beholden to them. Until you were worth nothing. Just domestic labour or hired help at best. What was the tipping point before Tasmanians said, 'Enough. We're slowing this thing down. We're upping the prices. We're limiting numbers. We're protecting our special places. Book in next year, or the year after.' JC would never do that. It was all short-term thinking for short-term gain.

Dan Macmillan's words came racing back from this morning. 'You and your family. You sure you want to belong to them?'

I loved my family.

But you live in New York, that other voice inside my head said. Can't love them that much. Let's face it, your mother kind of screwed you up.

I'm not blaming her. I just can't do proximity, I replied to the voice. Look what happens. I'm back to smoking dope and drinking too much.

You do that in New York too.

But for different reasons, I argued.

You sure about that? the voice asked.

Max had laughed when I'd asked if she could score for me. 'I know a supplier,' she'd said. 'Provides medical cannabis for people with epilepsy, chronic pain. She's a saint. Never charges anything. I'd like to give some to Mother for her nausea, but I don't dare to raise it. I can just see her telling her friends, "Maxine gave me marijuana!" And it'd be on the front page of the paper. So past time it was legalised.'

I want to love my family. I do love my family. And, yes, I belong to them. If I didn't love them, what sort of person would I be?

The voice said nothing.

This is why I left Tasmania, I thought. Because you get really small out here on the perimeter of life, and life gets way too big-picture.

The voice laughed. The sky was a zillion fairy lights. A rim of green light was rising up behind me as an aurora began to dance in the sky.

In my next life, I'm going to be a note of music or a sparrow or a strange blue jellyfish. I'm tired of worrying about people. Who really cares if we have world peace? And even if we got it, how long would it last? A day, a week? Humans are disaster-making machines. We love drama. We're wired that way. Radical Muslims are way more worrying than the Chinese.

I've seen what Daesh do. I've been to Mosul. You can't grow a hand back once it's been lopped off. Mind you, those stories of organ harvesting in Chinese prisons . . . hard to find another kidney.

The radical Muslims are out-of-control men armed to the teeth. The far-right Christians are out-of-control men armed to the teeth. How can Christians be pro-life, pro-guns, but anti-refugees? How did that work? Most people were anti-refugees, it seemed. Yet in a single moment of disaster, it could be any of us with no home and nowhere to go.

I poured another wine.

At least the Chinese are consistent. No human rights, no refugees, yes to abortions and no to guns. Yes to world domination. Why did it have to be about that? The world was just a giant James Bond movie. There was always a bad guy trying to take over.

I looked up into the lurid green and purple sky waving its fronds of light as if someone was hailing me from another galaxy. Definitely a movie. But if so, where was the dashing hero? Maybe I was the dashing hero come to save Tasmania from something. Or someone. My brother, perhaps.

Something was happening here with this bridge and I couldn't get my head around it. There was no fair go in Australia anymore. It was everybody for themselves. But here in Tasmania people were hanging on. For a moment longer, people were still saying hello to one another while walking the beach, trading a glut of their zucchinis for their neighbour's tomatoes, being kind to people in the traffic, and taking out the bin of the lady down the road who taught you in grade two.

I'll never get a straight answer from JC, I thought. He's about as useful as eyebrows on a dolphin in this situation. He doesn't seem to grasp that he's a pawn. But if JC is a pawn, who's the queen on this chessboard? It sure isn't America. Make America great again! And the US had fizzled into factions. After two hundred and fifty years, the government had finally let the Constitution undo them. Why hadn't Lincoln risen from the dead? His GOP had gone MIA when the country needed it most.

Was it China then? One in every five people in the world was Chinese. That was a lot of breakfast, lunch and dinner to provide. And if they did one thing very well, the Chinese provided. In a hundred years, one in three people might be Chinese. It was the economics of exponential growth. Which brought me back to the bridge. Why were the Chinese involved in building a bridge to drive people to Bruny? There was too much money involved. Something was wrong.

I thought about all those Chinese workers down there on the bridge right now, and who might fall tonight. How many before it became a thing that couldn't be covered up? Three? Five? Twenty?

'It's the yellow peril,' I could hear my mother saying. She said it a lot when we were kids. This idea that the Chinese were going to invade at any moment. They were invading Vietnam at the time. But it wasn't so much a fear of invasion here. More a sense that Tasmania—maybe even Australia—was being outwitted on the world stage. I had a bad feeling that, in five years' time, people would be saying, 'Why the hell didn't we see that coming?'

The vast bucolic wonder of Tasmania, with only half a million people and enough rich arable soil to support millions more than that, with an abundance of water and a perimeter of ocean with several deep-water ports, had to be a sitting duck. Unless you had a powerful ally. Maybe JC was right to cosy up with the Chinese.

You really want to belong to your family? I heard Dan Macmillan say again.

Do I care? I wondered. I could just say, 'To hell with your bridge, I'm going back to New York.' I'd be sent to another hell-hole because that's my work. Did I care that, on election eve, JC would stand on the bridge and look like a hero? What happened when the next worker died? When all is said and done, and I'm dust on the breeze, I wanted to leave something good behind. You see, I'm a hypocrite. I like altruism in me but not in anybody else.

Altruism is like vitamin C, that other voice in my head said. It staves off the scurvy but it won't stop the ship from sinking.

I'm like a vegetarian who still eats red meat, I thought. I pretend I'm committed, but I don't want to give up my bolognaise.

I had to get some human company, I decided. And because I was buzzed and a little drunk, I had lost my inhibitions. I didn't want to consider the ramifications of my next move. I got up off my balcony and wandered across the paddock, past the wallabies who hopped away, and went down the hill.

CHAPTER TWENTY-TWO

I pushed open his gate and saw the light was on in his house. Out on the deck, I found Dan Macmillan quietly rolling a joint.

He didn't seem surprised as I came up the stairs. I took the freshly rolled joint from behind my ear and put it down on the table next to his.

'You want to share?' I asked.

'Sure,' he said.

I put a new bottle of red wine on the table too.

'You come bearing gifts,' he said.

'You're not down there tonight,' I said.

'I was told to take a night off. I was offered longer, but I said a night would do.'

He indicated the other deckchair. 'Have a seat.'

I sat and gazed away from the bridge and down the channel at the water and the hills and the stars, the moon hurrying away from cavernous clouds.

Dan went into the house and came back with two glasses.

'It's good here,' I said. He offered me the joint but I told him to go ahead.

He lit up and took a long drag. 'Paradise,' he said.

'Why are we letting paradise get invaded?' I asked.

There was a long silence.

'Because we're little people,' he said slowly. 'And we can't stop it.'

'Are you sure we're little people?' I asked.

'Absolutely,' he said. 'Even if some of us do have connections.'

I thought about that for a while.

'I don't want to be little,' I said.

'I never thought I'd be anything else,' he said.

'That can't be true. You were a paratrooper.'

'Littlest people of all, in a way. They train us to be legends, but at the end of the day, we're fodder,' he said.

'What did you want when you were a kid, Dan?'

'I wanted a motorbike,' he said. 'I wanted a horse, actually. Watched a fair few cowboy and injun movies as a kid. And later I wanted a motorbike and leathers and a long road ahead. Had a bike for a while. Sold it eventually. Didn't come home enough to ride it. What did you want to be?'

'I was going to be an actress. But then there was this girl, Melissa, who was so good in year twelve that I realised I would never have what it took. I wasn't wild enough somehow. Couldn't let go the way she did.'

'So you decided to save the world instead.'

'And now I'm breaking the law.'

'You and me both. Bonnie and Clyde up on our hill while some poor bastard is down there feeding the crabs. I wonder what the penalty is? Not reporting a death . . . to say nothing of covering up a workplace accident. They'd throw the book at me.'

We were both silent.

'What if it leaks?' he said. 'If the media get hold of it? Am I the fall guy? I guess I'm the fall guy. I was right there. That's my crew. But what proof will they have? I'm sure they'll find another somebody to be worker number one hundred and seventy-seven if need be.'

'I'm so sorry, Dan, and I know saying sorry doesn't do anything. I'm numb about this. I'm still in shock, I think.'

'Rock and a hard place, you and me both,' he said. 'I feel like I should be raging.'

'Me too,' I said. 'I feel like I should have raged this morning.'

'Just our word against—what? The Communist Party of China? Can't see that going well.'

We were both silent again. There were crickets somewhere close by making cricket love with their wings.

'I didn't mean to take it out on you this morning,' he said. 'Well, I did, but you're not the right target.'

'I deserved it. I didn't come here to do this. I'm not an apologist.'

'Surely you must have known it was going to go this way. How did he do it, your brother? Appeal to your sense of family?'

I took a deep breath. 'Duty,' I said.

'Ah, that's the one. Duty and family. Bolted on, those two.'

'Goes in deep, this place,' I said.

'That it does.'

'I like to forget, when I'm away, but it's always a magnet. Luckily my family is the repellent, otherwise I might never leave again.'

I passed the joint back to him. He took it from me carefully.

Alarm! Alarm! my body was saying. *You're attracted to him.*

Who cares? my brain responded. *He doesn't need to know. He'll never know. Except you walked over. Clearly not a work thing. A social thing.*

'I didn't mean to interrupt your evening,' I said. 'Well, I did. But I was going a bit stir crazy up there.'

'Really,' he said. 'What does stir crazy look like to Astrid Coleman?'

'I was talking to myself. Got to thinking about beef, weirdly.'

'Beef?'

'Yeah, I'd tangled up world peace with giving up meat . . .'

'No bolognaise,' said Dan.

'That was exactly where I got to.' I laughed. 'You understand my misery.'

'I don't do misery anymore.'

'How do you avoid it?'

'I avoid miserable people,' he said.

'You can do that?'

'Unless they walk onto my deck.'

'I will hold back all misery until I return home.'

'Control at last.'

I smiled. And he smiled.

'Really, I've interrupted you,' I said.

'Yep, so you better stay and make it worthwhile,' he said. 'Seriously. I didn't think I could just walk over, so it's good you did.'

'Why not?' I asked.

'Because you're kind of the boss. And you're intimidating. Charming but intimidating.'

'Can I not be? Here? On my deck or yours, can we forget that? Can we just be . . . two people?'

We'd lived through something, Dan and I. There was a man's body in the D'Entrecasteaux Channel and we had no idea who had loved him, who would miss him, but there would be people. And we were complicit.

'What do people call you?' he asked. 'Do you have a nickname?'

'Ace,' I said.

'Ace,' he repeated.

'What do they call you?'

'Mac. Nothing very original.'

He went in and brought me out a blanket. I took it and spread it over my legs. I hadn't realised I was getting cold. I breathed in, and then I let a long breath out. I felt like I hadn't breathed out that deeply in weeks. Maybe not since I'd arrived.

'I've been going to see my dad late at night,' I said. 'He's in care and the staff have got used to my visits. No-one in my family knows I go. It's this private thing just for me and him. It's me making up for years I can't make up for. He's rarely asleep and, if he is, I sit with him and watch him breathe. If he's awake, I read to him. Shakespeare or John Donne. Some nights I lie down next to him and share my earbuds and we listen to Tchaikovsky or Chopin or Rachmaninoff—his favourites. There's something so surreal about it. The nursing home with its long hallways and dried flower arrangements. Dad and I sharing monologues and sonnets from four hundred years ago. He had a stroke, you see. He can't really talk any more. It's all Shakespeare, but it makes sense. Eventually I get sleepy. Sometimes he nods off. Sometimes we doze off together. Sometimes when I wake I have no idea how old I am. Time seems to go backwards and forwards.'

I stopped. I had no idea what had made me say all that, but it was done now.

'It's going to be okay,' Dan said, his voice easy in the quiet that had fallen between us.

'I'm not so sure about that.'

'Me either, but when we're on this deck, it's going to be okay.'

'Okay,' I said.

And the aurora went on like a green disco behind us.

CHAPTER TWENTY-THREE

Sunday lunch came around again. It was coming around way too often. But I went, the dutiful daughter. I had thought that coming home, the work would be the thing. But of course it wasn't. Family was the real thing. Sometimes I am more stupid than anyone I know.

We propped Mother up on the couch and plied her with champagne, which wasn't recommended, but she assured us it helped with the nausea.

'I'd rather be pickled with this than whatever they give me at the hospital,' she said. 'And those wafers that are meant to stop me vomiting, they make me feel like a horse has kicked me.'

'Would you like me to come with you this week?' I asked.

'I can't imagine you'll find time,' she said.

'Yes,' I said, 'I will. What day?' I looked to Phillip.

'Wednesday,' he said. 'Nine am.'

'I'll pick her up.'

'Oh, dear,' Mother announced to everyone. 'I must be dying. Astrid is actually making time to take me to the hospital.'

Stephanie said, 'Oh, don't be like that, Mum. You know we all love you. Astrid's working very hard. Now, for those of us who would like to sit at the table, lunch is ready.'

We all sat up, even Mother. As we settled in to roast chicken and gravy, roast vegetables, cauliflower cheese and peas, our father declared, '*Love sought is good, but given unsought better.*'

'I know that one,' I said to Ella, who was sitting beside me. 'It's from *Twelfth Night*. Olivia and Sebastian are twins. They get separated in a storm and each of them thinks the other is dead. Dad used to read it to your dad and me. It's the play that has the quote: *If music be the food of love, play on.*'

'Ah,' said Ella, quickly writing all this in her phone notes. 'You don't look alike, you and Dad.'

'That's because we're not identical twins,' I said. 'And because he got so fat,' I added quietly.

Ella giggled and then looked slightly mortified that she had laughed at her father. 'Can we play tennis this afternoon, Aunty Ace?'

'*If music be the food of love, play on!*' Ella said theatrically, and raised her glass to the table.

'Don't you start,' said Mother.

And everyone laughed.

∾

JC strolled out onto the deck after lunch. He was carrying two glasses of whisky. He handed one to me. The dead worker from last week was a silence between us. It had to remain a silence between us.

'I have to play tennis with Ella,' I said.

'I'm Ella's secret weapon,' he said. 'A nip or two for Aunty Ace and she's gonna beat you.'

'Very likely,' I said.

'How are you doing, Ace?'

'You know this will ruin it,' I said to JC. 'Bruny might be the one last place in the world where almost nothing happens. Pretty quiet by day, dead quiet at night. People down there, and up here, they're sad about the bridge. Not everyone, but a lot of people. They feel . . . bulldozed.'

'Paradise lost,' he said. His gaze was curiously tender as he looked across the Derwent River.

'Why did it have to happen, JC?'

'Because this place needs progress, Ace. And that bridge is part of a brighter future.'

'Why would a bridge to nowhere make a brighter future?'

'Ah, Ace, you know I'd never build a bridge to nowhere.'

'So what are you doing?'

'The thing everyone is missing is Antarctica. The Chinese have already expressed interest at the highest levels at exploiting whatever is under the ice there. I know it's not allowed. But when the treaty is up in 2040, they are going to need a serious base. That could be Argentina or Chile. But we're the closest. There's enormous money involved. After 2040, it may become another place to mine. There will be harbour fees for their Antarctic vessels and runway fees. The Chinese in Antarctica are going to need food, machinery, fuel. I'm thinking long term. Something politicians are not meant to do, Ace. We've got to make these alliances good and strong, and a long way out. It's a win-win.'

'And it's not Antarctica, is it, JC?'

He chuckled. 'Tasmanians like to imagine that it will stay this way. And it would be nice if it did. But let's face it, Ace, Tasmania is, at most, two generations away from high-rises on all the best beaches. Mining in the middle. Fish farms in every estuary and around the coastline. There'll be a few wilderness theme parks for the greenies. The rest of it is going to be supporting three times our current population, if not ten. Climate change will do that. All sorts of people are looking for what's here, and they'll come. They're already coming. That's the way it is, whether you and I like it or not. So, while I can, I'm going to take care of Tasmanians. And that's why I have you, sister, to ensure we deliver as smoothly and quietly as possible.'

That's why I hate Liberals. It's all money and power. I hate Labor as well, because they'll sell out on anything—workers, refugees, artists, freedoms—just to get power. Look at what Labor signed off on with the Liberals back in 2018 to bring in those counterespionage laws. Once the fine print emerged, Australians discovered that no-one was free to reveal government secrets either—even if they were whistleblowing. It was also a crime to assist foreign spies working in Australia. Which suddenly made any chance of working with the CIA or British intelligence, or any of our old allies, a crime that carried life imprisonment. That had made a lot of jobs a whole lot harder.

I don't want to hate my brother. I don't want to hate my sister. I love them. But the whole world is getting conservative and governments are getting more authoritarian. It isn't religion that's the opiate of the masses in the twenty-first century. It's fear. Fear is the new opioid. It makes us dull, paranoid, selfish and jittery, and we're fed it on the front of every newspaper, all day long on radio and TV and any online news. Whether you've got ten million dollars or ten cents, these days fear drives everything. It was grinding me down. A tiny handful of people are getting so rich. And they're squeezing the rest of us dry. I see it everywhere. Even in northern Europe, and they've been about the best at caring for people.

JC kept turning the whisky in his large hand. 'I just want to get the thing finished, Ace. And don't feel too sad for the locals. Property down there has trebled in value in the past four years. You, in particular, ought to appreciate that.'

'Not Maggie Lennox's retreat.'

'Maggie Lennox does very nicely out of this government. Did she tell you we put half a million into *Solitude*? We market it everywhere for her. Maggie Lennox understands development. She just didn't see this coming. And when she did, she couldn't stop it. That's what she's upset about.'

'And once the road is open, it won't be *Solitude* anymore.'

'Well, maybe she'll have to change the name. *Proximity*, or something like that.'

'And the boutique operators who'll be squeezed out by big hotels and big retailers?'

'The price of progress,' he said. 'Let them all compete.'

'Whatever it is you're doing, do the benefits outweigh the costs?' I asked. 'You just let a foreign government run rough-shod over our rules and regulations.'

'Ace, in the end it was my call. China doesn't intervené in the affairs of other nations. When Edward Snowdon got out of the US, he went to Hong Kong. China let him pass through to Russia. They didn't interfere. With a project this size, there were always going to be contingencies.'

'A life is not a contingency. And a way of life is not a contingency, either,' I said, finishing my whisky. 'You don't understand how mad the world has got out there, JC. We are a hair's breadth away from World War Three on any given day.'

'You're not going soft on me, are you, Ace? Look, there's a lunch tomorrow with a couple of investors. Come and meet a few people. You still with me?'

I sighed and nodded.

He walked back inside. 'I'll tell Ella to come whip your arse.'

'I'll go get changed,' I said.

As I ran downstairs to the apartment, I thought of what our dad used to say whenever me and JC began fighting. *'We came into the world like sister and brother, and now let's go hand in hand, not one before another.'* He adjusted it a little for the circumstances, seeing that we were sister and brother, not brother and brother. But still, it was a rule of sorts, long before Shakespeare was our father's only form of communication.

It was from *The Comedy of Errors*.

I was hand in hand with JC again. I wondered what Dad would make of us now.

❦

On the tennis court my niece was a good player in the making. She had a mean serve and an awesome backhand.

It took my height and strength to keep the score level. But she wanted victory more than me, and I wanted it for her. Still we slugged it out, 7/6, 6/7 . . .

It was a warm afternoon with a sea breeze coming in across the Derwent, twenty-six degrees and hardly a cloud in the sky. From up here, we looked down on a river arrayed with sailing craft of every size and variety, from dinghies to maxis. Some were racing, others were just pleasure craft. The harbour, the Derwent, the channel, it was all a sailing paradise.

'Might have to bring you over to New York and get you a coach there,' I said, as we finished up and I took a long slug from a water bottle.

'Thanks, Aunty Ace, but no thanks. I like it here.'

This made me think JC and Stephanie might already have suggested it to her.

'There are good places beyond Tasmania, Ella. And lots of opportunities if you're willing to take a few risks. You know, I left here for uni when I was eighteen on a scholarship.'

'My friends talk about where they're going to go when they leave here, but I don't want to go anywhere. Not for long, anyway.'

'What if you could be a really great player? If you went overseas to school?'

'That might be fun, but I'm just not sure it would make me happy.'

I looked at her and smiled. This was why I liked teenagers. They weren't yet full of everyone else's ideas.

'What do you think success looks like, Ella?' I asked as we wandered back through the rhododendrons to the house. It was always the great unasked question. If people got whatever they wanted, what would it look like? I used it often in my one-on-one sessions with clients and the answers always surprised them. It wasn't obvious, but when they unearthed it, it changed their ideas about life. So often it wasn't being in charge, having the best weapons or the greatest wealth. It was something simple. Holding a long-anticipated grandchild. Taking a trip. Dying without any regrets.

'Being with the people you love, I guess,' Ella said. 'And being here,' she added.

'What do you love about Tasmania?' I asked.

She shrugged. 'I don't know. It's just home.'

Then she said, 'What would success look like to you, Aunty Ace?'

I stopped. I pushed my racquet into the toe of my shoe and thought. 'You know, the first thing that comes to mind is sitting on my balcony at Bruny, watching the sunset over the channel.'

'When the bridge is finished, we can go from our place to your place in half an hour, Dad says.'

'I guess that's true,' I said.

'Aunty Ace, one of my friends says that the Chinese are going to take over Bruny Island. Is that true?' Ella asked.

'Not as far as I know. Does your friend's family have a shack there?'

'Her family lives there. She's a boarder. Her dad says there's all this land clearing going on out of sight.'

'Really?' I asked.

Ella nodded. 'Do you think my Dad is taking care of Tasmania?'

'That's a big question, Ella. Why do you ask?'

'People at school say things.'

'That can't be easy,' I said. 'What's the thing that most gets to you?'

'Calling me a princess. Saying the Colemans think they're the king and queen of Tasmania. Aunty Max and Dad.'

'What! Nothing about me?'

She smiled. 'My friend Millie says you're here to spy on us all.'

'How did she know?' I said, laughing.

'Sometimes I just don't understand, Aunty Ace,' she said.

'Me neither, sweetheart,' I said. 'None of us really do. You know what Grandad used to tell me and Aunty Max and your dad when we were small?'

'What?' she said.

I sat down with her at the table on the deck.

'If you can keep your head when all about you
Are losing theirs and blaming it on you,
If you can trust yourself when all men doubt you,
But make allowance for their doubting too;
If you can wait and not be tired by waiting,
Or being lied about, don't deal in lies,
Or being hated, don't give way to hating,
And yet don't look too good, nor talk too wise . . .'

And I remembered it all, right down to:

'If neither foes nor loving friends can hurt you,
If all men count with you, but none too much;
If you can fill the unforgiving minute
With sixty seconds' worth of distance run,
Yours is the Earth and everything that's in it,
And—which is more—

'But,' I said, 'I changed the last line for my kids. I like to say, *"And—which is more—you'll be content, my love."* My kids have always loved that poem.'

'Are they coming for Christmas this year?'

I shook my head. 'We decided it was going to be such a busy time with the bridge and all. But soon.'

'I want Tavvy to teach me how to bead my hair.'

'I can show you that,' I said.

'Really?'

'Really. Where do you think she learned in the first place?'

Ella giggled. 'People think I have the coolest cousins.'

'You do,' I said. 'And they do, too. They're both so busy with their work, and in America most people only get two weeks' holidays each year, so it's hard to come all this way.'

She nodded.

'I'll get a copy of *If* for your bedroom wall. That's how I learned it. We had it on the back of the toilet door when we were children.'

'Thanks, Aunty Ace. That'd be cool.'

'Beaded hair and Kipling. You'll be ready for anything,' I said.

Then we went inside.

CHAPTER TWENTY-FOUR

The lunch JC had invited me to was held in a private dining room at a winery out of town. The food was impeccable, the wine superb, and no-one mentioned dead bodies. But I was still on edge. Rattled deep inside by the sound of a man falling to his death before the sun came up.

The meal was a twelve-course degustation that began with a seared Wagyu beef carpaccio with pickled baby vegetables paired with a local pinot, then wild abalone with braised mushrooms and samphire served with a pinot gris. And so it went on. There were eight of us in a private room: two Chinese investors, Senator Barney Viper, Andrew Wong (head of the China–Australia Relations Institute), May Chen, JC, me, and a man called Edward Lowe—Dr Edward Lowe—a government business consultant to JC.

I suspected someone had been bumped when JC included me. Maybe Frank. Opposite me was one of the businessmen, Henry Liu, and to my left another businessman also called Henry—Henry Xiang. Henry Liu spoke excellent English with an international school accent. Henry Xiang spoke English less well.

I can get by in Spanish, French and Arabic. Even a little Italian if you mostly want to talk food. We'd never been offered Asian languages back when I was at school, and I hadn't worked in China or Japan or Korea, so I hadn't needed those languages, but I regretted that gap now.

Henry Xiang, I learned, had made investments in Tasmanian salmon farming, and he had also bought the state's biggest dairy farm. It was a heritage property, a flagship of Tasmanian agriculture for two hundred years. He intended to expand it. He flew fresh Tasmanian milk to China every day.

'It was Mr Xiang's planes that flew in the bridge workers,' said May Chen.

JC was on my right. He explained how Henry Xiang's farm had the state's biggest wind power plant—the one Amy O'Dwyer had been all worked up about. Built by the Tasmanian government with taxpayer money, and transferred into private ownership when the heritage property was sold to Xiang. Xiang's company's major stakeholder was none other than the Chinese government. When I'd pointed this out to JC on the way to lunch, he hadn't seemed at all concerned.

Through lobster risotto matched with a Tasmanian east coast chardonnay, Xiang talked of the roaring forties that whizzed about the planet, buffeting the west coast all year round. He also talked of the reliable rainfall in the north-west, and the fertile soil for the raising of cows, and the proximity to Asia for export. He lived in Hong Kong and he told me he had many investors. When I prodded him about the Chinese Communist

Party's stake in his company, he chuckled and said he didn't know I was also a journalist. And then he engaged in conversation in Mandarin with May Chen, well aware I could not understand. Henry Liu and I began a conversation.

Henry Liu told me he'd been born in Hong Kong but had attended international schools. His family was in finance and he'd invested in this winery we were dining in. He was also the owner of the one-hundred-year lease that encompassed the entire beach and undeveloped foreshore of Stanley, on the northern coast of Tasmania—which, he said, was surely one of the most beautiful places in the world.

'I didn't know that had been leased,' I said.

'Your brother is very generous with Tasmania,' he said.

I asked him what he intended to do with this parcel of land, and he said, 'Maybe nothing. Maybe I will just take care of it so it stays exactly as it is. I do not have to make all my investments profitable.'

Here Henry Xiang laughed at him, then turned back to his conversation with Miss Chen. Liu continued, dismissing this interjection. He said he felt extremely privileged to have discovered Tasmania and to feel so instantly at home here.

'So you are colleagues or rivals, you two?' I asked of him and Henry Xiang.

'We are speculators,' said Henry Liu. 'Perhaps I have a longer-term strategy . . . I am hoping to become an Australian citizen,' he added.

Xiang said something in Chinese to May Chen and she interpreted. 'Mr Xiang is telling Mr Liu that such a thing is not possible unless he marries an Australian woman, because it is not easy getting citizenship in Australia. He says maybe you can introduce Mr Liu to some suitable women.'

Xiang said something else, but May Chen did not interpret. So Xiang said, 'I hear you are single, Doctor Coleman', and guffawed.

Mr Liu smiled regretfully.

'And you would live here?' I asked, without missing a beat. 'In Tasmania?'

'I have built a home on my land at Cloudy Bay, on Bruny Island.'

At this Henry Xiang guffawed again. There was a quick exchange between the two men in Chinese. I looked puzzled but nobody translated.

'Why Bruny Island?' I asked Henry Liu.

'It is a little bit of heaven,' he said. 'It's good to acquire little bits of heaven.'

JC was exhibiting all the bonhomie of a man who had married off his daughters in spectacular matches. During a course of delicate dumplings, the director of the China–Australia Relations Institute, Andrew Wong, thanked me for all I had done to smooth the way for the workers. Senator Viper said, 'It's very good of you to come home, Astrid, and serve Tasmania in this way. We need our good people here at a time like this.' There was something about his delivery that came across as a vague threat.

'China wants to continue our long and very cordial relationship with Tasmania,' said Andrew Wong. 'We are very proud to be assisting Tasmania in this way, to realise this project of state and national significance with the help of people such as yourself, Astrid. To forward good relations between our countries. I feel there is much we all have to contribute in the coming years. I think everyone at this table agrees with that.'

JC raised his glass and everyone followed suit. The matched wines were beginning to have an effect on everyone. The waiters were discreet and very efficient.

'To you, Ace, for getting us this far without any more bombs!'

And everyone laughed and we toasted again. I caught the eye of the man beyond JC. Edward Lowe. JC's bulk almost entirely obscured him, but in that moment, as he smiled and raised his glass, he caught my eye and something passed between us.

JC suggested I swap places with him, so Edward and I could get acquainted.

'You two have things in common,' JC said. 'America, I think, for one.'

'Tell me something about you that would surprise me, Edward,' I said.

'I've been creating a model train park. A folly,' he said.

'As a tourist attraction?' I couldn't help smiling.

'Oh, no, it's a personal thing. It's in the . . . well, the back-yard—for want of a better term. I have forty acres.'

'Like a Hornby thing?'

'No, they're all ride-on miniatures.'

I looked at Edward Lowe. With his greying hair, dark eyes and rimless glasses, he reminded me of Colin Firth. I thought of ride-on model trains. I assessed his impeccably ironed shirt, the suit that was possibly Tom Ford. And a model train park. Eccentric. Good looking and eccentric. Probably gay. I like gay men. They make excellent friends, in my experience. As do gay women. They seem to know themselves.

In Tasmania, I had discovered, most everyone had a hobby. The protection of hooded plover nests on beaches; the training of racing pigeons; the knitting of convict bonnets; the quilting of Aboriginal stories; the use of feral cat pelts to line Antarctic vehicles. You name it, it went on in someone's backyard, sun room or garden shed, or on a plot of land they had in the bush.

Like me, Edward had grown up in Tasmania and then left. We talked about Harvard. He'd done a PhD there in economics. We talked about Manhattan, where he'd lived on the Upper West Side while he was working at Bain. His parents had both died a few years back, and his brother was suddenly in charge of packing up an enormous house in Hobart and dealing with the estate. Edward had come home to help and realised, once he'd returned to New York and found the plants dead on his balcony, that he really didn't want to leave Tasmania again, so he flew back.

'That was six years ago,' he said.

'Should I take that as a warning?' I asked.

I'd drunk a little too much. But at the same time, I wasn't sure I cared. I felt like I'd been in control a very long time. We all are, more or less. Some days it's hard to keep pretending that it matters.

'Tell me, Edward,' I said. 'What's the next big economic opportunity for Tasmania, then?'

'This may surprise you, but we need a football team,' he said. 'We need a Tasmanian team in the AFL.'

I laughed. The Australian Football League. He was right. That was not what I'd expected him to say. Australians are mad about football. More so even than Americans. It's the true religion. A funny-shaped ball, four goalposts and eighteen very big, very agile men a side. There was even a women's league, finally. But Tasmania was the only state without its own team in the national competition. Tasmanian players played for every other state, but they couldn't play for Tasmania.

'It stacks up,' Lowe continued. 'The economic case is very sound.' Within five minutes he had convinced me.

We had arrived at the first dessert—a vanilla bean panna cotta with a berry compote matched with an iced riesling.

'How is America doing, do you think?' he asked. 'You must get a unique perspective from the world stage.'

'Right now, America has an isolationist, neo-conservative president who doesn't believe in American strength being used to stabilise the world. Quite the opposite. He considers it the chief weapon to assert dominance. And he's in his second term. He's turned his back on America's allies because he doesn't believe in that framework. Now we're seeing the fallout of that approach and it's crippling international relations, the global economy, the American economy.'

'And Russia? China?' he added, quietly.

'Russia isn't a threat to anyone. It's a nation that's been in decline for many, many years. It's weighed down by sanctions. It depends heavily on oil. Its military power is not in the realm of the US or China. But it's a convenient and familiar enemy. And China?' I considered the company I was in and said, 'Maybe ASIO agents are feeding the left-wing press conspiracy theories . . . stirring up trouble with what they know . . .'

He gave me a very particular look, and the waiter came around and refreshed our glasses.

'You're not worried about the Russian intervention in elections?' he asked.

'At last count,' I said, 'I think the United States has interfered in forty-two elections, that we know about. Since the Second World War. Demonstrable, actual evidence. Allende in Chile. Iran. Guatemala. We've plotted assassinations and supported brutal governments—anti-communist, of course—in Latin America, Asia, Africa. Right now, we're seeing the decline of the empire and the rise of a multi-polar world. What people don't like is that the US is no longer the boss.'

'So you do think of yourself as an American,' he observed. 'You said "we".'

'If I could have a Tasmanian passport, I think I'd prefer that to anything,' I said. 'How do you think America is doing?'

'Like you, I don't think democracy, in general, is doing particularly well,' he said. 'Maybe better in some countries. Scandinavia always seems to do things better. The last Tasmanian election was an interesting test case,' he said. 'The next federal election will be telling.'

Despite Edward's discretion, Viper pricked up his ears at this. His pale face was a little sweaty and his eyes had grown small and glassy.

'The ABC made outrageous allegations about the last Tasmanian election. They're a leftist front paid for by this government. I doubt they'll survive past the next federal election. The Tasmanian people supported strong leadership in 2018. Your brother can't provide that unless he wins this next election too.'

'I couldn't agree more,' I said, smiling.

❧

As we were making our way out, Edward Lowe said, 'I look forward to the next conversation. We must have lunch.'

'That would be good,' I said. 'In the new year.'

He handed me a card. I could almost hear my mother saying, 'Such a handsome man.'

JC and I travelled back to Hobart together.

'So is Edward Lowe working for ASIO?' I asked him.

'What on earth makes you say that?'

'There's got to be one floating about you, you do know that, don't you?'

'Oh, yes, Ace, I forgot, every premier has a spy in their midst.'

'Well, you do have Frank.'

'You're funny when you've drunk too much. You don't think it's because he looks like George Clooney that you think he's a spy?'

'Not Clooney,' I said. 'I thought . . . oh, I can't remember now. Not Colin Farrell. Colin Firth! Is it very obvious I've drunk too much?'

'Only to me,' he said. 'I've put him on my team leading into the election. He's good on strategy. He's an old friend of Becky Walton.'

'Becky Walton! Now there's a name from the past.'

'Anyway,' said JC, 'Edward might be useful to you. Understands a lot about Tasmanians.'

'I got a bit carried away talking to him.'

'Give away any state secrets?'

'Nothing anyone will miss,' I said.

'I like having you on the team, Ace,' he said.

'Why?' I asked.

'Because I can trust you.'

I nearly said, 'What a shame I can't trust you.' Which surprised me, because until now that may not have been true. Sometimes I wonder what will happen if I ever get Alzheimer's. Will I begin confessing all the things I have learned over my lifetime? All the secrets I've kept? It's probably best that people like me take ourselves out, if dementia ever threatens. Save a lot of people a lot of trouble.

'JC, what will become of Tasmania if Tasmanians no longer own the parts of it they love?'

'What do you mean?'

'You sold a lease to the beach at Stanley. What were you thinking?'

'Jobs and growth, Ace. That's what keeps people happy. Jobs and growth. That's how elections are won.'

'And what's with closing the camping grounds at Freycinet? Is that true? Someone mentioned it yesterday.'

Freycinet is a peninsula of pink granite, white sand, tiny coves and she-oak forests, the playground of wealthier Tasmanians. It's also home to the world-famous tear drop of Wineglass Bay.

JC stretched out. 'Campers are low-value tourists, Ace, let's face it. Let them hire a cabin and at least contribute to the economy. The world's got more crowded. And tourism infrastructure costs money. Tasmanians have to accept that.'

'But if there weren't so many visitors, we wouldn't need more infrastructure.'

'So shall we tell people not to come, so a few locals can camp? It's not their God-given right,' JC said.

'It *is* their God-given right, those campers. You think Spring Beach is *your* God-given right,' I said. Spring Beach, where JC and Stephanie had built their very glamorous beach house.

'We pay rates, Ace. We're landowners.'

'These camping grounds are places families have been going for generations. Not everyone can afford a cabin, let alone a shack.'

'Shhh,' he said, taking my hand and waving his other at the rolling hills of grapevines through the tinted windows. 'This is what prosperity looks like, Ace. The place is pumping.'

'Am I here to create better relations between Tasmania and China?' I asked.

'Jesus, Ace. They're pouring a fortune into the place. Would it be so much to ask? Whatever you're doing, it's working, anyway. We haven't had a protester in *The Mercury* for weeks. Did you really get Farris and the salmon industry in the same room?'

'I did.'

'And why, exactly?'

'Well, the BFG are against more fish farms in the channel. So if I can get them to feel like they're getting somewhere on that, it distracts them—momentarily, perhaps—from the bridge.'

'Thanks, twin,' he said. 'It can't have been easy to drop your life and come home. Hey, do you want a little fun over summer? I'm sure we could set you up with someone. Stephanie will know who.'

'Need I remind you that I have a huge job to do for the premier, our mother is dying of cancer and our father is very fragile?'

'It's been three years, Ace. Got to get back on the horse one day.'

'I'm not so sure about that,' I said.

'Do you think she really is dying? She always seems like she's going to get away with it, somehow.'

'I'm taking her to chemo on Wednesday,' I said.

'You're a good person, Ace.'

'I may be, but I'm not a very good daughter.'

JC shrugged. 'I don't know,' he said. 'You came when we all needed you. You sure we can't interest you in staying? Couldn't you base yourself here? There'd be work, too . . . if you wanted it.'

'I'd die of claustrophobia. Everywhere I go, it takes people about one minute to work out who I am. It's all so close. I need my anonymity.'

He nodded. 'Is that why you're down at Bruny so much?'

I shrugged. 'Well, it is my job . . . but yes.'

'Thought you might have found a bloke down there . . .'

'Don't be ridiculous,' I said, and giggled.

CHAPTER TWENTY-FIVE

I picked Mother up at 9 am and took her to 8A at the Royal Hobart Hospital, the day oncology ward. JC was right. Mother was doing her best to avoid dying. Phillip had been busy for hours getting her ready. Today she was in a Doris Day wig with a pink gingham shirt, three-quarter white pants and a little orange scarf tied about her neck. Her make-up was perfect and her nails were done. I loved his dedication. Nurses are almost, without exception, the most generous people. Max had met Phillip when he was a student. Then she'd come across him again a few years back and offered him this job. He was a godsend.

It was strange visiting the old family home in Taroona, the suburb downriver from Sandy Bay. Pulling into the driveway, I was suddenly sixteen again, trying to sneak back into the house at four in the morning after going out drinking and fornicating with my boyfriend. Or I was eighteen and wondering if I could make it all the way down the hall without Mother appearing from the kitchen with a drink in her hand to say something suitably disparaging about my appearance. 'You look like a psychedelic giraffe', had been one of her favourites.

Phillip opened the door and said she would be ready in five minutes. 'Make yourself at home,' he said. 'Sorry,' he corrected. 'It is your home, of course.'

'Was,' I said, and smiled. 'A very long time ago now.'

I hadn't been able to get away fast enough after year twelve. I got three jobs once I knew I had a place at NYU and six months to save up. I worked a checkout at the supermarket through the week, pulled beers at a pub in town Thursday, Friday and Saturday nights, and all day Saturday I worked at Salamanca market selling second-hand books for a friend of Dad's.

The furniture in the house was exactly the same. The same sofas, the same paintings on the walls. The liquidambar now shaded the entire deck. Granny's flat was still there, closed up now. The tyre swing was gone, as was the bald patch we'd rubbed into the earth beneath it. Now it was all smooth clipped lawn and nothing to indicate children had ever lived here. The pink tiles in the bathroom were still the same, and my old room was as it had been the last time I was here. Homogenised white linen, cream walls and a wicker chair with a cushion bearing an image of the Eiffel Tower. No hint of the girl I had been, which was a relief. I didn't need her back.

Everything smelled as if it had been polished with lemon verbena. Perhaps it had. There were silver-framed photos of us all on the hall sideboard, but we were ghosts, somehow, in that house. JC's bad moods, Max and her bushwalking friends laying out their wet tents to dry on the back lawn, me with my world map on the wall and pins in all the places I was going to go. Gone too were all the nights when Mother and Dad argued, Mother working her way up into a fever pitch of rage at whatever she felt was unfair right then. So many dinners where she said not a word. And all the while, through our teenage years, this feeling that she wasn't really there. Her secret life of lovers and drinking and spending money—all of which I only pieced together later, but it made sense of it all. I remember Max ringing me on my twentieth birthday and saying, 'Well, now Mother is the only teenager left in the family.' Some women aren't meant to get married. Or be mothers. I don't know why we place that expectation on them, our daughters. It's a huge job and we all know that it takes everything to do it well. Not everyone has everything to give. And we expect them to keep doing it all their lives. I think my mother only ever wanted her freedom. Born in the wrong generation. I didn't make things easy for her. And then I left.

Mother was looking more like a ghost every day. She'd exhausted all her options. She'd had two rounds of chemo and it had shrunk the tumours, but then new ones appeared in her lungs. An experimental treatment had worked for a few months, but not anymore. Her last chance was this next round of whatever it was that came in a drip over the course of an hour once a week for six more weeks, a new drug, expensive, with tough side effects. It was unlikely she'd ever taste food again.

On the drive to the hospital she told me that it was very nice to be taken for treatment by her *daughter* because so many *other daughters* took their mothers. I mentioned that other people's *daughters* were not the leader of the Opposition, but she assured me that *other daughters*, even very important ones like Maxine, found time to take days off to be with their mothers.

'Verity has come with me a few times,' she said. I had discovered that Mother slightly despised her friend Verity because Verity could use the internet. Usually it was Phillip, *my boy*, who took her.

A nurse welcomed her and settled her into a reclining chair. There were at least a dozen patients all being set up, each with the gaunt, slightly flushed look of the deeply unwell.

'The staff seem very nice,' I said.

'They know who I am,' said Mother. 'One day they left me waiting in reception. I was not impressed. I rang Max and told her it wasn't good enough. It hasn't been a problem since. When you're waiting to die, any other sort of waiting becomes intolerable.'

I wondered about the book I'd brought in my bag. At what point would I be able to bury myself in it? We waited for the drip to be fitted and treatment to begin.

Mother looked at all the other patients in their blue vinyl recliners, their drips and trays, several of them hairless. One woman was in a blue cap.

'Oh, she's got the freezer bag on,' said Mother, a little too loudly.

The other woman looked up from her magazine.

'It's designed to stop your hair falling out,' Mother said to me. 'They tried it on me. Hideously painful. The most excruciating headache. And fine lot of good it did.'

'It won't work,' Mother said to the other woman. 'You may as well save yourself the pain.'

From the look the other woman gave her, she thought Mother was referring to the cancer, not the hair loss.

'Look at us. A bunch of drug addicts!' Mother announced loudly to the other patients, who all looked a little startled to be addressed in this way. I could see most of them knew exactly who she was—mother of both the premier and the leader of the Opposition. One younger woman smiled as if a show was about to begin. The room was set up to allow a collegial feeling among the patients, the chairs all facing inwards, as if this was a meeting of sorts.

'Did you see that young girl in the paper the other day?' Mother said to me. 'The one that held up that corner store—for a tin of baby formula! What's the world coming to?'

I'd read about it. The ever-reliable *Mercury* newspaper—a mix of bad puns, skewed facts and small-town stories.

'I thought she had a pretty good reason,' I said. 'Not for armed robbery as such. But she was clearly desperate.'

'But the tattoos. No wonder she can't get a job.'

'I don't think she was wanting a job, Mum,' I said. 'She's a new mother. That is a job.'

'I know that, Astrid. I've got cancer, not stupidity. I mean that she wouldn't need to point a gun at some unsuspecting boy, even if he was a Muslim, if she had a job.'

'I don't think him being a Muslim was the point.'

'It's not like they're not pulling guns on *us* these days.'

'Well, not here in Tasmania,' I said quietly, glancing at the nearby patients. 'Not that particular young man or his family.'

'Oh, you can't be sure about his family. They just fly off and become radicals. Then they come home on their Australian passports and the next thing you know you have another mass shooting. Or more stabbings of perfectly innocent bystanders. It's no different to the communists in the fifties. They infiltrate, these people, and before you know it, they're in parliament, making changes to the rules. And then it's too late. And we're all having to get down on our knees and pray to Allah.'

'So you think the girl was probably right to use a gun, seeing he was a Muslim?' I asked.

'No, I'm not saying she was right, Astrid. I'm just saying that if you were needing to steal from a store run by a Muslim, I can understand that young girl taking a gun, just in case.'

'Like the Australian who took a gun and killed all those New Zealanders in a mosque?'

'Oh, you still have to make every conversation an argument, don't you?'

I said nothing. Sometimes it was the only way. After a few moments, my mother said, 'I mean, what's going on when mothers can't afford milk for their babies?'

I thought we would leave it at that, until my mother said, 'Mind you, that sort of girl, they don't like to breastfeed. Probably a smoker too.'

'But you didn't breastfeed, Mum, did you?' Sometimes going over old wounds is strangely cathartic. Like scratching a mosquito bite long after it has scabbed.

'When Maxine was born, they completely understood that I didn't want to breastfeed. Gave me tablets and my milk dried up in a few days. But that was Sydney. Down here . . . goodness, you'd think *they* were in charge of my body. As soon as I got home, I put you both on the bottle. I mean you didn't want to feed at the same time, or sleep at the same time.'

'Until Dad discovered we'd sleep if we were put to bed together,' I said.

'Oh, I think it was his mother who sorted that out.'

This was a blatant lie. It was one of Dad's stories. How on a bad night, when we were only a few weeks old, he'd wrapped me and JC up together as if we were back in the womb, and it had worked. We didn't sleep apart until we were five. Squashed into the same cot, then the same bed. Apparently, JC wouldn't fall asleep until he had my hand in his.

'Your grandmother,' said Mother. 'She was a help with you all.'

This was an extraordinary compliment coming from my mother. You are mellowing, I thought. Death is working on you.

'I loved Granny,' I said. 'I missed her so much after she died.'

'I can't imagine you'll miss me. I doubt you'll even come home for my funeral.'

'Don't say that, Mum. Anyway, I'm here now.'

'Yes, but I'm not dead. I know you, Astrid. You only do something if it suits you.'

Maybe not mellowing after all.

'Cup of tea, Mum?' I asked, getting up.

'That would be nice. Ask a nurse.'

'I'll sort it,' I said.

Outside in the corridor, I rested my forehead against the wall. Then I texted Max. *With mother in chemo. Where can I find the fentanyl? Need to hook myself up.*

Max sent back the crying with laughter emoji and the halo face emoji.

I had wondered, as children of unhappy marriages do, why my parents stayed together. I'd asked my father on one of his trips to New York when my children were small and I was beginning to realise how hard marriage was.

'I loved her,' he said. 'As soon as I saw her, I thought, I have to take care of you.'

I'd asked Mother too. It was after yet another fight where Mother had said something needlessly insulting and Dad had left the dinner table. She'd had the decency, on that night, to appear a little remorseful.

'Why does Dad stay with you, Mum?' I'd asked. I was eighteen. Granny was dead. I had my scholarship in the US. I was almost out of there.

'Oh, Astrid, can't you see? The poor man loves me.'

I had tried to become only my father's daughter. But my mother taught me everything I know about manipulation.

CHAPTER TWENTY-SIX

It was late Friday afternoon. The past week had blown all the records for heat across Australia. In Tasmania, bushfires had been burning in the World Heritage area down south and the Tarkine up north. The wind had picked up and now smoke had obliterated the far hills, giving the world an eerie amber glow. All day I'd had meetings with people who had been ill at ease, worried for the week ahead when the temperatures were predicted to rise, and no rain in sight. A hot northerly had been blowing all day and the air smelled of smoke.

I'd taken a swim and, as I walked home, I found Dan cleaning flathead under a gum tree. When we were children, it would take half an hour in the morning to pull up enough to feed us all for breakfast. I'd heard again and again from people that those days were long gone. Now you were lucky to get a feed in three or four hours. Recreational fishing had taken its toll on the channel.

'They look good,' I said, sitting down on a log beside him. He was working at an old communal table, weathered and whitened by sun and salt.

I watched his hands as he ran a knife up the body of the fish, shedding scales and washing the board down when that bit was done.

'How was your day?' he asked.

'Actually, I spent the afternoon with the Recreational Fishing Club.'

'Ah, what do they have to say about things?'

'They mostly talked about the fish farms,' I said.

'It's the biggest employer in the state,' he said. 'After tourism and the Catholic education system.' He was now slicing up the fish and pulling out the innards under the gills. 'They'll be the biggest primary industry in the state soon. The broken nets and rope, and all the stuff that washes up on the shore, that's nothing compared to the havoc they wreak underneath the water.'

'So I've heard,' I said.

'When we were kids,' he said, 'I learned to dive in the Huon Estuary, and the bottom was amazing. We used to see cray-fish and abalone and sharks—all sorts of stuff. I remember watching documentaries about the Great Barrier Reef and the Mediterranean, but the Huon Estuary was way more vibrant because of the mix of warm and cold temperatures. A lot of algal life, a lot of vegetation, and a lot of fish life as well.'

'But it's not anymore . . .' I said.

'Everyone used to have nets. We'd net heavily. It was just part of the culture. It's what we did.'

'So it's not the fish farms?'

'It's industry too. I mean, we like to think it's somebody else, but it's all of us. There was a crazy scheme in the sixties that dredged the scallop beds. People want to think everything recovers eventually, but it doesn't. You can get a few if you dive for them now, but this channel, it was scallop heaven.'

I watched him wash down the weathered table with another bucket of salt water, scrub away the last of the fish remnants, leave it shipshape for the next person.

'I've got to get these home,' he said. 'Mind if we walk and talk?'

We headed back across the road and up the flight of stairs. At the top of the narrow path, we came to our road and walked side by side.

'Since I was a teenager,' he said, 'most of the Huon Estuary has, at some stage, had fish pens hovering over it. The bottom is suffocated with waste. They've killed the harbour over at Strahan. That won't come back for years now, if ever. Now they've moved into the channel, it's suffering the same fate. The east coast estuaries will be next. Because of pressure from conservationists, they're pushing out into the open ocean, which is where I'd prefer them to be. But it's more dangerous. Know a bloke who lost a thumb out there a few weeks ago.

'Now that you've got me started,' he said with his trademark grin, 'did you know they feed mackerel to the salmon? They use a lower-value fish to make a higher-value fish, which seems nuts to me. I mean it's questionable, when you're eating your bit of salmon, whether you're eating anything healthy at all. They're putting that colour in the feed, too—anthocyline, or something like that—to make it look pink. So there's people lining up in the Sydney markets to eat this Tasmanian salmon, and it's a filthy industry. But that's not a fight for us to worry about. I'm not going to give a rat's arse about anything anymore.'

'Really?' I said. 'Is that going to be your new year's resolution?'

'You just become such a grumpy bastard as you get older, if you're not careful.'

'Is your dad a grumpy bastard?'

'Probably. He died a few years back. Reckon he's still complaining somewhere.'

We had arrived at his gate.

'I think you'll just get happier as you get older,' I said.

'Do you now?' he said.

Sometimes it feels like my job is to help my clients find the parts where they don't know themselves, and the parts where they do, and get them to talk to one another. Sometimes it's like the divide between justice and mercy. Usually, people are harder on themselves than anyone. My gift is that people talk to me. Maybe it's because I've learned to ask questions. But mostly it's because I've learned to shut up. It's amazing what people will say if you give them the space to say it. But when a person is attractive, that can be deceiving. Some of the most ruthless men I've known have been handsome. It's almost a sociopathic marker. Dan was good-looking but not typically handsome. He was big and rough around the edges, and he wasn't needy. He didn't seem to be making up for any great hole inside him.

We both turned then and looked out at the smoky evening sky.

'Not looking good for the next few days,' he said. 'Badly need rain.'

The northerly was dropping and the channel was a milky pale blue.

'Another day in a life,' I said. 'When you add them up, there aren't that many of them.'

'Maybe there's enough,' he said.

'Do you think?'

'If you make the most of them,' he said. 'Yeah.'

We could hear the bridgeworks going on, muted at this distance. Generators, drills, the rumble of the barges that traversed the channel from the manufacturing plant at North-West Bay. Voices on the air.

He said, 'I've gotta get these into the fridge. They're for my mum. Seeing her in the morning.'

'I could make dinner one night,' I said. 'If you want.' I suddenly felt nervous.

He looked at me and his eyes twinkled. 'I'm not turning you down,' he said. 'But I'll cook for us. Not tonight. Another night. Soon.'

'You don't trust my cooking?' I said.

'Not sure I want to see you all domesticated. Wouldn't be right, somehow.'

'So have you got a hot date?' I asked.

'You really love to ask the questions, don't you?'

'That's why they pay me the big bucks.'

He laughed and walked through his gate and was gone into the dusk.

It was the lovely thing about the island while ever there was only access by water. If it was past 7.30 pm, you knew no-one was leaving. Short of your own runabout, or a kayak, you were all here for the night because the ferries had stopped running.

I walked across my paddock and up onto the deck. I went inside, made a salad and opened a beer. I saw Dan drive away in his ute. Then I sat down with my laptop and began another report on the day's activities. When it was done, a software program encrypted it and it winged its way to America, where it would be opened by an analyst who worked in a remote corner of a famous building. Hidden from presidential faithfuls, some of us were watching the axis move from democracy to tyranny in the United States and, oh, so many other countries. That's why I had come. JC had asked, but so had they. I had been sent back to my home town to see just what it was that had the Chinese government so very interested in Tasmania. Since I'd arrived, I'd amassed a few theories, but that was all they were. I needed to get closer to May Chen. I suspected she knew exactly what was going on. I also needed to work on my brother.

CHAPTER TWENTY-SEVEN

Max and I were out on JC's deck sitting side by side, shelling peas and broad beans, and drinking a very lovely Tasmanian sparkling wine. It was almost cloudless, twenty-eight degrees and still. A hot Christmas Day. There had been Christmases with snow in Hobart. Plenty of grey, blustery Christmas Days too. Plenty of memories of running about with new surfboards, or new bathers, in rain and hail. But this long, hot spell was not budging. Bushfires were still burning. Houses had been lost, and the water levels were down in the dams across the state.

JC's balcony had an uninterrupted one-hundred-and-eighty-degree view from Mount Wellington all the way down the river. You're hard-pressed in Hobart, squeezed as it is into the narrow band of land between the foothills of the mountain and the Derwent River, not to have a view of either the mountain or the water. But to have both was especially good.

Today, despite the heat, we were in floral dresses and shirts and ties, looking like some kind of throwback to the fifties. Stephanie was setting the table inside with the girls and keeping our mother occupied folding napkins into some elaborate design. Frank Sinatra was singing Christmas songs.

I'd just asked Max how her love life was going.

'You know what it's like,' she said. 'There's no time. Even if there was someone the least bit suitable in Hobart, which there isn't, can you imagine what they would have to go through?'

'I'm sure your wish list and mine are pretty similar,' I said. 'And that makes our chances of meeting the right person here about 0.002 per cent.'

'I think your odds might be a little optimistic, Ace. And in both our cases, *The Mercury* would want to feature them in the Sunday magazine. No. It's not going to happen.'

'Do you miss having sex?' I asked.

'Goodness, it's Christmas Day. Are we supposed to talk about sex?' Max elbowed me.

'That was the plan,' I said. 'We were going to find great sex. Fantastic sex, actually. Remember?'

'Is that what we said?'

I nodded. 'We made a pact. We were up the liquidambar and you said you thought your boyfriend—what was his name? Rick?'

She nodded. 'Rick with a silent P.'

I laughed. 'That's right! You said you thought he was a dud. And I said that I had the same problem. Two seconds and the whole thing was over. So we agreed we were going to find fantastic sex.'

Max pulled a face. 'I've found sex to be pretty overrated, personally. As I get older, I wonder if I'll ever be bothered again. Men are . . . well, messy. Demanding. Smelly. You?'

'I've discovered the wonder of vibrators. No premature ejaculation, no snoring. Bliss.'

'No being unfaithful either.'

I sighed. 'True. And no nastiness.'

'I'm still angry with Ben, I want you to know that,' she said.

'Maybe the fact I have better sex living without him indicates that things weren't exactly right between us.'

Max laughed.

'He said I wasn't very much fun anymore,' I said.

'Oh.'

'I loved him.'

'He was handsome . . .'

'We looked good. We had that going for us. He could magnetise a room, people hanging on his every word. And then he'd come home. Very different man behind closed doors.'

'You know none of that was about you, really, don't you?' said Max, pulling a face.

'The house was never tidy enough. The kids never quiet enough. He didn't like my work schedule. Or that I earned more. Travelled more. He resented my friends.' I sighed. 'No wonder I stopped being fun.'

Max squeezed my hand. 'I'm not going to give you sympathy, Ace,' she said, 'because I think what you do is awesome, and you don't need sympathy. Ben's an arsehole. He had a meanness with the kids. Like they were actually a nuisance. Took up his time. Got in the way. I never understood that. I didn't like it when I saw it. In fact, I hated it. But when it's someone's marriage, even your sister's, it's hard to say anything. He could be a bully, frankly. I watched how you ran around doing all this stuff to keep him happy,' she said.

'I thought that was how you were meant to do it,' I said. 'All those years watching Dad keep the peace.'

'Yes,' said Max.

'It's still bewildering that Ben found a new family. Ignored his own children. Particularly Tavvy. But she's stronger for it. I'm not so sure about Paul. I think he's worried he'll become like Ben.'

'We all have a parent we don't want to become,' said Max.

'One day I'd like to get softer,' I said.

'Have you at least had a fling?'

'Haven't even had a date. I look at men and I think, no, no, no. Tavvy says I have PTDS. Post-traumatic divorce stress. I think it's actually post-traumatic divorce shame. I feel ashamed that I couldn't see who he really was. It's possible I was really stupid.'

'Okay, Ace,' said Max, 'you have nothing, *nothing*, to be ashamed about. You'll know yourself better next time. And I'm interviewing any man you think is future relationship material! You know I love you, don't you? We all love you. It's over. You're here now.'

I cried then. And she held me. Anybody who might have considered coming out on the deck just left us to it.

'Do you have to be based in New York?' she asked at last. 'Could you work from here?'

'Oh no, I'm not coming back,' I said, wiping the tears away and laughing. 'That's not happening.'

'Why not?'

'The kids are there. And I made a promise a long time ago.' I sighed.

'What promise?'

'That I'd go live another sort of life.'

'Than what?'

'Whatever Mother had planned for me. But I do love it here. That's the hard part.'

'It is,' Max agreed.

'It kind of seduces me a little bit more every day. I sit up on my balcony at Bruny and it's so peaceful.'

'You still get the nightmares?'

I nodded. 'But at Bruny I've been sleeping better than I've slept in years.'

Stephanie appeared, bringing a fresh bottle of champagne and removing the bowls of shelled peas and beans.

'Can we help?' I asked.

'Lunch will be half an hour. Keep talking. You two don't get enough time to catch up,' she said, then she kissed me on the top of the head.

'We should come help,' said Max.

'If it's a should, then you must never do it,' said Stephanie. 'That's what I tell the girls.' She laughed and disappeared back inside.

'So,' I said, 'to completely change the subject, what's your latest conspiracy theory on the bridge?'

'I've decided it was a CIA job.'

'Do tell,' I said.

'Well, some people in the US government have got to be deeply annoyed at our swing towards China, whatever the official line is. People have been saying current policy will change, no doubt with a new president in two years' time. Thank God for fixed terms.'

'No saying it won't be more of the same,' I said.

'It would make the disappearing act understandable, though,' she said, 'if it was the Americans. The way that boat just vanished down the channel. They know how to get in and out, those guys.'

'How did it happen again, the bridge funding?'

Max raised her eyebrows. 'It came out of a COAG meeting. Council of Australian Governments. All the premiers from every state get together with the prime minister a couple of times a year and they float projects and negotiate deals. I'm sure they were pitched the bridge as a way to save Tasmania from sliding into economic paralysis. There was a lot of talk at the time about rising unemployment and the need to create a young skilled workforce here.

'Western Australia was looking at seceding because they thought Tassie was benefiting unfairly from its GST contributions,' she continued. 'I don't think it was particularly serious, but in Canberra they started to believe it. They have a habit of believing very silly things up there, depending on who's spouting the hype. What you have to remember is that Canberra operates in a bubble. No traffic jams or parking problems. Everyone can afford to send their kids to private school. It's a group of intelligent, affluent, middle-class people totally removed from life in the rest of Australia.

'I mean, you only have to sit in parliament and listen. All those years of travelling back and forth as head of the Nursing

Federation, I watched them make crazy policies. There was actually a hospital in Victoria that had been built and was totally operational, but it didn't have any patients. There were admin staff, but there wasn't enough money to have patients. At the time, nobody in Canberra seemed to think that was a problem. It was like an episode of *Yes, Minister.* So I think someone sold them the idea of the bridge and they bought it.'

'But who pitched it?'

'Aiden Abbott, I'm told. And Senator Barney Viper.'

I grimaced.

'Frank Pringle worked for Viper back then. But once the bridge was announced, Pringle went to work for JC and he's been there ever since.'

'Ah,' I said. 'So that's how he happened.'

'Viper's good at getting dirt on people and that's not restricted to his own party. He's a real manipulator. I'm still not sure he didn't undo my predecessor.'

'Has he got stuff on JC?' I asked.

'Probably, but I don't want to know what.'

'We're talking two billion dollars.'

'Yep.' Max shrugged. 'All the research about the bridge was hugely exaggerated, totally unrealistic. But even so, none of it was enough to allocate two billion dollars at a time when we have failing education rates, failing health stats. Tasmanians are getting poorer, fatter and more stupid. Actually, that's true of the whole country unless you're in the top one per cent. We're thirty years or so away from using up our coal reserves, fifty for our iron ore reserves, and then what are we all going to live on?'

'Maybe that was the gambit,' I said. 'I mean, the design and the whole international focus . . . the world stage. Get the focus off the domestic picture.'

Max shook her head and sighed. 'It could have been a simple, straightforward four-lane single span. But instead they have to do the six-lane flyover from Kingston and the new highway on the Bruny side. This massive design. It's as if they're expecting a million visitors, not another hundred thousand. It could have cost a quarter the price but instead it becomes this huge thing that totally overwhelms the landscape.'

I nodded. 'Maybe climate change is going to make Tasmania so attractive, six lanes is foresight.'

'Yes, except it isn't,' said Max. 'Sometimes I don't know if I can keep caring, Ace. The blokes in my party, the constant bickering and infighting and the power plays, it feels like a current I'm swimming against day after day.'

'You're tired, Max. It's Christmas. You're allowed to be. And you might be a bit paranoid.'

'But I'm not.'

'Should I tell you if I think you are?'

'I'm relying on you.'

When JC walked out onto the deck, Max turned and said, '*Nĭ hăo.*'

'You might regret that,' he said. He glanced at me, but he knew I'd never tell Max about the fatality on the bridge. That's the bit where discretion is the better part of valour.

'*Uneasy lies the head that wears a crown,*' said our father, who had followed JC out with Ella.

Max turned and said, 'I love you, Dad.'

JC said, 'So, Shakespeare, what other pearls of wisdom would you like to share?'

'Don't speak to him like that,' said Max.

'Well, he speaks to me like that,' said JC.

Our father wandered off into the garden, smiling, saying something out of earshot, but Ella was on to it. Tapping away on her phone, she recorded the quote and came back and showed me the screen.

It read: *Th' abuse of greatness is when it disjoins remorse from power. Brutus in Julius Caesar (2.1.19–20).*

'*Et tu, Brutus,*' I said quietly to her. 'It's a great play. You'd enjoy it.'

'I have one hundred and ninety-one!' she said.

Our grandfather had been a union man for twenty years until the workplace accident that killed him when our father was still in primary school. Dad had hated the area school he went to, so he'd followed in his father's footsteps and gotten a carpentry apprenticeship. His first job was making sets for the Theatre Royal, Australia's oldest theatre, in the heart of Hobart. Reading Shakespeare might have bored him in class, but on the stage it mesmerised him. He started being cast in minor roles. In his early twenties, he went to night school and studied to complete his Higher School Certificate. Afterwards he got a job in a union office as a clerk, and not long after that was asked if he'd be interested in running on the Labor ticket. People remembered his father. He campaigned well and he had the Coleman name. He missed out that first time, but he won the next election. He retained his love of acting even after he was in parliament. It created quite an affection for him among voters.

'I would have liked to play Julius, or Othello,' he once said to me. 'But I wasn't a leading man. Same in politics. I'm good at being stage left, sweeping up the mess, dancing on the table.'

When we were children, he'd always get us tickets for opening night, and we'd see our father decked out in fern fronds or battle gear or sitting about rolling drunk. He'd take us to every Shakespeare play that came through town, amateur and professional alike. In his early seventies, he began forgetting his lines. By then he'd retired from politics.

It was no wonder Shakespeare had stuck in his brain. It's possible that, this whole last phase of our father's life, he's playing the ghost in *Hamlet*. Trying to communicate with his son. Maybe, if Max is not paranoid but perceptive, something *is* rotten in the state of Denmark. Not murder, but something fishy.

'So when are you two beginning campaigning in earnest?' I asked.

The election date was set for Saturday, March 5th. They were already out there, jostling for media attention every day, but soon the real ruthlessness of an election would begin. Any camaraderie would be put on hold for the ensuing weeks. And I will almost certainly be caught in the election crossfire.

JC will be all about jobs and growth. Max will be all about health and education. JC will counter by promising to lower the payroll tax and invest in tourism. Max will parry with better public housing, upgrading services, new investment in schools. And on it will go. Everything becomes predictable in politics if you live long enough.

JC was standing by the railing. Max and I went to stand either side of him.

'So my guess,' Max said, 'is you'll bring the PM down about January twenty-sixth. For Australia Day. What do you think, Ace? With the biggest infrastructure project in the country going on here, I'm sure the PM will be wanting some Australia Day bridge shots . . . might even set off a few fireworks himself.'

JC scoffed.

'I think we should have the oysters out here—it's so lovely,' Stephanie said, coming onto the balcony. 'JC, could you make sure everyone has a glass?'

Then she looked at the three of us. 'You're not talking election, are you? Oh, you are! Stop it. You know it's forbidden today.'

CHAPTER TWENTY-EIGHT

Profound thought upon waking on New Year's Eve: *The thing that frightens me most is the next time I take off my clothes for someone.*

I had returned to Bruny. I'm not a crowd kind of person. I don't want to think about the past year. I don't make resolutions for the next one. I'm happy to hear the sound of revelry from afar, but I don't have any desire to be amidst it.

I was sitting on the edge of my deck, taking in the sky beginning to do its evening spectacle of red, crimson, orange, vermillion. The channel was darkening and soon night would be seeping through the gum trees. I listened to the birds chaperoning the sun to bed. The bushfires had been contained for the moment, the sky had cleared, but there was still no rain. It had been thirty-one degrees again today, a record-breaking streak of hot weather. Clouds had rolled in from the west, huge and black, but the promised thunderstorm had not arrived. The air was charged with heat and the prickly sense of unreleased energy.

I had been thinking about my kids back in New York, and my friends, and how I was almost halfway through this job, when Dan walked across the paddock, startling the wallabies grazing on any green shoot they could find in the parched grass. He was carrying two beers dewy with cold.

'Had a feeling you might be hiding out up here,' he said.

'Party of one,' I said.

He eased himself down beside me and, pulling the top off, handed me a beer.

'Nice night,' he said.

Dan was in a pair of long, faded navy shorts and a worn white t-shirt, which showed off his tan and a Celtic sleeve tattooed down one arm.

'You're my first visitor,' I said.

'Cheers to that,' he said, and we clinked our bottles together. 'It's a good view.'

'It is a good view,' I said. The mountain was silhouetted to the north. Two yachts—a ketch and a sloop—were sailing down the channel. Birds were carolling in the trees. It all went well with the coolness of the beer.

'How was Christmas for you?' I asked.

'I thought it might be my turn to ask the questions,' he said.

'Did you?'

'You're very good at it, don't get me wrong, but every time I walk away from you, I realise that I'm the one that's got almost no information. I reckon you need to give me ten questions.'

'Oh,' I said. 'That makes me nervous.'

'Excellent,' he said. 'So can I start?'

'Can I choose not to answer?'

'Of course,' he said. 'But I'd like you to sweat a little.'

'I'm already sweating.'

'Perfect,' he said. 'So, single, relationship, married?'

'Divorced.'

'How long ago?'

'We broke up three years ago.'

'Married for how long?'

'Twenty-five years.'

He nodded. 'Kids?'

'Two. Paul—he's twenty-seven now, and Tavvy—Octavia—is twenty-four. Both in New York.'

'Favourite food?'

'You planning on a career as a quiz show host when the bridge is done?'

'Maybe,' he said.

'Grilled cheese on toast. Cheese soufflé. Cheese omelette. Cheese anything. I love Thai and Japanese too. And Mexican. But if things are going badly, it's grilled cheese all the way.'

'Favourite cheese?'

'Something soft and smelly. A ripe Taleggio. Roquefort. There's a soft sheep cheese I get at the local deli back home with jalapenos . . .'

'Favourite book?' he asked.

I looked at him. The title of every book I had ever read went out of my brain. He had really good arms. He had good legs as well, with just the right amount of body hair. The beer was obviously relaxing me. It was actually my third for the evening. And his eyes were unsettling me. So ridiculously blue. But none of this was getting me to a book, so I said, 'That's too hard.'

'C'mon, you're going to a desert island. You can take one book.'

'The dictionary.'

'Is that cheating?'

'Nelson Mandela's *Long Walk*?'

'No, no, you only get one. You get the dictionary. All right, favourite movie.'

'*Casablanca*. That's not exactly true, because I love so many, but it's the first one that comes to mind.'

He looked at me. '*Here's looking at you, kid.*'

I grinned. What was he doing here? It felt like he was flirting. Was he really flirting?

'Favourite parent? Although I think I know this.'

'My dad,' I said.

He nodded again. 'Best night of your life?'

I took a breath. 'Other than the night Paul was born, my fiftieth. We had it on the roof of a hotel in New York. It was a beautiful night. It was cold and everyone was rugged up and there were braziers burning. We had this jazz band and we danced. The kids made a film. It took them months and all these photos came out of nowhere from old friends and places I'd been posted. My dad came with Maxine. JC and Stephanie were there with the girls. I was happy. I was so happy.'

Stop talking, I told myself. Stop talking right now. But my mouth went on. 'It started snowing. And we all stood out there between the fire and the snow, and I just loved New York. I loved my husband. I loved my children and my friends and everything hard in the world fell away.'

'And then?'

'Well, life went on . . . and here I am,' I said.

He nodded. 'You want to go for a walk?'

'Is that included in the questionnaire?' I asked.

'It's optional,' he said. 'I can leave you to your quiet night.'

'Let's go for a walk,' I said.

Beyond the lights of the houses, the night was velvet and warm. At his gate, he went inside and retrieved two more beers.

'It's New Year. Figure we should live it up a little,' he said.

It felt good to walk beside him.

'Strange seeing it quiet,' I said, looking over at the bridge, dark but for the navigation lights. Tonight, Christmas Eve and Christmas Day: they were the only days the men had off. Every other day, the bridge continued.

'What happens for you after this?' I asked.

'Ah, there's a whole lot in the pipeline, but I'm thinking I might take off. Go find some breaks.'

'You're a surfer?'

'Put me in the sea and I'm happy. You?'

'I love the sea too. And it's so easy here.'

'That's the word for it. Easy.'

'I swim most every morning,' I said. 'Either at Sandy Bay beach or down here.'

'I go down to Cloudy Bay,' he said. 'As far from that thing as possible.' Cloudy Bay at the far end of South Bruny, where I'd gone the day the Chinese worker died. Fifty kilometres from the bridge.

We crossed the road and went down onto the sand. It was such a warm evening. Rich, velvety heat and the air was almost crackling with static. There was a deep rumble from the clouds in the west. We waited. It felt like any moment there would be lightning. But none came.

We continued to the far end of the beach, past the shacks along the inner edge of the dunes and the boatsheds. Some of the houses were dark, others were occupied by New Year revellers. Music of different varieties accompanied us, snippets of conversation, laughter and barbecue smells. We reached the low sandstone cliffs that fringed the shore. It was very quiet here but for the odd burst of laughter caught on the air, and the beat from a distant sound system up on the hill. From here on it was rocks all the way to a distant point that took the shoreline south.

'I used to play down here as a kid,' I said. 'Me and Max used to make jewellery for the mermaids. Shells and seaweed . . .'

'I like your sister. She has really good calf muscles for a woman her age.'

'You know that's an entirely inappropriate thing to say,' I said.

'Oh, are we going to do appropriate? Damn, I hoped we wouldn't.'

'Have you met her?' I asked.

'No,' he said. 'A distant admirer.'

I laughed. 'I'll tell her.'

'No, don't!' he said. 'But it's your brother who's your twin, yeah?'

I nodded.

'So you're closer to him?'

I said. 'Not really. Maybe, yes. It's hard to explain.'

'Pretty complicated—that's how it looks to me.'

An almost-full moon had skirted the north of the island and was shedding tinsel on the water.

Dan flipped the lids on the two beers and handed one to me.

'Happy New Year, Ace,' he said, clinking bottles.

'Happy New Year, Mac.'

He was staring out to sea. I remember Tavvy telling me when she was about fourteen that what mattered in a man was a good jawline. Dan had a good jawline.

'So do I get ten questions?'

'Why didn't I see that coming?' he said.

'Favourite parent?'

He reached for a hand-sized rock and placed it in front of him. And another.

'My mum,' he said. 'Olive. Makes a mean lamb roast. Country girl. Kindest person I know.'

'Dumbest thing you ever did?'

'Yikes,' he said. 'There must be a ledger somewhere. I reckon my old man could list a hundred.'

'But . . .'

'Maybe leaving the army for love.'

I nodded. So that was part of it too, not just that our paratroopers had been reassigned. There'd been a relationship.

'It didn't work out?'

'Nah.'

I already knew he didn't have kids. I wanted to ask him why, but I didn't.

'What's the one thing you would change in the world if you could?'

He placed another rock.

'You're not going to like this,' he said. 'But maybe we could slow down the human population. Make it an opt in, not an opt out. With rules.'

'Such as?'

'Well, at one end, we ought to be able to die whenever we're ready. At the other, one kid each. Enough to replace ourselves. There's way too many of us already.'

'So you're a Farris supporter?' I hadn't taken him for that. 'Is that why you never had kids?'

'I just wasn't sure. About me, really. Not about anything else. And then, well, she was sure. So that wasn't a fit. Now she's got two kids and she's happy.'

'Any regrets?'

'Haven't been to Antarctica.'

'Favourite film?'

'*Dr Strangelove.*'

I nodded. Kubrick. I loved that film.

'Least favourite thing in life?'

'Swearing.'

'Swearing?'

'I know, but I just find it ugly. I know I do it all the time. But I don't like it. It doesn't feel right. I think it's . . . well, most of it's unnecessary.'

'You are quite an old-fashioned guy,' I said. I worried suddenly that he might be a Christian.

'Religion?' I asked.

'The sea,' he said. 'Actually, religion is the second thing I'd change. Abolish it. No organised religion.'

'In my line of work,' I said, 'I find two things: the good people have faith and the bad people have faith.'

'There you have it,' he said. 'Welcome to the human race.'

I suddenly realised he had done this deft thing and built a beautiful arc of stones there in the dark. A bridge. How had he made it balance so beautifully?

'He builds things,' I said.

'I'm a pretty simple guy,' he said.

'Really?' I asked.

'I love my mum.'

'I'm not sure I do,' I said. 'I want to, but it's not easy.'

'That must be tough,' he said.

'I've got used to it.'

'What happened?'

'Let's not go there.'

'Swim?' he asked.

'Now?' I said.

'Yes, now.' He laughed. 'It's hot.'

'It is,' I said.

'She's a little bit shy,' he said.

The thunder rumbled again. Closer this time. I looked at his rock creation.

'It's going to be a good bridge, Dan. I don't know what it will do to Bruny, but it's going to be a good bridge.'

'Everything has a price. I've learned that.'

'Me too,' I said.

'Come for a free swim,' he said, offering me a hand up. 'We might get zapped,' he added, looking up.

'I'm not worried about that,' I said.

'Really?'

'It's not how I'm going to go.'

'Good to know you're certain about that,' he said. 'You can get undressed here. I'll go over there.'

I didn't let him within a metre of me. I floated on my back. He did too, and for a while we just drifted. The clouds parted and stars appeared. The moon came out. The water was soft and fine. It must have been forty years since I'd skinny-dipped.

You work together, the pesky inner voice said. Whatever this is, you can't get physical. Okay? You got that?

Okay, I said to myself.

I realised I hadn't asked Dan if he was seeing someone. Not enough to see them on New Year's Eve, anyway. But men like him, tall, good-looking men, they weren't usually single. Maybe there were . . . issues. Erectile dysfunction. Very small penis? I'd had a few friends on the dating circuit who'd told me stories. Whatever his story might be, I wasn't finding out about it tonight. But swimming in that warm sea under a canopy of cosmic wonder, it was almost better than sex. The stars glistened. The water glistened. I saw phosphorescence. It danced as we moved. Dan started laughing. I could see his smile in the darkness. It made me laugh too. And for a while we swam about laughing recklessly, with crazy delight at the sparkling luminous water and the possibilities of fish and sharks and jellyfish against our naked skin.

Afterwards we dressed silently, a respectful distance from each other. We walked back along the beach with our feet in the water. Not something you can do in a lot of places. But here, the greatest danger probably came from a bold crab.

The electrical charge in the air seemed to have settled in my body. Despite my resolve, I thought that if he took my hand, I wouldn't refuse it. Yes, I would, I thought.

He's the bridge manager. You cannot have an affair with the bridge manager, said the inner voice.

But I'll be gone again, I replied to the sensible Astrid. No-one needs to know.

Everyone will know, the other voice said. It's visible in that invisible way, no matter how good you are at acting. You've probably already made it difficult for yourself, more than him, just doing this tonight. You know that, don't you?

'You run out of questions, Ms Coleman?' he asked.

'I'm not sure,' I said.

'I guess kissing you is out of the question?'

I stopped and looked at him in the darkness. He was less than a metre away.

'It's out of the question,' I said.

'Let me know if you change your mind,' he said, and we resumed walking.

'You're younger than me,' I said, keeping pace beside him. 'You're twelve years younger.'

'That's your resistance?'

'And the work thing.'

'You can resist on work grounds. You cannot resist on age.'

'Okay,' I said.

'I am wildly attractive, though,' he said. 'You've seen me naked.'

I laughed. 'It's dark. I didn't look.'

'I did,' he said. And I could feel him grinning beside me.

We walked up the hill and, at his house, he left me. We didn't hug. We didn't touch one another. He just said, 'Thanks for the walk.'

'You too,' I said.

'And, Ace?' he said. 'Have a great year.'

'You too, Dan,' I said.

When midnight came, I was out on my deck. No doubt he was out on his. I blew a kiss to the sky.

'Happy New Year,' I told the air.

As I was turning in, the rain came, big fat heavy summer rain that lulled me deep into sleep.

In the morning, the sky had cleared and the grass on the paddocks was looking relieved to have been watered. I walked the same way down to the sandstone cliffs. Mine were the first footprints on the shore. The tide had knocked his stone bridge down, and it was scattered about as if it had never been.

CHAPTER TWENTY-NINE

P rofound thought of the day: *Risk is always opaque and cata-strophe is more imminent than you think.* I guess that's the basis of the insurance industry.

Max and I had walked morning after morning since New Year, through sun, wind, calm and even an unseasonal fog that came in one morning from the Southern Ocean. Max was focused on fitness, going into election mode. It was never an easy thing to be a woman in politics. Aside from the culture of men, there was the looking good. Men had it so much easier in that regard. No daily make-up. No hair done. Well, minimal hair done. No polishing of nails or eyelash extensions. So few wardrobe decisions. So few shoe decisions. Very little waxing. Far less criticism of their visual imperfections.

We set a good pace, the two of us and, from 5.30, walked for the best part of an hour on the track along the river. We barely passed a dozen people. It was still the strangest part of being back in Hobart. Compared to New York, it was seriously lacking in population. Even with all the tourists, downtown Hobart after 8 pm was a quiet country village.

On Sundays, you had to wonder if there hadn't been a mass alien abduction.

At 5.30 am Max's brain was already on. Apparently the water was getting warmer and scientists had discovered that a long stretch of kelp forests had died down the coast. Kelp forests seemed particularly vulnerable and Max was distressed.

'The warmer water isn't just bad for kelp,' she said. 'It has major ramifications. New South Wales is still recovering from Cyclone Pauline.' Cyclone Pauline that had wreaked such havoc on the New South Wales coast last summer.

'Why aren't you a Green, Max?' I asked.

'Because they'll never be in government. You know that.'

The newspaper had reported the arrival of a new poisonous jellyfish in the Derwent, a traveller from warmer waters. Several people had been hospitalised. There had also been a sewage leak from the out-of-date sewerage plant beside the city. Ten million litres straight into the Derwent River. Increased visitor numbers were blamed. Strangely, Hobartians weren't making much of a fuss. Everyone seemed to have accepted the notion that effluent into the river was just fine. Even normal. It had happened before. Sandy Bay Beach and a string of other beaches down the Derwent had been deemed fit for secondary contact only. Meaning no swimming and every day it was over twenty-five degrees. The city was waiting for cool weather and a big rain. It had been dry since the thunderstorm on New Year's Eve.

'The closer we get to completion, the more I have this gnawing feeling,' said Max.

'You sure that's not because election day follows?' I asked. The official political party launches were yet to happen, but it was pre-election events morning, noon and night across the state. Between her and JC it was a Coleman blitz. Election signs were up in gardens bearing the trademark photos of people desperate for you to like them. Billboards were blazing messages of jobs and growth or education and health, depending on the party. Gilbert Farris had a big one at the main roundabout by the ABC, declaring Tasmania for Tasmanians. He was running as leader of a new party of the same name. They had candidates in every electorate.

The television was blaring ads, and every time I checked my social media there was a message supporting or denigrating my brother or my sister. JC was outspending Max ten to one again, it was clear.

'Who's funding him?' I asked. 'The gambling laws got stitched up last time . . .'

'Ask *him*. Maybe this is the reward for getting the gambling laws through. The Liberals get funded through every election cycle until 2043. I'm still outraged. If I get elected, I'm going to do everything I can to undo that. A monopoly until 2043!'

'It was Labor who first allowed the monopoly . . .'

'I know, I know,' said Max, shaking her head.

Tasmanians lost more than one hundred and fifty million dollars a year to pokie machines. On an island with a population of half a million, with thirty per cent of people living below the poverty line, the maths was steep. That was a lot of school lunches. And a lot of horses and art for the one family behind all the machines—who did not, of course, live in Tasmania.

'You know, Max,' I said, 'for all the speculation about the bridge, I wonder whether it's just that Tasmanians have been so unloved on the federal stage for so long that any investment, let alone a two-billion-dollar one, seems to smell. Frank Pringle said it when I first arrived and maybe he's right. It's like the kid who is so used to being punished, or shamed, that when something good comes along, they flinch and wait for the blow.'

Max frowned.

'Look at what has happened over the past ten years or so,' I said. 'South Australia got that huge deal to build submarines. Nobody protested there—well, other than the people who weren't awarded the contract. Queensland got that nightmare coalmine. A fair few people protested but it still went ahead. Western Australia got some massive new highways and, other than a few environmentalists trying to save the spotted pardalote or whatever, no complaints. Victoria got more power stations. Residents got a bit upset because coal is such a backward step, but again, not enough to change anything. New South Wales got power stations too, and dams and the Murray–Darling Basin, which it's managed to destroy almost entirely.'

'And now we're up in arms when it's our turn,' said Max. 'The difference in all those instances is that those projects created a lot of long-term jobs. They used local subcontractors.'

'Well, the bridge is doing that too.'

'For a moment, but after that, what is it really doing?'

'Ferrying tourists?'

'Yes, ferrying tourists to an already overrun very popular local destination. When two billion dollars could have brought every single child out of poverty here in Tasmania. Funded every government school, built a new hospital . . . Tasmanians don't want a six-lane architectural folly messing up the view.

They want their kids to have smaller class sizes. They want their hips replaced and their catheters removed without having to wait two years for it to happen . . .'

I'd mapped it all out—the groups and sub-groups, the interested parties and the key players. They were all on the wall at Bruny. I'd built dossiers on everyone, too, and where I thought they fitted. Liberal Party, Labor Party, the Greens or the People's Republic of China. Or agents of seemingly insignificant groups like the Hunting and Fishing Party, who, since the bombing, had been advocating for citizens being able to own assault rifles to protect themselves against terrorist threats. They were also running a candidate in every electorate. I felt like the NRA was just a hair's breadth away in Australia. There had been a horrific massacre here in 1996. Thirty-five people died when a young man opened fire with a semi-automatic weapon. Since then Australia had banned guns. Unless you were a member of a gun club. But when I looked into it, I'd discovered that membership of gun clubs had soared since 1996. It was only a matter of time before those owners became a lobby group and then you had an armed minority edging their way into power. Mussolini's black shirts had been of that order. Hitler's brown shirts for that matter.

Democracy is a privilege. Madeleine Albright, ex-Secretary of State, once said democracy was the most stable form of government in the long run, but the most vulnerable in the short term. It's easy to forget. Look at the US and the state of emergency when the president couldn't get his way. That's what autocrats do. In France there would have been a rebellion. But in America there were just more homeless trying to find a space under a bridge to sleep the night. At least in Australia voting is compulsory. The results might be no better, but everyone has to take responsibility.

Max looked at her watch. 'I'm on the ABC after the seven o'clock news this morning. What does your day look like?'

Things had momentarily slowed for me. Tasmanians were on holidays. The public servants were at their shacks. JC and Stephanie had taken the girls to their holiday house at Spring Beach. Their last break before the election was officially called. Kids were doing what kids had been doing for sixty thousand years in Tasmania: mucking about in water. At the swimmable beaches beyond the Derwent, in pools, in their backyards under sprinklers. When we were kids, Dad used to set up a long sheet of plastic in the backyard. We'd rub detergent all over ourselves and slide down it at speed with the hose on. My sloping paddock at Bruny would be just the place for that, too. I wondered if I'd ever have grandkids there. Would Paul and Tavvy always be in America?

The Bruny Bridge was back on track. The damaged caisson had been re-sunk into the riverbed and the tower rebuilt. The damaged cables were being re-strung and the roadway was being replaced, coming in sections on the barges from the manufacturing plant night and day. No more 'incidents'. Other than the odd minor injury, bridge life was going smoothly. Dan was looking weary when we intersected briefly at the cafe. He seemed preoccupied and he probably was. Or maybe it was because I'd been rather cool to him since New Year. I just figured it was best. There was no future there. Yes, maybe a fling, but then what? I was going back to New York in March.

Did I really want to get involved with an ex-army tradie from Tasmania twelve years my junior?

To Max I said: 'I'm having lunch with the Chinese.'

∽

Max dropped me at JC's and I watched her drive away in her Subaru all-wheel drive, the car of choice for Tasmanians. Back in my downstairs apartment, I made a berry smoothie and sat out by the pool to drink it while I considered my lunch date.

May Chen and I saw each other every week at the Friday bridge meeting. JC or Frank, or both, Mick Feltham, Chen, the government PR people . . . it was the weekly update and incubation chamber for good-news stories all the way. Last Friday, May Chen had invited me to lunch. She had texted me an address on the waterfront in Battery Point, a little heritage suburb right beside the city.

Were the Chinese involved in Australian politics? Their main focus appeared to be infrastructure and economics in Africa, in the Middle East, in the Pacific and southern Europe. No different to any emerging power historically.

There were also many different sorts of Chinese. Mainland Chinese, Hong Kong Chinese, Malaysian Chinese, Cambodian Chinese, Filipino Chinese, Thai Chinese, Vietnamese Chinese, Australian Chinese, American Chinese. There were a lot of them. A pretty significant part of Australia's population was Chinese. Didn't they deserve representation? And, ultimately, was it any different to a whole lot of Anglo-Saxons taking over the world two hundred years ago?

With the US in protectionist mode, the likelihood of global warfare was escalating. The Chinese and the Russians had been in a standoff in the South China Sea since the US had withdrawn. In the last two thousand years, we'd had the rise of the Greeks, the Romans, the Ottomans, the Spanish, the British, the Germans, the Japanese and the US. Now it was China's turn. I was interested to see what they would make of the task.

There was logic in Australia allying with China. If China ceased the flow of students to Australia, or the flow of tourists, it was going to hurt big time. Australia was vulnerable. A great continent sitting pretty in the southern hemisphere with all its land, its mineral riches, so few people, so little forward thinking, and no sovereign wealth fund. Despite one hundred and fifty years and more of pulling resources up out of the ground, Australia was vulnerable to the vagaries of world economics. It could have been robust. Could have shaved a profit off everything dug up and sold and put it into a fund, like the Oil Fund in Norway. That would have made Australia a major player investing internationally. Could have protected Australia from every market fluctuation. But that golden opportunity was gone. Instead, Australian governments stumbled about looking for quick ways to make money, and some of those decisions looked very flimsy. Was the Bruny Bridge another one?

I'm trained to analyse variables. Across the world, populist leaders have risen up on the discontent of the disenfranchised. Some of those leaders were left, some right, and some supposedly centrist. Lots of them were building their platform on religious doctrine. Voters were increasingly incensed at the world's failure to deliver the better life they were promised. And women were always the first casualties of extremism and war. The women most affected by domestic violence in the US came from Christian homes. The women most violated in the Middle East and Africa lived in Muslim homes. A hundred years ago, Bertrand Russell wondered why women, once they got the vote, voted for men at all.

People were always frightened of losing out, of having what was theirs taken away; they were resentful at being overrun, of never getting ahead. If someone in Tasmania could sell the family farm, then so be it. It was a free country. Everyone for himself and herself.

Australian foreign land ownership rules let almost anyone buy anything. That wasn't the case in smarter countries. But Australia's best farming and grazing land had been sold off with not a thought to food and water security for Australians over the coming generations. Energy security too. In Western Australia they'd just privatised their grid and given forty-nine per cent ownership to a Chinese consortium which, when a journalist looked into it, was basically funded by the Chinese government. That's globalisation.

As for the Chinese, they were buying up assets wherever they found them: Greece, Turkey, Africa, South America, the Pacific and now Tasmania. The Belt and Road Initiative was about buying cooperation by way of Chinese investment in ports, rail, bridges, roads, oil and gas pipelines. It still felt like Bruny was a very out of the way place for China to want to connect to, but maybe it was the Antarctic thing . . .

The bombing of the Bruny Bridge had been the impetus for the passing of the foreign labour laws. The Chinese got to sell us more steel. Now there were Chinese workers arriving by the plane load in mining areas in remote parts of Australia through summer. There was talk of bringing in foreign teachers, too, because there was a shortage now in inner-city Melbourne and Sydney. But this wasn't really about a skills shortage. It was about the cost of labour. The corporate sector didn't want to reduce profits and increase wages. The government didn't want to increase taxes. People weren't paid for the wealth they helped generate. They were paid whatever amount they were desperate enough to accept. The lack of long-term planning by government after government was biting Australia hard. Everything felt like a kneejerk reaction. I'd watched that in the US after Obama. Kneejerk politics got dangerous fast.

Australia was educating Chinese students at a vast rate. It left the whole education sector vulnerable to any shift in policy from Beijing, but nobody seemed to think it was a problem. I'd met with the vice-chancellor of the Tasmanian university, and we'd chatted at social functions too. He was well-meaning. Academics always think they're well-meaning. But the real world chews up altruists and feeds them to the narrow-minded. One word from the Eternal Fragrant President and a billion-dollar river of students flowing to Australia could be diverted to India, the Middle East, or simply back to China again.

The Chinese Communist Party espoused very different values and loyalties to those held by the everyday Australian. But who was the everyday Australian now? Was it the second-generation Australian born of Indian parents? A fifth-generation Queensland farmer? Was it an outer suburban couple in Melbourne both working full-time with their three kids at state schools? The single mother juggling work and uni to get a better qualification? The indigenous grandmother in Alice. Or a gay couple in Sydney with their European car and annual skiing holiday? There was no everyday Australian, no matter what politicians told us.

'What are Australian values, now?' I'd asked Max.

'Jeepers,' she'd said. 'Kindness? I'm not so sure. Europe has done integration of immigrants so much better than us. At least until recently.'

I agreed. In the seventies, Australia had been the nation of the fair go—an idea embraced from the prime minister down. One wins, we all win. Me, Max and JC had grown up in that era. There was free university too. A whole lot of very smart kids from poorer homes got educated. But it was bled dry, that national heart. And the person who drained that goodwill was a little man called John Howard, a tracksuit-wearing conservative prime minister who, over the eleven years of his leadership, persuaded an optimistic nation to become pessimistic. How did he do that? With fear. And the greatest fear facing Australia? Refugees. Not the droughts, floods and fires predicted by climate change scientists. Nor the loss of food production that would flow from that. Refugees.

Millions of refugees running from impossible landscapes, from cities bombed to dust, from terrible regimes, from the fear of never being able to offer their children a better life. Or simply because they could no longer grow food in a place where it hadn't rained in ten years. Millions of refugees were wanting to come live next door to you, if you believed the John Howards, and the Murdoch press. What a legacy Rupert Murdoch had left in his wake. Dumbing down the national conversation in the US, the UK and Australia to three-word headlines and shock-jock opinion. Intelligent commentary and reporting had withered on the vine, save for a few notable exceptions. The political left splintered into a hundred self-interest groups. The right sprouted a whole lot of hatred. And big business kept getting bigger.

I thought about the Chinese and Antarctica. What no-one knew was how difficult it might be to stop the Chinese if they did begin mineral exploration down there without consent. We hadn't stopped the Japanese and their whaling, despite diplomatic pressure. Mining in the subcontinent was way more problematic. I wanted to believe it wouldn't come to hostilities. I am, despite everything, a great believer in diplomacy.

Mind you, nothing had stopped the Chinese marching into Tibet. The world had let that happen because it was China. So there were going to be things to negotiate.

People worried about the Russians because of their intervention in western elections, but Russia wasn't a consideration. Australia's exports to the US were a tad behind Russia's, but the new US tariffs were killers, worse for Russia than Australia, and toughest of all on China. Current US foreign policy was like the bully who climbs a tower and lobs rocks at everyone below, and then wonders why he's unpopular. At some point, that tower is going to get stormed.

Standing with China was the wiser move for Australia. Whether people liked it or not, they were the emerging power. A thousand years ago a Viking was a king in England. A whole lot of Christians were off on crusades, running amok fighting the Turks in the Middle East. The Muslims were in their Golden Age. The Holy Roman Empire was Europe's most powerful state. Jewish people were being persecuted and black people were slaves. There were incredible kingdoms in Cambodia, China and Japan. A lot can change over millennia. And some things don't.

What came to light over the next few weeks, I could never have predicted, sitting there on that benign Monday morning drinking my smoothie and considering the current global picture. It completely blindsided me. And it blindsided Tasmanians too. But not JC. Oh, no. My little brother, at that moment up at his cliff-top beach house reading the morning paper, my brother the traitor, knew about it all along.

CHAPTER THIRTY

May Chen's apartment overlooked the harbour. The company she worked for, Shoughan International, was majority owned by the Chinese government. They had projects all over the world.

The food was simple and elegant. May had invited the businessman Henry Liu and Andrew Wong, head of the China–Australia Relations Institute, both of whom I'd met at the lunch at the winery before Christmas. It was just the four of us.

May raised her glass before we all commenced lunch and said, 'I thought that this was a good opportunity to get to know one another a little better. We spend all our time in meetings . . . so, Astrid, we are keen to know more about you.'

Not a topic I'm good at, but I have the required patter. Still, I kept wondering when it was going to come up.

And then, after the main course, Andrew Wong said, 'I heard we had a tragedy, Astrid. On the bridge.'

I looked at May and she nodded almost imperceptibly.

'Your discretion is valued,' said Wong. 'We want to reassure you that his family has been compensated. It is taken care of.

There will be no further events of this nature, you can be assured.'

A son in China is a very valuable thing. If he had been under forty years of age, he may have been the one child his mother had been allowed to have. Or keep.

Were they all Beijing operatives? Wong, of course. May Chen almost certainly. MSS or 3PLA, China's two branches of secret service. But Henry Liu? Henry Liu was a man trying to escape something, and it may have been the Chinese Communist Party. If so, why was he here, and not a hundred miles from May Chen and this bridge?

Wong had to excuse himself at the end of lunch to catch a flight to Melbourne, and so it was just the three of us. I was still wondering why this lunch had taken place here and not in a restaurant. Was Chen trying to disarm me? Was it all being recorded? There was another agenda, clearly.

May took me on a tour of the apartment, showing me her collection of fifty rare Japanese prints detailing a walk from Tokyo to Kyoto six hundred years before. When we re-joined Henry, he had made tea. He suggested we take it out onto the balcony. The balcony caught the afternoon sun and was furnished with soft-cushioned couches. Across the harbour an enormous white cruise liner was moored, dwarfing every building on the waterfront.

The balcony was entirely private and, but for a very long lens on the deck of that cruise liner, this was a balcony fit for private purpose. Perhaps it was also free of recording devices. If I was about to have the 'other' conversation, I wondered what it might be.

Henry presented me with a large wrapped gift.

'For the new year,' he said.

I opened it to find a framed watercolour of the view from my home. It was strikingly beautiful.

'Where did you get it?' I asked.

'I painted it,' he said. 'I like that hill above your house.'

'Ah,' I said. So he knew about my house. It was Hobart. Word got around. Word got around even faster on Bruny, even if Henry's place was at Cloudy Bay and I was on Dennes Point fifty kilometres away. Still, was this picture a warning? *We are watching you.*

'You didn't include the bridge,' I said.

'It's a very precise moment in time,' he said. 'I did this painting several years ago before the bridge was announced. I had it framed for you when I realised where you lived on Bruny.'

'You are a wonderful artist, Henry,' I said.

'He is,' said May. 'It's what he really loves about Tasmania. He has time to paint.'

'I want to be like Winston Churchill and spend eternity mastering watercolour,' said Henry. 'Because a lifetime isn't long enough.'

'How do you feel about the bridge, Henry?' I asked.

Henry paused.

'He feels the same way I feel about it,' said May.

'But I have the luxury of being able to voice my opinions,' said Henry.

'Perhaps a better question,' said May, 'is how we both feel about Tasmania.'

'So how do you both feel about Tasmania?'

Henry said, 'When I first arrived, I kept wondering when it would all go wrong, and I would wake up to find it crowded and polluted with no blue sky. But it hasn't gone wrong. It's so quiet at night I feel I can hear creation. When I first left China it was to go to the University of Chicago. My apartment was tiny, at the back of a building, but even in Chicago, and in my own tiny place where no-one else lived, it was the first time in my life I really heard silence. And it was Chicago! So here—here—it's as if this is where they invented sound.' He smiled and I nodded.

'There is a Chinese saying,' he continued, '"When you drink the water, remember the spring." I think Tasmanians are lovely people. Generous. Kind. But they do not keep enough of an eye on the spring. When I left home, I didn't know there were places that were uncrowded. If the thing that makes you unique can be protected, then that is what Tasmanians must do.'

May said, 'We both came here with very different ideas. I am here—like you, Astrid—to ensure the bridge project proceeds with maximum ease and community support. But my loyalty . . .' She hesitated. 'Our government is not known for its benevolence. If it sends workers, if it offers special prices on steel, if it aligns with the Australian government, the Tasmanian government, then there is a very substantial reason. The Bruny Bridge is very important.'

'What does this bridge have to do with the Belt and Road Initiative?' I asked. 'This is not a key location in the world's shipping or transport. There are no resources, at least not that we know about.'

'Of course, water will be much more valuable than coal or zinc soon enough,' said May.

'The bridge is something to do with water? Is there a plan to ship Tasmanian water?'

'We will see,' Henry said enigmatically.

There was a long silence. Nothing else was forthcoming.

'Tell me, May,' I said, 'I am intrigued by Mr Gao. We have not seen him again. Will he be returning from China soon?'

She smiled. 'Forgive me, Astrid. I brought him to the meeting only because we know that in Tasmania, in a room full of men, a young woman would never be taken seriously—let alone an attractive Asian woman. Regardless of who I represent or my credentials. So I posed as his assistant and interpreter.'

May Chen was Shoughan's lead here. Of course she was. All these weeks she had been posing as his representative after Mr Gao had been called back to China.

'May is thinking of staying here in Tasmania, beyond the bridge,' said Henry.

'You're going to move to Tasmania?'

'I think you should tell Astrid about your father,' said Henry.

'My father is at Cloudy Bay,' said May. 'At Henry's home. He is my only family. My father's brother, my uncle, was the mayor of a small town in China. He disagreed with a plan to build a large shopping centre. Six men grabbed him off the street and held him down while a cement truck ran over him. There were witnesses but his death was ruled accidental. The official finding was that he had stepped in front of the truck. Stories circulated that he had taken advantage of state funds. His wife had to make a public apology. My father, his older brother, is an academic. He is an expert in late Ming Chinese literature. Because of his brother's alleged corruption his social score was going to be lowered to the point where he would have no longer been employed at the university and he would have been unable to travel. You know about this?'

The Chinese government had mapped every citizen and scored them. The score was drawn from everyone they associated with, all the suppliers they used and all their online interactions. If you were considered a good consumer and citizen, aligned with Communist Party ideals, your score was high. If you stepped out of line, or you were associated with the wrong people or groups, your score dropped. If you had a low score, you were unable to enrol at certain schools, be employed by certain institutions or companies, and you weren't allowed to travel, either within China or overseas.

'He did not travel here under his own name,' May said.

May Chen had just told me she had helped her father flee China.

'But he is safe now,' said Henry.

'My father is Gao Enzhu,' said May. She smiled at Henry and he smiled back.

It was only then that I realised May Chen and Henry Liu were in love. So maybe Beijing didn't come first. Love did.

I looked again at Henry's painting. 'What don't I know about the bridge?' I asked.

'The long term,' said May Chen. 'None of us do. But I am sure you have your doubts, as do I. What I do not know is how far those doubts will take you. You too have a loyalty to your family. But perhaps, this time, Astrid, it is misplaced.'

CHAPTER THIRTY-ONE

JC and Stephanie were back from their time at Spring Beach and JC was rarely home before eight. With the girls still on summer holidays, the evenings were slow and simple. The weather was still hot, but it was also damp and balmy. It was an unusual combination for Hobart. More suited to the tropics. Stephanie made an excellent pre-dinner margarita. It seemed like the right summer for tequila.

'Everyone said climate change would be good for Tassie,' said Stephanie. 'I do love warm weather, but not this damp sticky heat. I just want blue skies again! If I wanted this, I'd live in Queensland.'

'God, I had to battle my way through Salamanca this morning,' I said. 'I feel like we need resident car parks beside the disabled spots so people can simply live their lives. Where are all these tourists staying?'

'One in seventeen Tasmanian homes are now registered on Airbnb,' said Stephanie. 'I know so many people who have rented out their home and gone interstate, or camping. Did you hear how today eight thousand passengers came ashore off the cruise boats?'

We could see the new ships in the distance, moored at the dock in the city.

'Apparently both ships rang ahead to advise that, between them, they had more than three hundred passengers restricted to their cabins. So the hospital chief rang the health department begging for the ships to be quarantined.'

'What was the problem?' I asked.

'One ship had gastro,' said Stephanie. 'On the other they'd all come down with a severe flu. The hospital only has four isolation beds. But the health department refused to quarantine the passengers.'

'They came ashore?'

'Yes. Totally blocked up the emergency department. It was a nightmare, I'm told. I mean we are this close'—and here she held her fingers about a centimetre apart—'to a major epidemic sailing into Hobart and we simply don't have the medical facilities to cope.'

'Because the tourism department . . .' I began.

'That's right,' said Stephanie. 'Because quarantining a ship would be bad publicity. I'm fed up with it. I actually rang Max. I thought, if JC is too busy to turn his mind to this, then Max needed to know.'

I observed Stephanie for a moment. 'Will you tell JC? That you rang Max?'

'He's got enough on his plate, don't you think?' she said.

'You're a brave woman, Stephanie.'

'Thanks,' she said, smiling. 'There have to be benefits to my sister-in-law being the ex-head of the Nursing Federation.'

'And the Opposition leader?'

'Well, yes . . .'

'I'm rather touched you trust me enough to tell me.'

'Why wouldn't I trust you?'

'Well, you're trusting I won't mention it to JC.'

'Oh, Astrid, if I didn't know that, I don't think you'd be here at all.'

I decided not to enquire further.

'Do you think that headline was right today?' she asked. 'You know, "Coleman Inc."?'

The front cover and a double-page spread of *The Mercury* had featured the three Coleman children and their roles in present-day Tasmania. Gilbert Farris had basically accused JC and Max of colluding to run the state as a Coleman family business, stitching up government policy between them. Amy O'Dwyer questioned their united front on the bridge when there were still so many questions around why the project was greenlighted. There was a bit about Max's support of me and the alleged quarter of a million dollars I was being paid for my role. There was even a picture of the three of us on the balcony on Christmas Day, taken by someone with a long lens.

JC and Max had issued statements confirming their commitment to the bridge as a project of state significance that required exceptional circumstances following the bomb. That included the appointment of a specialist in conflict resolution, someone the Tasmanian people could trust. But I knew the money I was being paid would not go down well. The fact it wasn't true was immaterial now. I could hardly say that it was under by fifty thousand dollars, including my success bonus when it was all done. I'm expensive. Peace is. I'd be sure to get a few cold, hard stares onsite. And maybe a new respect. Men liked money and I was always dealing with men. I suspected Frank Pringle of leaking the information about my contract, but I hadn't anything but my gut to prove it.

'I think Viper will be annoyed that he wasn't featured in some way,' I said.

'Sidelined by Coleman Inc.,' said Stephanie, using her finger to dab at the salt around the edge of her glass. 'Mind you, he's always got something up his sleeve. You watch him reassert his significance in the coming weeks. He has a way of coming out of left field.'

'What does JC make of him?' I asked, observing with interest this shrewd Stephanie who was rarely on show when JC and the children were about.

'JC knows Viper's a snake in the grass. But he also knows that he can't run the jungle without him. I'm actually in a book club with his wife. She's very smart. Don't know how she puts up with him. But, then, I'm sure there're people who think the same about me.'

We sat in silence for a little while. The thunk of balls and the screeches of the girls could be heard from the tennis court.

'I'm going to have to get a screen put up, aren't I?' said Stephanie. 'Whoever took that picture on Christmas Day, they can do it again. It's endless sometimes. But on we go.'

I nodded.

I was thinking about how I had crossed the channel with Dan at 7 am. Then I had watched Dan have a heated exchange in the morning meeting with Mick Feltham over pushing the teams to work faster. Dan was coming off night shift and he was in no mood for a fight. I could see he was right at the edge of saying, 'So you want another fatality?'

Feltham must have known about the Chinese worker. But we had never discussed it. Event. Incident. Fatality. There was no official name. There had been no event. We were all meant to have amnesia. But both Dan and I had found a bottle of very limited edition whisky on our Bruny doorsteps a few days after the event. I had yet to open it.

The works across the Channel at North-West Bay had been hit by lightning in another storm a few days back, and it had caused problems with some of the machinery. There were delays on bridge sections. Dan was explaining to Feltham that speeding things up, once the delivery schedule was back to normal, wasn't the answer. I could see that the public glory of a statue had begun to colour Feltham's thinking. The wellbeing of a few workers—their hands, eyes, backs, lives even—was becoming less of a concern to him. After all, someone had died and no-one had made a fuss. Collateral damage.

At times like this, watching Dan and Feltham struggle to communicate with each other, I thought how there were eight billion people on the planet with very little idea how to communicate effectively. I was meant to feel okay about this because at the grocery store there was an excess of lettuce varieties, sheep's yoghurt and coconut ice cream, artisanal tomatoes and paleo muesli varieties. But if I had a poor social media score, or wanted to cancel an automatic debit, it was bad luck because there wasn't anyone to call. There were just Frequently Asked Questions and chat rooms and layer upon layer of opacity and bureaucracy. In my darker moments, I felt as if twenty-first-century existence had been assessed by a quantity surveyor who had determined we were all just parts, not people.

When I had complained to my son Paul about how I'd been unable to solve a double-billing problem at a company, he'd said, 'They're not focused on in-bound traffic, Mom.'

Not focused on in-bound traffic. Someone seemed to have forgotten in all this that the in-bound traffic kept the machine running. That great traffic jam every morning on the freeway going into every city was filled with the people who made the machine work. No doubt, soon enough, we would almost all be replaced by robots, and the rise of the billionaires would be complete. The people who owned the robots, who employed the techies ignoring in-bound traffic, those who could afford high-protein, low-carb medical care and organic sex, they were going to be sitting pretty in their driverless cars. They would be the ones the car would save when it had to choose between the wellbeing of the driver and the life of a pedestrian crossing the street. There are people working on those algorithms right now. Whose life is worth more when we are in driverless cars? That's one of the things facial recognition software will give us. The ability to instantly recognise the rich from the poor. If both you and a billionaire were crossing the road, you didn't stand a chance. The driverless car would avoid the billionaire and kill you. The GOP had proved that to every sick kid in America.

This was the problem with growing older, I thought. Even with two politicians in the family, I felt powerless. And that was why a 7 pm margarita had been invented, no doubt. So that when you got old enough to realise what was at stake, you could also anaesthetise yourself against the pain.

'You're very quiet,' said Stephanie. 'You okay?'

'Do you think JC has sold Bruny to the Chinese, Steph?' It had been nagging at me ever since the lunch with May Chen.

'God, I can't believe people are saying that,' Stephanie said. She'd obviously heard the rumour. If it was true and she knew it, she was a marvellous actress.

'He would never do that. He loves Bruny,' she said.

But does he love it more than his political career, I wanted to ask her. What was the long term May Chen had suggested? What did JC really want for Tasmania? What would it cost?

'Seven weeks,' Stephanie said. 'Then you can escape all this, lucky thing.'

'Are we prisoners, the two of us?'

'Political wives are all prisoners, Ace,' she said. 'Everywhere I go, people remind me where JC is doing badly, what's going to bring him undone. Tennis parents, coaches, at the supermarket, at the fish shop, at the health food store, when I'm buying school supplies, on the phone, via email. It's a never-ending one-way dialogue. I don't mean to complain. I know this is what he does, what he's passionate about. He's cut out for it, but I'm not sure I am. It will go on for another four years, unless Max pulls a rabbit out of her hat. And can you imagine how awful he'd be in opposition? I doubt he'd resign, if Max wins.'

'Did you know JC wanted to go into politics, back when you were, well, making plans together?'

'Yes,' she said. 'I was rather starstruck by that at the time. I was only twenty-four. He told me he wanted to be premier of Tasmania. Felt it was his calling. He and your dad had talked about it many times. Then he told me he was going to run for the Liberals. He thought your father would never speak to him again. I was sure that wasn't true.'

'But you offered to step in, keep us all together, no matter what?'

'Yes,' she said. 'So you see I'm caught in my own ideals. The perfect wife.'

'You are the perfect wife,' I said. 'At least from over here, that's what it looks like.'

'Even if I've caused my husband some nasty headlines in the paper tomorrow?'

'And possibly saved an epidemic,' I said.

She poured us another round from the cocktail shaker and raised her glass to mine.

'To missions accomplished,' she said.

And we clinked.

CHAPTER THIRTY-TWO

Two days out from Australia Day, JC announced that the prime minister—his friend, Tasmania's friend—was flying in to Hobart to officially launch JC's election campaign. And our mother went into hospital. Phillip had settled her into Calvary, the Catholic hospital she preferred, and her oncologist was monitoring her. Max had rung me to let me know and we'd all agreed to meet at JC's.

'Her white cell count is too low,' Phillip explained. I had come home from another meeting on Bruny. With the school holidays nearing an end, several groups were planning a last hurrah on the bridge protest. At least I was informed, which meant JC was informed.

'They may keep her in for a week or two,' said Phillip. 'She's asked me to stock up the Hendrick's.'

'I'll go see her after dinner,' I said.

'I'll go in tomorrow,' said Stephanie.

Max and JC looked at one another. We all knew their schedules. There wasn't time for a sick mother in all this. But it would play to the sympathy vote. So who would pull that card first?

Max said, 'How about we do a doorstop on the hospital steps together declaring our mother is unwell. We find a great picture of her—from twenty years ago. She'll be delighted to be in the news, and we're back on the campaign.'

JC shrugged. 'Sounds fine,' he said, although I could see he thought he'd missed an opportunity. But having agreed to it in front of me and Stephanie, he wasn't going to default.

When Max and Phillip had left and Stephanie had gone upstairs, JC and I had a last drink together in his office.

'By the way,' he said, 'the dinner with the prime minister? Becky Walton will be there. She's one of his advisers.'

'Becky Walton?'

'Rebecca Standish,' said JC.

'Rebecca Standish?' I said.

'The same.' JC smiled. 'She's not married anymore but she kept his name.'

I looked at JC and a wave of memories washed over me.

'I told her you were here,' said JC.

'How is she?'

'Done well for herself. You knew she was in government, yeah? Well, now she works for the PM.'

We stood and stared out at the lights of Sandy Bay and the city.

'Is she here often?' I asked.

'No . . . yes . . . a few times a year. Obviously not since you came, or I would have told you.'

'So, how are you two these days?' I'd remembered how he'd mentioned Becky after that first lunch with the Chinese.

JC turned away and I could feel him blushing. Even if I couldn't see his face, I knew the way his shoulders moved when he blushed.

'Does Stephanie know?' I asked.

'Know what?'

'JC . . .'

'I've never mentioned it.'

'You've never mentioned it? Never introduced them?'

'They've been introduced. Functions, you know.'

'So Stephanie doesn't know that this is the girl you were madly in love with for about ten years, who caused you so much grief? You've never mentioned that to your wife?'

'As I said, it never came up, Ace. I told Steph the truth: she's an old family friend. Jesus, quit with the inquisition.'

I observed my brother. 'Once a politician, always a politician,' I said.

'And what's that supposed to mean?'

'Everything on a need-to-know basis. Even with your wife.'

'Drop it, Ace. It's nothing. It was years ago.'

I nodded, took another sip of whisky, felt it burn all the way down my throat. JC was lying.

'Have you sold Bruny to the Chinese?' I asked.

He did not have his face organised. I saw sheer panic and then he laughed. 'Fuck, Ace, where did that come from?'

'Have you sold Bruny to the Chinese?' I repeated.

He was rattled, angry. 'No, Ace, I haven't sold Bruny to the Chinese.' He sat down behind his desk.

'You've done something, haven't you?'

'You're paranoid, Ace. I thought you were better than that.'

'You don't get to turn this around,' I said. 'This isn't about me. This is about you. If I find you've screwed me over here, JC, made me cover for some plan you've hatched that you're keeping secret . . .'

'I wouldn't do that,' he said.

'It's like Becky, isn't it?' I said, running a finger along the edge of his desk. 'Choosing what people need to know.'

'Becky thought it best nobody knew. Keep the past in the past. So that's the way it is,' he said.

'She still has you on the run.'

'It's not like that, Ace. She's just really private. Please.'

He stood up and came around the desk, pulling me into a hug. 'We're on the same team, you and me. We've always been on the same team, Ace. Don't let all this conspiracy shit get to you. It's bullshit. You know how much I care about Tasmania. And Stephanie and the girls. All of it.'

Being single for so long, physical contact has become a little strange. Like I'm out of practice. I let him hug me. I sank into that big body of my twin brother and remembered for a moment what it was to stop. To find rest in another person's affection. When we broke away, he looked emotional. I had a bad feeling about that.

❦

There was a fine mist as I arrived at Government House, enough to wet the fronds of grass and the leaves of ferns, but not enough to fill dams. I stood for a moment in the driveway and took in the grand Georgian sandstone house and its grounds. It might have been from *Citizen Kane*. It looked like the home of a wealthy media magnate. The stone had been cut from a quarry on the land. The quarry had filled with rainwater over time, and was now a sunken garden and ornamental lake. I wandered over to the stairs that descended to the lake, and watched a mother duck lead nine baby ducks across the water.

'Can we help you, madam?' came a voice. I turned to find a man in a dark suit. Very *Men in Black* with his earpiece and dark glasses. He was extending a large open black umbrella to me.

'I'm here for the reception,' I said. Obviously, I wanted to add, my blue silk dress and high heels surely giving me away. I had already passed through security. Nothing like the old days, when guests to Government House simply had to present an embossed invitation at the front door. Now it was all photo IDs before visitors even made it inside the front gates. 'I've always loved the lake.'

'Shall we go in?' he said. 'We don't want the guests getting wet.'

I sighed, lamenting the loss of my private moment, and followed him. It was the prime minister, after all. Best not to be late.

∽

Inside the front doors, my ID was checked again and I was helped out of my coat. Then, along with several other guests, I was chaperoned along the hallway into the corner room that overlooked the Derwent River. The room was buzzing with people in conversation.

JC spotted me and indicated that I should join him. He was standing with Edward Lowe, who looked pleased to see me and kissed me on both cheeks.

'You look stunning,' he said.

JC winked at me. Then he introduced me to the governor, her husband and several parliamentary colleagues, federal and state, whom I had yet to meet, and their husbands and wives. Stephanie was in a dress of pale smoke and pearls. She is strikingly beautiful, Stephanie. She can look almost plain in her track pants and t-shirts. And then she does this. Puts her hair up, adds a little make-up, and she's amazing. I wondered what she made of all that weight JC had gained. I wondered if she still found him attractive. She was loyal, I sure knew that about her. Well, until it came to biosecurity in Tasmania. Everyone has a point where loyalty wavers.

It had made the front page of the newspaper. BIO-SCANDAL! The whole fiasco of the cruise ships and no policing, no ability to quarantine sick passengers and get medical help to them on board. The risk of an epidemic, if they were allowed into our hospitals. It wasn't going to die down quickly.

Max had been quoted saying that, being an island, we needed biosecurity to be robust. Fruit fly had caused millions of dollars of damage a few years back. She was committing to biosecurity at all entry points into the state, if Labor was elected. It was now a core promise of her election campaign. Code for: it may well change. I don't mean to be cynical, but we all know that's true.

Waiters were carrying silver trays bearing sparkling wine, beer, gin and tonics or sparkling water. I chose the sparkling water. I thought I might need my wits about me.

Then the prime minister arrived and everyone turned to gaze at him. He was a businessman before he went into politics, and he wore a multimillionaire's suit, a shirt that cost a nurse's weekly salary and a silk tie that probably cost four weeks of unemployment benefits. Beside him were Aid-n-Abet and Barney Viper. I reckoned Viper had maybe one more election in him before he'd be wanting to retire, which always made a politician, like a chief engineer, give acute consideration to his legacy.

And there was Rebecca Standish who had once been Becky Walton. When I'd last seen her, she'd been an earnest bespectacled student who chose study over exercise and loved Jethro Tull. She'd also been a smoker at fourteen. And she had driven JC wild. His first love. I'd seen that girl emerge from JC's bedroom, adjust her spectacles, tighten her ponytail, and look to all the world as if she'd still be a virgin when she was forty. Now there she was, in an impeccable black evening dress and heels, a sassy pixie cut and no glasses. She had a killer curve to her figure. She remained at the PM's side as he moved about the room and JC flanked his other side.

When the PM's party reached me, I saw Becky's face light up, but I discreetly shook my head in warning. She didn't miss a beat. We shook hands as if we were distant acquaintances, and she said, 'It's lovely to see you again, Astrid.'

The PM said to me, 'I hear you've got the community settled down.'

'It's a fragile truce,' I said. In photos the PM could almost look handsome, but in real life he resembled a koala. 'Everyone has been keen to ensure they are not suspects, Prime Minister. It's made them a little more malleable than they might otherwise have been.'

'Just keep them quiet for another five weeks, that will do,' said the PM. 'Isn't that right, John?'

'It is, Prime Minister,' said JC.

Then a bell rang, and we were all ushered into the adjoining dining room.

I found my place setting. Scanning the people on either side, I saw I was between Scrutiny Australia and Scrutiny Tasmania. Scrutiny Australia was a government initiative to oversee Very Large Projects and eliminate pork-barrelling. That is, ministers putting projects into their own electorates to curry favour with voters. Scrutiny Australia was already engaged in a conversation with his local equivalent from Scrutiny Tasmania when I sat down between them. Then Rebecca Standish took her seat opposite Scrutiny Australia.

I watched her carry on a polite conversation with Scrutiny Australia while I engaged Scrutiny Tas. All the time I was remembering the cigarettes Becky and I had shared at age fourteen, the first time we had tried marijuana together (also at fourteen), the first time we had got drunk (on tequila no less, again at fourteen), the mad crush JC had on her, the sleepovers in my room where she'd climb out my window and into JC's, climbing back into mine in the morning, always refusing to call him her boyfriend and always remaining steadfastly my friend through all kinds of dramas I've worked hard to forget. And then I left for university in the US. Becky had kept up the correspondence for several years after she'd moved to Canberra and landed a job at Parliament House. She'd done a Masters in politics up there and we would have had lots in common over the years, but I got weary of all the drama between her and JC. Somehow all his relationships came unstuck over her. Finally, he'd moved to the UK and there he'd met Stephanie. Becky had sent me a birthday card for many years, but things had tapered off. It had been me who had let the friendship go, along with all the other parts of Tasmania I had shed as I cemented my life overseas.

There were twenty-four at the table. JC was seated to the right of the PM with the governor to the left. Stephanie was between Edward and the Governor's husband. Rebecca became engaged with the person beside her and Scrutiny Australia turned to me.

He was heavyset with a sinking face and kind eyes. He said he'd had a site visit at the bridge today and how amazing it was. I agreed. Then he said, quietly, that in truth it remained extraordinary to him that the government had invested so heavily in the project.

'Didn't you have to greenlight it?' I asked.

'No, that was done from above,' he said. 'Let's hope it creates the kind of flood they're all anticipating.'

'Tourists?' I clarified.

'It will take half the world to get a return,' he said. 'But still, if it's good for Tasmania . . .'

I frowned. 'That's a thing?'

He looked into his wineglass. 'That's the talk. If it's good for Tasmania, then it's good for Australia.'

'I didn't know the island had assumed such a prominent position in federal strategy.'

'Indeed,' he said. 'I guess it was Western Australia a few years back. Now it's Tassie's turn.'

We discussed the timeframe, and other major projects around the country. He shared a few pertinent stories, and I shared some too from the various hot zones over the years.

'This must seem tepid, after all that,' Scrutiny observed.

'Not in the least,' I said. 'I always find family the most treacherous location.'

He chuckled. 'I wondered how things were in Camelot.'

'So, seeing as I've asked everyone else over the past three months,' I said, 'how do you feel about the level of Chinese investment in Australia?'

'Oh, it's not nearly as high as people make out in the media. You have to look at percentages. Gina Rinehart might have a Chinese joint venture, but only thirty per cent of that is actually from a Chinese company. I think it's still a bit of the yellow peril. We've never had our major trading partner be neither a democracy nor an ally, so I think it's wise of the PM to make them an ally. It's the new order. Without China, this country would be in dire straits right now.'

'And elsewhere? In the Middle East, for example?'

'Well, China built that port in Pakistan. Now that was done for two reasons. First, to frustrate India; and second, to establish a beachhead in the Indian Ocean. No doubt China wants to extend its influence. But it's not the same as when the US goes into Syria and says, "We're going to regime change here."'

'What do you make of the Eternal Fragrant President?' I asked.

'Hmmm,' he said. 'It's a concern for China. Strongman leadership is never a good idea. Most of them aren't benevolent.'

'And for Australians?'

'You and I might be discussing this, but out in the suburbs Australians aren't discussing the Chinese. Maybe not even here in Tasmania,' he said.

'What do you think they *are* discussing?'

'*Married at First Sight?*'

I nodded.

'I remember intelligent TV,' he said. 'I'm sure you do too. BBC. *Civilisation*. *Brideshead Revisited*. What people watch now, it's the last days of the Roman Empire. It's the lead in the water.'

After the main course, the governor suggested we all move about to ensure we could catch up with as many people as possible. She was a delight, this first female governor. Made diplomacy look like a warm summer breeze.

I got into a conversation with the wife of Barney Viper, who came to introduce herself. She was, apart from being in Stephanie's book club, a member of the Tasmanian Bird Society, which supported the Bruny Friends Group—although of course being Barney's wife, she reminded me quietly, she couldn't say anything publicly. She said she was very appreciative of the work I'd done to align the Bruny Friends and Birdlife Bruny with a nature preservation strategy.

When dessert arrived, Viper came over and joined us. Together with Scrutiny Australia, we all discussed the bridge and how wonderful it was to see it nearing completion. An architectural feat. A triumph. A truly remarkable Australian achievement. I was thanked again for my role. And then I caught

Viper gazing at Becky Walton. Becky was in conversation with JC at one end of the table.

Viper said to me, 'We Tasmanians never fly far from the nest. Not in our hearts.'

I shrugged.

'Useful, of course, for your brother,' he said, in his mean oily voice, as he continued to gaze at them.

So Viper didn't like JC having a personal line of contact with the PM. Seeing JC and Becky there together, I glanced around for Stephanie. There she was, also observing JC and Becky. Ah, I thought, she senses something. Women need to trust that instinct. We have a great radar.

Then I noticed Edward Lowe also observing JC and Becky. He had an entirely blank expression, schooled, calculating. Who are you, Edward Lowe, I wondered. Then he glanced at me and smiled.

Viper said, 'Your brother may need you to stay on after the election. Have you made return plans?'

'Not yet,' I said.

'Good,' he replied.

∽

Tea and coffee were served. Edward came over and we chatted for a few minutes. We arranged a lunch date for the following week. The PM took his leave and the party broke up. Edward and Becky walked ahead up the driveway to the waiting cars and cabs. They were clearly good friends. JC, Stephanie and I travelled home together, but when we got there, JC said he had to go back to the office for a bit. It was election time. Things happened day and night. He dismissed his driver and took the car. Stephanie and I chatted for a little while then said goodnight and went our separate ways to bed.

I thought of Becky feeling the piece of paper in her coat pocket. I wondered if she'd waited until she was back at her hotel room to unfold it. I had written: *Meet you at the cave 5.30 am tomorrow—alone. Tell no-one.* There was no number but there was a small drawing of a quarter moon.

CHAPTER THIRTY-THREE

Back at the apartment, I took off my make-up and evening attire and put on my sweats. I wasn't tired, so I walked down the hill to see Dad at the nursing home. I told him about Mother going into hospital and her low white cell count. He nodded but remained silent on this. Then I told him about the dinner and the PM. I told him about Barney Viper and Scrutiny Australia and Becky Walton being there. He nodded at all this too and said: *'When sorrows come, they come not single spies, but in battalions.'*

It was close to 1 am when I left. Navigating the garden path, I saw a car I recognised pull into the facility. It was JC. I turned to go back and meet him, then I realised he was not alone.

From the passenger's side stepped Becky Walton. JC walked around to take her hand. Then he leaned down and kissed her. It was a lover's kiss. It may have had recent sex in it too. I took out my phone and photographed them. They walked towards the door hand in hand. I photographed that too. When he pressed the buzzer, they dropped hands, stepped apart, and a nurse came and let them in. By the time I had walked up the hill again, my rage at his deceit had settled into the pit of my stomach.

Viper knows, I thought, remembering how he had observed the two of them. *We Tasmanians never fly far from the nest. Not in our hearts.*

Did JC know he knew? I was enraged for Stephanie. I remembered Ben waiting by the kitchen table with a bag packed when I flew in late one night. Like some scene from *Heartburn*.

'What's this?' I had asked him.

'Astrid, there's someone else. I need to be with her.'

I'd been calm at the time. I had been reasonable.

'How long? How long has it been going on, Ben?'

'Six months. I'm really hoping we could all be family together, somehow.'

'Is she married?'

'Divorced.'

'Children?'

'Two.'

'How old is she?'

'Thirty-four.' That had stung a bit.

'Why, Ben?'

'You know, you stopped being fun a long time ago.'

'Please leave.'

'I am.'

I came home one day and he'd taken every wedding present we'd been given. When I'd asked him why, he said they'd come from *his* friends. We'd been married for so long, I didn't remember things like that anymore. I thought of everything as *ours*.

I had requested we see a counsellor. She told him to stand up and imagine a circle around him. That's your personal space, she said. Now imagine that Astrid has the same circle. So if you want to come into Astrid's space, you need to ask. That means the family home now. That's Astrid's space.

It was after that he took the paintings. Tavvy rang me. 'Mum, I just came home and there's all this art missing off the walls.'

I changed the locks. Everyone should have to get divorced from the person they're married to, just to see who that person really is.

All of that went through my mind, thinking of JC and Becky and Stephanie. Had it been going on all these years? Or had it started again recently?

∽

I waited for JC to come home. I heard the car come up the driveway half an hour later. I heard the door shut quietly and his footsteps on the side path.

I said, 'JC?'

'Jesus, Ace, what are you doing awake?'

'Come sit by the pool with me,' I said.

'Now?' he said.

'Now,' I said.

It was a warm, moist, big sky night with a waxing moon, a week from full. The pool was scrotum-shaped with lights that changed colours from blue to purple to red to green to gold.

'JC, I didn't tell you this, but I've been going down to see Dad at night. If I'm restless, can't sleep. I went tonight, after the dinner.'

I could sense him stiffen.

'I saw you with Becky. I saw you kissing Becky.'

'Ace,' he said.

'Are you fucking mad?'

'Jesus, Ace,' he said.

'JC, you're the premier. You are going to get caught. It's going to be everywhere. You think people don't talk?' I don't know why that was my first concern, but it was.

'We're really careful. It's only once or twice a year. I . . .'

So it wasn't new. It was very old.

'You're a pig. You do not deserve your wife. You do not deserve your girls,' I said.

'Easy, Ace.'

'She gave up her career for you. She keeps us together as a family. You have to stop this.'

'You know how it is with me and Becky, Ace. It's . . .'

'Oh, yes, I remember. I remember when you were fifteen and seventeen—but you're fifty-six and you're married and you're the premier of this state.'

'Ace, I don't know how to . . .'

'Why the hell didn't you marry Becky?'

'Because she wouldn't have me.'

'What does that tell you?'

'You can't say anything, Ace. You can't tell Steph.'

'Who else knows, JC?'

He was silent.

'Viper?' I asked him.

He said nothing.

'You stupid idiot. He's got that over you?'

He said nothing, just sat there silhouetted against the pool lights, his big bulky frame with the lights behind him going blue, purple, red, green.

'Has he called it in?'

'Maybe,' he said, so quietly.

'Maybe?' I was beyond furious by now.

'Yes,' he said. 'He called it in.'

'What did you have to do?'

He was silent. Then he stirred and stood up.

'I had to get the bridge finished by election day,' he said.

CHAPTER THIRTY-FOUR

It is immensely difficult in Hobart to find somewhere discreet you can meet. She was having an affair with my brother. She was the other woman in Stephanie's life. I had hardly slept at all. But that wasn't why I was meeting her. I wanted information from Becky.

I had come all the way from New York to help JC. And to help causes bigger than JC. Becky hadn't been a friend for a long time, but she had been my closest friend growing up. As the PM's adviser, she would almost certainly know what was really going on here. Even if JC didn't. Would she turn up? I was pretty sure she would.

When she emerged from under the she-oaks above the cliffs, I walked to meet her. She hugged me. 'It's so good to see you, Ace.'

'You too,' I said. And it was, despite everything.

'Beck, turn off your phone, please,' I said. 'I really mean off. Mine is off too.'

She lifted her eyebrows. She did as I asked and I shoved both our phones into a Faraday bag.

'You're not taking any chances,' she said. And I knew then that she knew something and she knew I knew something. This was going to get interesting.

At 5.30 am the light was low and the place was deserted. In another hour there would be walkers and joggers making their way between Bellerive Beach and Howrah Beach. Here on the cliff edge, away from the track, we were almost invisible. But she was right, I wasn't taking any chances.

I motioned to her to go first and followed her down over the edge on a tiny path to the cave that made us entirely invisible unless you were a seagull, or someone out on the water with binoculars. But it was early and there were no sailors, and here in the cave we were in shadow. The cave mouth looked all the way down the Derwent and we could just make out the arc of the bridge as it curved across to Bruny.

Becky said, 'I remember you having sex with Lance Van der Laan just over there.'

'Oh, God, I remember that too,' I said.

'All those ways you invented to get out of the house to see him. I was always in awe of your nerve.'

'I learned from the master,' I said. 'Mistress.'

She said, 'Should I be nervous?'

'I saw you and JC together last night at the nursing home. He knows. I've told him.'

She blanched. In her face I could still see the messed-up younger Beck. She'd had much older step-siblings and bitter parents. Our house had been her home too. Our mother had always liked Becky, mostly because Becky's mother was the centre of a certain old Sandy Bay elite that mattered. And Becky had a way of being charming that always took our mother by surprise. She remembered our mother's birthday and found just the right scarf or piece of jewellery. Her parents didn't give her their time or their interest, so they made up for it with a hefty allowance, enough for good presents and all the best drugs. And a fancy car on her seventeenth that allowed us to escape to places like this.

'Ace . . .' she said.

'I love Stephanie,' I said. 'This will ruin their marriage if she finds out.' I wasn't sure it would, but it was worth saying.

'I had to see Angus. I begged JC to take me. I was so worried I might never see him again. He's so fragile now.'

Our Dad had treated Beck like one of his own. 'Ah, the third daughter is here,' he'd say when he found Beck at the dinner table.

I waited for whatever was coming next.

Beck said very softly, 'He's always been my weakness. JC. You know that, Ace. I don't know why. Young, not so young, fat, thin, he's under my skin.'

'Why didn't you just marry him?'

'Because I didn't—I don't—believe in marriage . . . I tried. After he and Stephanie got married. But it only lasted six months. I don't want that sort of life, Ace. I don't want anyone to own me.'

Oh, I knew that feeling now.

'You need to stop, Beck. It will ruin him. It might already be ruining him. Viper knows.'

'He doesn't.'

'Oh yes he does.'

'Shit. Shit shit shit,' she said.

'But that's not why I asked you to meet.'

'Okay,' she said.

'What's going on with the bridge?'

'What do you mean?' she asked, a shade of contrived innocence in her voice.

'The Bruny Bridge, Beck,' I said.

'I can't, Ace,' she said. 'It's too dangerous. For me. For you. You don't want to get involved.'

'Believe me, I do.'

'I won't—' she began.

'I have photos of you and JC last night,' I said.

'Fuck, Ace, who did you become?'

'Someone who needs to know.'

She paused. I waited. She got a little teary. Then she reached out and took my hand. We'd been sisters of sorts.

'If I tell you, I'll be breaching the Official Secrets Act and the counterespionage laws. There's new legislation. I'll get a life sentence if anyone finds out it came from me. You understand? Twenty-five years, Ace. You too. We'll both go to prison. So if it's a choice between my name getting splashed about for having an affair with your brother or this, that's the choice you're giving me.'

If that was the truth, then it was worse than that, far worse than she could know. But I needed her to go on. I needed to know what the PM's adviser knew. Tasmanian to Tasmanian in a cave from childhood with our phones off and the sun just risen.

I pulled down the sock on my left foot. There was a quarter moon tattoo. Beck did the same. There was hers. A trip we'd taken to a backyard parlour for my eighteenth birthday. When my mother glimpsed it a few days later, she had been furious. Which had been the whole idea, of course.

'Break the rules,' said Beck.

'Break the rules,' I said. Our motto all those years ago.

'When I got your note, I thought maybe you already knew,' she said.

I looked at her. 'Beck, I need small steps. From the top?'

'You'll destroy the photos,' she said.

'Done,' I said.

'I'm not doing this to save my own skin, Ace,' she said. 'Or even JC's. I'm doing it because it's been burning a hole in me ever since I found out. I'm doing it because . . . well, you'll understand in a minute.'

'Okay,' I said.

She stared down the river, took a deep breath and let it out. 'The government is selling Tasmania to the Chinese government.'

I couldn't speak for a moment. Then I managed a feeble, 'What?'

'They're selling it,' said Beck. 'The Chinese government are going to put their high-value people here. They're also going to bring some of their most sensitive technology here, away from mainland China, to keep it safe. Agriculture, aquaculture, IT. It's a big plan.'

'To live here . . .' I repeated.

'You understand about their ranking system, yes?' she asked.

I nodded. The problem May Chen's father had run into.

'Chinese citizens chosen for this project will have an initial two-year stay. If these first residents maintain their social score, they'll get another five years,' Beck said. 'Like convicts. But the reverse. A reward, not a punishment. If they do well here in Tasmania, they'll continue to improve their social score. And they'll be the first to be able to cache their ranking for inheritance by their children. Nobody knows the input or the algorithms—it's made up of all the personal stuff about a person . . . but it extends way beyond that. Every business that interacts with China also gets a score. So this is a way for Australian businesses to grow their status in China by doing business in the new Tasmania.'

I looked at her, waiting for more. 'I don't understand,' I said, frowning.

'To stave off dissent, of course,' she said. 'Those people are going to pose the greatest threat to the Communist regime. They'll be the ones who'll get restless and want to experience capitalism. They'll urge for democracy. Want a free economy. The Communist Party is getting more and more pushback, especially since the Eternal Fragrant President announced his lifetime tenure. The CCP keeps trying to clamp down on dissidents, but the world is watching. They can't hide their concentration camps and prisoner abuse so well. So they're taking a gamble.'

'They've sold Tasmania?' I was still back at square one.

'Sold,' she said. 'As soon as the bridge is opened, it all goes into play. The Chinese have already been making significant investments here. In the past five years thousands of homes and over half a million hectares of agricultural land have found their way into Chinese hands. All either private investment, or investment that can be traced back to the Chinese government. All up, almost a third of all agricultural land and around fifteen per cent of private dwellings. They've been smart. They use Chinese already living here to buy stuff so the stats don't look so bad for foreign ownership. Students who got fast-tracked citizenship.'

'Keep talking,' I said.

'About ten years ago,' she continued, 'pressure was put on the FIRB—the Foreign Investment Review Board— to tighten the eligibility rules. A few people had started to notice that great swathes of agricultural land beyond the Blue Mountains, up in Queensland, south of Perth, were being bought up in parcels below the two-hundred-and-fifty-two-million- or even the fifty-five-million-dollar thresholds. It's all online. Every decision is made individually.'

'So someone has been stacking the Foreign Investment Review Board?'

'Well, they get politicised by government. But Beijing started taking a great interest in the members of FIRB. And our politicians, too. Suddenly there was a lot of travel to China, people being wined and dined at expensive restaurants in Canberra, Sydney, Beijing, Shanghai, Melbourne. Absolutely no different from what's happened in the past with the British and the US, let me say. The same as the Chinese telcos. Very good at throwing money around for trips and conferences for politicians and advisers.

'FIRB is not under the spotlight,' she said. She had always been like this. Super smart. A debating champion. When she was interested in something, she was articulate. 'By the time anyone finds out about these deals, the crops are already in the ground, the cattle off to market. It's a slow-burn kind of situation. Until someone noticed that the fire was starting to run wild. Suddenly big, heritage grazing land, farms with generations of history, some of the most prized land in the Hunter Valley, was going into foreign ownership. Not just any foreign ownership. To the Chinese.'

'Like the Japanese buying the Gold Coast back in the seventies. Or America buying our mining interests,' I suggested.

She nodded. 'But then the Yanks stepped away. They were our biggest investor. And our protector.'

'And how is the federal government dealing with this?' I asked. A weight was settling in the pit of my stomach.

'Cabinet already fell foul of Beijing when they tried curtailing foreign ownership in our energy plants and limiting the telcos. Beijing was getting very unhappy. If we lost the students, it would have a devastating effect on Australia's economy. The same with the tourists. They did it to Taiwan. China instructed citizens to cancel their travels plans and Taiwan lost a third of their tourism industry almost overnight.

'They did the same to South Korea,' she said. 'When South Korea put in a missile detection program with funding from the US, China ceased accepting imports, banned tourism, even did petty things like blacking out the faces of South Koreans on Chinese television shows. And South Korea backed down. The Philippines are in the same boat. Japan too.'

I squeezed my eyes shut for a moment. Beck went on. 'Russia and China have both begun to look like capitalist societies, albeit with dictators as heads of state. People like to imagine real communism is dead. And in Australia, we have no sense what the retreat of individual freedoms feels like because we've only read about it in history books—and most of us don't read those. So people can't see it coming. Then the US gets that president, and we see the values we relied on America to uphold trickle away like sand. We've all heard about the dangers of speaking out in China. Being a journalist, or a lawyer, or even a movie star who dares to question the status quo. You disappear. In America the same thing is beginning to happen. I actually like our PM, but he had to choose.'

'Choose?'

'America or China,' she said. 'We're already completely reliant on their economy. It was a small step, really. China offered a lot of money. I'm guessing the PM was convinced that the Chinese had too much leverage. Australia stood to lose too much if we didn't.'

'Sell Tasmania?' It was barely a whisper.

'Yes,' she said. 'There's a contract but nobody seems to realise that when the Chinese do a deal, whatever happens in writing won't happen in reality. Very rare that things are as they appear. Unlike here, there is no central legal system in China. Agreements are made to get the job done but they're always fluid. Once the thing is signed it's "Okay, now what we're really going to do is . . ."'

'You've talked to the PM about this?'

'I can't breathe a word. I found out another way. If I wasn't told, I'm not meant to know. I've raised it delicately, the idea of doing business with the Chinese but, as we know, he's not very smart. This is a Viper masterplan. I'm sure you feel the same about him as I do. I've watched him working behind the scenes for years making everything grubbier. Setting people against one another. He's a dinosaur and they need to make those people extinct in the Liberal party. But it won't happen soon enough for this. That's why good people keep resigning from parliament. Especially women, once they work out that, ultimately, no matter how hard they work, they're just window dressing.'

'How did this even get mooted?' I asked.

'A few years back, JC hosted a little event called TasInvest,' Beck said. 'It was hatched by Viper. It was meant to be a way for Tasmanian businesses to connect with the greatest global market in the world. The Chinese president came. There were tours and talks. A great deal of schmoozing. Remember how the Chinese were in Tasmania in the 1800s for the gold rush? There was this sense of welcoming them back. That was part of the tone of the event. I was here because my minister at the time was Agriculture. The Chinese delegates—and there were hundreds of them—were shown the fish farms, the poppy farms, the dairy farms, the wineries, the tourist destinations, heritage homes, acreages, the vast unoccupied tracts of land throughout Tasmania and the many, many businesses who would happily take on a Chinese investor or two. They were shown the hydro schemes. And they were shown the wilderness, with its seemingly endless rush of pure, pristine water.'

I sighed. 'Did Tasmania benefit in any way from this?'

'It got Chinese funding for a longer runway so planes could fly direct from Hobart to China,' said Becky.

'No new trade at all?' I asked.

'Oh, yes. Some of the best farms are now Chinese owned and operated and the food they produce—vegetables mostly but fish and seafood, too—is flown straight from Tasmania to China every day thanks to the runway extension. All the abalone.'

'Crayfish. Lots of salmon. Milk. Yes, I've heard,' I said.

'And wine,' she added.

'Absolutely. Sitting ducks,' I said. 'But how do they expect to get Tasmanians to accept . . . how many Chinese?'

'Five million over the first five years. It will be a building boom,' she said.

'Tasmanians are never going to allow that!' I said. 'If this is true, it would be like living in a Chinese state.'

'Tasmanians won't be here, Ace,' said Becky. 'That's what the bridge is for. Tasmanians are being moved to Bruny Island.'

CHAPTER THIRTY-FIVE

I felt the world stop then.

'What?'

'Yes,' said Becky. 'That's what the bridge is for.'

'No!' I said. 'Tasmanians are going to leave their homes and move to an island with a current permanent population of six hundred people? How is that going to happen?'

She shrugged. 'How would you do it? You're the conflict resolution specialist. Imagine you're the Chinese.'

'Build facilities?' I said. 'Offer everyone a lot of money?'

She nodded. 'First a bridge to take them easily back and forth. And every Tasmanian will be offered three times the valuation of their home. Given the way housing prices have shot up over the last few years, a lot of Tasmanians are going to get rich. Plus anyone below the minimum wage will receive a universal basic income for the rest of their lives. It gets rid of the whole welfare burden, the pension burden. People here will be more comfortable, have more economic certainty, than any other people in Australia. It will be an excellent research model.'

She paused.

In the distance, growing clearer as the day brightened, was the huge arc of the Bruny Bridge beyond Tinderbox.

'The accommodation on Bruny will be varied,' she said. 'Some low level, some high-rise. Almost thirty per cent of Tasmania's population is over fifty now, so retirement enclaves will be the norm. With the bridge built, it's close to Hobart. Around an hour's drive for those who will still be required, or will choose, to work. Roads, hospitals, schools . . . it's all planned out.'

'Will money do it?' I frowned. 'I mean, these are Tasmanians. They're not going to go quietly.'

'Oh, I wouldn't rely on a few protestors to spark Tasmania to rebel,' she said. 'This is going to be way more complicated.'

'But surely,' I said, 'the rest of Australia won't stand by and see a part of Australia excised and handed over to a foreign power?'

'Ace, your altruism is showing. Why do we do nothing substantial about climate change? Why do we do virtually nothing to improve the lives of the poor? Or bother about those refugees on Nauru and Manus? We like our comfortable lives. We don't want to give anything up. We fear the loss of comfort. This Chinese deal means the rest of Australia is safe for the meantime. Think twenty-six million mainlanders against half a million Tasmanians. Most Australians have never even been here. Those that have think it's beautiful—nice art, good food. But they're not going to give up their Saturdays to protest. And with the new protest laws, who's going to want a five-thousand-dollar sting? I don't think we're going to see any great demonstrations in Federation Square or Martin Place.

Probably a few on the lawns of Parliament House here, but people get poor fast with five-thousand-dollar fines.

We'd found this cave when we were seventeen, the one place within half an hour of Hobart where we could hide from all the world. We'd smoked drugs, lit fires and brought boys here. Pretended everything beyond here didn't exist. Now it was almost forty years later, and we couldn't hide from the world anymore.

'You knew when you took this job,' she said, 'that there wasn't time to really do anything other than bury the bridge protesters under layers of better public relations than the protesters can manage. I don't mean to devalue what you've done. You've done it well. Their voices have been drowned out. And after the bombing, the Chinese look like our saviours. Bruny Island is half the size of Singapore with a tenth of its population. Singapore has almost eight thousand people per square kilometre. Hong Kong has nearly seven thousand. Tasmania has approximately seven people per square kilometre. Seven. If you put half a million Tasmanians on Bruny, you've still only got around fourteen hundred people per square kilometre. That's only a little higher density than Sydney. It looks like luxury to a lot of people in the world.'

'I'm going to need proof,' I said.

'It was delivered to me. The Tasmania/China Project. Top Secret.'

'Deliberately?' I asked.

'It looked just like Amazon had sent it. Before Christmas. I've been sitting on it all this time.'

'You haven't noticed anything else. Anyone following you? New people wanting to get close?'

'No,' she said. 'I have it with me. I haven't let it out of my sight. It's in the lining of my suitcase.'

'Okay,' I said. Not liking that at all.

'So I have a question for you,' she said. 'Can you do something, Ace? Can you find someone who will break it?'

'I thought you said it would make no difference.'

'We have to let people know. Give them a chance. Before the bridge is finished. Once it's done and the deal comes into play . . .'

'Break the rules,' I said.

'Break the rules,' Becky repeated. 'I don't want to have to perjure myself at some point in the future. But I'm a Tasmanian. And so are you. If this comes out, I want it to have been for something.'

'Maybe whoever sent it to you was a Tasmanian,' I said.

'I thought that too,' she said.

She looked at her watch. 'I have to go. And today we're in a meeting where we have to revert to being two people who, to all intents and purposes, know almost nothing about one another.'

'Okay,' I said. 'So how do you want to do this?'

'I could just give it to you today, at the end of our meeting. It's in a manila envelope now. Looks just like any large file.'

'No, not direct. Someone might put it together later. You could leave it somewhere for me to collect.'

'I'm having a drink with Edward this afternoon before I jump back on the plane,' she said.

Tasmania. Where everyone knows everyone.

'I could ask him to pass it on to you.'

'Can you trust him?' I asked.

'Of course. I've known him almost as long as I've known you.'

I'd have preferred a dead drop, but in light of the limited time, maybe this was a good solution. 'Okay,' I said.

We clambered up through the bush out onto the path. Back at the turn-off to the car park, she said, 'What comes next, after this, is up to you, Ace.'

'I'll do what I can,' I said. 'And, Beck, you need to end it with JC. I mean really let him go. It's time.'

'That's the choice I just made, isn't it?' she said. 'I don't want to wreck his life. If it came out, it would kill me. I'd rather share a state secret than that.'

I felt as if we'd both aged in that cave. Any vestige of still feeling seventeen had gone.

'He must know, Ace,' she said. 'I don't know how much, but he must know some of it. I tried to get a sense of that last night, but everyone on this is so tight. I can only imagine he's justified it as his way of saving the Tasmanian people. His legacy. You know how he feels about that. It's just that now it will be on Bruny.'

This almost winded me. The idea that JC knew. I wanted to scream. The duplicity. The underhanded, conniving, manipulative, deceitful . . .

Suddenly I was remembering all those little moments.

'Ace, you know I'd never build a bridge to nowhere.'

That meeting with the Chinese in JC's boardroom.

The lunch with the two Henrys and the laughter at the reference to Bruny.

Max saying, 'It was a COAG meeting.'

Max saying, 'Something about this bridge doesn't add up.'

Dad saying, '*Uneasy lies the head that wears a crown.*'

JC saying, 'We're part of the future. We promised we'd be that, and here we are. Changing the world, twin.'

JC saying, 'Don't let all this conspiracy shit get to you.'

Viper saying, 'Your brother may need you to stay on after the election.'

'Okay,' she said. 'I'm going.' It was barely a whisper.

I handed her phone back to her. She looked inexpressibly sad as she turned away. We both did.

There are better men. There are much better men, I wanted to tell her. But I wasn't so sure. She lived in Canberra.

Who knows what love is? Who knows what marriages are? Who knows what loyalty is? It was as if we'd both already been convicted.

I sat in my car and felt ancient.

CHAPTER THIRTY-SIX

That evening, Edward Lowe called me.

'I have something for you from Becky,' he said.

'I'm in town if you want to meet?'

'I thought we might make lunch this week instead,' he said. 'How's tomorrow?'

'Sure,' I said. 'I can do that.'

'Trio, midday?' he asked.

'Perfect.'

I don't just gather information for the UN. I do it for my other employer. The CIA. Deep in CIA headquarters, people have been keeping a very close eye on the axis moving from democracy to tyranny in the United States. With the current president there's been interference in our work at the highest levels. Everything has become political and there's an agenda running that's disturbed a lot of us. Our response had been to create black cells. Rogue units that are quietly protecting democracy wherever we see it being threatened. The blowing up of the Bruny Bridge and the passing of the foreign labour laws shifted something here in Australia. That's why I had come.

JC had asked, but the team back at Langley had instructed. *Call back your brother. Say yes. Tell him you changed your mind.* I had been sent home to see just what it was that had the Chinese government so very interested in Tasmania.

I chose to work for the CIA a long time ago. I was recruited during my time at Columbia and it fitted with the UN. It fulfilled something in me, this other part of my life that no-one knew about. No wonder Ben felt he never knew me. He didn't, but he could have. If he'd watched carefully. But he wasn't that sort of man. Maybe that was why I'd married him in the first place. Marriage can be a strange mix of hope and secrecy. Beyond loving Ben, our visibility gave me a veneer of invisibility. The very good-looking Jamaican with his flourishing academic career and his white Australian wife working for the UN. We were what we were. And not at all.

There had already been talk of sending me to keep an eye on this big bridge being built with Chinese money. I hadn't wanted to go. I didn't want to do surveillance on my own family. After the bomb, things changed. Enter the conflict resolution specialist stage right.

Those files I'd been amassing at Bruny, all of that had been going back to our team at Langley. Until Becky agreed to meet in a cave, everything I'd amassed was speculation. But now I knew. And I was about to know a great deal more.

❧

Trio had booths and I had already discovered their benefits. It was one of the rare places you could be private in public. I wondered why more Hobart cafes and restaurants hadn't invested in booths, so people could have the much-needed reprieve from always running into people they knew. Sitting in the farthest, quietest booth was Edward Lowe. I was on alert. This wasn't going to be a simple thing. I could see that in the blandness of his expression.

'Hello, Astrid,' he said, standing up to greet me.

'Hello, Edward,' I said.

He kissed me on both cheeks and we sat down.

Edward ordered a white that was good and local. We ordered food. I might have done better with someone like him. A straight version of him. I was probably quite useless at choosing the right men, I decided. It may have been a lifelong weakness.

'So Astrid Coleman,' he said, 'I want to know who you really are.'

'In what way?' I asked.

'I'd like to know what the premier's sister is doing playing the spy. Trading files with the prime minister's senior adviser? It's very intriguing.' Had I been set up? What did he know?

I saw a cold, highly trained Edward, just under his skin. Analyst. Observer. Operative. Ah, I thought, not such a nice guy after all. Perfect. But dangerous.

I feigned innocence at his question. Was he federal police or was he ASIO? If he was ASIO did he have eyes on Becky or eyes on me? Without the file, there was nothing anyone could prove. But he might have been wearing a wire.

As if he sensed my thought, he said, 'I'm not here to trap you, Astrid. If anything, I'm here to protect you. I could have had Feds waiting when I handed over the file.'

So he was ASIO. Fine.

'Becky and I go back a long way, too,' he said. 'We lived in a share house together in Battery Point when we were at uni. She was escaping her family and I'd come back to Tasmania after travelling for a few years. She used to talk about you, her friend who had left for New York. I first met JC then, too. She had him on the run.'

'She did,' I agreed.

'Does she still have him on the run?' he asked.

I had a feeling he knew all about JC and Becky. 'It was a long time ago,' I said.

He leaned back. 'You're a good sister, Astrid. Are you a good Tasmanian?'

'Is this a job interview?' I asked.

'Maybe,' he said. I wondered if he was going to ask me to work for ASIO. That would make things interesting.

He said, 'Answer the question, Astrid. If we put aside world peace for the moment and we ask you to choose between your brother or Tasmania, what would you pick?'

So many of the most terrible conversations have taken place in benign settings. This one was accompanied by gnocchi with blue cheese and a delicious sauvignon blanc. Millions of lives have been decided over poorer fare.

'Did Becky explain the contents of the file she wanted to give you?' He observed me carefully.

'You opened it?'

'I didn't have to,' he said. 'I am very familiar with that file.'

'You sent it to her?'

'We are the Tasmanian diaspora, Astrid. We go out into the world and sometimes we come home again. Believe me when I say this thing has stayed inside a tiny bubble of people in Canberra. Fewer than ten.'

'Meaning . . . ?' I said.

'Meaning, do you understand the counterintelligence laws?'

'I think so,' I said.

'Twenty-five years without parole for having this information in your hands. Twenty-five years for me handing it to you.'

'And if I said I knew nothing?' I asked.

'Do you have any idea what an interrogation feels like?'

I nodded.

'They train you for that?' he asked.

I nodded again.

He said. 'If I thought you were a threat, or that I couldn't trust you, I would never hand over this file.'

I wanted to say, 'Edward, I don't just work for the UN. Just like you are clearly not just a consultant. I'm almost certain you work for ASIO. I gather information for the CIA. We are both keeping an eye on the same thing. That the good guys win. We just work for different agencies.' But I didn't. While ever I could fly under the radar, I would. This thing didn't need to get any more complicated. An Australian agent handing top secret government information to a foreign agent—we wouldn't just get twenty-five years without parole. We'd be gone forever.

'You know one ridiculous thing the Chinese want in all this?' he asked.

'What?' I asked.

'They want to compete in the World Cup. They can't find eleven players from a population of more than one billion people to beat the rest of the world at soccer. The Chinese are good at individual, repetitive sport. They can do a million perfect dives. Win a million ping-pong games. But soccer is creative. No matter how much they've poured into it, they've failed. They understand that they have to manufacture creativity. It's never been done in China. They have had an education system that's dampened any such inclinations. So this is part of the experiment too. Giving their people, their high-value people, the chance to raise their children a little differently, and see what comes of that. Free them from some of the Communist strictures. Not many but a few. But don't think for a minute any of this is altruistic. China is, and will be for a very long time, a communist regime with supreme control over its citizens.'

'That's in the file?' I asked. 'About the soccer?'

'Oh, yes,' he said. 'And the selection process for high-value citizens. The dangerous ones who've sniffed the cocaine of capitalism. It's all in there.'

'I'm still incredulous,' I said. 'I mean, we're part of the Commonwealth. We're part of Australia. It's never going to fly.'

'That's where I went,' said Edward. 'Surely the King will save us! But the Brits are a basket case. We both know they'll never recover from Brexit. The King might have a fondness for us but, really, if the Australian government think it's a good thing, then he's not going to step in. The Queen might have been a different story. I think she was very fond of her Commonwealth—but he won't keep that vision alive in the same way.

'Hong Kong built a bridge too, a few years back,' he continued. 'From mainland China to Hong Kong. It killed the Hong Kong locals. And that was Chinese against Chinese.'

I thought of Hong Kong with its shabby high-rises, an air conditioner in every window, washing hanging from the balconies, the sea of people at every pedestrian crossing and one and a half billion people right across the bridge in China.

'India will outstrip China in population in a few years,' said Edward. 'Its need for food security will become pressing. Africa, too, but that will always be a basket case. China, they see the future and they take action.'

'Food production,' I said. 'Food security before India cottons on.'

'Indeed. And if you were looking for somewhere clean, green and pristine, out of the way, easy to defend . . . and you might solve an almost unstoppable urge from certain elements in your country for more freedom at the same time. Dangle a fabulous carrot for good behaviour.'

'It will never work.'

'It's a done deal,' he said. 'The flag goes down and everything goes into action once the bridge is completed. Is it any worse than the British who've been using their influence here since they invaded the place? Or the US and the UK dismantling the Whitlam government?'

'Your model train farm is going to be hard to relocate,' I said.

'My land is on Bruny. At Simpsons Bay. I thought my slice of heaven was well preserved. But it turns out it is not. People thought I was mad relocating to Bruny. In the deal, all current Bruny landowners will be given the right to subdivide. Imagine the building industry. This is a peaceful way to inspire a boom. And we didn't have to have a war first. Name one other way that has ever happened in the last five hundred years.'

'Tulips?'

He smiled then. 'Unlike the Dutch, the Chinese will ensure market stability. At least while it suits them.'

'You don't think economic theory has gotten in the way of pure common sense? I cannot believe for a moment Tasmanians will give up their homes to live on Bruny Island.'

'Astrid, it is shocking. I know that. But you know better than anyone that economic theory got in the way of common sense a long time ago. Very soon twenty-five per cent of the world will be over sixty-five years of age. Tasmania will reach that sooner than most places. People are tired. They'd like to stop. The Gold Coast has always been very attractive to Tasmanians. I think you'd get a fair few moving to the warmth. You can buy a pretty nice apartment for a million dollars on the beach in Queensland and you'd have a very stylish retirement. It's the people who don't move away I'm more worried about. The people who take the Bruny deal. A contract with the Chinese is always opaque. This deal, all the new infrastructure they're promising to build on Bruny . . . China do things on terms that will greatly benefit them down the track. They'll compromise you. They lend you the money but you'll never be able to pay it back. When the agreement suits them, they'll enforce it. Like Sri Lanka with their ports. There are Chinese warships in the harbour now, because Sri Lanka couldn't meet the repayments.'

'These are Tasmanians. There will be outrage. Did nobody notice? We don't go down without a fight . . .'

'The Aborigines got moved to Cape Barren Island. The government got away with that.'

'But half a million people? High-rises on Adventure Bay?'

'Yes, and schools, medical facilities, arts centres. There's sensitive technology that the Chinese want to ensure is no longer kept on mainland China. Too vulnerable. Safer out of the way. Tasmanian kids are assured of work in those businesses. Free university too, I believe. And the universal basic income for anyone over eighteen earning less than the minimum wage. Right now, we're looking down the barrel of Tasmania being the Australian Detroit in five to ten years. Unemployment for people under thirty is at twenty-five per cent and growing. Growing unemployment overall. Automation is coming and smart businesses know it. Everyone from doctors to drivers can be replaced with the right programming. There isn't enough left to cut down or dig up here to save everyone. Zinc smelting won't do it. Nor fish farms. I think you'll find most people could be pretty adaptable under the circumstances.'

I pictured the bridge and its six-lane capacity. I wanted to scream.

'How did this happen?' I asked. 'We're Tasmanians. We're never going to surrender this island. We're the most reluctant people in the world to embrace change . . .'

Edward tilted his head to one side.

'Have you heard about the TasInvest conference?'

'Yes,' I said.

'Do you know the greatest mistake I think they made, your brother's government?' he asked. 'They disregarded the arts. There wasn't a single cultural reference. No Tasmanian

Symphony Orchestra. No theatre. No films. No dance, poetry, art. It was all PowerPoints and economics. The Chinese saw this place as a cultural wasteland. And that makes you a prime target for anything like this. The Chinese know they haven't done Hong Kong well. It was a jewel and now it's not. It's become tarnished and chipped under their rule. Some would say cracked. Anyone who dares to talk of independence is howled down as a heretic and bundled back to the Chinese mainland for re-education. This is a different experiment. This is a different sort of re-education. This is a toe in the water of capitalism under communism. It's never been attempted before.'

'I hardly believe a play or a symphony could have made the difference,' I said.

'Nobody with a strong culture looks like they can be bought,' he said. 'There's no price high enough for people who have land and community in their blood. Haven't we learned that from every indigenous culture that has clung to their ways and their land to the death? This government, at a state and a federal level, they've hammered the arts for years. They've eviscerated it. How the ABC have hung on is a miracle, and now, with all these hyenas circling, they'll almost certainly be forced to privatise. And then it's over. No national public broadcaster. The right-wing press will win. Every theatre company or film production company in this country—unless it's making a Marvel movie—has been defunded. That's our cultural expression, and if we don't have that, it weakens everything. It's a bit like leaching. We're wilting with cultural anaemia. The sheer determination of artists, practitioners and administrators—that's what's keeping Australian culture going. But in so many cases, it's been death. Organisations and festivals, magazines and journals and, ultimately, possibilities. This is where it's got us. Selling this little island to prop up the rest of Australia. What next? Norfolk Island? You can bet those people would go down fighting. Fraser Island? Rottnest Island? Why not the whole of Western Australia? I mean, would anyone really notice? Easy enough to make a border across the desert. Build a wall.'

'I think this is the worst lunch I've ever had,' I said.

'Astrid, don't get me wrong. I'm not telling you this so we acquiesce. Do you understand that?'

'No,' I said. 'I didn't understand that. So what are you suggesting? We start a revolution?'

'Let me tell you something. A few years back I was commissioned by your brother to assess the role sea changers could play economically in Tasmania's future.'

'And . . . ?'

'Well, this didn't go in my report. Every person I interviewed had some kind of spiritual undertone to their move to Tasmania. I interviewed hundreds across the state. All of them felt that they had found a place that was good for their soul. They might not have used that word, but they all referred to a sort of spiritual wellbeing. This wasn't about religion, I might add. It was something bigger than that.'

'Any Chinese?'

'Twelve. The rest were from everywhere else. Iceland to Argentina.'

'Hippies?'

'Not at all. Most are affluent, older, middle-class people wanting a quieter lifestyle.'

'Why didn't you put it in your report?'

'I didn't know how to couch that language,' he said. 'It seemed to be inappropriate somehow. But I think they're emblematic of the greater Tasmanian population.'

I thought of Dan Macmillan saying that Tasmanians had already given up a lot to be here. To stay here. But did Tasmanians see more than money? Surely some of them must. Would there be a tipping point? If, say, fifty per cent of Tasmanians took the deal, made three times the value of their homes, moved to Bruny or Queensland or wherever they thought life looked good, would the other half roll over?

'I think they'll fight to the end,' I said. 'And what about Bruny landowners? What if people don't want to develop their land? Compulsory acquisition?'

Edward smiled. 'Remember the resident population is only six hundred people. There's a great deal of state forest and Parks and Wildlife land on Bruny. That will be reassigned for development.'

'How will the government force relocation to Bruny? I mean, they're not going to get out the army, are they?'

'It must have been considered. But clearly they're relying on the money to make people docile, compliant, supportive of the whole thing.'

I shook my head.

'You're the expert. How do we fan these flames of protest?' he asked. 'And, most importantly, how does it happen without anyone going to jail?'

'I'm meant to stop it?'

Edward said, 'I would guess, over and above your loyalty to country and family, you came home because the world was wearing you down, Astrid. The conflict is endless, isn't it? At least here no-one is going to murder your best friend and put their head on your doorstep. You don't have to see women who haven't had the right medical help after their genitals were cut away. You don't meet young men who've been trained to be suicide bombers but mucked up and lost their arms or legs. Or had them hacked off by militia. The wars, the bombs, the rapes, the children, the sex slaves, the refugees, the families trying to rebuild a life together . . . all the horror in this world. It's no wonder you're spending as much time as you can on Bruny. You're getting a sense of what you left, and probably you're considering whether you'll go back to New York at all. Because waking up here in Tasmania, you're hoping you are a long, long way from the next terrorist attack. You are a long way from rush hour in almost any form. You rarely have to queue. You don't have to park and ride. You can park right outside most anything you want—even Salamanca, if you get there before the tourists. Every time there's another mass shooting in the world, we all become a little more numb. But here, in Tasmania, it's as if we get some feeling back. The sky is beautiful at night. The light is magical. Sunrises, sunsets, the sea—it all works on you, doesn't it? And, like me, you want to believe it can stay this way.'

I wanted to cry. How had he done that? Had he accessed my file from the UN? I hate the world sometimes. I hate how you can't escape it and you can't escape yourself.

'Astrid, you're maybe the one person on this island who can make this thing go away. But time is of the essence. I think Beck was very clever when she chose you. You have connections. Anyone who can settle conflict down must have a pretty good idea of how to start it as well.'

I wasn't going to correct him. Let him think Becky chose me, not that I gave her an impossible choice.

'I'll deliver the file to you at your house on Bruny. Wear gloves. No-one is getting prosecuted over this. When's a good time?' he asked.

It was Friday. 'I'm there tonight. Tomorrow night, too.'

'Tomorrow night is good. I'll come by at six o'clock.'

'Edward, do you think the person who sent Becky the file also knows who blew up the bridge?' I asked.

It was the first time I'd seen his eyes sparkle.

'You're rather clever, aren't you?' he said.

I walked out of the restaurant with Edward.

'We are two friends,' he said. 'We know nothing. We just had a delicious lunch. Look happy.'

'Of course,' I said.

My phone was buzzing in my bag. I reached for it and saw that both Max and JC had been calling. Twelve missed calls. Texts saying: *Call me.*

I wondered if we were about to be swooped upon by federal agents. I wondered if something had happened to our mother in hospital. 'Oh no,' I said, and called Max.

'Shall I wait?' Edward asked.

'No, of course not.'

'Yes, of course,' he said, ushering me to a bench in the public space by the fountain.

'Ace . . . Ace, I'm sorry to have to do this on the phone. Are you sitting down?' Max said.

'Yes, yes,' I said.

'Where are you?'

'In Salamanca Square. What happened? Is it Mother?'

'No, no, no . . .'

'What happened, Max?'

'It's . . . it's Dad . . . He had another stroke and, Ace—he died. I'm so sorry. Just half an hour ago. We're coming to pick you up, okay? JC is with me. We're coming to get you.'

CHAPTER THIRTY-SEVEN

According to the writer Douglas Adams, there are two hundred and thirty-two types of rain. Grief is the same. It comes in droplets and squalls, drizzle and downpour. I felt as if I was submerged and all noise came at me in a weird slowed-down soundwave that I couldn't understand.

I remember Max getting out of the car. I remember finding JC breaking down out by the rhododendrons near the tennis court and holding hands with him as we walked back inside. I remember Max holding me and me holding Max. I remember being hugged by Ella and Grace.

At some point I was sitting with Stephanie and the girls at their kitchen table. Stephanie and Max were trying to discuss funeral details with me. The archbishop from St Mary's came, but I can't remember what was said. Frank Pringle came and went and JC poured us all whisky. Stephanie fed us chicken soup. Max came and crawled into bed with me and stayed all night.

It was on the front of the paper the next morning, a picture of Dad from his life as one of Australia's longest-serving elected representatives. There was a picture of JC, me and Max with

Dad when we were kids. From all sides of politics, Tasmanians had liked Angus Coleman. There was going to be a state funeral. He wasn't ours in this moment; he became everyone's.

In the morning I went with Max to clean out his room at the nursing home. We didn't need to do it so soon, but we both felt we had to. We wanted to be with whatever was left of him. We packed up his books, the photos, folded his clothes. We packed up his bathroom items. A toothbrush. A hairbrush. A comb. The soap he liked—Imperial Leather.

When we got back to JC's with Dad's stuff, I got a text from Dan Macmillan. It said: *So sorry about your dad. I'm in town this afternoon if you'd like a lift down.*

I read it a couple of times and then I replied *Yes*. I sent him the address. He sent back: *3 pm?* I said perfect. And then I remembered that, despite everything that had happened in between, this was the night Edward was dropping the documents to the Bruny house at 6 pm. And the final road section was being delivered to the bridge. All of it came back to me in a crushing, roaring wave.

Suddenly I was hearing again. I needed to be in action.

'Thought you might stay in town,' JC said.

I looked at my brother standing there in his blue denim shirt and his chinos—his Saturday uniform, as he called it—and I saw him for what he was. A turncoat. A thief. A liar. A traitor. Someone who had duped me and was going to dupe Tasmania. What was his election slogan? *Growing a brighter future.* What a joke.

'What?' he said.

I gathered myself. People's lives relied on my discretion now. He would guess Becky in a flash.

'I'm sorry, JC. I'm distraught. I need to go hide for a day or two. I'll be back Monday. I'll miss Sunday lunch tomorrow. I'm sorry. I need to be alone.'

꿍

Dan came up the driveway and I was out the door with my bag before he'd stopped the car. I knew everyone's eyes were on me and Dan and they'd all be thinking they'd missed something. But let them think what they liked.

'You rescued me,' I said.

'Good,' he said.

And we didn't talk after that. Not until the ferry, when he handed me a pouch of rolling tobacco.

'How did you know?' I asked.

His blue eyes regarded me. 'Anyone who rolls a joint as well as you do has clearly had practice. Thought it might be time.'

I had smoked for years, until I had the children. After Ben and I split, I'd often rolled a cigarette or something stronger when I poured a glass of wine at the end of the day. Coming back to Tasmania, I'd determined that it was a slippery slope, and I needed to give it up. But it was perfect right now.

I went through those familiar motions of paper, tobacco and filter then I got out of the car. There on the top deck, I lit, inhaled, and looked up the channel to the bridge. It was getting precariously close to being finished.

They'd completed the roadworks from the Hobart end, too. Not opened—but all ready to go. The final stretch of the

Dennes Point road from the top of the hill down to the bridge would be finished next week.

The nicotine and the salt air rushed through me, along with the despair. My father was the first person I would have told about the deal with China. He was the first person I'd rung with any news. Passing my uni subjects. Getting engaged. Being pregnant. First steps and words for Paul, first steps and words for Tavvy. When a UN mission did or didn't go well. Getting divorced. Now I couldn't. There was no-one to confide in. I tried to imagine what he might have said, but there was only silence and the breeze.

Dan came and stood beside me. 'You going to be okay to come down and watch the last section go in? I'd like to see it, but we can stay home if you need to.'

I shook my head. He put his arm around me and pulled me close.

'I'm really sorry about your dad,' he said.

And then I leaned into Dan Macmillan and cried on the Bruny ferry.

CHAPTER THIRTY-EIGHT

Dan offered to whip us up some food. His house was fascinating inside. I hadn't expected that, and then I didn't know why I hadn't expected it. I'd sat on his deck. I'd seen beyond the windows into the dimmed interior. I had known that it had bookshelves. But I didn't know it had so many novels, military history, political history, philosophy, poetry. And curiosities. Several pieces of carved scrimshaw. A very old set of backgammon made with inlaid Huon pine. It was peaceful and rustic in the way houses can be when they're uncluttered and unpretentious. There was a view from every window and nooks that I was sure were perfect suntraps during the day. I asked him who had designed it all, and he said he had, and I was surprised. He put on Nick Cave and I was surprised. He made cheese on toast. It was a delicious Taleggio and he served it with a mug of tomato soup, and it was just what I wanted. We went out on the deck with wine and tobacco and it wasn't cold, but he brought me a light blanket anyway and I wrapped myself in it. Day two of life without my dad.

'What time's the section being delivered?' I asked.

'We'll see it come across,' he said, looking towards North-West Bay. 'Around seven pm, I'm told.' The money shot at golden hour, the perfect light for the camera crews and media. I'd discussed it with JC's team.

'Dan,' I asked, 'why aren't you in a relationship?'

'Who said I'm not?'

'Are you?'

'I was,' he said. 'On and off. Until recently.'

'What happened?'

'Jeez, you ask the questions.'

'Sorry.'

'Let's just say I met someone who clarified my thinking.'

'Ah,' I said.

'You leave someone in New York?' he asked.

'No,' I said.

There was a pause.

'See,' he said. 'I know when not to ask the next question.'

I nodded. 'You might have to teach me that.'

He smiled.

'I have to go to my house at six,' I said. 'But I'll be back. It won't take long.'

'Sure,' he said, and he didn't ask why.

'Tell me about your dad,' he said. 'He always seemed like a nice bloke. Old school.'

So I told him about my dad. How he loved being with us as children. How he read us poetry from as early as I can remember. How he took us to all sorts of functions and events that children might not normally have attended, but it was there we all learned about public life. How his enduring question at dinner every night was: 'Who did you help today?' How, despite their differences in politics, he was so proud of JC and Max. How he'd officially adopted Max when he married our mother and, even if she'd had a different father, he'd never, ever treated her as anything but his beloved eldest daughter. When she entered politics 'for the right party' he campaigned for her, walking the streets for months handing out leaflets and telling people about her, and what excitement there was when she was elected. How he came every year to New York to see me and came twice a year when the children were little, and how he'd come right away each time I gave birth because he believed that, if he got in early, they'd always know him. And how they didn't just know him, they loved him. And how he had taken them to the Met, and the Guggenheim, and the opera, and the orchestra, and for walks in Central Park, and how he'd taught them to love Shakespeare too. How he'd worked as a carpenter in the theatre, and then took bit parts, and how even when all he could do was talk in Shakespeare quotes, he still knew just what to say. And how he'd stayed with my mother for nearly sixty years, even though she'd had affairs, which must have made his life so tough, but despite everything he'd kept loving her, until the strokes, when a less compliant Angus had showed himself. How he'd gone to the nursing home. How the last thing he'd said to me, the night before he died, was, '*My crown is called content, a crown it is that seldom kings enjoy.*' And I had really known, then, that he was ready to go.

Dan listened to all of that without interruption. Then he went inside and got me tissues. He said, 'I don't want you to go, but it's ten to six, Ace. Do you want me to walk up with you?'

I said, 'No. But I'll come back.'

≈

I went up to my house and waited. Edward Lowe pulled up in a car. He came down the path and I opened the door and let him in. He was carrying a manila envelope. It was bulky and had no name or address.

He said, 'Are you okay?'

'Put it there,' I instructed, referring to the hall table. Then I took out a scanner and assessed that he was not wearing a wire. I asked for his phone and checked it was off. I took it into the kitchen with mine and ensured neither could send or receive signals.

When I returned, the cool pragmatic Edward met me. 'Why didn't you tell me at lunch?'

'I wasn't sure I needed to, but I think we're beyond that now.'

'How long have you been . . . ?' he asked.

'Since Columbia in the early nineties. You?'

'1994.'

He studied me for a moment.

'So this whole thing?' he asked. 'You've been here as . . . ?'

'As a conflict resolution specialist. And to observe. I would never have taken the job on its own terms. The timeframe, the politics, the family connections. I turned JC down. But orders. You understand.'

'US foreign policy isn't doing Australia any favours right now . . .'

'US foreign policy is downright dangerous to global security. So some of us are doing what needs to be done. I felt it important you understand the resources I could make available if the circumstances arise.'

We had walked into the lounge room and were looking down at the bridge, waiting for the last piece of the puzzle to fall into place.

'Who was it?' I asked. 'The bombing?'

'The PM needed a way to introduce the Chinese. Slide them in under the radar. Get people comfortable. Make them appreciative. Nothing to fear. Your brother never knew. Only a handful of top people. Incredibly quiet. There was a submarine down south that picked up the boat and the crew.'

I nodded. Of course it had been our government. The whole thing was *our* government. People might fear the Russians, the Chinese, even the Americans, but when you were at home, it was wise to keep a sharp eye on what was happening with the government you voted for. 'There's no darkness except ignorance . . .' *Twelfth Night*. Shakespeare.

'That's when I came across the whole thing,' Edward said. 'I sorted the money. That's what I do. I watch money, I move money and, from time to time, I stop money. Once I got hold of the file, I sent it to Becky because I trusted that she would not stay silent. She would find a way of getting it out. And she did. Turns out, I could have just handed it to you.'

'Edward,' I said, 'how brave are you feeling?'

'I'm not sure brave is the word,' he said. 'More an absence of fear.'

We continued to look at the bridge.

'We are both thinking the same thing,' I said. 'Aren't we?'

'We are thinking the same thing,' he said.

'You know what to do? What to organise?'

'I do.'

'You won't have second thoughts?'

'No, I won't,' he said. 'As soon as I read that report, I knew what side I was on.'

'I always wondered if I could be like them. I was never sure. But I am sure now,' I said. 'We spend our days trying to stop conflict, but when it's your place, your people, I see their perspective entirely.'

'You are willing to live with the consequences?' he asked.

I took in the bridge, and beyond the bridge I absorbed the sky, the channel, the hills, the sea, the idea of dolphins and the reality of Pacific gulls and the smell of gum trees and wood smoke and the sheer quiet, unpopulated beauty of it all.

'Yes,' I said.

'Strange how it feels like sanity. Like the only clear, reasonable thing to do,' he said. 'It'll take time to organise. But the story needs to break soon, well before the election.'

'I'm on it,' I said.

He handed me a card which bore only a phone number. 'Send me a list,' he said.

The warmth came back into his eyes.

'Have you got good people around you now?' he asked. 'Losing a parent is very hard.'

'I do. It is,' I said. I appreciated that he didn't conflate the two things. The death, and what we were planning on doing.

Then we walked to the front door, and he got in his car and drove away.

∽

I locked the envelope in a safe I'd had installed months ago in my bedroom and went back to Dan's. We walked down the road and passed through security. On the bridge, the workers were hard at it. It was noisy and floodlit. An immense structure that, any moment now, would bridge the entire D'Entrecasteaux Channel.

We arrived at the gap over the water. A barge was by the side of the bridge. Men on the barge had the final section of roadway ready to go. The crane on the barge lifted it into the air and, as it was swung in towards the bridge, the riggers guided it down.

It was the Chinese night crew, but to ensure a PR win they'd created a mix of Tasmanian and Chinese workers. Everyone not on the shift was being paid to turn up. This was the moment. The media was there in full force. Golden hour was beautiful, the channel calm. The horizon was beginning to offer up tangerine and pale rose, and the whole thing might have been a Spielberg movie. *The Bridge of Lies.* The last section was fixed into place and it was done. Everyone cheered, the sirens sounded. When the signal was given, the crowd on the Tinderbox side and the crowd on the Dennes Point side walked towards each other until we all met in the middle.

At the two BFG camps, a steady drumbeat started up, but someone switched on two big loudspeakers on the bridge and Queen's 'We Are The Champions' erupted, drowning the protestors out. Workers began twirling in their fluoro on the completed roadway. One took another in his arms, and soon a whole lot of men were dancing. There was much laughter. Mick Feltham had come across from Tinderbox and he looked so proud. He seemed surprised to see Dan and me standing together, but neither of us explained. Then the media moved in on him, and he was lost behind cameras and journalists.

It should have been a great moment. It was a great moment in engineering. In architecture. It was a great moment for the men who had built this thing. For everyone involved. Even those, especially those, who had died. But the bridge was a death sentence for Tasmania. I had a file that proved it. How could I even begin to mobilise action? Who could I trust, so that nobody ever knew it was me who leaked the story? So nobody would ever trace it back to Beck, or Edward, or me, when I took the action I knew I had to take?

On the way back up the hill, Dan said, 'It's not just your dad, is it? Something else is worrying you.'

'No, I'm fine.'

'No, you're not.'

'How did you get good at that?' I asked.

'I've been watching you for months.'

'I can't talk about it.'

'That's okay,' he said.

After a while he said, 'When's the funeral?'

'It's going to be a state funeral. They're planning it for next Friday. JC's people, Max's people—there's a whole lot of protocol that goes into action now.'

He nodded.

'My children are both flying out. They arrive Wednesday,' I said.

Back at my house, on my deck, he hugged me again and he smelled so good that I wanted badly to invite him in. To take him to bed. But there was a terrible secret in my bedroom and I had to prioritise it. This wasn't the time for romance.

'Thank you,' I said. 'You've been . . . so great, Dan.'

'You need to go over in the morning?' he asked. 'Sunday lunch?'

'Can I borrow your car?' I asked. 'Early?'

'Tomorrow?' he asked.

'I'll be back by mid-morning.'

'Sure,' he said. 'I'll leave the keys in the letterbox at my place.'

'Thank you,' I said.

'If you need me in the meantime, you know where to find me,' he said, as he stepped down off the deck.

'I'll try not to need you,' I said.

He looked up at me. 'Well, I think that's a start,' he said with a grin.

CHAPTER THIRTY-NINE

I read the documents. There, in black and white, I read the plan outlined across one hundred and ninety-four pages of a central document and an accompanying one hundred and eighty pages of appendices. It was thoughtfully done—in the bureaucratic way that things are thoughtfully done, without any regard for the real world.

> Thirty per cent of Tasmanians live below the poverty line. Ninety-two per cent of all working Tasmanians rely on government in the form of employment or for government contracts. Fifty per cent of Tasmanians are functionally illiterate and innumerate. This reflects a mendicant state. And a state that will offer little educated resistance to the project. We believe that, with a concerted public relations campaign, the Tasmanian people will welcome this transition from economic hardship to economic certainty.
>
> The living precincts planned for Bruny Island will offer residents an unparalleled lifestyle, making them the envy of the Australian people. We envisage negative migration with

an increase in the sea-change population wishing to take advantage of the many benefits the Bruny lifestyle affords.

Laid out was the injection of capital into the Australian economy by the sale to the Chinese. Over a hundred billion dollars was to change hands through the course of the ten-year transition. The metrics of Tasmanian exports (negligible after zinc) against the cost of supporting all those Tasmanians on welfare, pensions and in the public service (substantial and getting worse into the future). The projections were compelling. The federal government came out ahead. Significantly ahead.

Some thought had been given to the strategic nature of Tasmania in the Southern Ocean. The People's Republic of China, it said, was an ally of Australia. A joint presence in the Southern Ocean and the Pacific would prove beneficial in protecting Australia from the arrival of illegal immigrants, which Australia was not sufficiently resourced to do on its own.

Australia will maintain a naval presence in Bass Strait. While diplomatic in nature, it is felt that this safeguard will reassure mainland Australians concerned by the Chinese presence on their border.

The secession of Tasmania from Australia is seen as a win-win. Landowners with a turnover in excess of $1 million per annum will be given the opportunity to remain as employees on their land, while enjoying the significant benefits from receiving three times the property value, a share of profit and the universal basic income as a safety net. It is thought that all Tasmanians will transition from the island within the next ten-year period, resettling on Bruny Island, or moving to mainland Australia or a foreign destination.

And on it went:

The Tasmanian people are benign in character. Activism, while given a lot of media coverage, has involved a very small percentage of the population . . .

Tasmania's secession as a state of Australia will have little bearing on the Commonwealth alliance . . .

Tasmanians who have experienced a significant gap in wages and living standards over the past thirty years in comparison to mainland Australia can expect a significantly higher standard of living . . .

And this:

A random ballot will determine the first wave of homeowners offered relocation. Sale and relocation is the basic eligibility requirement for receipt of the universal basic income. All other Australian government subsidies and pensions will cease. Two further ballots will complete the process over a five-year period. At the end of the five-year transition period, any remaining residents will have their property compulsorily acquired by the incoming administration. Any legal challenges will become a matter for the incoming authority. Tasmanian residents unwilling to relocate beyond the five-year period will lose all Australian government benefits. (See Strategy for Relocation Appendix H, Managing Resistance Appendix M).

And this:

The project will make efficient use of material resources and human capital; Chinese entrepreneurism in Tasmania will focus on capitalising on forms of knowledge that meet modern consumer demands for functional and attractive goods and services.

And this:

The Tasmanian hydroelectric scheme is underdeveloped. Expansion of the scheme will allow significant upscaling for increased demands for both domestic and industrial use . . .

There were charts with water volume targets in gigalitres and projections of net revenue over the next fifty years. There were future projections on the expansion of agricultural outputs too: wine, cheese, fish, seafood, beef and sheep.

On and on it went. The detailed analysis. The transition strategy. The business case. I thought of all the times I had heard my dad quote Benjamin Disraeli: 'A conservative government is an organised hypocrisy.'

I thought about what came next. I made a couple of calls. It was late in Tasmania, but it was early elsewhere. I was on the 8 am ferry. I was at Officeworks at 8.45 am. I returned to Bruny on the 10.30 am ferry. I set up the scanner. At no time did

I touch the documents with my bare hands. While the TOP SECRET header and footer on every page had been cut off before the documents came to me, I wasn't taking any chances. When the scans were done, I transferred files onto two USB sticks.

The next day, I borrowed Dan's car again and got back on the ferry. I drove to a post office in Cygnet, by the cafe where I'd met Amy O'Dwyer. It had no surveillance or CCTV. There I express posted the USB sticks to two international destinations. At no time did I touch the parcels or use my real name or my regular handwriting.

Back on the island, I made some calls to old friends and together we made a list. I texted it from my second phone to the mobile number Edward had given me. I carefully took down the web of photos and names, the threads and pins, the ideas and theories I had mapped on the wall of the spare room. I took my notebooks, too, and the original documents from Beck. I burned everything in the fireplace until it was white ash.

I met Tavvy and Paul off the plane when they arrived at Hobart airport and there was much joy and also grief. He had loved them well, my dad, and because Ben's mother had visited rarely, and my mother had never visited at all, Angus Coleman had really been the only grandparent they'd known. I took them to Salamanca and we had lunch, and then we all went back to JC's. They slept for a while, then JC came home and Max arrived with Mother.

For a woman who had just lost her husband of almost sixty years, Hyacinth Coleman was remarkably chirpy. She had been allowed out of hospital under strict instructions. She was wearing a light brown wig today, the colour of her real hair a long time ago. It was done in a French roll, and her dress and shoes were navy. Phillip had obviously tried to set the tone for a grieving widow.

'Goodness,' said our mother, when she saw Tavvy and Paul across the lounge room engaged in conversation with Grace and Ella. 'I'll never get used to it.'

'What's that, Mum?' I asked.

She hadn't seen them in ten years, so I thought she was referring to their having become adults since their last visit.

'Well, they're black, Astrid. How could you do that to the family?'

And because my father was dead, and my heart was broken, and the whole world felt upside down, I couldn't hold it in.

'I did it to annoy you, Mum.'

'That'd be right,' she said. 'So they wouldn't feel like my grandchildren.'

'That's okay,' I said. 'I don't think you feel like their grandmother.'

'How ridiculous,' she said, stiffening. 'Of course I'm their grandmother.'

At this she set off across the room in her high heels, unsteady but certain, and went up to the little group. She kissed Paul and Tavvy, asked how their flight was, and insisted they sit on either side of her at dinner.

'Did Grandma take nice pills?' Tavvy asked, when Mother was distracted in conversation with Paul.

I nodded. 'Seems so.'

JC raised his glass. 'I propose a toast to Angus Coleman, lately of this table, lately of this world, always of this family. Rest in peace.'

I wanted to hate JC. I wanted to hate him, but he's my twin. And I could feel Dad shaking his head. 'Not the time, Astrid. Not the time.'

'Well, at last I'll get all the attention,' said Mother. 'High time, too.'

Tavvy turned to her and said, 'Grandma, sometimes it's better not to say certain things aloud.'

'Oh, I'm far too old to subscribe to that,' said Mother.

JC continued his toast, 'And to our mother, matriarch of the Coleman family, may she long say everything she wants to say.'

'Hear, hear,' said our mother, raising her champagne glass.

'Any words to say about Dad, Mum?' Max asked.

'He was . . . well, I don't know,' she said. 'He was Angus. Always the same. Never changed.'

'Shall we put that on his headstone?' I asked.

'Actually, it's a serious question,' said Max. 'What do you want on his headstone, Mum? A Shakespeare quote, maybe?'

'Really?' Mother said, looking at all of us. 'Haven't we had enough of that?'

We all exchanged glances.

'Oh, well, if you must. God, I'll have to read it every time I visit,' she said.

'Were you planning on visiting?' Tavvy asked.

'Goodness, you're a chip off the old block, aren't you?' our mother said, and chortled.

'So what will it be?' Max asked, looking at me.

I shook my head and looked at JC. 'Have you settled on anything?'

He shook his head too.

Then Ella perked up. 'Can I leave the table, Mum? I've got an idea.'

Stephanie nodded. Ella ran out. She came back and stood at the head of the table beside JC, scrolling through her notes. JC put his arm around her. A look passed between him and me. He was unfaithful to his wife and he'd sold Tasmania. How would I ever trust him again? I guess I didn't have to.

'You must send me all of those,' I said to Ella.

'Okay, I will,' she said. 'Here it is. I know he really liked this one because he said it to me and Grace often.' And in a voice Angus would have commended her for, she read, '*A good heart is the sun and the moon; or, rather, the sun and not the moon, for it shines bright and never changes.*'

There wasn't a dry eye at the table. Even our mother looked moist for a moment.

'That's the one, Ella,' I said.

'*Henry the Fifth,*' she told me.

'That's the one, sweetheart,' said JC, and he hugged her to his side.

Tavvy put her head on my shoulder. 'I'm really going to miss him.'

'Yes,' I said. 'It's going to be a hole.'

'I'd rather hoped,' said our mother, 'he might have stopped on the way and taken me with him.'

We all looked at her.

'Mum,' said Max.

'Well, as always, he made it look easy, didn't he?' she said.

'Dying?' I asked.

'Yes,' said our mother.

It was then that I realised our mother was afraid. And alone.

I reached out and took her hand.

'We're all here, Mum. We know cancer sucks. We're all here for you.'

'About time,' she said, lifting her napkin and dabbing the tears away.

CHAPTER FORTY

The day after Paul and Tavvy flew back to the US, the story of the Bruny Bridge broke across the world. It hit the front page of the *Hong Kong Standard* with the headline CHINA DOWN UNDER and detailed the bold plan to move half a million Tasmanians from their homes onto a smaller, more southern island so that five million Chinese could be the first settlers. Within an hour, the *Guardian* picked it up and ran it online in the UK. It went live on the *New York Times* website too. Then it ran in the *Financial Times* and the regular *Times* in London. With the cat out of the bag abroad, variations on SOLD FOR BILLIONS! ran on the front page of every major paper in Australia. No journalist could be prosecuted for revealing classified information if the information was already public knowledge around the world. And the stories were all run very carefully under the guise of syndicated copy—one of the rare benefits of a Murdoch press.

The story reached the readers of the Hobart *Mercury* last. *The Mercury* headline wasn't SOLD FOR BILLIONS! It was TASSIE

MILLIONAIRES! The front page included a big headshot of JC and an interview declaring his full support of the plan.

'This plan,' JC was quoted as saying, 'allows us to take care of Tasmanians. People complain that politicians don't think long term. Well, this is long term. We're all going to be millionaires. What could possibly be wrong with that? And we'll be in charge of our own destiny.'

When it was pointed out that Tasmanians would no longer be in charge of their destiny because they'd be living not in a state of Australia, but a state of China, JC refuted it. 'We'll still be Tasmanians,' he said. 'That's our identity and no-one can take that away. We'll have state-of-the-art facilities on one of the most beautiful islands in the world. Right across the bridge, we'll have services and industries the Chinese are looking to develop and the jobs that come with that. Tasmania may yet become the next Silicon Valley with the technology the Chinese are looking to bring here. Tasmanians will be laughing all the way to the bank. That's way better than being the poor cousin nationally.'

Every day that week, it made the front page, and numerous pages within. The letters section stretched to three pages by the Saturday. Online the discussion ran like wildfire. All over Australia people were debating the pros and cons of Tasmania being sold to the Chinese.

The mainland shock jocks promoted the government line. What's good for Tassie is good for Australia. The words 'mendicant state' were touted. A drain on the federal coffers. Unemployment. All the economics of a remote destination with failing educational standards, high youth unemployment and the health stats of a poor, badly educated, ageing population. It was best to detach. Remove the weak link. 'Like plucking a bad grape from the bunch,' one of them said. 'Australia will be stronger without Tasmania.'

Barney Viper featured heavily in the conversation. JC was out every day spruiking the deal. And Max prevaricated. Behind the scenes, her party was completely divided. Some saw it as the ultimate solution for Tasmanian families doing it tough. The old communists in the party embraced the whole scheme. More progressive members were adamantly resistant, calling it a vicious betrayal. Max had to somehow walk that tightrope and it wasn't easy. She agreed that this was a way to lift every child out of poverty. But she did not see this as a brighter future for Tasmanians.

Amy O'Dwyer, leader of the Greens, was unequivocal. Her anger was incandescent. She came out in full force, declaring a giant conspiracy had been enacted on the Tasmanian people. She gave a speech on parliament lawns. 'People call us Greens optimistic as if it is an insult. Because optimists fail to recognise the reality of forces at work beyond optimism: economic realism. Well, this is what economic realism looks like! Our ineffective federal government and our obsequious state government would have us surrender our values, our sense of place and our heritage. They would sell Tasmania to a foreign power that has no respect for human rights, democracy or the rule of law. Being Tasmanian is more than being from a place. It is our identity. We are Tasmanians first, Australians second. We love our island and our community. We will never surrender.'

#NeverSurrender became a meme with every kind of interpretation. #SaveTassie began trending internationally on all the social media platforms.

Farris, the BFG, Bruny in Action and every other group, both pro and anti the bridge, aligned against the deal too. All over the world, people were posting their photos of Tassie, sharing their stories of Tassie. Brilliant seascapes. Wild surfing breaks. Dolphins and whales. Wine and cheese. The deep wonder of rainforests. Wild rivers. Mountains. Bushwalks. Fresh air. Auroras. Fishing. Kayaking. Everyone who had ever been to Tassie was suddenly online. There was a global outpouring of Tassie love.

JC fought back valiantly, telling Tasmanians they needed to carefully consider their finances. This was a way to realise their investment in Tasmania—an offer that would never come again. An offer that could make their family wealthy for generations. They could choose to give up work.

The real estate industry was enthusiastically declaring the deal a win for all Tasmanians, but Amy O'Dwyer declared it just a win for their commissions. Amy's partner, Charles Lee of Tourism Tasmania, was reporting a sudden spike in bookings from people wanting to visit before it all disappeared.

Barney Viper encouraged all the homeowners wanting to become millionaires to rally on the Parliament House lawns the following weekend. But a sit-in began on the lawns days before that, and it wasn't those wanting to get three times the value of their properties, as Viper had expected. It began with a few Tibetans, but within two days the crowd had swelled to thirty thousand people. And because of the protest fines, it wasn't a rally. It was a knit-a-thon. Needles and yarn of every variety were brought out to create a community event. People began knitting maps of Tasmania. Soon, not a ball of wool could be found in Hobart. Jumpers were being unravelled. Second-hand shops sold out of knitted garments, toys and blankets. Anything crocheted was being unwound and re-knitted at a great rate. Craft shops were awaiting new stock from the mainland. Relatives and friends in Melbourne, London, Sydney, Brisbane, Hong Kong, Perth and Adelaide sent parcels. Map-of-Tassie knit-a-thons began in other towns and cities. The owner of the famous art gallery outside Hobart offered to turn the maps into a permanent installation and funded the purchase of more wool.

Barney Viper was enraged at this peaceful uprising. When asked if he felt that this takeover of Tasmania by the Chinese government was another version of Tibet, Viper called the Dalai Lama a shuffling old monk and a CIA-funded fraud. He called the protestors the Anti-Everything Brigade. Then he harangued the Tasmanian chief of police, insisting that he issue five-thousand-dollar fines to the knitters on the lawns of Parliament House. But the police chief, a man who had seen a few protests in his time, said on ABC TV, 'Senator Viper needs to remember that this is Tasmania and people can knit wherever they like.'

The Eternal Fragrant President gave an interview saying that the historic links between our two countries had been at the heart of the project. His government had responded to an offer by the Australian government in good faith. It had never been China's preference to hide the deal from the Tasmanian people. China had done so only at the request of the Australian government. He also said that the notion of the sale of Tasmania had really been an exploration of how the two countries could better ally themselves. China had always had a presence in Tasmania, and it valued Tasmania as a jewel of the Southern Ocean. No disrespect was ever meant to the Tasmanian people. He stood by the offer outlined in the proposal and said that any Tasmanian wishing to sell their property to a Chinese investor was no different to anyone selling to any willing buyer. This was the face of democracy that he knew Australians respected. The transition process from an Australian to a Chinese territory would have to be reviewed, but he was sure that a solution was possible.

The journalist of the *Hong Kong Standard* article had disappeared. Word was she'd been whisked away to mainland China for re-education. But she popped up instead in New York, seeking asylum, with all the China Project paperwork, and a whole new media frenzy began on the details that had not yet been revealed.

The betrayal of government, the duplicity of politicians, the notion of community sovereignty, the infiltration of the Chinese Communist Party into Australia, the problem of overpopulation in the world, the making of backroom deals in the Australian parliament, politicians riding roughshod over due process, Tasmanians becoming wealthy and the upcoming Tasmanian election—all these issues were in hot debate on every media platform. As was the behaviour of another summer cyclone hitting the coast south of Sydney.

Sydneysiders were battening down the hatches. Cyclone Pauline last summer was vivid in people's minds and this one was behaving with similar ferocity. It was causing massive three- and four-metre storm surges, flooding coastal properties around Batemans Bay. It had flattened crops and destroyed roads, bridges and marinas. There was talk of it moving inland, towards Canberra, and blowing itself out. There was the chance it could move north towards Sydney; that got everyone very worked up. But it didn't. The cyclone continued down the coast of Victoria until it hit the Tasman Sea. Meteorologists declared that now it would blow itself out. The cyclone was named Angus.

By the time the crowd of knitters had swelled to fifty thousand, and Salamanca was overflowing with picnic rugs, thermoses and knitting needles, Viper's would-be millionaires were vastly outnumbered. JC decided to give it one last shot. He switched his charm into overdrive on every media channel as he attempted to convince the Tasmanian electorate that he was not a traitor, and that he had always, *always*, had the best interests of Tasmanians at heart. He said the vision to develop Bruny Island with all the benefits of a rich society—with investment in architecture, design, housing, the arts, sport, lifestyle—all this could be an inspiration to the world. Tasmania was yet again leading the way, benefiting from foresight, just as it had in becoming a clean, green destination.

Amy O'Dwyer came out and reminded the world that the Green movement had begun in Tasmania, and it was her party that had set the agenda for a clean, green destination, and Liberal and Labor had done everything they could to dismantle that vision, and never more so than now.

BRUNY

'Clean,' she said, 'ought to also reflect the behaviour of our politicians. Never has such an insidious deceit been brewed in the darkness of both state and federal parliaments. What will be next? Will we sell the Blue Mountains, Uluru, the Opera House? Why stop there? What price Western Australia? Or, for that matter, our whole country?'

WHAT PRICE OUR COUNTRY? was on the front of many newspapers the following day.

It turned out that the rest of Australia was rather fond of Tasmania. New Zealand was too. An ex-head of the Australian armed services came out and said, speaking only as a private citizen, he believed that a Chinese presence, able to launch ballistic missiles from nuclear-powered ships and submarines off the coast of Tasmania, was clearly not something that had been thought through at the highest levels.

CHAPTER FORTY-ONE

On the Monday before the Tasmanian election, the federal government was still trying to spin the Tassie deal, declaring it a plan by Tasmanians for Tasmanians. Viper was spruiking the Tasmanian election as a referendum on Tassie's future. A vote for JC, a vote for the Liberal government, was a vote for wealth and progress. Which was just a variation on jobs and growth, Amy O'Dwyer pointed out, and Tasmanians were too smart to buy that when the only jobs and growth were going to be in Chinese factories if the Liberals had anything to do with it.

The PM began back-pedalling on the Tuesday, no doubt receiving polling numbers on the hour. He contradicted Viper, saying that despite the China Project being a Tasmanian-inspired initiative, indeed *the vision* of his esteemed colleague Senator Viper, and a project co-funded by the federal government for the good of the Tasmanian people, he had never really been sure that this was what the Australian people would want. And he had been proved right. 'Which just goes to show,' he said on ABC TV's *7.30*, 'that all research is flawed.'

'Are you saying, Prime Minister, that there was research done to ask Tasmanians if they were willing to settle on Bruny Island, in a new high-rise city with a population density of Sydney, while the Chinese took over Tasmania?'

'I believe so,' he told the ABC journalist. The research was not made public.

He was a prime minister who had vacillated on so many issues that this became simply another of his flip-flops. He admitted that, in light of both local and international concern, his government may have to review the contract. A multi-billion-dollar land sale, even if it was for the good of all Australians, probably required deeper consideration. This didn't win him any friends. All over social media Tasmanians were posting pictures of themselves saying: *We are not land*. The following day the PM suggested (not to disagree with his esteemed colleague Senator Barney Viper, or interfere in state politics) that perhaps when the Tasmanian people re-elected the Liberal government in Tasmania, a referendum could be held on the deal.

Viper's role as the mastermind of the China Project burned like wildfire through the media. Viper finally had his moment in the sun and, like Icarus, he fell. No matter that it may not have been entirely true. Aid-n-Abet maintained a very low profile. The prime minister needed a scapegoat and Viper was it. The PM and his government were up for re-election within twelve months. Better to lose Tasmania, and a senator in his last term, than to risk further damage.

The bridge was to be opened on Friday, March 4th. The Tasmanian election was scheduled for Saturday, March 5th. Schools had been booked to bring their students to line the bridge. Local, national and international media were coming into Hobart for the opening. Celebrities and dignitaries from far and wide, and, of course, JC and Max and Amy O'Dwyer were all to be at the launch. So was I. But Cyclone Angus had other plans.

Cyclone Angus had increased in size by entwining itself with another low-pressure system forming in the Tasman Sea. Now Angus was mammoth and meteorologists were predicting it would hit Tasmania's east coast within twenty-four hours. On Friday morning, March 4th, Hobartians awoke to a cyclone warning for all southern waters. This was without precedent. There had never been a cyclone this far south. But the ocean temperature along the east coast of Tasmania had never before reached twenty-six degrees; at least, not since records had been kept. We had become cyclone territory.

I had been beside JC all week through the media storm. I had watched Frank Pringle assure JC that things would settle down. It was just a matter of riding it out. Tasmanians needed some time to get their heads around it. Beyond that it would all be fine, and JC would be hailed as a visionary. Let the people get to the election, have their say in the privacy of the ballot box, then JC would know it had all been worth it.

JC had the sense not to buy it. The polls on Thursday had him at seven per cent. Even lower than the Labor premier whose resignation had made room for Max to become leader.

'What we need is for someone to blow up the bridge,' JC said to me. 'Where's a bomber when you need one?'

The beautiful thing about living an international life, moving from war zone to conflict zone, from rebel stronghold to terrorist headquarters, from corrupt government to outposts of hope, is that you meet some very talented people. Talented recruiters, talented ballistics experts, talented divers.

On Thursday, when the cyclone was circling in on our TV screens and the bridge opening was delayed until the storm had passed, I told JC I was going to Bruny.

'It won't hit Tasmania,' said JC.

'It's never going to reach land,' said Max. 'Let alone Hobart.'

'It's not looking good,' said Stephanie. 'You really sure you want to go to Bruny?'

'I'll go first thing tomorrow. I need to make sure the house is all battened down,' I said.

'Why is it named after Grandad, Aunty Ace?' Grace asked.

'Cyclone Angus? Because Grandad has a sense of humour,' I told her.

You coming back to the island? Dan texted me.

Yes, I replied.

Pick you up at Tinderbox at 7 am, he texted. *Not safe after that.*

At Tinderbox the sky had the look of a week-old cork bruise. The sea was getting wilder. The wind was increasing. All the bunting for the launch was strewn across the paddocks. Up on the hill, the BFG camp was deserted but for a few cars parked beside the farmhouse. The marquee and tents were all gone. There was no-one in sight. The worksite had been evacuated, too, all those prefab buildings full of office equipment and bridge paraphernalia were empty. Even the security guards had been sent home, the temporary structure of their offices deemed unsafe for the forecast wind.

Dan had brought a large power boat across. 'Not trusting the Zodiac today,' he said.

'Don't suspension bridges wobble?' I asked as we left the shore.

'They engineered that out,' he said over the wind. 'But, yes, in a wind they used to start twisting. This one's designed to move up and down about five metres, but the caissons go down to bedrock. No wind is going to knock that thing over. Now hang on. It's going to be a little hairy mid-channel. Must be nearing thirty knots.'

I surveyed the bridge as we passed along its length towards Dennes Point. I looked at the scale of the thing and thought about metrics. All the engineering specs I'd memorised over the last few months.

Total length of bridge including approaches from abutment to abutment: 2052 metres.

Length of suspension span including main span and side spans: 1474 metres.

Length of main span portion of suspended structure (distance between towers): 960 metres.

Length of one side span: 257 metres.

Width of bridge: 27 metres.

Width of roadway between kerbs: 19 metres.

Width of footpath: 3 metres.

Total weight of each anchorage: 54,400 tonnes.

Total weight of bridge, anchorages and approaches: 811,500 tonnes.

～

At 9 am the ferry service was shut down at Kettering. By then, the wind was over forty knots. Out on my balcony I took a few pictures to accompany my report. Once it was encrypted and despatched I took my second phone and removed the sim card and fried them both in the microwave. I then took the melted remains to the old outdoor toilet and let it all fall into the long drop.

I had thought long and hard about what life could look like beyond the election. I had thought long and hard about Tasmania and Tasmanians and the bridge, JC, Max and my family. I had thought about my dad. I had thought a lot about my dad. I had thought about Dan Macmillan.

I made a call to Stephanie, who had picked up Mother from the hospital and taken her home to their place with Phillip. Phillip had brought several bottles of Hendrick's with him, and everything was just fine. Stephanie said all southern coastal properties less than three metres above sea level were being evacuated. Which turned out to be a lot of homes around Hobart. Stephanie had opened their house for anyone needing to relocate from lower Sandy Bay.

'It's a little crazy. We have three families here already and another two on the way. The kids are going silly with this wind, but it feels good to be helpful,' said Stephanie.

'The election has been postponed,' she added. 'They're predicting power blackouts across southern Tasmania.'

'So you're speaking to JC again?' I asked. I had never imagined Stephanie angry, but her rage about the bridge and the deal had taken on the kind of hostility that might well have summoned Cyclone Angus. She hadn't spoken to JC since the day the news had broken.

'You know, Ace,' she said, 'JC has lived his life just as he's wanted. I have stood by him. But I'm not blind. And I'm not stupid. I happen to value family above everything else. But Tasmania is my family too. That's where he went wrong. What on earth did he think he was doing?

'I blame Viper,' she said. 'And I know JC. He wouldn't have come around to this easily. Whatever Viper knows made him pliable. I don't need to know. I suspect you do, because you have a way of knowing. He's going to lose the election. He's going to lose everything he's worked so hard for. Everything *we've* worked so hard for. He's going to be remembered as a traitor. And I'm the traitor's wife.'

'Oh, Stephanie,' I said.

'You can go home to New York and nobody will know about this. But I have to live with it,' she said.

'Maybe you and the girls might like to go live at my place for a few months?' I said. 'You're welcome to stay as long as you like, actually.'

'You're not going back to New York?' she asked.

'I think I'm going to stay here. For a while at least. Until the dust settles.' I hadn't been sure until I said it, but now I was. Somehow, I knew I wasn't going anywhere.

'Let's get through this storm,' she said. 'I mean, both storms. I still can't believe it's called Angus.'

'God works in mysterious ways,' I said.

Dan had tried to insist I spend the night at his place, but I wanted to be alone. If anything went wrong with the plans Edward and I had made, I wanted to be the first to know. And in truth, I still thought it was all going to be okay. Cyclones lose power over land. To come into the Derwent River, the storm needed to cross several peninsulas and waterways. By then, it would be wind and rain. I was high on a hill. I had gum trees around the house that might fall but there was nothing to be done about that now.

No house in this part of Tasmania was built to protect it from easterly weather. West is the prevailing direction for any storm. Tasmania didn't get cyclones. Sydney didn't get cyclones, until it did. The chance of Angus doing any real damage was low to nil. That's what everyone said.

But Cyclone Angus wasn't playing by the rules.

At dusk that day, Cyclone Angus crossed the hills and peninsulas and hit Hobart. One of its first victims was the mobile tower on Mount Wellington. Every phone in a hundred-mile radius lost coverage. That included Bruny Island. By then, the power had been out for hours.

CHAPTER FORTY-TWO

Someone was banging at my back door. I shone the torch in the eerie darkness and there was Dan.

'What the hell are you doing out in this?' I asked.

'Checking you're okay,' he said, his face wet, his oilskin dripping.

'Maiden in distress?' I asked.

'Not quite a maiden.' He grinned. 'But if you could act like one, it might be fun.'

This whole conversation was carried on at a shout over the banshee wind.

'Come down to mine,' he said. 'I've got the car.' His house was more protected. Lower down the hill.

And then a terrific rush of wind made us both jump, followed by a tree branch crashing through the kitchen window. The whole house shook and groaned, the wind screamed. I dropped the torch. I had an image of Dorothy hurtling out of Kansas, airborne in her flying house.

'Too late,' he said. He had already grabbed my arm and was pulling me into the hall.

'Bedroom,' he said.

'I thought you'd never ask,' I replied, but he didn't hear.

Dan began dragging the wardrobe across the window and the chest of drawers in front of it to anchor the wardrobe more securely.

'Grab the bedding,' he said. 'We have to get under there. These old sleigh beds, they're made to go the distance.'

We pulled pillows, the doona and blankets into the space below the bed.

'I'll be back,' I called over the wind.

I scuttled back to the kitchen where rain was sluicing the floor. I crawled under the branch and looked about with the torch beam. There it was. I pulled my backpack from the remains of what had recently been the kitchen bench. My roof, I thought. The branches and leaves on the newly arrived tree branch shivered and quivered in the torchlight. The wind was making the most hideous howling sound, as if a thousand grieving spirits had been loosened from the dark caves of the underworld. Glass was shattered across the floor. Back in the bedroom, I tossed the bag in under the bed and crawled in after it.

'Supplies,' I said to Dan.

'You're a nut,' he said. 'What was so important?'

I pulled a gyro lantern out of the backpack. I turned off the torch and wound the lantern awkwardly in the confined space. It gave a gentle glow to our cocoon of blankets and pillows. The dark space beneath the wooden slats became a cave. His proximity was a little disturbing. His eyes were dark blue in the lamplight, his teeth very white. My hand searched the backpack and found the zip. I brought out the bottle. I handed it to him. Suddenly I felt giggly. I'm in shock, I thought.

It was the whisky we'd been given after the death of the Chinese worker.

'I thought if we died it would be a shame to waste it,' I said.

'What else have you got in there?' he asked. I smelled the damp, good smell of him.

'A book,' I said. 'I just figured if it was my last night, I'd rather spend it doing the things I like.'

'So what book?'

I showed him.

'*One Hundred Great Ghost Stories*,' he read. 'Food?'

'Biscuits and cheese. Chocolate. Couple of apples. Packet of mixed nuts.'

'Right now, you are the most attractive woman on earth,' he said.

Once the lamp burned down, it seemed pointless to rewind it. We checked our phones. Both on low battery now. We lay side by side in the pitch-black, the blankets beneath us not doing much to soften the floor. He took one of my hands and held it. The storm raged on, a symphony of catastrophic proportions. The whisky was warm in me. I closed my eyes.

'I don't want to be crushed to death,' I said.

The skin of his hand was a little rough. I curled my hand into it, and he stroked his thumb near my thumb.

'This house was built in 1939. It isn't built to withstand a cyclone,' I said. 'It's too close to the trees. We shouldn't even be having a cyclone. Or a super storm, or whatever this is.

It's not right. It's not even possible. Everyone knows that. What's happening to the world?'

He pulled me closer. I reached my fingers up through the bed slats and felt the mattress.

'I don't want to suffocate either. I don't want to be crushed to death. What if the legs give way? Are you sure the legs won't give way?'

'Pretty sure they won't,' he said.

'It'll be like a sandwich press. I don't want to die that way.'

Dan offered me another slug of whisky and took one himself. Somehow this seemed the most sensible thing to do. I had never lived through a severe weather event. But I had seen the aftermath of hurricanes and tsunamis. 'Severe weather event' seemed an improbable term for whatever was happening outside. I had worked with people who had lost everything. Their homes, their businesses, their churches and schools, their children and elderly: all washed away in storms or blown towards death by wind or water on an unprecedented scale. Except now there was no unprecedented. There was whatever happened next.

I thought of how the media would measure it against other storms. It would be explained by changing currents, warmer temperatures. An act of God. When we couldn't explain it any other way, it was always an act of God. Even insurance companies called it that, trying to explain the inexplicable. A medieval God perhaps. An ancient vengeful God of Chaos. Something freed by an archaeological dig, ripping through this part of the world at forty degrees latitude and unleashing an ancient might.

Lightning cracked, sending shards of light across the floor and about the bed. Then it blinked out and the thunder broke once more. I had seen those illustrations on weather charts of warming water and the effect this had on cold air and precipitation, and how it lifted then travelled and gained velocity. The rain was pounding on the roof. Thunder sounded again. Very close. So close we felt it reverberate in our bodies.

'Fuck,' Dan said, squeezing me closer. 'Whatever is going on out there, it's going to pass. It has to. It has to drop out eventually.'

'What if this is it?' I said. 'Hypothetically.'

'I don't think it is,' he said. 'Hypothetically.'

'But if it is,' I said, 'what should we be talking about?'

'Well,' said Dan, 'if this were the last hour of my life, I think it would be the time to confess to anything I'd never confessed before.'

I stayed silent. He waited.

'Well?' he said.

'You go first,' I said.

'I think it's a ladies-first moment.'

The wind was a moan now, a things-coming-apart kind of moan. I'd had all the edges knocked off me with death and falling trees and his body so close to me, the whisky inside me and the urge to be loved. I told Dan the thing I'd never told anyone, not even my best friend at the time, Becky Walton.

'When I was seventeen, I got pregnant,' I said. 'You couldn't get an abortion in Tasmania back then, so my mother took me to Melbourne. At the clinic, when they asked her to sign the

forms for the operation, she wouldn't let me have any anaes-
thetic. Usually they give you a general, or at least a local. But
I wasn't allowed anything. She told the doctor that she didn't
want me to forget it. So they stuck a hose inside me and there
was this lovely nurse, an older woman, who held my hand and
cried the whole time. It was really painful, but it was harder
watching her. All the nurse kept saying, over and over, was: "I'm
so sorry, sweetheart, I'm so sorry." Later that day, my mother
took me to a fancy restaurant she'd heard about. She seemed
surprised that during the meal I could think of nothing to say.
I haven't really had anything to say to her since.'

Dan seemed frozen momentarily, then he pulled me very
close and held me.

'Ace.'

'It was a long time ago.'

He kissed my forehead. The first kiss he'd given me. He
ran his hand over my hair and I felt the warmth of his face
against my cheek. After a while, I said, 'Your turn. Something
you've never told anyone.'

'Well,' he said, 'I'd tell you I'm in love with you.'

I was now the frozen one.

'And I'd wish I'd told you sooner, so that at least there might
be the possibility of sex. But of course, you may not feel the same
way. And now we're in this situation where even if we wanted
to, sex would be seriously awkward, and when the next tree
comes down, we could be pinioned together when the rescue
workers discover our dead bodies in the morning.'

I could feel my heart beating and the blood in my veins.

He said, 'You going to help me out here at all?'

I didn't know what to say.

'Play the game, Ace,' he said.

It made me smile, that.

'Oh, God, don't tell me it's all me?' he said, groaning. 'You're killing me here.'

There was another gigantic drum roll of thunder. The wind reached a top note of operatic shrillness.

'I'm out of practice . . .'

'What?' he asked.

'I might be . . .'

'In love with me?' he asked. 'A little bit?'

'Yes,' I said.

'Say it, Ace. You're about to die. This is what people say to each other when they're about to die.'

'I might be in love with you, Dan Macmillan.'

'Good girl,' he said. 'I don't think we are going to die, by the way.'

'Fuck you,' I said.

'I'm waiting.' He grinned.

And then, as he was kissing me, really kissing me, the gum tree by the front fence surrendered its roots and came through the bedroom roof. Ceiling plaster, beams, all of it came crashing down on top of the wardrobe and the bed.

Rain began cascading onto the floor around us, and there was a vivid smell of eucalyptus. I reached my hand out beyond the bed and felt wet leaves with the tips of my fingers. The tree groaned and settled. The bed sighed above us, as if burdened by a great weight. One leg groaned in an almost human way, but the frame held. I realised, in the next flash of lightning, that I was looking into the yard.

'The wall's gone,' I said. 'Are you sure we aren't going to die?'

'I'm sure,' he said. We both reached up and felt the mattress pushed hard between the slats. Wind was rushing into our cave in freezing blasts.

We took several more slugs of whisky. Then we pulled the blankets and doona closer about us, up over our heads. We huddled in there, and I thought of all the walls caving in. I thought of Tavvy and Paul.

'Kiss me again,' I said. So he did.

After some time, as the creaking and groaning of whatever was above us continued, I managed to turn over. I pulled Dan's arms around me, and he curled his body against me, tightening the blankets about us.

'Don't let me go,' I said. I prayed silently then, one of the only prayers I remembered. Hail Mary, full of Grace, the Lord is with thee, blessed art thou among women and blessed is the fruit of thy womb, Jesus. Holy Mary Mother of God, pray for us sinners, now and at the hour of our death. And then I added, Just let us get through the night. Do whatever you have to do to me tomorrow. Just let us get through this.

Improbably, I slept. It might have been the whisky. It might have been him. It might have been the prayer. At some point, deep in the wee hours, as the storm was leaving, an almighty noise was heard across the channel. It woke me. I listened to it rolling on and on. It seemed to go deep into the core of the earth. There was a wild screeching and wailing, high-pitched and cruel. I wondered if those awake thought it was the storm giving its last hurrah. I lay there for a long time, listening to Dan's gentle breathing, feeling him close to me, until sleep washed me away.

CHAPTER FORTY-THREE

Dawn had come by the time we woke. The floorboards were awash. The bedding was half sodden. But I was warm in his arms. The quiet was eerie.

He squeezed me.

'Did you sleep?' I asked.

'I did,' he said. 'It was actually kind of nice.'

We crawled stiff and sore from our quarters to discover a new skylight that was the whole of the roof. There was a turbulent clouded sky hurrying west, wind still blowing but with none of the force of the night. Everything in the house that hadn't been destroyed was wet and harried. Pictures on the walls had fallen to the floor, windows were shattered, leaves and other debris had blown onto the furniture and into every corner, electricals were dangling from the roof remains.

We managed to clamber out to the balcony. There we took in the scene before us. Dan's truck had escaped the tree but the forest beyond looked as if someone had banged about with a large stick. Flattened patches of trees were dark against those still standing. Across the street I could see another house missing part of its roof. There was a caravan rolled over in the street and the power lines were ripped and dangling. The sky and the sea were a violent mauve. And the Bruny Bridge was gone. It was a glaring omission in the landscape. Or, rather, the seascape. No bridge. All that remained were two roadways reaching out high above the water, but everything in between—wire, cable, caisson, roadway and railing, all of it, every screw, bolt, rivet, every last metre and tonne of it—had disappeared.

Dan said, 'What the . . .' He rubbed his face and looked at the gap again, as if expecting that it was a trick of the light.

'No way. Fuck. No way.' He started along the deck. 'Come with?' he asked.

'Shouldn't we check your house first?'

'It can wait,' he said. 'I've got to see this.'

On the foreshore other residents, as dishevelled as we were, stood staring at the absence of the bridge across the channel.

'I think it's the first time I've ever believed in God,' said Gilbert Farris.

'Where the hell did it go?' Dan asked. 'There's no way . . .'

'I guess it's all down there,' said Farris.

'It's not possible,' said Dan. 'The thing was over-engineered to buggery. Unless the steel . . .'

'The steel,' said Farris.

'Chinese steel,' said Dan. 'Quality issues. We had problems early on. But we were testing constantly.'

'It sleeps with the fishes,' said Farris's wife, Barbara, coming to stand beside her husband.

'I think, whatever it was, Angus got the better of it,' said Farris.

'How did you fare up there?' Barbara asked me.

'Not great,' I said. 'You?'

We all turned to look at the Farris's. Two gums had come down right beside the house.

'Four inches to the right and we'd have lost the eaves,' she said.

'Five feet to the right and we'd have lost the TV,' said Farris. And we all laughed.

The BFG camp was tossed and scattered along the beach. Fragments of the temporary buildings were visible all the way up the hill.

'We better check on everyone,' said Dan.

There was still no mobile coverage. If there was going to be any help, we were it. We went from house to house, searching for survivors. We clambered over debris and tree branches, called out for any sign of life under flattened walls and caved-in roofs. Dan and Farris used chainsaws to cut away branches and free doors and driveways. The people we found had the bright eyes of survivors and the conversation of those who've escaped the firing squad. Farris had a complete inventory of residents. Apparently he'd gone from house to house in the days before, confirming who was here on North Bruny and who wasn't. It occurred to me, then, that he had taken this notion of Bruny Friends very seriously.

Eventually we came to my house again. By now there were eight or nine of us, a small troupe of dishevelled islanders, hoping against hope that the only thing we'd find today was wreckage, not dead bodies. And so far, we'd been in luck. Other than bruises, scrapes, wide-eyed children and a dog with a broken leg who had been seriously terrified by the storm, there were no casualties. My house looked like something from a disaster movie. The highest house on the hill, it had taken the full force of the storm.

Farris shook his head. 'My,' he said. 'You won't be sleeping in there any time soon.'

Dan took my hand and we all walked down the hill to his house. There was a fair bit of debris in the yard and on his deck. Someone's plastic bucket was caught under the steps. A cover from a boat had blown against the side of the house. But somehow the macrocarpa hedge and the random effects of weather had saved it.

'We'll leave you two to it,' said Farris. 'Get some rest. We'll take a couple of cars and see how things are further afield.'

'I've got a freezer full of fish that's been defrosting since the power went out,' said Dan. 'I can get a fire going. Everyone's welcome for a feed in, say, an hour?'

Farris and the others nodded, and they went on.

Inside the house the carpet was wet where rain had blown in under the door. Dan set about getting the wood heater going. When it was burning brightly, he said, 'You think someone might have come back and finished it off? Whatever they began back in November?'

I sighed. 'Another bomb? Hard to say.'

'Could have laid the charges before the storm came in,' he said. 'Could have laid them any time, I guess. Might have been down there for a week. Or more. Until someone pressed a button.'

He went to the gas stove and lit it with a match. He filled the espresso maker, put it over the flame, took down two cups. Took down a bottle of brandy. Put a measure in each cup.

The coffee steamed, the cups were filled. He put milk in his and handed the black one to me.

'You're very quiet,' he said.

'My house is destroyed,' I said.

'My bridge is destroyed,' he said.

'Well, cheers,' I said.

'Well, cheers,' he said.

❧

The clean-up after the cyclone was immense. Cars had been upended and blown into fields. Roofs and walls were missing off houses and shed. Boats had fled their moorings. The Brooke Street Pier in Hobart had sunk, leaving just the rear end above sea level, like a moment from *Titanic*. School buildings had been flattened. The Tinderbox worksite had been right in the path; the BFG farmhouse over that side looked like it had been split for firewood.

It took days to work out what had happened to the bridge. The weather was erratic and diving too dangerous. People assumed it had been the storm. Suspension bridges had a history, after all.

When divers assessing the wreckage discovered the bolts hadn't given way, the metal cables hadn't snapped, the caissons hadn't fallen, that in fact the bridge was lying in a million tiny pieces across the bottom of the channel, the government went crazy trying to pin it on the Greens and on Farris. Maggie Lennox came in for some harsh interrogation. Farris was held for three days for questioning. Every member of every protest group was hauled in. They found chemicals in Farris's shed capable of making a bomb.

I was called in too; no-one had better contacts with all the protesters. I spent two days with the federal police going over everyone on their books. It was hard to tell if they thought of me as someone providing useful information or as a possible suspect. They were very polite. They called me back a few days later, but after an hour clarifying some details, they let me go. On the way out, I saw Edward Lowe in a meeting room. He made a show of coming out to speak to me, kissing me on both cheeks.

'A terrible business,' he said. 'So lucky no-one was killed. I hear you lost your house too?'

'Yes,' I said.

'You will rebuild?'

'I will.'

'Good,' he said.

He introduced me to the senior detective from Sydney, whom I had met briefly on the previous visit.

'No-one worked harder to make the bridge happen for this community than Astrid,' he said.

I said goodbye, and after that I didn't hear from the feds again. The feds were sure to know Edward was ASIO. If he was vouching for me, they knew he'd done his homework.

❧

Meanwhile the Chinese workers disappeared. They all got back on their planes to Shanghai and Beijing. The Chinese Buddhists lay low. They weren't out helping to rebuild. They disappeared to their property on Bruny behind the gates with their lion statues, and were not seen for weeks.

In the national media, there were endless theories. Dams and forests and fish farms had taught Tasmanians well. Separate, divided, they were like any other rabble. Disorganised. Ill-informed. Not enough money or resources. But when they coalesced—in this instance around a plan by both the federal and state governments to move them from their homes—they were unstoppable.

Gilbert Farris was quoted as saying, 'There's nothing more formidable than island people.' He was still awaiting formal charges, but word was they had no case. Apparently the chemicals were the same as those most landowners had in their sheds. Put together, they could never have done what it took to destroy a bridge that size. There were no large transfers of money from his accounts. No evidence of any activity that suggested he had friends or allies capable of such a thing.

There have been a few famous underwater sabotages. The *Rainbow Warrior* in Auckland in 1985, bombed by French frogmen. The Waal Bridge in 1944, attempted by German Special Troops. And the VC campaign against South Vietnamese and US forces in 1967, which had mixed success. But there had been nothing like the Bruny Bridge.

It took a lot of experience, skill and money. The dive sets needed to do the job were twenty thousand dollars each. The three propulsion vehicles to get them in place were five thousand dollars each. The delivery craft cost forty thousand dollars, including the specialist crew with four divers. The extra equipment cost some two hundred thousand dollars, including firing devices, diving gas and pumps. Plus military-grade explosives. All done covertly. That cost more still.

But we had good information. We knew exactly how deep the caissons were. The exact strength of the cables. Exactly where the stress points were. Exactly how to avoid security.

The boat dropped the divers and all their equipment in the water four hundred metres up-current from the bridge, below the Tinderbox cliffs where Frank Pringle and I had first stood admiring the view. Tide and shipping had been researched meticulously.

The divers had to change their sets to a mixed-gas mode at about eight metres below, then they descended to the thirty-metre mark. They used inflation bags to make the bombs neutrally buoyant, and walked them towards the caissons. The main risk was that the current might separate the primers from the main charges. Empty sandbags were filled to hold the charges down. It was dark when all this happened, just to add to the complexity of the task.

The primary firing device, connected to a phone, was activated remotely. The secondary was manual, but it hadn't been required. On land, the cables were severed on the Tinderbox side. Without them tensioning the structure, and with the towers blown, it all went down as one. It was timed to the second.

The team we employed came in the week before the storm. Bearded, urbane, well built. It's impossible to tell a smart terrorist from an art enthusiast these days. It took them three nights to prep everything and lay all the charges. They were gone days before the storm hit, by plane from Hobart and Launceston, and ship from Devonport. They're people who don't leave a trace. It just needed the remote signal. One phone call. And they had a perfect cover, thanks to a super storm bearing my father's name.

There had been no risk of sightseers. No security either, thanks to the storm. No casualties had been the first order, other than the fish, crabs and sharks caught in the explosion. Collateral damage, but still, I did feel bad about that.

Edward had sorted the money. Edward is a money man. He knew how to find it and he knew how to hide it. I ran the international team.

Gore Vidal was right: the US is a corrupted democracy, but it's still the best chance humans have of living peacefully. Regardless of who's in that chair in the Oval Office, there are interests that need protecting. Interests beyond America. As they say in the real estate game, location, location, location. The US is still the biggest economy in the world and it's the heartland of democracy. There was no way our black cell at Langley was letting a competing foreign interest that close to Australia. That's all I can tell you.

All my life I've worked to bring people together. To end conflict. To champion the notion of community, peace and reconciliation. And I've lived another life beneath all of that, infiltrating, learning secrets, trading information. Usually those two parts of my life, the public and the secret, are aligned. But not this time. It had been JC's bridge. It had been Dan's bridge. But it was going to be Tasmania's death knell. Two billion dollars' worth of metal and labour and concrete was now resting in pieces on the bottom of the channel.

I had fallen for an ideal. An ideal called home. And I'd created an act of violence to protect it. It took me a long time to realise that the shame I felt wasn't for my part in it. It was because I didn't feel guilty. I didn't feel guilty at all. I had done what it took to survive. For Tasmania to survive a little longer.

Break the rules. Me and Becky forging our mantra for life with our matching tattoos.

Is a place enough to believe in? Maybe not.

Is a people enough to believe in? Yes.

Is a way of life enough to believe in? Absolutely.

> If you can force your heart and nerve and sinew
> To serve your turn long after they are gone,
> And so hold on when there is nothing in you
> Except the Will which says to them, 'Hold on!'

Well, I had held on, and it had taken heart and nerve and sinew. But here was Tasmania and everything in it was okay. That's what I learned coming home. This is my doctrine. The sea. The sky. The light. I am a jihadist for my faith. Inside everyone, behind the light, is the darkness. On my dark side, I'm a spy and, for a little while, I became a terrorist. I put fear into the heart of this government. That's what a true terrorist does. Not into the hearts of ordinary citizens. No deaths or injuries. Just activism that frightens the daylights out of a government that thinks it can run roughshod over the people.

CHAPTER FORTY-FOUR

Once he put it together, enough to look at me with new eyes, Dan was silent a very long time. So long I felt as if time had stopped and he, we, might never speak again. He went off for a long walk. When he came back, I made us both tea. We went and sat outside on his balcony.

'The moment I saw you walking along the road towards me that night down at the pier, I thought, here's trouble,' he said.

'I know it was your bridge.'

'I hated that thing, you know that. I hated it even more when I knew what I'd built. If I could have blown the thing up myself . . .'

'You know if this ever . . .'

'You'll have to kill me.'

'Yes,' I said.

'Not if I kill you first,' said the ex-paratrooper.

I wasn't smiling. But he was. 'Astrid Coleman,' he said, 'conflict resolution specialist, you have outdone yourself. I don't think there's going to be much conflict after this.'

Of course there was but, in the wake of it all, I saw the good more than the bad in people. When Tasmanians finally went to the polls six weeks later, they voted in ways they never had. Afterwards, as they exited the polling booths, they didn't give anything away. They just shook their heads at the media and smiled that kind of slow, quiet smile Tasmanians have when they are amused by life.

A year later, the broken roadways leading to the Bruny Bridge had been removed and replaced with viewing platforms where people could come and observe the sea and think on what nearly was. A statue was erected on the Bruny side of a man and a woman, both more than three metres tall, staring back towards Tinderbox. It was called *Resistance*—a memorial to whoever had rid Tasmania of the bridge. The artist received an anonymous commission. The rest was up to her.

The federal government won't rebuild that bridge any time soon. Apparently, the payout crippled an insurance company in London. After the first bombing, no-one had thought there'd be a second.

The sale of Tasmania to the Chinese is not going ahead either, at least not in the foreseeable future. Far too much public outrage. More than I might have expected. Dan had been right. Tasmanians were not driven by money. They'd given that up a long time ago. They were driven by something else. Belonging. Community. A simpler life. Beauty. A whole lot of things that money can't buy.

The election outcome? Labor won eight seats, the Greens ten

and the Liberals six. It was the Liberal's worst loss in history. Labor's too. And Gilbert Farris was elected as the twenty-fifth member of the new parliament.

The Mercury predicted that Coleman brother and sister would form a Liberal/Labor coalition, but that was never going to happen. Amy O'Dwyer and Max began negotiating. Then Max did something unexpected. The week after JC stepped down, she held a media conference and resigned. She said that Tasmania had borne enough from the Coleman family and, from now on, she'd be returning to private life.

She took a trip to Western Australia, where she met a wine grower she'd been corresponding with. The only thing to add is the wine grower is a woman, and Max has never been happier. They've bought a vineyard three hours from Hobart. Max and JC have vigorous discussions about the alcohol market when she and Sandra come south.

The new Tasmanian parliament changed the rules for development applications and lease agreements. It changed the rules on foreign home ownership, too. Government compensation was negotiated for those businesses that had to surrender their Chinese partners and were returned to local ownership. Private leases in national parks and on Tasmanian beaches in foreign hands were also returned. It was considered a wise investment.

The rest of Australia was in uproar about the Tassie deal that first year and into the next, a lot of people worried it might be them next. Western Australia put their hand up and said they'd be grateful for a similar offer, but the federal government wasn't having a bar of it. Too many mines in WA. Couldn't have all those resources in foreign hands.

Farming land across Australia that was foreign-owned was secured by new laws, ensuring that half of anything produced on it had to stay in Australia. Power schemes that were foreign-owned were slowly returned to majority Australian ownership or state control. A recession came, but it was no worse than the last one, and somehow people got through it. Amy O'Dwyer secured the universal basic income for Tasmanians as a ten-year trial. Gambling licenses were wound back, so people couldn't give it all to pokie machines. Already the metrics on health and education are improving. More than that, it's as if whole suburbs have a new sense of pride.

Further afield, the very rich keep getting richer. The middle class keep sliding a little further behind. A lot of people have learned again how to fish and grow potatoes, how to cultivate their front yards, darn their clothes and make do with less. The global mechanisms continue. More governments are becoming dictatorships. Wherever that happens, women's rights are rolled back. More and more jobs are mechanised. Unemployment is increasing. There's more outrage, more unrest, more refugees, more climate chaos, more religious extremes, more terrorism. More depression and anxiety. Especially in young people. Nothing anyone didn't expect, if they'd been thinking at all.

Maybe it's only a matter of time before another deal is proposed. There's been some recent talk of water being shipped to China from Tasmania, but everyone is nervous now about Chinese deals.

What will it take to stop the next major threat? I have no idea. Hopefully by then I'll be an old lady up on the hill and my children and grandchildren will make those decisions.

CHAPTER FORTY-FIVE

Profound thought: *Living with your sins is not worse than dying for them.*

Our mother Hyacinth died three months after the bridge disappeared. It left more of a hole than I thought it would. I was glad for all the times I'd gone and sat with her, and all the G&Ts we'd drunk after the drugs stopped working in the final weeks. If she hadn't been the mother I'd wanted, what did it matter? We all disappoint someone. Another profound thought: *Your heart is with you your whole life.*

Before she slipped into her final sleep, she said, 'You're a good daughter, Astrid.'

'Thanks, Mum,' I said. 'If you knew all the things I'd done, you might not think that.'

'Oh, I know a few of them,' she said. 'Don't go waiting until you're in my position to forgive yourself. Or other people, for that matter. No-one is going to do it for you. Leave it behind, dear. Otherwise it just weighs you down.'

Then she said, 'I did my best to love you all. I don't think I was very good at it.'

'That's okay, Mum,' I said. 'We love you. We're all fine. You're not so fine, but has it been okay?'

'Life?' she asked. 'It's been a little disappointing, to be honest. Now, is there any champagne?'

Those were her last words.

JC was devastated by her loss. It was then that he begged Stephanie to come home from New York and she agreed, but only if he promised never to enter politics again. He invested in a gin and whisky company. It's called Truth Serum and the irony is not lost on anyone. He's dropped a lot of weight.

'I guess we're the grown-ups now,' I said to Max, after our mother's funeral.

'That didn't occur to you before?' Max asked.

'Strangely not,' I said.

It was a crazy time but, nearing sixty, life is allowed to be kind of crazy.

I bought a campervan after Mum died, and Dan and I headed off, finding out-of-the-way places to camp and fish all up the east coast of Australia. Once the worst of the winter was over, we went home to Bruny, and when we closed the curtains, lit the fire and turned on the music, we could forget what had nearly come to pass.

The light is beautiful in the mornings and, often on our walks, ours are still the only footprints on the beach. The shearwaters still nest in the dunes and take flight on the last warm wind of summer. The dolphins still leap in the channel. The sea eagles still nest in the great gums along the coastline. Wallabies graze in the paddocks, and rabbits too. The breeze still blows cold from the west and warm from the north. The fish farms continue.

I often wake surprised to find I am still in Tasmania. Being here and smelling the air, seeing the landscape and the light change through the seasons, I wonder why I tried so hard to stay away. This life now wasn't what I'd planned. Nor was falling in love with Dan. I'd thought that when I finally did start another relationship, I'd be wary. Jumpy. But Dan made it easy. Looking back on it, he treated me like a stray with wounds. He was kind and steady.

Tavvy met a Tasmanian in New York, and they are considering moving back to Australia. Tasmania is going to be the first place in the world to be totally mapped for a virtual reality game, and my son Paul is one of the team working on that. Years ahead, if chaos does come, if the forests are finally felled and the oceans turn toxic, my great-grandchildren might have that other reality where they can see the Tasmania that was mine, that was ours, when the world was simpler.

I think often of my dad. I remember him telling me that you become more of who you are the older you get. And it seems that in this, like a lot of things, he was right.

❧

Amy O'Dwyer, the first Green premier in Australia, and her husband Charles Lee were both at the Boxing Day lunch Stephanie and JC held the next Christmas. She has been doing an admirable job of running a multi-party government.

'So much easier this way, infiltrating Australia,' Charles said to me as he poured champagne. 'Marry an Australian.' We clinked glasses and laughed.

Max was there too, with Sandra. Tavvy and Paul had come from New York for Christmas with their partners. And Dan was there, of course. So was Edward Lowe, with a man called Tarif, a chef from Oman with a quiet sadness. They were an intensely good-looking pair, those two, and I wondered what Tarif knew. Did he have any idea? Was he one of us? I saw them out on the balcony surveying the view. There was something so world-weary about both of them, and I thought how that same thing was in me, even if I couldn't see it.

Henry Liu, May Chen and her father, Gao Enzhu, were also there. May and Henry were expecting a baby in June. They'd asked me and Dan to be godparents. I liked May's father very much. He was teaching me Mandarin.

One Saturday, Dan and I drove to the RSPCA and bought a dog and a cat. Wheeler and Riley. If you were to look in the window you might see us by the fire, curled up with our books, our wine or whisky. We don't watch TV. We don't even own a TV. I check the *New York Times* every few days and we read the papers on Saturday, but it's enough. The world is here, and we only have so many years. Some nights you might see us chatting out on the deck or heading down to the beach for a moonlit swim in the channel. Or you might see us in Hobart going to a movie or for dinner.

There is one thing about old age. It takes a long time. It started creeping up on me around fifty-three and it hasn't let go. Keeps having a word with me here and there and, no doubt, one day it will be the only conversation I'm having. But it's a long way away, that moment. And I think Dan is my lucky charm. He keeps me young. There's not a day goes by that he doesn't make me laugh.

I thought of Angus and how he would have been so proud of us all. And I imagined our mother surveying this scene. Max being gay, me hooking up with Dan, JC abandoning politics. The whole multicultural assortment at the dinner table. Worst for her would have been the Greens running the state. She would think the world really had come to an end. But it kind of does, here, in Tasmania. Or maybe it's the beginning. I wondered what Shakespeare quote our father might have summoned up for it all. Perhaps: *We know what we are, but know not what we may be.* Ophelia. *Hamlet.*

I had moved into Dan's place while mine was rebuilt, but now we live between the two homes. I still like my own space. My house is mostly an art studio now. Wheeler and Riley live with him. I like the way Dan walks across the lawn and up onto the deck at the end of the day, as if we're still just neighbours. In the mornings, I make him spirulina smoothies and he calls them hippie juice, but he drinks them. He looks well. He's bought a Harley which vibrates like a wild thing. In our black leathers, with the wind in our faces, I feel like I'm seventeen again. Until I get off the bike, and I'm almost too stiff to walk.

Once upon a time, people like my ancestors and Dan's came to Tasmania having no choice. Convicted for stealing a loaf of bread, a silk handkerchief, or for cutting someone's throat. Transported to the other side of the world and nothing familiar in it. But when they had the chance to leave, after they'd served their sentences, they didn't go back to where they'd come from. They decided to stay and make a life here. They built homes, grew food, raised kids and imagined a future. And they did their best to forget the people who had been here before, who must have loved it too. The people who had died so they could live this way.

We're still doing the same thing a couple of hundred years later. It feels like half the world is trying to do the same thing. Find somewhere peaceful to live and forget the past.

I took leave from the UN after the bridge, and then I resigned. In truth, when you've done what I've done, it doesn't feel quite right to go around trying to encourage people to get along. I'll remain on the books for my other role. Our cell is still active. I don't spend time wondering what will come next.

I think Henry Liu is the only person who suspects. He said to me one night, at Cloudy Bay, with its two-hundred-and-eighty-degree view over sea, beach and hills, and the most brilliant aurora lighting up the sky, 'We have bought our peace at a high price, Astrid.'

'We have,' I agreed.

'There are certain truths that never escape us.'

I nodded.

'But we are safe here, among friends,' he said. 'And I maintain excellent surveillance. I have our family to consider. Our extended family. You, more than anyone, understand family, Astrid. Like you, I would never let anything happen.'

I realised that, in his way, he was thanking me.

I started writing a memoir, thinking to exorcise all I'd seen out there in the world, but dredging up those images was all too hard. So I enrolled at art school. I started to work in metal. Turns out, with a little tuition, I'm kind of handy with a welder. So there are sculptures in the front yard and a pretty elaborate fence going up around my house. Dan cooks most nights. We're okay. We're better than okay. When I see him walk in the door, I think: That's him. That's who I want. I sleep really well. And the sex is fantastic.

Coming back wasn't what I'd planned. Nor was falling in love with Dan. Nor was blowing up a bridge. We never speak about it. We've put it aside. Just like we did the death of the Chinese worker. Sometimes I am still quietly thrilled at myself. And sometimes that shame of not being ashamed registers in me, playing its song. I like to think my father might have understood. Not the act itself. Never that. But the strategy.

'Who did you help today, Astrid?'

'Well, Dad . . . I did a very bad thing. But I did it for all of us. So this place could be what it is a little longer.'

I could hear my father say, '*I never did repent for doing good, nor shall I now.*' Shakespeare. *The Merchant of Venice.*

Out there, beyond Tasmania, the world is getting crazier, more destabilised, more vulnerable. Climate change has gone from greenhouse to hothouse and there's no winding it back. The Middle East is getting drier; southern Europe, northern Europe, North America too. India will have a bigger population than China before long. Soon enough clean water, good soil, regular rainfall, it will all be worth more than oil. So we're sitting on a goldmine here. But it's possible to forget, if you don't read the news, if you don't pick up your phone. It won't last, this Tasmania. The crazy will come. But for now it's all clouds and sea, wind and stars, solitude, peace and the beautiful illusion it will go on forever.

ACKNOWLEDGEMENTS

Many very experienced and well-informed people gave me their time and knowledge for this book. They shall remain anonymous but you know who you are and you have my deepest appreciation. Your observations and stories proved invaluable.

To the friends who read drafts, gave feedback, made tea, delivered vegetables, brought wine and food, shared wisdom, lured me to movies and dancing, sent texts, took me to dinner, remembered the things I forgot, were surrogate mums, ferried the cat and the hockey bag, hung out on my back deck, shared your homes, and kept me laughing through the intense process of writing this book, I love you all.

In 2017, the Australia Council gave me a grant to create the first draft of this novel. I am enormously grateful.

In 2018, Carol and Alan Schwarz gave me the most beautiful house and the gift of solitude to finish the second draft.

The Stella Prize community has been the warm breeze at my back during the writing of this novel.

Jane Palfreyman, Ali Lavau, Christa Munns, Christine Farmer, Sandy Cull and the entire team at Allen & Unwin have been a powerhouse of professionalism and care.

Gaby Naher, my agent, has given me twenty years of guidance, passion and belief.

My mother Dawn for the early magic of words.

My father Kevin for a lifetime of writerly support and inspiration.

My children Belle, Byron and Alex have made every day a gift beyond measure.

My island home of Tasmania—and the brilliant community I live amongst—I wrote this for you.

Thank you all.

Nothing Bad Ever Happens Here

HEATHER ROSE

Believing and belonging occupy a great deal of human life. What to believe? How to belong? All of it is a mystery that we fill with stories.

Growing up on the remote island of Tasmania, Heather Rose falls in love with nature, but a tragedy at age twelve sets her on a course to explore life's mysteries. Here is a wild barefoot girl born for adventure, a curious seeker initiated in ancient rituals, a fledgling writer who becomes one of Australia's most highly awarded authors, a business woman and a mother whose body may falter at any moment. Heart-breaking and beautiful, this is a love story brimming with courage and joy against all odds.

Nothing Bad Ever Happens Here is a memoir. It's the exploration of a life through four lenses—Heather's relationship with nature, wild spiritual adventures, the bonds of family and the lessons of pain.

ISBN 978 1 76106 632 0

SKY

May I speak to you
Like we are close
And locked away together?

HAFIZ

Here she is, standing in the schoolyard. She is six years old, dressed in a crisp green uniform. Other children are on the swings and seesaw, but she has taken herself off to stand alone under the eucalyptus at the edge of the playground. She gazes up through its broad branches to the sky above.

Hello, she says. *I'm ready. Tell me what to do. Make use of me.*

She might have chosen to do this at the small church where she attends Sunday school, but instead she does it here, because it feels as if this big tree must have a direct connection to whoever is in charge.

Does anyone answer back? They do not. Yet she feels better for having declared herself willing to be of service. She has reported for duty.

—

Physicists suggest that 70 per cent of the known universe is dark energy. Dark matter is another 25 per cent. Once we thought we knew all about life, but it turns out everything we think of as reality is less than 5 per cent.

Crumpets and honey, hockey sticks, sailing boats, temples, shopping centres, literature, the pharmaceutical industry, mathematics, every scientific discovery, every plant, animal or virus below the sea and above, the planets and the stars we can name and all those we can't, this galaxy and the 200 billion other galaxies that comprise the known universe, everything that has been created, constructed, calculated, measured or observed by humans amounts to a mere fragment of existence. Ninety-five per cent is hidden from us, invisible, unknown, only to be imagined or sensed. Yet it's present everywhere, in every moment, in everything around us, and everything that *is* us.

—

Believing and belonging occupy a great deal of human life. What to believe? How to belong? All of it is a mystery that we fill with stories.

Standing under that tree in my primary school playground is not my first memory, yet it remains vivid. I will grow up and travel the world, and I will travel the inner places of heart and mind, always curious. What is this thing called life? Why am I here?

For decades now, I've asked strangers if something ever happened that they couldn't explain. Something outside the normal. To my surprise, I discovered that everyone had a story of a guiding hand, a strange connection, a reassuring presence, something life-saving or life-affirming, something more than a coincidence. Everyone had experienced something that gave them a sense that there was more to life than could be seen, touched or verified.

I could write a memoir about travelling, the writing life, or my love of baking cakes. But I'm still that girl under the tree who wants to get to the big conversation, to the heart of things. So here are some stories about life and death. About experiences that have no easy explanation, but which happened, nevertheless. The unknown, that 95 per cent – maybe it's an invitation for compassion. Life is a process of forgiveness for the choices we make in order to be ourselves.

FIRE

We do not 'come into' this world; we come out of it . . .

ALAN WATTS

Here is where memories begin.

My mother is on a ladder watering the roof of our orange-brick house with a hose. The house is newly built and overlooks a wide blue river. I live on an island at the end of the world, just a week's sailing from Antarctica, though I do not know this because I am only two and a half years old. I do know, however, that my mother standing on a ladder and watering the roof is not a normal thing.

I hear her gasp. The forested hill behind us has become a wall of flames, a ridge of leaping red and amber spiralling up into billowing clouds. It is 7 February 1967. The wind blowing across Tasmania, birthed in the lizard heat of Central Australia, has become a firestorm travelling at more than 130 kilometres an hour, dropping millions of sparks. There is no rural fire service in 1967, nor a volunteer service. There is a small fire station over the hill but it has only limited equipment.

I am delivered to the home of our neighbours down the street while my mother retrieves my two older brothers from school. A goat, a sheep and chickens are in the neighbours' laundry. In their lounge room, I sit beneath a clothes horse and breathe in the scent of drying linen as I eat a delicious oatmeal biscuit.

By 3 pm the sky is black and the city of Hobart has emptied. The temperature is 40 degrees. Across our sylvan state there are flames hundreds of feet high, fireballs, exploding gum trees, roaring wind, melting roads. The power is out and communications are down. My dad is home early from work. He and a friend go to fight a fire nearby, using sacks to beat back the flames. Mum and my brothers return and soon everyone in our small community gathers on the beach to stand in the sea. Huge particles of ash fall about us.

In one day, fires burn through some 652,000 hectares of land; 1300 homes are incinerated, and 7000 people become homeless; 64 people die and more than 900 are injured. It takes three months for the power to be reconnected across suburbs and rural areas.

—

Our house does not burn down, nor do those of our friends and neighbours on the perimeter of the forest. Six months after the fire, I turn three, and six weeks after that, my mother gives birth to my sister. Now we are four children: two boys and two girls. My mother reads aloud to me as she breastfeeds my baby sister, turning page after page of Little Golden Books and *Mother Goose* until, one day, the words from her voice match the words on the page, and I am reading too.

—

At age four I am at the kitchen table scrawling squiggly line after squiggly line across the page with a crayon. My mother asks me why I am ruining the butcher's paper she's given me to draw on.

'I'm writing,' I reply brusquely.

It is lucky that I begin writing early because I have a long way to go. I've done many jobs in my life, but writing has always been my favourite thing to do. It's also been the hardest. It's required the greatest discipline, the longest hours and the deepest commitment. Writing has said: *Look more closely, go this way, dig deeper, learn this, know yourself better.* It has been a pathway into the unknown, the fascinating, the heartbreaking and the wonderful. I give myself to writing and it bends me, sharpens me, whittles me and sculpts me.

—

But first I am very young. My mother's voice is high and musical. She recites limericks, smokes cigars at parties and has an extensive repertoire of rude jokes. She loves The Goons, Monty Python and Walter Mitty. She makes her clothes from French *Vogue* patterns. She makes our clothes, too – even our school uniforms. Her sense of the ridiculous, her delight in the silly, is infectious. I am often in paroxysms of laughter. She can draw anything and make it look real. As a teenager she wanted to become a graphic artist, but there was no money for further study. When my younger sister begins kindergarten, my mother returns to work as a secretary. Along with a career, four children and a husband, she bakes and cooks, sews, preserves, sings, embroiders, gardens, arranges flowers, decorates cakes, and makes kayaks and pottery. Only on Sunday night does she forsake her culinary wizardry and feed us cheese on toast or Heinz tomato soup. (Anything from a packet or a tin is a treat in our house.) She is slender, elegant, dark-haired and beautiful. She gets chest infections and her back is often sore.

My father is handsome, reserved and serious. Dad grew up poor and started full-time work at fourteen. In his twenties, he completed high school by attending night school. Later, much later, I will ask him why he stayed in the tax department for forty years when he wanted to do other things. He tells me that he was making a bridge for his children from the lower class to the middle class.

Dad loves reading and music. My mother loves music, too. She is an atheist while Dad is a Christian. He takes us to church while Mum stays home. He is an introvert while she is an extrovert. She leans politically right, he leans left. Mum is sunny while Dad can be moody. He whistles when he is displeased and retreats into silence.

From Monday to Friday, Dad catches the 7.45 am bus to work in the city. Until they build the new highway, the journey takes almost an hour. A bus returns him home again by 6.10 pm. I watch out for it and run down to meet him, walking home holding his hand.

—

Childhood is kelp and sand, birds and sky, and boats pulled up from the tide. Rainy days are for reading in bed, playing games, cooking, doing craft. If it is fine, we are sent outside to play. There are seasons, neighbours, weekly library trips, the radio playing in the kitchen, the fire at night and the habit of growing things. Everyone in our cul-de-sac grows things. We have a vegetable garden that provides much of our food, and a Golden Delicious apple tree in our backyard. Roses of every scent and colour line our front boundary, as if our surname requires it.

Our house is the first on a new subdivision above a curve of beachside shacks. We are surrounded by farms, apricot orchards, paddocks and dams. Throughout the sixties and seventies, a new house is always being built, a new family moving in. Kerbs and bitumen arrive, washing lines and paling fences. Our neighbours are public servants, business people, stay-at-home mums, teachers, academics, architects and retirees. There is a small government primary school.

Both sets of grandparents live close by, as well as cousins from Dad's side of the family. We children roam the farmland that is yet to become suburbia, building forts in sandy embankments, climbing the seaside cliffs, catching tadpoles in the dams, kicking the footy on the oval, playing beach cricket, swimming in the sea, exploring rock pools and riding our bikes everywhere like mad things. In winter we take cardboard and slide down the icy paddock behind the house. Only rarely does it snow, down there so close to the sea, and when it does we are awestruck.

There are neighbourhood barbecues, bonfires and fireworks, fancy-dress parties and dinners where the adults walk between homes for various courses, my mother's laughter rippling on the night air. On hot days, Mum and her girlfriends lie on the beach, laughing and chatting, rolling their eyes at the habits of their husbands, while we children swim, play and listen. There are Boxing Day gatherings down the street where a television broadcasts the start of the Sydney to Hobart yacht race. Days later these yachts sail up our river to the finish line. We watch them from our house, taking turns at the telescope. We do not own a television. Books and games, music and friends, the radio and the outdoors are our entertainment.

My brothers and I, and children who live along the way, walk to school together, a kilometre and a half each way. No one locks their doors. We are welcome in everyone's houses. We must be home by the time the streetlights come on.

—

The River Derwent is an enormous river travelling more than 200 kilometres from its birthplace in the highlands until it passes through Hobart beneath the watchful gaze of Mount Wellington. It can appear benign, but the river is quixotic, changing from calm to asperous in moments.

From our house, I watch the sun rise on the river's far shore washing the sky in tangerine, vermilion, peach and gold. Throughout the day, clouds stride in from the west, full and white, lean, brindled, feathered. On breathless mornings, the river is liquid satin. In winter it is wreathed in a high rolling fog. Full-moon tides crash below my bedroom window, low tides leave sand flats that mirror the sky. Seagulls and shorebirds wander the water's edge. Mount Wellington, always in view, changes from grey to blue to mauve throughout the day, until sunset turns the mountain into a silhouette. Every day there is a breeze, or many breezes. Tasmania is a place of endlessly changing weather.

As a child, I love the sea. I often spend dawn and dusk with my grandfather, waiting for the tug on my handline that signifies flathead, perch and, sometimes, a stripy trumpeter. I am mesmerised by light catching on ripples, by birds sliding across the sky and wind bringing its own shadow.

Solitude becomes my friend early: reading in bed late into the night; drifting on the swing in the backyard staring at clouds; sitting on the rocks by my grandparents' boatshed or on the shore below the family shack. At night I pull back the curtains to watch the moon rise over the river and wonder at all those stars. Every night I listen to the waves, the ceaseless metronome of my early years.

One day, when I am five, my mother mentions that her family came to Tasmania from Scotland a long time ago. I ask her where Scotland is. She says it's on the other side of the world. There is a globe in the lounge room which I love to spin, my fingers tracing the countries and oceans. For the first time, I grasp that I am at the bottom of this globe. Scotland is a long way away, far over the curve. I decide that as soon as I am grown up, I will go there.

All this lies at the heart of who I will become.